PET LIONS & WELL-DRESSED ELEPHANTS

A CIRCUS JOURNEY TO GREATNESS 1846-1873

Pet Lions & Well-Dressed Elephants

A Circus Journey to Greatness 1846-1873

Donna Lee Dicksson

CHARLES & ANNA WHITE'S
LIFE WITH THE CIRCUS

"Donna Lee Dicksson takes on the challenge of telling the lives of Charles and Anna White, who in the 1870s travelled with P. T. Barnum's Greatest Show On Earth. They moved by train across the country during the circus season and in the off months lived in the Bridgeport, Connecticut winter quarters. Charles White earned recognition over time for his unique care and training of felines, elephants and other exotic animals. Love blossomed under the circus big top as Charles married Anna Donovan, a seamstress on the show. Anna worked her way up to Wardrobe Mistress and was in charge of a dozen seamstresses on the circus. She was responsible for all the men's and women's costumes, as well for all the animal costumes from the largest elephant down to the smallest Chihuahua dog. *Pet Lions and Well-Dressed Elephants* gives a unique view into the life and times of the circus during the 1870s."

John Polacsek
Past President, Circus Historical Society

"A compelling read into early circus life along with the growth of a couple's love and other varied relationships amongst the pioneers of the traveling circus business in North America."

A.W. Stencell
Past President Circus Historical Society

A. W. Stencell is author of *Seeing is Believing: America's Sideshows* (ECW Press)
Girl Show: Into the Canvas World of Bump and Grind (ECW Press)
Circus and Carnival Ballyhoo: Sideshow Freaks, Jabbers and Blade Box Queens (ECW Press)

When I delved into the history of the circus in the United States, I found a miriad of books and resources, but not a single reference that told the broader story. This work attempts to knit together some of the pieces of circus history between 1846-1873.

I came across the wardrobe mistress who was with the Barnum show from its beginning in 1871 until it was sold to Ringling Brothers in 1907. What a life she must have lived! What stories she could tell! Who was she? Where did she come from?

Although this is a novel, most of the people, places, and dates were real and are as accurately recounted as I could write them. The births, deaths, accidents, routes, acts and events were gleaned from dozens of renowned circus reference books, old newspapers, the Library of Congress, The Illinois Digital Newspapers Collection, and the occasional circus historian who was kind enough to provide feedback. There are a few fictional support characters and all the personal moments that tie the story together are purely the fantasy of the author.

Dedication

This story is humbly dedicated to the memory of Charley White and Annie Matchett, circus pioneers.

Anna Margaret Matchett
August 14, 1842
August 15, 1935

Alasco Charles White
January 21, 1832
March 29, 1909

My sincere thanks to:

The circus people whose primary goal is to survive to work yet another season. I'll buy a ticket.

The animal keepers who devote their lives to caring for the creatures in their care. All I have met would gladly go without supper (and they have) to provide for their lions, tigers, bears, elephants, and more. Not only do they care for their own, but they also raise awareness and money for the wild animals in need of preservation.

The **Circus Historical Society**, bless them for keeping the magic alive.

John Polacsek, circus historian, for his patience, feedback and insight.

And the clowns… who took me under their wing and let me tag along.

PART I

PART 2

14 AUGUST 1842
OSWEGO COUNTY, NEW YORK

THE BEST PART OF DOING farm chores was not having to think about them too much. While the body is busy working, the mind is free to wander.

The boy's hands worked rhythmically, alternatingly squeezing and releasing the swollen teats of the family cow. Practice made him adept at landing every milky squirt directly to the frothy center of the half-filled bucket. The "shush, shush, shush" he heard was no longer milk in his mind's eye; it was the sound of steamboat paddles touching the surface of Lake Ontario.

Alasco's clear blue eyes glazed over as he sank deeply into his daydream. He savored every nuance of the fantasy. *The Lady of the Lake*, built in Oswego, had launched from the shipyard in April. She was beautiful and modern, one-hundred-ninety-six feet long and a full twenty-four feet wide. She had a one-hundred-horse-power engine, and could withstand any storm on the lake. He had never been caught in a storm on the lake, but he was sure there would be no problem. He imagined stepping onto the steamer, waving goodbye to his father and leaving to see the world.

Travelers crossed Lake Ontario from all around including Canada West, to shop, play, or journey onward to other destinations. Since the Saint Lawrence River flowed into Lake Ontario from the north, some boats came from Canada East and as far away as Europe by way of the Atlantic Ocean.

A boy could entertain himself for hours just watching arrivals and departures. If he was clever, he could make a penny or two helping people carry things. Once he had gone to the docks with his father to fetch carpentry supplies. He made seven cents that day helping off-load lumber with another boy. He still had all seven coppers. It was his savings, a seed of the traveling money he would need.

Sometimes a boat brought a circus to town. That was a red-letter day! If news of its pending arrival reached the farm, his father would take them all to see it. His motto was, "All work and no play, makes Jack a dull boy." It was rare that his father was so light-hearted, but Alasco reasoned that he liked the circus too. With those rare circuses came music, trained horses, acrobats, and clowns. Most of the time shows were made up of equestrians who did all sorts of gymnastics that were both marvelous and dangerous. Occasionally a circus would arrive with its own menagerie of exotic animals. He had witnessed many wondrous creatures the past couple of years but was still waiting to see an elephant. He could only imagine its size.

Most in northwestern New York were born on a farm and never left until they were securely planted under it. He had no intention of staying that long. He had, what Grandfather Hubbard called, "wanderlust." He didn't think that was a bad thing.

His two little brothers would soon be old enough to help father and then he could take off and have an adventure of his own. He was ten now. He could take care of himself.

He knew his father wanted to leave the farm, too. He had worked for the neighbors in their carpentry business over the past few winters and learned the trade. He wanted to stop farming altogether and do only carpentry, but the transition was difficult with small children and no money. They needed the farm to sustain them until his carpentry could support them.

An orange striped tabby cat purred loudly as it waited patiently beside the boy's boot. Occasionally a paw, with nails retracted, reached out and tapped the boy's pantleg to remind him she was there.

"Oh, all right Jingles," he laughed, "Here's a drink for you!" He pointed the teat toward the cat and gave a good squeeze. The milk stream found its way to the rough tongue of the barn cat. The aim was good. The catch was perfect. The few odd drops that dribbled down the furry orange chin were quickly licked away, safe and sound.

The job completed, he picked up the wooden bucket in one hand, the three-legged milking stool in the other and walked toward the barn door. He set them down and went back to release "Bell" from her milking stall. He fetched a little extra grain from the bin and put the tin pan down in front of her. "Good girl," he said, patting her on the rump. Closing the door behind him, he headed for the house, bucket in hand, whistling.

+ + +

Meanwhile, on the other side of Lake Ontario in Monaghan, Canada a small woman rested in a narrow cot, woolen blanket drawn down exposing the simple white linen nightgown her mother had made for her before she left Ireland some two and a half years prior. Hand-crocheted white lace adorned the wrists and neck and ten small buttons with loop fasteners closed the front. It was plenty enough to keep her warm because August, although half gone, was still stifling at mid-day in the attic of the little schoolhouse.

The log structure was eighteen feet wide and twenty feet long, making the available space on the ground floor three hundred and sixty square feet. The attic afforded about half that much living space given that the roof sloped steeply on both sides.

A small window stood open on the south end of the room and the rock chimney which rose from ground floor to rooftop dominated the north. Warm in the winter, if the schoolhouse fire remained well-stoked, and cool in the summer if one could live with the mosquitoes that came in through the open window, the attic was perfect for a single woman. She was the teacher and taught local children reading and writing, art and a little Irish dancing.

School was closed for the summer so children could help on family farms. She had kept the baby a secret as long as possible. There had been no need to worry the children or their parents before the child actually arrived. Margaret Ann Slingsby loved it here and she didn't want to leave. She hoped and prayed that if the citizens did not find out about the baby until it was too late to get a new teacher for the winter months, they would accept her situation. Schoolteachers were hard to come by in the new little township of Monaghan and she hoped this was enough to keep her employed.

A good neighbor had gone after the midwife when Margaret knocked on her door in the small hours of the morning. The baby had come easily, cried lustily, and was a good, solid, wee baby girl. Margaret smiled down at the little bundle in her arms and whispered softly, "We'll make the best of it, *Cáilín mo Pháistín.*"

The baby's father, Sandy Matchett, was one of the earliest settlers, a pioneer. He'd come from Ireland in 1825. He had a farm in Otonabee Township, a short distance from the Monaghan schoolhouse. For him, the baby was profoundly inopportune. He had two daughters, a four-month-old son, and a wife at home.

The new mother had drifted off to sleep but was awakened by the sound of the heavy wooden schoolhouse door opening. She waited, holding her breath, and listened as boots quietly ascended the steep stairs. Sandy Matchett, young, tall and handsome, appeared at the top of the steps and asked, "May I come in?"

She nodded and he emerged from the stairwell into the attic, the nursery, the living space of the schoolteacher. He had been here once before, but then it was dark. It looked different now. The room with its log rafters and bare wooden floors appeared crowded and uninviting. Wooden boxes, filled with bits and pieces of school-children's needs, lined one side of the room where the ceiling was too low to walk. On the other side, was Margaret lying on the cot with her baby.

She pulled the wool blanket up under her chin, a reflex of modesty fostered long ago in Ireland.

"She is so tiny," he began. "Is she well?"

"Yes, she is a strong *báibín*," Margaret whispered.

"Miss Slingsby," he began, looking into the young mother's eyes, "Have you given her a name?"

"Aye," she answered. "Anna, after my mother."

The man shifted from one foot to another as he worked his fingers around the brim of the felt hat he held in his hands. The floor groaned with the shift of his weight and the clock on the small table ticked off the moments of silence. He stared intently at the baby for what seemed like an eternity.

Clearing his throat, he said very formally, "I acknowledge that I am the father of this child. When the day comes for her to be christened, please write my name in as father in the church book and allow her to bear my surname."

Tears welled up and slid down her face, an emotional response to his words that she was unaware of until she tasted the saltiness on her own lips.

"I was a weak man," he continued. "I threw off the responsibility for my wife and children to enjoy the warmth of your bed. Please forgive me. God forgive me. I cannot leave my wife, nor abandon my children."

Margaret's heart broke a little as she stared into his face. It was over between them. It had been over since last winter, the moment he descended the attic stairs. They had both known, but now reality was spoken aloud, and all hope faded.

Her lips quivered as she tried to hold her composure. The task before her was daunting, to raise a child alone with no family on this side of the Atlantic to help her. She touched the cheek of the baby girl and then gently took a soft golden lock of hair between her fingertips.

"But," she stammered looking up at him and trying not to show her feelings, "You will give her your name?" She asked again, just to be certain.

He dropped his gaze and stared at his own hands to avoid the sorrow and disappointment he saw in front of him. It was his fault, but what could he do? He could never leave his family.

Finally, he looked up and declared, "Yes, I will give you an allowance to help you live while she is a child. But perhaps it is best if I am never in your lives otherwise again. She will know that I honor her because she carries my name. I must also honor my wife and hold myself only to her."

Margaret gathered strength as stubborn pride swelled within her. Somehow, they would make it through. The baby Anna stirred and stretched. She opened her beautiful dark eyes and stared directly at her father.

PART I

CHAPTER ONE

FOUR YEARS LATER…
MAY 1846
ONONDAGA COUNTY, NEW YORK

IT STARTED WITH A FEW quarter-sized raindrops bouncing randomly off the horses' backsides like crickets jumping to high grass. A solitary sunbeam found its way through a crack in the clouds and painted a watery rainbow over the road ahead. Alasco Charles White most often called "Charley," lifted the reins and snapped them down lightly, encouraging his team forward. He hoped to make it back to camp before the road turned to mush and daylight surrendered to darkness. He did not like traveling at night. Never had. Too much could go wrong.

Ominous black clouds growled and boiled as they ravenously swallowed up every last morsel of sky. A wind gust snatched the boy's hat from his head, but he grabbed it just in the nick of time and stuffed it under his rump. The storm grew quickly into full glory. A jagged bolt of lightning streaked across the sky followed by a reverberating explosion of thunder. The horses stopped in their tracks and listened. The boy urged them on.

Then it came, the squall line, with its pulsating wind-driven sheets of rain that against all laws of gravity, flew sideways instead of straight down to earth. He leaned into it eyes squinted against the pelting rain, and hoped the boys could find their way without his help. The horses, heads lowered against the onslaught of nature, claimed the road in front of them with strong legs and steady gait. Well-trained by gentle hands, they did not need a whip to tell them what to do. They knew. Go home.

Bobby and Billy, twin buckskin draft horses, had been cared for by their young master since the day they foaled. They had been so weak and wobbly when they arrived, the boy slept in the barn for a whole week to ensure their survival. They were seven years old now and Charley was fourteen. They'd grown up together. This was their first job away from home as a team. He was proud. Everything had gone well.

Earlier that spring the boy's father, a carpenter and woodsman, caught wind of a job coming to the Syracuse area, roughly forty miles south of their farm just outside Oswego. The Anderson New York Lumber Company had organized into a stock company in order to build a new kind of wooden road. It would replace a critical section of the decrepit Old Salt Road between Salina and Brewerton. The new "plank road" would be the first of its kind in the United States. Unlike corduroy roads made from logs laid down like dead soldiers in a long bumpy row, the plank road would be smooth. Builders would grade the earth surface flat and then lay stringers on each side like the side poles of a ladder. Eight-foot-long, four-inch-thick planks would then be laid across, creating a single-lane road. It would take a lot of lumber to cover the twelve miles of planned toll road and there was money to be made delivering it.

No one outfit was awarded a contract. All materials were to be delivered by competing independent suppliers. The road company would buy the lumber from whomever showed up first and when the road was done, the job was over. Suppliers who delivered their lumber quickest would make the most profit.

Charley's father, Benajah, wanted to supply as much of that lumber as he could. He struck a partnership with his sawmill-owning cousin down near Syracuse. Benajah, his cousin, and Charley's ten-year-old little brother Ben, would manufacture the lumber. Charley would deliver it.

They had been working the job for a little over two months. They had enjoyed good fortune, and all had gone well. The job would be done soon, and Charley was glad for that. It was lonesome driving back and forth all day, even if he did have the horses for company. His stomach growled. Supper would be waiting for him when he got back to the sawmill. He hoped it wasn't beans. He thought of his stepmother's Sunday chicken dinner and could almost taste it. His mouth watered.

The horses halted, pulling him from his daydream. Before he had time to figure out why they had stopped, a lightning bolt lit up the road ahead revealing the reason. The way was blocked by a crippled wagon and its struggling crew. Charley set the brake, slapped his hat onto his head, and jumped down from the wagon. In two long strides, he was alongside Bobby. He patted the horse on the shoulder, looked him in the eye, and told him to wait. The boy's feet slipped and slid in the mud as he scrambled forward to see if he could help.

A brightly painted circus wagon boasting "Sands, Lent & Co." in gold and white lettering stood crosswise in the road. The back wheels were in the ditch and the rear axle rested on the muddy roadbed. Two sturdy black horses were trying unsuccessfully to pull the wagon back onto the road. Several men had taken their places around the wagon and in concert with each effort the horses made to pull the wagon free, the men heaved with all their might. Charley joined the effort, but it was of no use; the wagon wasn't moving, and the horses were exhausted.

The rain stopped as abruptly as it had begun. The sky lightened. Bobby and Billy, still as statues, watched and waited for permission to continue. Charley walked back and unhitched the horses from his empty wagon. The circus men quickly removed their horses from the crippled wagon. Charley maneuvered Bobby and Billy into their place. He cradled Bobby's head between his hands and talked softly to him. He did the same with Billy. He looked past his horses at the men and wagon behind them and made an assessment. Then, while touching Bobby's shoulder with one hand and gesturing with the other, he gave the command, "ho… right." Both horses took a step forward, bearing toward their right. "Easy boys," he reassured as they dug in and struggled forward, "Easy." The big horses slowly began to move the wagon. First one wheel and then the other crept out of the ditch. When the wagon was square on the road, he shouted, "Whoa boys! Good Boys!"

The circus men came forward and each in turn shook Charley's hand enthusiastically, pumping and thanking, pumping and thanking.

"Welcome," he muttered repeatedly.

When the men headed off to join their own wagons, Charley released his horses from the circus wagon and walked them back in tandem to his own. He methodically checked and adjusted the assembly of traces, reins, and straps that made pulling a wagon possible. The load must be balanced, and nothing should pinch his horses.

One obstacle remained; the road was only wide enough for one wagon. And, since the circus caravan and plank wagon were headed in opposite directions, the plank wagon would have to wait while the circus went by.

The men from "Sands, Lent & Company" helped to ease the empty wagon off the road so the caravan could proceed.

Charley watched silently as wagon after wagon passed him, their drivers tipping their hats and nodding. What really caught his eye were the horses… not just the ones pulling the wagons, but the ones in small groups led by men on horseback. There was a big copper bay with black ears, mane, and tail that appeared to float down the road. Yet another horse, a tall and regal black one with white socks and blazed forehead, was led by a small man riding on a mule. Only his dark eyes could be seen peering out from beneath an oversized, rain-soaked leather hat. Behind him came Shetland ponies of different colors, a dozen at least and yet more small horses, brown, short-legged, sturdy fellows. These were foreign to him.

When the last wagon in the caravan passed Charley, it stopped. Two men jumped down and came back to help get the plank wagon back onto the road. The surface was now deeply rutted, but the horses were strong and with the wagon empty, they were back on track quickly.

Just as he lifted the reigns and opened his mouth to signal his boys to head home, a very large man on a small horse rode toward him waving his hat in the air. His white canvas overcoat flapped open in the front and trailed behind him making him look like a giant crane about to take flight. The big man jumped off his horse and stomped toward Charley. His boots splattered mud on both sides, but not once did he slip or slide. The man was a mountain. He walked up to the wagon and gave a hat-in-hand ceremonious bow.

"My good man," he panted, "please accept my deepest gratitude for your assistance! You have quite possibly saved tomorrow's show and so…." he reached inside his big white coat, pulled out a handful of cards, and handed them up to Charley.

The boy's eyes lit up as he read the top card, "Admit One. Sands, Lent & Company's American Circus!"

The big man coughed, cleared his throat and continued, "I would be most pleased to have you as our guest, in Syracuse! Free admission! No Charge! Bring your whole family! Are four tickets enough?" He asked without waiting for an answer. "We'll be there tomorrow and put on a show for three days. My name is Lewis B. Lent and," he waved his arm gesturing at the caravan, "This is my show!"

"You are welcome, Mr. Lent," he stammered, "I would like that very much!"

"What is your name?" inquired the dark-eyed giant.

"Sir, my name is Alasco Charles White, but my friends call me Charley."

"Well, if you can't make it to Syracuse Charley, we'll be in Jordon Village on the fifth." The man replaced his hat, turned, and started back toward his horse. He stopped suddenly, pivoted on one foot, and looked up at the boy.

"Young man," he said as he re-approached the wagon. "You're pretty good with horses and I saw how you handled getting that wagon out of the ditch. We could use a man like you. If you want a job, come see me after the show."

Charley found himself back at the sawmill without recalling those final miles. It was pitch dark and he'd hardly noticed. He released his horses and led them to the barn. He brushed them down, put the harnesses away, made sure there was plenty of water, measured out a portion of oats for each and pitched a nice pile of hay. After a last glance to make sure everything was as it should be, he headed off toward the little shack where his father and brother awaited him with a big bowl of steaming hot beans.

CHAPTER TWO

11 JUNE 1846
TUESDAY AFTERNOON

WHY HAD HE BEEN LEFT behind to shovel manure? He joined the circus because he wanted adventure. They hired him because he was good with horses. Nevertheless, he stood here, alone in a field, picking up horse dung. It didn't make sense and it wasn't much of an adventure. He bent down and lifted another forkful of steaming excrement from the grass and tossed it onto the canvas.

The "Sands, Lent and Company's American Circus" had packed up and gone down the road as soon as the afternoon show was over. They'd been gone about an hour already. He slid the pitchfork under the last remaining pile and lifted it. Pausing mid-scoop, he stared at the fork, thinking. As the truth dawned on him, he rolled his eyes and his breath burst from him in a spasm of laughter. He emptied the load onto the canvas and thrust the fork into the ground. He had been *tricked*! He'd been told to stay behind and clean up or the circus wouldn't get their five-dollar deposit back. They said the farmer who owned the field would be back around to deliver those five dollars, however Charley had not seen any man and he had not seen any money. It was tomfoolery and he was the fool.

Still smiling, he picked up two corners of the canvas and dragged it over to the side of the road to empty its contents into the ditch. Once done, he spread the canvas onto the grass and scraped off the clingers with the side of the fork. He folded the canvas in half and then, starting at one corner he rolled it up. He secured the bundle around his back with the rope that he used for holding up his pants. He walked over, picked up the pitchfork, and headed down the road after the circus.

"Not so bad," he thought aloud as he raised his face to the sky. This was the first time he'd been alone with his thoughts in days. Charley had been with the show less than a week, but it seemed like forever. They had set up in five towns since Syracuse, including Jordon Village, Skaneateles, Auburn, Seneca Falls, and Waterloo. The next town was Clyde about fifteen miles north on the Erie Canal. The sun was shining on his back despite the late hour, one of the blessings of living in the north in the summertime, and it made him sleepy. He hadn't gotten more than a couple hours of sleep a night since he hired on. He was tempted to take a nap in the grass beside the road, but he didn't dare; he'd never catch up with the show before breakfast if he did.

The circus that Mr. Lent had so proudly proclaimed his own that stormy night was in fact a joint venture between himself and Mr. Richard Sands, a very clever equestrian acrobat. Mr. Lent didn't actually travel with this circus. It was a fluke that he'd been with the caravan the night their wagon got stuck and Charley's horses pulled it out. When Charley had shown up in Syracuse to take advantage of the free tickets, Mr. Lent was already long gone. The troupe remembered Charley, of course. He travelled with them to Jordon Village that very night. His dad and brother headed back home to Oswego in the wagon drawn by Bobby and Billy.

He learned quickly that circus boys rested while the caravan was moving. When the wagons stopped, they started work. Cart horses had to be fed, watered, and staked out to eat and rest for the following day's journey. Show horses not only needed to be fed and watered, but also groomed. All the gear needed to be checked and mended before every show. Big towns got two shows, one at two-thirty and one at seven-thirty. Small towns got just one show. If it rained, the boys had to clean mud off horses and wagons. If it didn't rain, they had to clean off dust. Either way, it was a never-ending job to keep things bright and shiny and a show needed to be a bright and shiny if they wanted folks to buy tickets.

Charley had already made a friend, Jimmy. He was also fourteen but wasn't a hired boy; He was a trick rider. Jimmy's stage name was "Master Hernandez" which had made Charley chuckle. Jimmy was a New Yorker, not Mexican. He kept his curly auburn hair tucked under a hat, so the audience never knew the difference. Jimmy had been in the business since he was eight and had been taught by the famous John Robinson himself. Charley didn't know who Robinson was but tried to look impressed just the same.

Jimmy was educating Charley in the ways of the traveling circus. Although "Hernandez" had only joined up with Sands & Lent a couple of months earlier, he already had six years of experience. There was a system to setting up, tearing down, and traveling with a show that was efficient and clever. Above all else, the show had to give the impression of being fun and exciting in spite of stuck wagons, lame horses, or any of the myriad of things that could go wrong. When the show was in public view, everybody smiled like it was the happiest day of their lives.

He soon figured out what the circus advertised was mostly fluff. But if he wanted to fit in with the others in the show, he needed to know that fluff. He had snatched a handbill off a post as they were leaving Syracuse and stuffed it into his pocket. Every time he got a chance, he studied the names and descriptions. All in all, there were eighty horses and eight wagons, plus the Cinderella Coach which was hauled on top of one of the flatbed wagons. Mr. Mosely, the equestrian manager, doubled as an "English Equestrian." He acted out some characters from the Pickwick family of Charles Dickens' fame. For the most part, it was Mr. Mosely who gave Charley orders.

The handbill proclaimed that Mr. Richard Sands, equestrian extraordinaire, had performed all over Europe with his two young sons, Maurice and Jessie. The three of them presented a new type of gymnastics combined with a series of Classic Passes, Evolutions, Groupings, Tableaux, and flights of Aerial Grace. However, as his friend Jimmy explained, Mr. Sand's "beautiful children" were not really his children. Mr. Sands wasn't even married.

Mr. Aymar, also an equestrian acrobat, was advertised as, "Second only to Hernandez."

Mr. Perry and his "infantile" son Tom were equestrians of another sort. Their performance was more about being graceful and balancing rather than being daredevils. Mr. Perry's son was young, but not an infant.

It turned out that the beautiful bay horse Charley thought "floated" down the road was a special horse brought from England called May Fly. He was trained to take dainty steps and "dance" for the patrons of the show. The beautiful black horse was Pas Tempe, a pure-bred Arabian. The handbill described his dance as a "polka."

The equestrian acrobats had normal-sized horses, but the rest of the horses were small and sturdy ponies of thirteen hands or less. "The Lilliputian Troupe" that pulled the Cinderella coach, dubbed "fairy steeds," was made up of imported Burmese ponies. Two Shetlands, Damon and Pythias were the so-called "twin ponies" that did an entertaining routine of tricks and fancy footwork. The "fighting ponies," Deaf Burke and Tom Spring, also Shetlands, reared up on hind legs and turned circles. Their act was more like a horse version of pat-a-cake than fighting. Still, audiences loved it.

In-between equestrian acts came variety acts like singers crooning Ethiopian songs and choruses. Henry Conover did his "India Rubber Man" act by twisting and turning his joints inside-out. Charley found this act hard to watch.

Every outfit needed a top-notch clown and that was Joe Pentland. Joe had been in Europe with Sands the year before and was very happy to be back home in America. Although he was dead serious about his act, Mr. Pentland was easy to get along with. Charley had shared a wagon with him between Auburn and Seneca Falls and had enjoyed the talents of this master performer. He had shown Charley a few of his magic tricks, like throwing his voice. Joe was a good singer, too.

Sam Lathrop was the second clown and, since no circus guy did just one job, he was also a "Buffo Singer" which is someone who sings comic opera roles. Sam helped move horses from one place to another during the show and assisted the equestrians. In between set-ups he sang funny songs in a deafeningly loud opera voice. Mr. Lathrop always appeared very happy, relaxed and well… tipsy during the show; But as long as he did his job, nothing was said. The man snored like a disgruntled bull as he slept off his medicinal libations, a talent they all agreed kept the wolves away at night.

Mr. Henry Ruggles was the slack rope acrobat. A lithe and gentle man, he'd generously allowed Charley a chance to balance on his slack rope before it was packed up for the next show. Charley smiled to himself, "Not trying that again," he thought aloud. Even though Henry told him he had the right build to manage it, he'd fallen off repeatedly.

A crow swooped down close over his head and gave off a loud "cawl" startling him back to the present. He had been walking a good while and was thirsty. The cool weather brought by the rain yesterday had given way to a steamy hot sunshine-filled New York summer day. He stopped, bent forward, and with both hands reached behind himself to adjust the canvas roll. He listened for the sound of water flowing, hoping there was a stream along the road. Instead, he heard movement behind him. He turned. Shielding his eyes from the setting sun, he watched as a man mounted on a small dark horse leading two gray ones approached.

When the rider was alongside Charley, he stopped his horse. Sporting a big grin, he leaned over toward the boy and said, "You must be the new guy with Sands and Company!"

Charley returned the man's smile with one of his own, took his hat off and held it to his chest. "Yes sir! That would be me, Charley White, at your service."

"So? Did you pick up all the manure and throw it in the ditch?"

Charley grinned sheepishly, "Yes sir! But I think it was a joke played on me."

"Joke maybe, but also dead serious," the man said as he looked squarely at the boy. "It might be a stupid job and one that doesn't need getting done, but it is a good test to see if a boy is willing to follow orders. If you finished that job even though you knew it was a joke, then you just earned yourself a place at the table."

"Name's Michael!" he said, stretching out a hand, "Glad to meetcha! I work for Mr. Lent, and I am taking these two horses to him. These boys," he nodded at the big, beautiful steeds behind him, "are meant for Mr. Van Amburgh himself…well, for the show. I don't reckon he'll be riding any draft horses," he laughed. "That man always sits front and center of his fancy wagon like he's the Roman emperor." Michael took off his hat, scratched his head, and replaced it. "Seein's how he calls himself "The Lion King," I guess it's fittin!"

The man laughed again and leaned back in the saddle.

"Want a ride? You're skinny enough, my horse wouldn't even notice ya."

"Yes, sir! Thank you! But maybe I should just ride one of these big fellows?" he said, nodding toward the big gray horses.

"Well Charley White, I don't have a saddle and I am not sure they'll take on riders. They're wagon-pullers, you know."

"Let's try," said Charley, grinning.

He secured his pitchfork and canvas to the saddle pack behind the older man. He nodded at Michael, took his hat back off again and secured it in the waist of his pants. Eyes down and hands in his pockets, he approached the closest horse with slow measured steps. Once he was even with its great shoulder, he worked his way around to its chest.

He stood there quietly for a minute and let the horse smell him. His hot breath swept the side of Charley's face and neck. The soft muzzle and sparse whiskers touched his cheek as he stood fast, unmoving. Facing the horse without looking up, the boy touched the horse's neck and stroked him gently. His gaze lifted, and he realized that this was possibly the prettiest horse he had ever seen, dappled gray and massive, at least seventeen hands, probably more. The horse moved his head, resting his lower jaw on Charley's shoulder. This was either a defining moment of friendship or the precursor to a painful bite. The horse blew and nodded, lifted his head and relaxed.

Feeling confident, Charley worked his way to the left shoulder of the animal. He stroked him a moment and then gently reached up to grasp a handful of the horse's dark gray mane. He paused to measure the animal's reaction. The horse lowered his head and appeared relaxed. Charley whispered, "Good boy," and then, as gentle as a cool summer breeze, he mounted the horse.

Michael did not relinquish the reigns of the horse Charley rode. He really didn't know this boy from Adam, and it was serious business to get these giants back to Mr. Lent. They had traveled only a short while when they heard the babble of a creek swollen from yesterday's storm.

The riders dismounted and led the horses to the water. Three horses and two men drank side by side, ankle deep, in the rushing stream.

It didn't take long to catch up with the circus because horses by themselves travel faster than horses pulling wagons. Charley slid off the big gray leaving Michael on his own. He climbed into the end wagon, found a spot in the corner on top of a sack of flour and immediately fell into the kind of a deep sleep only the innocent can manage. The bumping and jerking of a wagon on the rutted dirt road could do nothing to disturb the sleep of the utterly exhausted.

Someone was shaking his shoulder to rouse him. He was momentarily confused. Was it milking time? Had he overslept? As the cobwebs of slumber melted away, he recognized the kind face of Max the cook staring down at him.

"Get yourself up, boy," he muttered.

They had arrived at the rented exhibition field. Since it was only midnight, chores could be done in time to get a little more sleep before morning.

There was a quarter-moon to light the clear warm night. Charley crept behind the cook wagon, found a bush a few feet away and relieved himself. Feeling better, he walked up to the lead wagon and awaited instructions. The crew scattered as jobs were doled out. Charley was surprised to be assigned to Michael, the young man he'd shared the road with.

"Get back to the new horses and make sure they're fed and staked out for the night," instructed Michael. "They might be a little spooky since they've just come from the farm. Settle them in. Then, come find me by the fire and I'll give you more to do."

Charley found the grays and walked them to a grassy spot within the half circle of the wagons where the night guard could keep an eye on them. He set the stakes and tugged on the lines to make sure they were secure. Next, he brought hay from the pile the advance agent had procured from local farmers. The Clyde River ran just west of the field. He got a wide-bottom wooden bucket and ran to fill it. He returned to the horses and watched as they drank. He ran back to the river, refilled the bucket and brought it back to leave for the night. He got a currycomb from the wagon and carefully brushed each horse lightly to make sure there were no cockle burrs, or ticks. He checked each leg, stroking gently to see if there was any tenderness. Satisfied that the horses were secure and well-tended, he returned to the campfire to await further instructions.

The rest of the crew had finished their chores. Everyone snuck off to get some sleep before breakfast. Charley waited by the fire as the camp grew still and quiet. Only the guards, staged at each end of the caravan, remained alert.

He fell asleep sitting on a stump with his elbows on his knees and his fists under his chin to prop his head up. He awoke with a start when one elbow slipped from his knee causing the whole sleeping-there-with-his-head propped-up thing to collapse.

Camp was dead quiet, the fire nearly out, and Michael was nowhere in sight. Charley made his way to the cook wagon, retrieved his bedroll, and returned to the fire. He had been told to wait and he would wait, but no one said he had to be awake while he waited. He put more wood on the fire, curled up next to it and fell sound asleep.

— Chapter Three —

12 June 1846
Wednesday Morning
Clyde, New York

THE SUN PIERCED UNINVITED THROUGH his eyelids. He could smell the side pork frying and heard random movements within the camp. Horses needed tending. Bladders needed emptying. He wondered why Michael never came back. He walked over to the big gray horses and found them standing nose-to-nose as if they were having a private conversation. They turned to watch as he approached. Again, he marveled at their size and beauty. The water bucket was empty, so he ran to fill it. The hay was depleted, so he replenished their ration.

The younger boys were arbitrarily expected to help the cook. Charley went after water and wood and stoked the breakfast fire. Others broke out dishes and utensils. In an efficiency that would put a farmer's wife to shame, Max had steaming hot meat, potatoes, scrambled eggs, and coffee ready to feed the thirty-odd all male outfit in a matter of minutes. Everything needed to be made ready for the "best show ever" and getting it done was much easier on a full stomach.

After chores, everyone took a turn at the river. A bar of soap, a bath, and a clean shirt were luxuries on the road and bathing rituals were attended to with much seriousness. A man was lucky if he managed to bathe once a month. Long hauls between shows sometimes made it impossible to indulge in undertakings of personal hygiene. When opportunity was limited, horses and performers were the only troupe members that didn't stink. They had to smell nice, or the crowds wouldn't come.

Charley looked around as he curried the big gray horse in front of him. No Michael in sight. He hadn't been there at breakfast and now it was nearly noon. Every horse at Sands and Lent was brushed shiny, well fed, and amply watered. The Cinderella coach was spotless. Halters, saddles, ropes, reigns and bits were inspected and ready. Costumes were checked, tidied, and mended where necessary. Wagons had been examined from stem to stern. Repairs were in progress for a loose wheel band on one wagon. The tongue of another had developed a small crack and was being splinted and rope-wrapped to reinforce it.

Locals had already started gathering in the woods around the camp, watching. Gawkers in every town were keen to catch a glimpse of the private life behind the public facade of the show. Although they usually stayed a respectful distance, Charley still wasn't comfortable with the watchers.

Joe Pentland always made a point of entertaining the peeping-toms. If they wanted to see him during his most private moments, he was happy to share. Charley watched as Joe stood at the back of his wagon, making preparations to shave. He was bare-chested. His clean shirt hung on a nail at the end of the wagon. Red suspenders, fastened to buttons at his waist, hung down loosely on both sides. He placed a washbowl filled with steaming hot water on a board that protruded out behind the wagon like a narrow table. He lifted out his white porcelain shaving mug with red-handled shaving brush from a recess in the wagon and placed it beside the bowl. He reached into another nook and pulled out a tin mirror which he propped up behind the washbowl. His hand disappeared into yet another cubby and pulled out a folded straight razor. This he placed beside the shaving mug. He stepped back, put his hands on his hips and looked over the setting. Then, with pointy fingers and much finesse, he adjusted every item. He tilted the mirror… peered into it… tilted it again. He moved the mug and laid the brush to one side. He opened the razor and peered down at its blade, twisted it and peered again. He began humming loudly as he lifted the end of the razor strap which was hung from an iron ring on the left side of the wagon. He stretched it taut and sharpened his straight razor by dragging the blade up the strap on one side, turning it, and dragged it down on the other in perfect rhythm with his humming of the Widow MaChree. At last, he held the blade up to the sun and turned it slowly, squinting and inspecting the edge.

Once satisfied, he turned back to the table, laid down the razor, picked up the shaving brush and swished it around in the hot water. He held the shaving mug steady on the board as he pushed the soggy brush into it. With the furor of a prairie dog digging a hole, he pushed the brush round and round and finally, with a loud, "ah ha!" removed the brush and inspected the astounding mass of bubbles adhering to it.

Gazing into the mirror, he carefully applied a lavish amount of foam to his face and neck. He laughed at his own reflection and turned to show Charley (and the audience) that he now appeared to be a grizzled old mountain man with a full white beard.

Just as he was about to apply the blade to his cheek, a cat meowed loudly, startling the man. The spectators could not see any cat and although Joe looked, he could not lay eyes on it either. He resumed his ritual, dipped the blade in the water, shook it three times, and watched as the water droplets fled far and wide. With exaggerated ceremony, he peered into the tin mirror, raised the razor to his left jaw and scraped upwardly gently…one, two, three times….

"It worked!" He exclaimed aloud, and with razor in right hand and towel in the other, jumped up and down, dancing a high-kicking Irish jig. His foot landed in a bucket, he half-fell, caught himself, shook the bucket off his foot and somehow got entangled in his dangling suspenders. He wriggled and shrieked and finally got his arm loose when he stepped into the bucket again, lost his balance, and landed on his backside in the grass with the shaving blade still in hand, pointing straight up at the blue sky.

The spies in the bushes laughed behind their hands believing they were still undiscovered. Their number had increased during the ordeal to more than twenty. They looked at each other shaking their heads, acknowledging this shaving man was a simpleton.

Joe stood up, brushed himself off and very carefully placed the bucket under the wagon away from his feet. He returned to his ritual and removed the remaining foam and whiskers quickly. Just as he toweled off his face and was peering into the mirror, the cat meowed again! Louder! Armed with a towel in one hand and razor in the other, the half-dressed man, suspenders dangling, sprinted around the whole wagon in effort to catch the beast. He shrieked unintelligible abominations as his bare feet met with twigs and stones. The watchers laughed unrestrained now, as did Charley. He'd seen it before, but it was still funny.

No one could see a cat because there was no cat. Mr. Pentland was able to throw his voice and make people believe there was a cat. Tall, skinny, and with a face that appeared ready to break into laughter at any moment, Joe the clown was everyone's favorite.

Setting his shaving instruments down, Joe turned to face the gawkers. "Shoo!" He said making shooing gestures with his hands. "The show doesn't start until two! Come back then! Goodbye!"

As Charley watched the crowd break up and move off, a big hand grasped his shoulder causing him to turn on his heels. The friendly face of the man he'd been waiting for stood in front of him.

"Hey Charley, are you ready?" Asked the blue-eyed man.

"Ready for what, Michael?" asked Charley. "What job have you got for me?"

"I see," said Michael, "No one talked to you about getting the horses to New York City?"

"No sir! I haven't talked to anyone about any such thing. I've been waiting here for you, just like you asked yesterday."

"Sorry about that," Michael said apologetically. "It took longer than I thought to line up transportation on the canal for us. I had to see some folks last night about fixing a spot on a line boat to Albany. I waited outside the boat office until this morning before anyone showed up. Then I had to convince them they had room for us."

"Room for us?" he inquired of his new friend.

"Oh yeah!" laughed Michael. "I forgot! No one talked to you yet. Mr. Lent, my boss, told me about you before I came to get the horses. He said that if you worked out with Mr. Sands, I should try to get you to help me bring the new horses back to New York City… you want to? Go with me, I mean?"

"Whoa!" exclaimed Charley. "Um, YEAH! I want to go, but I can't just quit if they need me here."

"It's all fixed, they just forgot to tell ya!" Michael laughed and started off toward the horses entrusted to his care. He got about ten feet, stopped, and turned around to say something more to Charley… who hadn't moved a muscle.

"You want to go, Charley? You don't have to if you don't want to. Mr. Lent just told me you were good with horses. You can come back after if you want." He paused, and then added, "If you want to travel, we'll pick up your pay and head out in the morning."

There was no question that he was going. NEW YORK CITY! He had never been there, but he had heard about it. The water, the boats, the canal, and hauling livestock on line boats weren't new to him. He grew up on Lake Ontario and had traveled the river with his dad several times. This sounded way better than shoveling horse manure.

The two shows at Clyde had gone on without a hitch. Charley helped get the caravan packed up and on the road to Lyons before nightfall. He hadn't been with the show very long, but he still felt a little sorry to see the wagons pull away. He'd made friends. He tucked his thumbs under the thick leather belt at his waist, a gift from Jimmy. "I have a new one," Jimmy had said to Charley. "I don't need two belts to hold my pants up!" Jimmy had reassured him they would meet again soon. Circus people were always parting and meeting again in another place. It's just how it worked out.

Michael and Charley looked around the empty field. They had stirred the fire pit to make sure it was cold and thoroughly doused it with an extra bucket of water. With three horses in tow, they walked off north, across the low bridge that spanned the Erie Canal toward the busy town of Clyde. They would camp by the canal and board the line boat at first light.

+ + +

"Wake up! Wake up!" whispered Michael somewhere in the dark. "Time to go. We have to hurry."

It took just moments to pull stakes and move the horses off toward the docks. It was obvious when they got there they were not the only passengers waiting to board the vessel. A half dozen or so people murmured and shifted as they waited for passengers and cargo to be unloaded first.

Commodities from inland traveled from west to east and goods from New York traveled from east to west along the canal. Many foreigners arriving in New York paid two cents a head per mile to transport themselves inland in search of a new life on new land. They came with children, cattle, sheep, and even chickens.

The trip to Albany would be slow as the mules on shore that pulled the boats could only move so fast. There were some thirty-odd locks on the Erie Canal between Clyde and Albany and each one took time to open, close, fill and empty. If the trip wasn't already slow enough, whenever a packet boat wanted to pass, the line boat was required to drop the ropes between themselves and the hauling mules and wait while the packet boat passed. Packet boats, filled with only human passengers, traveled faster and always took precedence over boats carrying freight or livestock. The disconnecting, waiting, and reconnecting took additional time.

Michael told Charley that they would replenish their supplies in Albany and then take a different boat to New York City. That leg of the journey was one hundred and fifty miles. For now, they had the canvas sack Max had given them with side pork, tough sour dough bread, hard boiled eggs and soda cake. The sun peeked up over the horizon in golden warm tones as 13 June 1846 arrived in all its summer splendor. Horses secured on deck, the two boys, one younger one older, sat on the sun-warmed boards of the canal boat filling their bellies.

CHAPTER FOUR

27 NOVEMBER 1846
OSWEGO COUNTY, NEW YORK

BENAJAH WHITE, AGED THIRTY-SIX, HAD spent the previous day celebrating Thanksgiving with three of his four children and wife, Johanna. Dinner was a bountiful feast of fresh bread with raspberry jam and salted butter, turkey and potatoes with gravy, whole roasted carrots, and warm apple pie drenched in fresh cow's cream. Although splendid, the day was not perfect. His eldest son was missing. They had set a place at the table for him. His chair stood next to his father's because he was the eldest. Even with the cheerful company of Ben junior, Emily, and William, ages ten, eight, and six respectively, Benajah caught himself staring at the empty chair. Was Charley all right?

The little circus his son had joined was routed through New York during the months of June, July, August and September. If all went well, Charley would stick with them and travel to Baltimore, Boston, and Philadelphia in October and November. It was a grand opportunity for the boy, a chance to learn things and make a little money. Although young, his boy was smart and careful. Benajah did not regret allowing him to go. He only regretted not knowing if he was alive and well.

The morning was clear, still and beautiful. Indian Summer, they called it. A week earlier, a gale had blown up over the lake. The storm wrecked several ships and ruined tons of cargo. Many farmers around him had lost livestock and some of their buildings were blown down. Benajah's buildings had held thankfully, and he didn't lose any animals. He was a carpenter. He knew how to build. He did, however, lose most of the hay he'd mounded up under the lean-to by the barn. He should have known a stiff wind would just blow it away. He wasn't a good farmer. He didn't like farming. He liked wood, everything from cutting it down in the forest to sawing it up into lumber. Cupboard-making in the winter was good work, and it paid well when folks could afford to buy from him. Charley had been his helper ever since he could fetch a hammer.

Benajah stopped walking, took in a deep breath, and asked the clouds, "Where are you, son?" He withdrew a piece of paper from his pocket, unfolded it and read it for the umpteenth time. The circus route was written neatly in his son's steady hand. According to the list, the boy would still be in Philadelphia and not home before the first of December. Somehow he did not believe his son was in Philadelphia. It nagged on him.

"I'm a fool," he muttered as he continued down the path toward town. Maybe today there would be a letter.

He had to buy nails to fix the chicken coup. That was the excuse he'd given his wife for coming to town. She thought he was foolish to worry about Charley. She thought it silly to walk to town every other day to check for a letter. Never mind. He was going to do what he wanted in spite of what she thought. Still, there was absolutely no reason to get on her bad side…so he'd lied. He didn't need nails, but he had better get some home with him.

Johanna was Benajah's second wife. His first wife, Ivanna, had died in childbirth when Charley was a little more than two. Ivanna and their baby girl were buried in the same casket the day after they died. Ivanna's family, the Hubbards, had gathered around to mourn her and comfort Benajah as he held tightly onto his little son's hand and stared at the coffin. His whole family, except for Charley, was in that wooden box.

His dead wife's family stood by Benajah. Johanna, Ivanna's older sister, cooked, cleaned and looked after Benajah and Charley for months. She came in the morning and left in the evening. It seemed natural for them to marry. They had their first child together a year later, in 1836. Johanna tried to love her sister's son as much as she did her own offspring, but she did not. Benajah tried to love all his children the same, but Charley was dearest to him. Joanna was secretly relieved when the boy left.

Hearing a boat whistle in the distance, Benajah realized he was already at the edge of town. The three-mile walk always passed quickly. He liked walking and he wasn't opposed to a little daydreaming. Benajah nodded at several of the locals on the boardwalk on his way to the letter office. He braced himself for disappointment as he drew open the door and stepped into the building. The little bell over the door tinkled merrily even as he walked to the far corner where letters were handled.

There was a letter for him. The clerk handed it to him and turned his back, returning to his business. There was no postage due. Benajah stared at the envelope in his hand. It was thick and heavy, and he recognized the careful handwriting of his son. A warm wave of happiness swept through him. He pushed the letter down deep into his coat pocket and made his way over to the hardware store.

He exchanged pleasantries with several men. Most of them stopped in for the sole purpose of getting away from the missus. Gossip was an extra benefit to the outing. He was no different. This man-place was an oasis. He weighed out his nails, paid, poured the nails into his leather pouch, and headed home.

He was mindful of the unopened letter in his pocket as he milked the cow and fed the chickens. He did not forget it as he rattled the oat bucket at Billy and Bobby to call the horses to come to him. There was still grass in the field, but they needed their grain. Benajah scooped oats from a barrel and put a measure into each of their pans. He smiled as he quartered two sweet apples for the horses.

Benajah touched the letter in his pocket during supper, and even once while bringing wood in for the fire. It was reassuring to know it was there. He didn't tell his wife about it. He wanted to be alone in the barn to "check on the animals" to read the letter in peace and quiet.

As his wife was tucking the little ones into bed, he lifted the lantern from the nail on the wall, lit it and headed out the door. "I'll be back in a few minutes," he called softly, just loudly enough for his wife to hear.

He led the horses into their stalls and shut the barn door. November nights were chilly and some of the heat would stay in. He hung the lantern on the nail over his workbench and pulled up a stool to sit on. He looked around, reassuring himself that he was alone, and withdrew the letter and slit it open with his pocketknife.

"Dear Dad," it began…

I hope you are well, and mother and the children. I miss you all, especially Emily. I do not want you to worry about me. The carrier said that you should get this letter in about a week. I hope you received it in good time. Things did not work out as planned this summer, but I am working and doing well.

I am in Brooklyn right now. I am working at the Van Amburgh show and not with the circus I started out with. I will stay here long enough to help this outfit get moved to Baltimore where they will stay for the winter. As soon as they are moved, I will come home.

Here is what happened. Mr. Lent, the man I met when I pulled out the stuck circus wagon, said he liked how I handled my horses. Do you remember that Mr. Lent was not in Syracuse when we went to the show there? Well, he told Mr. Mosely, the horse boss, to hire me if I showed up, which he did. Mr. Lent manages another traveling show, the Van Amburgh & Company Menagerie, and he travels with them most of the time. He was only up north where I met him because he was buying some horses to pull Van Amburgh's wagons. He could not transport them himself, so he sent his man, Michael O'Donnell. Mr. Lent told him to catch up with the Sands & Lent show and see if I could help him move the horses.

We got the horses to New York City and were supposed to deliver them to a livery on Bowery Street, which we did. I was supposed to travel back upriver to rejoin the circus. When we got to the livery, Mr. Titus, Mr. Lent's boss, asked us to deliver the horses to the Van Amburgh show in Massachusetts. We said we would. We took a boat to New Bedford and arrived June twenty-second.

I thought I could catch up with the Sands & Lent show in North Danville. It did not work out that way. When the man came to get the horses, Mr. Lent was with him. He asked us if we could stay with the Van Amburgh show for a few weeks because the man who takes care of the harnesses for all the horses broke his leg and needed boys to work for him.

Michael did not want to stay, so he got his pay and left right away. He wanted to fight the Mexican War in Texas. He has no family except his brother who is already there. I decided I would stay for a few weeks to help Mr. Lent out. I am glad that I did. I am learning new things and making good pay.

I will tell you a little bit about the job. The eight horses pulling the bandwagon are great black ones called Flemish horses. They are graceful and walk as if they are prancing. They hold their heads high and proud. The wagon they pull is big and heavy. It holds a large brass band that plays wonderful music. The horses pull the wagon easily and do not seem to mind the noise. They are finer boned than our boys, but taller at the shoulder. They wear ornaments on their harnesses made of silver plate from Germany. Mr. Jones, the harness man, taught me how to inspect the harnesses and make sure the ornaments are secure. I polish them every day.

There are other horses that pull the cage-wagons with the menagerie animals. These are called dappled gray draft horses. It was two of these that we delivered from up north. Every piece of leather harness and trapping for every horse needs to be checked and fixed every day because the outfit travels from one town to another and has a parade in every one of those towns. The menagerie has a lot of interesting animals, but I am most often around the big cats. They are calm as kittens in their cages. It is only when Mr. Amburgh is with them that they sound dangerous. The crowd thinks Mr. Van Amburgh will be killed, but I think the cats are afraid of him.

Anyway, Mr. Jones' leg got a terrible infection and the poor man died. Now I am in charge of the harnesses until they find someone else. That is why I cannot come home until the menagerie is in Maryland and settled for the winter.

I hope to be home in a week or two.
Your son,
Alasco Charles White

Benajah read the letter twice, folded it up and put it back in the envelope. He lifted the lantern down from the hook and headed toward the house. He was proud of his son for taking on such responsibility and content to know he was well and coming home soon. Inside the house, he extinguished the lantern, hung it on its nail, pulled off his boots, hung his coat on its hook, and went to bed. Johanna was already sleeping. He would tell her in the morning.

CHAPTER FIVE

TWO YEARS LATER…
NOVEMBER 1848
BROOKLYN, NEW YORK

THE BOY WALKED SOUNDLESSLY THROUGH the maze of cages, making his way from the dining tent through the animal tent to the camp area. All eyes were on him as he passed. The animals drew closer to the sides of their enclosures where he walked, not to challenge him, but to greet him. Young Charley often had a treat and if there should be such a good bit in his hand today, they would be available to take it.

Charley was a person of habit. He had always saved something back for the animals. He supposed he got that from his dad. Tonight, he had cut up an apple into small bits and stuffed the pieces into one side of the brown leather pouch on his belt. Bits of beef gristle from the evening meal had also made their way into the pouch, treasured tasty bits for the big cats. He had fashioned the bag for just this purpose, transporting treats for the animals. One side was "wet" and had small holes drilled in it so it could air out and dry. The other side was kept "dry" for nuts, sugar cubes and leftover bread bits. A stranger might speculate as to what he carried in the pouch and would probably guess money or valuables, perhaps a bible or diary. The critters of the Van

Amburgh & Company Menagerie were not so deluded. They were mindful of "the pouch" and keenly aware of its treasure.

Of course, he could never have enough scraps to feed every animal every evening, so he made sure that his not-so-random handouts were spread evenly over time. He offered up chunks of apple with open palm to zebra and deer alike but gently tossed meat or fat through the bars to the waiting animals with sharp teeth. The polar bear, made famous the previous month by his antics, was a stark reminder that most of these seemingly calm captive animals were still wild beasts at heart. The story of the bear's adventure was carried in newspapers throughout the northeast. Bruin, when offered a piece of candy by a young boy in Cleveland, took not only the offered sweet, but also the boys' right index finger. There was nothing to be done about it. The finger was severed, clean as a whistle, and swallowed. It's doubtful Bruin even realized he'd harmed the boy. Menagerie signs had been posted on every cage in big black letters, **"DANGER! WILD ANIMALS! KEEP BACK!"** The boy had not heeded the signs. In any case, it seemed that there truly is no such thing as *bad* publicity. Since the incident, Bruin's visitors had quadrupled. The white bear had been a part of the show for years without being very significant, but now he was famous and a *main* attraction. It didn't take long for the signs on his cage to read, **"DANGER! MAN-EATING BEAR! STAY BACK!"** That was proper selling. Mr. Lent was good at that.

The extensive and much-admired exotic animal collection of John June and Lewis Titus had split into two parts in March. One part, "Van Amburgh & Company Menagerie," toured through the northeastern United States while the other half billed as "June, Titus & Company," made its way through the British provinces.

November marked the end of the traveling season. The Van Amburgh half of the collection with Charley arrived in Brooklyn on the fourteenth. They had pitched their tents across from the new city hall on Joralemon Street for a four-day exhibition. On the fifteenth, the second half of the June/Titus collection arrived from Canada. The shows merged to become one. Now there were twice as many animals for the public to enjoy at one low price.

After the four-day exhibition in Brooklyn, the entire collection would move to the Zoological Hall at 37 Bowery Street on Manhattan Island. The animals would winter there. Their owners hoped that paying New York crowds would bring in sufficient income to sustain them.

Charley's job was to take care of the tack for all the horses including those that pulled the wagons in street parades and moved the show from one town to another. Without parades or moves, there was no work for him once the transfer to winter quarters was made. He would pack his few belongings and head back upstate to work the winter at the sawmill alongside his dad, in Onondaga County about twenty-five miles south of Syracuse. It was colder up there, but it would be nice to be with his family.

With all the equipment packed down and stored, dinner settling in comfortably and the contents of his treat pouch empty, Charley tended to his own needs. Before retiring, he always sat by the campfire in the company of his friends. He pulled out his little knife and scraped the day from beneath his fingernails. Habits were comforting and gently closed the circle of the day's living, neatly and securely.

The knife was small, the blade less than three inches. The deer horn handle fit his palm perfectly and was useful for innumerable small jobs, like cleaning fingernails. He had come by it through the death of his friend, Michael O'Donnell. It had never occurred to him that when Michael joined his brother in the Mexican War in Texas, he might not make it home alive.

Liam O'Donnell had returned to New York, wounded but alive, and delivered his brother's knife to Mr. Lent to hold for Charley. When

Charley pulled the knife from the leather scabbard a hand-written note came out with it.

"If I die, please see that my friend, Charley White, gets my knife. I hope he remembers me."

He read the note once before folding it carefully and tucking it into his wallet. He could never forget Michael, nor could he brave reading that note again. He was constantly reminded that it was in his wallet however, as the edge of it showed whenever he took out money.

The knife always hung from his leather belt, the one Jimmy Hernandez had given him, also in 1846. Jimmy said the name his mama gave him was Mickey Kelly. On the belt's inside, scrawled in a small child's best attempt at branding, was unevenly burnt in, "M. Kelly." He'd been orphaned before he was five and taken in and trained by John Robinson. With the help of someone whose name he'd forgotten, he'd burnt his real name into the leather so he would never forget where he came from. Jimmy was currently riding with Dan Rice's Circus and headed to New Orleans. Show life, such as it was, their paths would surely cross again before long.

This was the end of his third season traveling with the Van Amburgh show. He had loved almost every minute of it. Mr. Lent was a good leader, a hands-off kind of fellow. He gave you a job to do, you did it, and he made sure you got paid on time. As a bonus, Charley got to spend his spare time in the company of animals and, although it wasn't his job, he often helped take care of them.

This season had been unusual, he thought, as he carefully cut a ragged edge from a thumbnail. This year brought its fair share of trouble. That was life though, some good, some not so good. Some things you can fix and some you cannot.

The challenges began the previous December, two days before Christmas, 1847. Charley was at his father's home in upstate New York while Van Amburgh & Company Menagerie wintered at the Roman

Amphitheatre on Calvert Street in Baltimore, Maryland. The "Roman Chariot" bandwagon that was seventeen feet high and twenty feet long, painted black and red and gilded in gold had gone up in flames while awaiting a fresh coat of paint. Twenty other wagons had been consumed along with the bandwagon inside the coach maker's shop of Mr. George C. Potts on Fayette Street. The wagons were insured, so money wasn't the immediate problem; time was the issue. It had been a valiant race against the calendar to get twenty-one colorful wagons and cages built and decorated in time for the spring run. By the time Charley showed up to travel with the show that spring, the brand-new bandwagon stood complete and ready to transport "Post's famous New York Brass Band" in the year's first parade. All Charley had to do was ready the tack, polish the silver-plated harnesses, and hitch the eight black Flemish horses to the front of it. The menagerie went parading through Washington D.C. on the tenth of April, just shy of four months after the fire as if nothing bad had ever happened.

The exhibition tents had been erected right in front of the brand-new Smithsonian Institute and remained for four days. The partnership between the Smithsonian and the menagerie was for mutual benefit. The Smithsonian would naturally attract intellectuals who might not otherwise be inclined to frequent an animal tent. The menagerie, on the other hand, would attract many curious visitors, some of whom had little formal education, who might normally avoid visiting a scholarly museum.

Both concerns hoped that they could double the volume of citizens in the vicinity of their perspective attractions and that those citizens would be inclined to buy tickets for both the museum and the menagerie.

The resulting cross-over of visitors from menagerie to the Smithsonian was less than enthusiastic, but not without merit. On the other hand, the arrangement was a huge success for the Van Amburgh show as indeed most who visited the museum were delighted to relax and enjoy the "educational experience" of the exotic animals.

Isaac Van Amburgh was not part of the Van Amburgh & Company's Menagerie the summer of 1848. While the outfit bore his name, it was not his. The whole kit and caboodle belonged to June, Titus, and Company. They employed both Mr. Lent (to manage) and Mr. Van Amburgh (to be lion tamer and wild animal procurer). Van Amburgh had been sent off to Europe to retrieve some new exotic animals for Mr. Titus. He then stayed overseas the whole year to entertain the populace of England and Scotland.

Every week or two an article from London would find its way into the local newspapers where Charley and the crew would read about the adventures of Mr. Van Amburgh. And, while Charley loved hearing about the lion-tamer, he was not sorry the man was absent this season. While Van Amburgh was not evil or mean to the animals, his posture was cold and deliberate. His very presence cast an aloof, unpleasant shadow on the otherwise pleasurable experience of being in the company of the magnificent felines.

Mr. Van Amburgh's replacement this year was another veteran animal trainer, Mr. Brooks. He had been hired to oversee the menagerie and to do a show with the lions, tigers, and leopards for curious crowds, twice daily. His presentation was not very exciting, never having anything unexpected transpire, but it did lure customers into the tent, which paid the bills.

Competition between different traveling shows to get patrons into their tent was fierce, especially between Raymond & Waring's and Van Amburgh's menageries. In 1846 Van Amburgh rolled out the "Roman Chariot" bandwagon. The grandeur and beauty along with the glorious "Shelton's Brass Band" lured visitors to watch the parade, follow it, and buy tickets to the show. However, it wasn't long before Raymond & Waring's menagerie responded with their own "Roman

Chariot" bandwagon twice as long, three feet taller, covered in gold and "superior to Van Amburgh's or anything ever constructed, both in carving and gilding."

The competition mounted. No expense was spared for advertising and poster plastering. It was an ongoing battle for the public's attention. And what got the public's attention? They flocked to see shocking things, and terribly frightening scary things.

Raymond & Waring's got the jump on Van Amburgh's show when they introduced Miss Adelina, a female version of a lion-tamer. Women were almost never a part of any show as they were considered too delicate and refined, so what Raymond & Waring's did was bold and unprecedented. What could possibly be more alarming than seeing a defenseless damsel alone in the cage with ten or more wild cats?

Miss Adelina was dubbed the "Lion Queen" and garnered a lot of attention. Attendance was never better for Raymond & Waring's Menagerie. One could not dream that it could be better for them, until it was! Miss Adelina who, not unlike Bruin the polar bear, became a colossal sensation because of one frightening incident. As Miss Adelina was presenting the big cats of Raymond & Waring's in Connecticut, a severe storm blew the tent canvas right down right on top of the big cat cage with her trapped inside. It was all very shocking according to the papers. The cats roared and it was believed that the little lady was being eaten alive. When the canvas was finally removed from atop the large enclosure, one leopard was dead, and another was in the deadly jaws of the young male lion. The woman, although pale, was standing there in absolutely perfect health. It was subsequently reported that Miss Adelina had been heroically saved from the savage leopard attack by the brave loyalty of the young male lion. The story spread like wildfire and multitudes thronged to Raymond and Waring's tent to see for themselves, this mighty heroic lion and the little woman who dared to be in the same cage with him.

Mr. Lent's answer to the extraordinary popularity of Miss Adelina was to introduce "Miss E. Calhoun," woman lion tamer, also dubbed "Lion Queen." Lent utilized the notoriety of Miss Adelina's story to draw in his own audience. It was highly unlikely the public would know which "lady lion tamer" had been saved by the heroic lion. It could have been this lady, right? There could only be one lady lion tamer, correct? Calhoun's costume was that of a Roman gladiator, even though Roman women were unlikely to be gladiators. There was a beautiful lithograph produced to advertise her bravery. Small copies were sold after her show that exactly duplicated the posters plastered on every barn and fence along the menagerie route. The lithograph depicted her standing on the back of a growling female lion while simultaneously being embraced by a large male lion on one side and a tiger on the other. Several lions, tigers, and leopards were arranged behind her. "Miss E. Calhoun. The Celebrated LION QUEEN, as she appears with her Group of 9 Lions, Tigers & Leopards now attached to VAN AMBURGH & Co.'s Magnificent Collection of living wild animals."

Miss Calhoun was a good-sized woman, half a head taller than Charley. Up close, she did not seem small or defenseless, but she was a *woman* and that is what mattered to the public. Calhoun showed respect for the felines, but never fear. Twice a day, she entered the big cat cage where the lions, tigers and leopards were assembled for the show. She stood amongst them and handed out chunks of raw meat. Since the beasts were fed to bursting just prior to her show, the meat offered was just an extra bit of goodness, of which cats were always willing to partake.

While Charley was not overly impressed with how Mr. Brooks and Miss Calhoun showed the animals, he was pleased with how they respected them. He had even gone so far as to purchase one of the small lithographs of Miss Calhoun to take back home to his little sister, Emily.

Mr. Brooks and Miss Calhoun were both willing to share their knowledge of the big cats, and Charley was eager to learn. Whenever possible, he helped with feeding and cage mucking. He hurried with his own chores so he could help deliver the large portions of raw meat that he would slide into the cage via floor-level trapdoors. He grew to love the big, rumbling kitties. He generally took his lunch sitting by the big male lion's cage. Samson watched him intently, awaiting that little "snack" that Charley always saved for him. Mr. Brooks even allowed Charley to join him in a cage with Samson a time or two. To Charley's surprise, the cat rubbed his head on his pantleg in much the same manner as the old barn cat had done back in Oswego. Mr. Van Amburgh had never allowed anyone near the big cats, so his absence was good in many ways.

Although working with the animals helped soothe Charley's soul, he was still mourning a significant loss. On November seventh, the night before the menagerie was set to move from New Jersey to Brooklyn, calamity struck. This time the fire burned a hole right through his heart. The stable where the black Flemish horses were temporarily housed had gone up in flames. The inferno killed all eight horses and four dappled grays. The silver-plated harnesses perished with them.

The show, no matter how devastated by the tremendous loss, made its way to Brooklyn without so much as a hiccup. In Brooklyn, the new advertisements touted the "100 DAPPLE GREY HORSES" that would pull the wagons of the menagerie in the parade. No mention was made of the horses that perished.

It was hard enough for a menagerie to capture the fantasy of the public in normal times, but fervor over the presidential election made it even harder. Amusement advertisements got lost amongst the news and opinion articles about who should be the next president.

The election was scheduled to take place on the 7th of November, a Tuesday. It was the first election where everyone was to vote on the same day in every state.

Shows in Brooklyn were quick to capitalize on the situation where every man in the area would be out voting on the same day. They put up posters and handed out flyers creating their opportunity to be a part of the occasion. "Bring your family along and after your voting is done, come see the…" circus, menagerie, museum, or whatever said advertised entertainment was.

Clay, Scott and Webster lost out to General Zachary Taylor of the Whig party. And, although the Whig party platform was against the Mexican War, their candidate, General Taylor, had been part of the leadership in said conflict. The new president, as a candidate, would never say if he was "for" or "against" the conflict and maintained a middle-of-the-road posture.

Charley knew that Michael and Liam had served under this man, so he was convinced that General Zachary Taylor was the best choice for president. Someday he would serve his country as Michael had, but for now it was in good hands with General Taylor.

Today marked the last day in Brooklyn before the short hop to Bowery Road. As soon as the menagerie was settled there, Charley was free as a bird to do as he pleased, and he had plans.

Sands, Lent & Company's show was set up on the lot where Niblo's Garden used to be before it burned down, just off Broadway. He wanted to stop there to see his old friends Mr. Sands and Joe Pentland and see who else he knew in the show. A lot had happened to him since he joined them in upstate New York. Maybe they had news of Jimmy. After that, Charley planned to visit Barnum's American Museum off Anne Street and Broadway. It was twenty-five cents, but he knew it was well worth the price. He liked animals and odd things and he'd been told the museum was chock full of them.

As Charley slipped the little knife into its scabbard, footsteps approached. He looked up and found Mr. Lewis B. Lent, ever attired in black coat and hat, standing in front of him.

"And Charley, what will you be doing this winter? Will you be back in the spring?"

"I'm going home to my fathers' for the winter, sir. And yes, I do plan to be back here next April," he explained as he stood to face the man. "That is, sir, if you would have me back."

Mr. Lent coughed into his hand and cleared his throat. "I'm sailing for California come January. I won't be managing the show next year, Charley."

The news was disappointing, but not altogether surprising. There was gold in California, and many had spoken of nuggets big as hen's eggs just lying around in creek beds waiting to be found.

"Charley, I am going on an adventure. I have not been to California before and while I know how to do this," he gestured at the animals now relaxing for the night, "I should like to try my hand at other endeavors. Life is too short to be bored. Sometimes one has to take chances."

"Sir," Charley responded, "You are right, of course!" He drew himself up to full length and looked the older man in the eye. "I wish you Godspeed, Mr. Lent. I know you will master the task."

Charley offered his hand and Lent took it in both of his and shook firmly.

"Thank you, Mr. Charley White," the big man said and tipped his hat. "I'm sure they'll have you back in the spring. You do a good job and are steady." He turned to go and halted, waved his left hand over his shoulder and said, "We'll see you when we see you, Charley! Take care!" And he disappeared into the night.

The move to the Zoological Hall on Bowery Street went without a hitch. The building was beautiful, spacious, and had just been completely renovated by June, Titus & Company. The combined menageries of exotic birds and wild beasts, also the property of June Titus & Company, could rest. No parades. No new towns. The people of New York were welcome to come to them for the next four months or so, but the creatures were staying put for a while. As for Charley, well he would head back north to spend the winter with his family just as he had the two previous years. This time, however, the trip would be a day shorter. His father had finally moved from the farm in Oswego to a little town called Fabius, just south of Syracuse. Charley had a job at the sawmill if he wanted it.

Chapter Six

2 April 1849
The Bowery
Manhattan, New York

A THIN LAYER OF FROST HAD painted the sooty streets of Manhattan a ghostly gray. He had made his way back to New York City by way of the canal (Syracuse to Albany) then on the Hudson (Albany to New York City). The freighter he'd caught a ride on had arrived hours before dawn to be off-loaded at the docks, reloaded and quickly sent back upstream to Albany. Charley had bartered his labor in exchange for passage, thus two hours passed between docking and his release. His arms ached some. He had rushed to get the boat empty, so he could continue his pilgrimage.

He finally arrived at the back door of Zoological Hall at 37 Bowery Street at quarter past seven in the morning. A thick mat of frosted straw crunched under his feet as he approached the blood-red ten-foot barn doors of the hall. Straw had been spread out to help marginalize the effect of the boot-sucking Manhattan mud. "It must be ten-foot deep by now," he muttered to himself. No one ever removed straw, they just kept adding more. Layers of sawdust and straw and mud were the very foundation of any menagerie or farm for that matter. Wet feet caused sickness, so every attempt was made to provide a stable dry surface for both man and beast.

He shifted his bag and raised a fist to knock against the heavy wooden door. His knuckles very nearly smacked into old Dan's forehead as the guard managed to open the door at precisely the same instant.

"Well, I'll be!" Exclaimed the old fellow. "If it ain't young Mr. Charley coming back for another year of madness. Come in! Come in!" The white-haired gentleman opened the door wider and gestured for him to enter. "Good to see you, boy! How are you? Let me look at you," he said as he put a hand on each of the boy's shoulders and looked at him, face to face. "You've grown! You must be half a hand taller!"

Charley laughed and raised his hand to shake Dan's.

"It is good to see you, Dan. At least you're still here. I'm almost afraid to go inside and see how things have been switched around for the summer."

"Always changing Charley, you know that. The public is fickle. They want new, new, new… all the time. Since Mr. Lent is off hunting gold in California, it's June and Titus who schemed up this year's combinations." He closed the door and dropped the latch into place. "You go on now, find yourself some breakfast. I'll see you later."

Dan couldn't leave his post at the back door. His job was to keep ne'er do wells from coming in to sleep or steal. The door was always locked, and Dan was always there to let the right folks in and out.

The ode-de-menagerie surrounded Charley like a dense ocean fog. The mingling of straw, sawdust, food and fodder, excrement, liniment, wool, feathers… not to mention a waft of bacon, coffee, and pancakes coming from the large kitchen… awakened an excitement in him. He thrived on working with the animals and being in the company of others who also loved it.

Breakfast beckoned. He passed by the animal cages, glancing sideways at the still sleepy inhabitants as he made his way to the dining room. He stopped in the doorway and paused a moment to observe. His friends. His people. The room buzzed with conversation and then quieted as each man in turn noticed him standing there.

"Hey Charley, get your backside in here!" hollered John-John the bird man. The six-foot farm boy with thick blonde hair that stuck straight-out like straw rose from the table and went straight toward him. "Good to see you, buddy!" He said shaking Charley's hand. "Come on, get in here and get some breakfast."

The crew that wintered the June-Titus menagerie rarely changed. They were mostly older guys, trusted men that could keep the animals well-shod, fed and tended during the winter months. They were a tight group, not prone to letting just any newcomer into their inner circle. Lots of circus men with ten years or more under their belts still found themselves to be "outsiders."

Charley was lucky. Although no one had ever said it out loud, he was accepted as one of the insiders. It hadn't been because of his years with them or because of his fine work that got him in. It was because John-John trusted him…and everyone trusted John-John. The blue-eyed bird man had grown up on a chicken farm and was the kindest, gentlest fellow on the lot. He looked like he could bend iron with his bare hands and yet he got downright sissy when he started talking about his birds. He'd been working for the American Museum at Broadway and Ann Street taking care of Mr. Barnum's exotics when Mr. Lent talked him into coming to work for him. Now he took care of all the exotic birds in the hall, cleaning pens and feeding them all by himself. It wasn't unusual to see him sitting on a stool in a bird pen with a fancy chicken perched on his knee. "Birds are downright affectionate," he would say as he stroked its head. You had to agree with him when you saw just how relaxed that chicken was, eyes closed and making noises that sounded a lot like a cat purring. Neither was it unusual for John-John to take off on his free time to trot over to Barnum's to visit his old flock. One day he had taken Charley with him. John-John knocked on the back door of the museum and the door-guard waved him in without paying. When the guard moved to stop Charley from drafting in behind him, John-John put his big hand on the guard's shoulder and said, "He's with me, Mike. He's one of us."

The African Grey Parrot, Merlin, was his favorite. When they had approached the bird's cage, it flew closer to them and said, "Hello pretty boy!" in what seemed to be a perfect copy of John-Johns' surprisingly soft tenor voice. John-John planned to have his own flock one day and he dearly hoped to save enough money to buy Merlin off Mr. Barnum. These African birds live very long lives, so he had time to save up.

Charley got a stack of pancakes and while he ate, the fellows filled him in on the plans for the upcoming summer. Once the collection of animals had been divided, they would take off in different directions. The "June, Titus, & Company" outfit would route through New York, Pennsylvania, Maryland, and Washington D.C. They were starting out the 16th in Brooklyn. They'd signed on several acts Charley hadn't heard of and some he had. Sam Lathrop who had been with Sands & Lent in '46 when Charley started out, was now a clown and George Beasley, was the lion tamer. They would take the Asian elephant Romeo with them.

The "Van Amburgh & Company" part would journey farther east starting off in Connecticut and ending up in Massachusetts. Mr. Langworthy would take his performing war elephant, Bolivar. He also had trained monkeys and ponies. Mr. Brooks was named as the lion tamer and Miss E. Calhoun, the lion queen. Although Van Amburgh had recently returned from England, he was not performing at the Zoological Hall and would not be attached to the show with his name on it. Instead, he was performing at the Bowery Theatre enacting a dramatic spectacle called "Morok" where he played a beast tamer straight from the imagination of Eugene Sue's "Wandering Jew" novel.

"Worth seeing," John-John grinned, "the cats he has are really pretty, especially that new black tiger."

Almost as if there had been a silent whistle, everyone stood to leave the table and get to work. Animals were hungry, stalls needed mucking, and the arena needed readying before the first show at one-thirty.

Charley made his way to the office to confirm his summer employment and get his assignments. He imagined there would be a very long list of "fetch this" and "carry that." The hustle was always on during the first week of April. Not only did the boss have to manage two public shows a day, he had to get ready for the summer.

Wagons that had been repainted during the winter needed fetching and double-checking. Horses they would use to pull the wagons, including the 100 dappled grays, needed to be repatriated to the menagerie from boarding barns. A team of farriers was already making their rounds working on the more than one hundred fifty horses that were needed. Quite literally every piece of hardware needed rechecking, everything from cage bars on the animal wagons to wheel bands and spokes. And, every single piece of the show must be clean and polished, for who would wish to follow a procession of dirty animals and wagons and pay twenty-five cents to get into the show?

Mr. Jacobson sat at his desk, bent forward over the stack of papers in front of him. He'd arranged himself so that the high window in the room was behind him and the door to his office was in front of him. His thick eyeglasses were perched on the end of his nose so he could make out the details on the lists in front of him.

Mr. Jacobson was already peering over the top of his spectacles in response to the sound of approaching footsteps when Charley knocked on the door frame.

"Charley!" He laughed, "Good to see you! Come in! Come in!"

Charley walked over to the man, who stood and shook his hand.

"Sit! Sit!" he said, as he motioned to the wooden kitchen chair at the side of his desk.

Charley sat, as instructed, knowing that this was likely the last time he would have a moment of peaceful time with his boss until the day he collected his pay after the menagerie was once again securely put into winter quarters in November.

Mr. Jacobson was earnest in his discussion. "I could use three of you, Charley. There is much to do and few experienced men to help get it done." He summarized the summer strategies for the two shows and who would be in charge of what; G.C. Quick would manage the "June, Titus, & Company" and Jacobson himself would manage "Van Amburgh & Company."

"Now Charley, you can choose to take up with either one of these shows. It is your choice. We could use you in both. Brooks and Langworthy are the animal men going with the "Van Amburgh" outfit. I'm hoping you'll choose that one."

"Well?" asked Jacobson.

Charley didn't have to think about it. He'd made up his mind back in the dining hall when the boys had filled him in.

"I'll go along with you, of course, Mr. Jacobson. I get on with Mr. Brooks and I've heard a lot of good things about Mr. Langworthy. What of Mr. Van Amburgh?" asked Charley, wanting to confirm what he'd heard at breakfast.

"Van Amburgh is doing his show over at the Bowery for a while. Word is he doesn't want to go on the road just yet. He just got back from England. Tired, I guess," muttered Jacobson.

"And what of Mr. Lent, sir? Have you heard from him?" asked Charley.

"Oh, my goodness, yes!" laughed the older man. "Lent got hisself off on that packet boat in January, but the damn thing ran into a bad storm three days out…paper said they were lucky to come out alive… floundered just off of some island. Last we heard he was waiting it out in Rio in Brazil, South America for ship repairs. Funny business, that… floating halfway around the world in hopes of finding a little gold." Mr. Jacobson sat up straight in his chair; catching-up time was over.

"So! Here is what I'm thinking. You have some good experience and I know I can trust you, so I'm going to give you more responsibility. I'm going to hire some boys to help out again this year, only difference is," he paused for breath and effect, "You are going to run 'em for me." Mr. Jacobson leaned back in his chair again and eyed Charley. "That work for you?"

Charley nodded at his boss, "Yes sir! I can do that. Where do I start?"

"Well, right now I need you to go check on Mr. Langworthy over there" and he waved in the direction of the far side of the arena. "He is in immediate need of an assistant. His elephant needs his feet worked on before we head out. Run on over and see if he'll have you. Come back later and I'll give you a list to get working on." Mr. Jacobson turned back to his desk, leaving Charley to fend for himself.

He took a shortcut across the arena and let himself through a side door into the livestock holding area on the other side. He stopped in his tracks. A muscular black and white bulldog stood near the opposite wall, growling at him.

"It's okay, buddy," Charley spoke softly. He closed the door behind him and stood in place, waiting for the dog to approach. He murmured reassuring nothingness all the while the dog sniffed at him. Boots, then pants, and finally, standing on hind legs with forepaws on Charley's legs, he inspected the human's hands. With a snort, the dog dropped down on all fours again and sat down. Charley, whose eyes had been non-confrontational, now focused directly upon the impressive canine seated in front of him. The dog's eyes were soft, but inquisitive. He tilted his head and while looking right at Charley, let out a soft, "woof."

"Hey boy! Okay if I come in now?" The dog seemed to understand, got up and headed back into the shadows of the cavernous space. Charley followed. Only the dim morning light from the high windows thirty feet away penetrated the darkness. It was probably a good thing the dog was there for him to follow.

Charley watched as the short-legged creature disappeared behind a dividing wall. He knew he must be almost to the outside walls of the building because although he'd never been in the elephant area before, he had two years of experience in and out of the building and had a sense of its size. Besides, it had become lighter. He slowed his pace and advanced quietly trying to relax and eliminate any anxiety he might have felt. He whistled ever so softly to let the creatures, whatever sort they were, know that he was coming, and they had nothing to fear.

Following the dog, Charley found the double doors leading to a giant room. One door was open only a crack for the dog. Charley opened it wider to let himself in. The room, ablaze with the light from the rising sun temporarily blinded him. He stood still for a second to let his eyes adjust. Even half-blind, there was no mistaking the silhouette of the backlit giant in front of him. This had to be the elephant that Mr. Jacobson had told him about.

A man's voice greeted him, quietly. "Please, come with me."

The dog emerged from the shadows and followed the man at his heel. Charley followed them a short distance to a small tack room. The familiar smells of liniment and leather met him as he walked through the door. Dust particles danced randomly in a sunbeam that found its way through the high window to light the opposite wall, a wall covered in harnesses and halters.

"Sit! Sit!" instructed the man as he pointed to a chair. "Who are you and what business do you have here?" The man sat in the opposite chair and waited.

Charley explained who he was and that Mr. Jacobson had sent him. All the while the man nodded affirmatively.

"You are Mr. Langworthy, correct?" asked Charley.

"Yes. Yes. Of course. That's me." The man smiled and gestured at his dog, curled up on a sack on the floor. "And you've met Turk, of course?"

"Yes! He showed me how to find you." He continued, "Will you have me help you today, sir?"

"Oh yes!" laughed the gentleman in front of him, "I will always be grateful for a helping hand! The question is," and he gestured toward the big room where the elephant was, "Will Bolivar like you? Have you been around elephants before, son?"

"No sir, not really. I've seen them and I've heard lots of stories. They are powerful animals, sir, and I believe you must be very careful with them."

"More than that," Mr. Langworthy continued, "they can kill you. If you make 'em mad, they can kill you in an instant." He looked at the boy, trying to judge his reaction. Was he frightened? Was he of good character?

"Elephants can tell good people from bad. They can be tolerant if you're stupid, but they will kill a man who is mean. They cannot leave, you see. If they don't like something in the wild, they can just leave, get away from the evil. But here," he gestured into the elephant room, "the elephant is trapped with both good and bad. The only way he can escape the bad is to crush it. You understand?"

"Yes sir!" answered Charley, "I don't know if he will take to me or not sir, but I would like to give it a try."

"Okay then. There is a wooden chair in the other room. I want you to stand behind it and stay there. Do not approach Bolivar. I'm going to go tell him that you are a good guy and while I am standing by him, he can eyeball you and judge for himself."

The two re-entered the elephant parlor. Mr. Langworthy put a hand on Charley's shoulder and walked him over to the wooden chair about fifteen feet from the elephant. He made the boy stand behind the high back of the chair, take his hands out of his pockets and place them on the back of the chair where the elephant could see them.

"Now, don't say anything until I say so, got it?"

Langworthy searched out Charley's eyes and as soon as the boy nodded, he headed over to the front end of the elephant. Turk followed right behind him.

Langworthy muttered soft nothings to the mammoth beast as he approached. As Langworthy reached the elephant, he held out his hands in front of him. The trunk extended and encircled the man's head softly and then reached down to smell the hands of his trainer. Charley's scent was all over Langworthy. As if the elephant were contemplating the flavor of this new person, he sniffed and snorted and sniffed again, finally dropping his trunk and just standing still by his keeper. Only his eyes moved, first to Langworthy, then Turk, and then a side-glance at the stranger behind the chair.

"Okay, Bolivar!" Said Langworthy as he petted the giant, "I'll be back in a bit and have you work for the rest of your breakfast."

Bolivar rocked back and forth gently in a barely perceptible movement and dropped his trunk into the bale of hay in front of him. Langworthy, followed by Turk, returned to Charley.

"Come on, son." He gestured out the other end of the room. "Let's go meet my ponies and see what you think of them."

"Sure," said Charley, "but, what about your elephant? Jacobson said you needed some help with his feet?"

"Plenty of time for that Charley. Bolivar has to get to know you first and so do I," he said as he steered the boy toward the ponies.

When they entered the holding area with stalls for the ponies, there was an awful screeching that startled Charley. He looked at Mr. Langworthy questioningly.

"That's the monkeys, Charley. They're excited to see us!"

Mr. Langworthy let out a laugh and walked by all the pony stalls to the end where a large, barred cage stood. Two small monkeys stood on the foreside holding the bars in their spidery little hands.

"They're smiling at me, sir!" exclaimed Charley as he got closer.

"Keep a distance, Charley. Smiling can mean they're nervous and trying to look submissive, so you don't hurt them. If you get too close, they might get scared and bite, probably not, but we ought to introduce you before you get too personal with them."

Langworthy and Charley spent the day together, cleaning out pony stalls, feeding the monkeys carrots and apples and even three more trips to Bolivar. Langworthy was a gentle man and a good teacher. He showed Charley little things that his ponies could do for him. He got one of the monkeys out and stuck it on a pony. Neither pony nor monkey was shocked by this, but Charley was. He had a lot to learn about the animals in the menagerie and he dearly hoped Mr. Langworthy would teach him. They were traveling together this summer, so there was time to learn.

When Langworthy took Bolivar out for the 1:30 performance, Charley watched the show for the first time. The big bull elephant knelt on the sawdust when asked, appeared to "dance" when instructed to do so and to Charley's utter amazement, gently lifted his keeper off the floor with his long ivory tusks before setting him back on the floor unharmed. Bolivar and Turk returned to quarters and Langworthy brought out his ponies and monkeys. The audience showed unfettered joy as the two small primates rode, clinging to the manes of the well-trained ponies and then leaped effortlessly from one mount to another without touching the ground. This miniature equestrian act was a favorite of the audience. Mr. Langworthy pretended to leave the arena with his animals, but to the surprised delight of the audience, returned for an encore.

There was no time for Charley to sit around and watch Mr. Brooks and the big cats. He'd seen Mr. Brooks in the cages before and there was plenty of time to see his act when they were on the road, and Miss Calhoun's. He found Mr. Jacobson and got the list, read it, and got on with it.

This first day back with the menagerie was better than Charley could have imagined. Mr. Jacobson was raising his pay and giving him more responsibility. Mr. Langworthy seemed a good man and had expressed a willingness to teach him more about training animals. At seventeen, Charley was a man with seemingly boundless opportunities in front of him. And to top it all off, he was happy to meet his friends once again, especially John-John the bird man.

CHAPTER SEVEN

MARCH 1850
FABIUS, NEW YORK

WHEN HE MET MR. LANGWORTHY the previous spring, Charley thought he knew quite a bit about horses. He had felt downright cocky when he introduced himself. He'd been training horses since he was seven and had been with the menagerie several seasons. He fancied himself something of an expert, an equal to Mr. Langworthy when it came to horses.

He was wrong. He was an idiot. It took half a day with Mr. Langworthy for Charley to recognize his own ignorance. In reality, he knew very little about horses, and half of what he did know was wrong.

What he knew, he'd mostly learned from his father. And, while he was never mean, he had learned to snap the whip on the back end of a horse when it wasn't moving fast enough. Sometimes he became impatient and hollered when an animal wouldn't take the bit as submissively as he thought it should. In short, most of Charley's attitude toward horses was dominance. He loved them, but in order to make them work, he'd been taught that one had to lord over them.

Mr. Langworthy, however, never raised his voice and although he carried a quirt, he never hit a horse with it. He boasted that his trick ponies worked for him because they wanted to. He paid them, of course, and that's why they worked. "As a trainer, you have to figure out what your horse is willing to do for the payment you are willing to give him." Then he added, "I have a working relationship with my animals, Charley. That means they do what I want because it's their job and they want to, not because they have to."

Charley spent as much time as he could with Mr. Langworthy during the nine months the menagerie was on the road. Whenever he had a moment, he sought out the trainer, observed and listened.

+ + +

December through April when the menagerie was wintering and Charley was living at his father's house, he practiced the basic techniques he learned from Langworthy on a five-year-old filly named Penny. To get her to do what he wanted, he first began to grow a relationship with her. He went to her stall before and after every shift at the sawmill. He would approach her and say, "Are you pretty, Penny?" After that, he would wait for her to move her head. As soon as she did, he would say "good girl" and give her a chunk of a carrot. At first Charley didn't care how she moved her head; she just had to move it a little bit and then she got the carrot.

Penny caught on quickly. She liked carrots. She would start bobbing her head like crazy every time Charley showed up in the barn, expecting a carrot in return. He would ignore all of the random head-bobbing until she gave up and stopped. Then, while making sure that she was paying attention to him, he'd say, "Are you pretty, Penny?" The instant she bobbed her head *after* the statement, he rewarded her with a "good girl" and a chunk of carrot. It didn't take her long to learn the sequence of talk-nod-treat that Charley wanted

The next step was to teach her the correct head movement, an up and down motion that resembled a "yes." To do this, he would ask Penny the question and watch her closely. She would move her head all over the place trying to please him to get a carrot. But he would wait until the head movement loosely resembled what he wanted. At that instant, she was rewarded. Charley repeated the sequence over and over again, each time waiting until the head nodding was a little closer to a perfect 'yes.'

In a week's time, she had it.

Over the next four months, Charley taught Penny nodding, whinnying, and bowing on request. He gave a demonstration for his family and told them they needed to work with her to make sure she didn't forget her training. He hoped his father would quit yelling and try teaching his horses instead.

If Mr. Langworthy's wisdom was the best of what Charley took away from the 1849 road season, the pipe-organ-wagon introduced by another outfit was the worst. Chaos had ensued when the Spaulding and Roger's Circus procession, complete with their monster "Apollocon" pipe-organ, passed in front of them on a cross street. The organ, enclosed in a decorated circus wagon nearly two stories high and drawn by thirty-six unfortunate steeds, gave out a long string of noises unpleasant enough to wake the dead…and scare any man or beast within earshot of it. It had taken a long while to calm the horses. The Baltimore Sun newspaper described the sound as, "a mixture of gong, bag-pipe and feline falsetto." It was only funny in hindsight.

Over the winter months, Charley pondered long and hard about whether he should return to the menagerie. It was hard labor and long hours and meant traipsing all over the countryside for nine months of the year. Sure, he'd learned a lot and had made a lot of friends, but it had become familiar and a little mundane.

He could be in Syracuse in one day's travel and find work on the docks. If he wanted greater adventure, he could easily sign-on to a boat crew. Transport vessels moving cargo on the Erie Canal connected with other waterways and bigger ships that went to places like Ohio, Michigan, Missouri, Louisiana and all the way up through Canada to the Atlantic Ocean. It was a dangerous job, but the pay was good. The world would be his oyster should he sign on to the right vessel. He had always dreamt about seeing the world by steamboat.

Whether he chose the Canal or the menagerie, he wanted something that would take him away from Fabius and a pretty girl named Lucinda. He had never had the nerve to court her. He should have spoken up. Their eyes had met a couple of times in church and he'd felt the butterflies in his stomach long after he got home.

However, the blissful spark of youthful infatuation was quickly extinguished by a harsh reality: Lucinda married a farmer named Seth the week after Easter. He was a widower, at least thirty, with an infant son. "Helpful Neighbors," the local church charity, had come forward to assist him when his wife passed shortly after her child was born. Different girls had shown up to tend the baby in the daytime so that the man could work in his field. Lucinda had been one of those young women. She fell in love with the farmer and they were soon married in a private ceremony on the farm.

When they came to church as a family the following Sunday, the parishioners swarmed around them, oohing and awing about what a blessing it was. Lucinda glowed as she stood there, baby in arms, flourishing in her new role as wife and mother. Charley had slipped out the side door, skipping the sermon.

As bright green blades of new grass poked up through the mud along the roadside heralding the coming of spring, Charley made up his mind to return to New York City. He felt confused about his feelings, not understanding why it felt like someone had died.

He was lonesome and longed to be with friends and familiar work. "Hard work cures most things, boy!" His Grandpa White's wisdom echoed in his head.

He got back to the Bowery by mid-March and there he found Mr. Langworthy along with John-John and most of the other regulars. Jacobson gave him his briefing on the year's show. Brooks would be in charge of the animals and perform with the cats. John-John was still in charge of his birds. Miss Calhoun was not coming along this season. Jacobson showed him a newspaper clipping with the headline, "Frightful Death of the Lion Queen." The paper said Miss Ellen Bligh was killed in England when a male tiger sprang upon her and tore her throat wide open. She was eighteen years old, the same as Charley. Her family had witnessed it.

"We cannot have women getting killed in the cat cage, Charley. I don't think they hold the same dominance over the beasts as men do," he muttered unintelligibly as he filed the news article on top of the pile on his desk.

Charley stared at his hands and took in a deep breath. "God in heaven," he muttered, "That's awful." He knew animals could be dangerous, but this made it really sink in. He liked the big cats and spent as much time around them as he could. He'd have to think about whether he wanted to continue to do that…or not.

"Our route will take us through a lot of little towns in New York, Connecticut and Vermont," he continued, "and the show will be twice as big this year. Mr. G.C. Quick, the fellow who managed the "June, Titus, & Company" show last year, has purchased the entire collection of animals and intends to keep them together in one giant show."

Then he added, "Van Amburgh is taking off with one of the three Raymond shows. "They're calling that show "Raymond & Company and Van Amburgh's, or something like that. We won't run into 'em, probably. I hear they're doing Pennsylvania and Canada West this year." Gossip about what shows were out there and who was doing what was as common as the sun coming up in the morning. It felt good to be back and to catch up.

Jacobson shuffled through more loose papers on his desk until he found what he was looking for and handed it over to Charley.

"We are officially employees of the "G.C. Quick & Company's Mammoth Menagerie," he said as Charley glanced over the print. "You will be in charge of some of the younger boys like last year. Suit you?" he asked rhetorically.

Charley opened his mouth to answer but was cut off.

"Oh! One more thing," Jacobson injected, "do you remember that damn organ of Spaulding & Rogers,' and how our animals spooked, and what a time we had getting them settled?"

Charley nodded affirmatively.

"Well, guess what? We're getting one… getting delivered next week. They're calling it the "auto-ma-to-deon." Say that three times, real fast!" Scoffed Jacobson. "Well," he continued, "the public wants new stuff and that's what Mr. Quick's giving them. "We'll need a couple of your boys willing to ride in that organ wagon and pump the pedals during processions. I'll leave that up to you to figure out."

Charley laughed softly as he rose from the chair, "Well, where is that list you have for me?" Jacobson shuffled the chaos on his desk again and found what he was looking for. He stood and handed the handwritten pages to Charley.

"Mighty glad to have you back, son. Now get out there and let's get this show on the road, huh?"

Mr. Jacobson had turned his back and was already bent over his desk reading before Charley made it out of his office. There were so many details that needed tending to before the show headed out, Charley was certain a great deal more would be added to his chore list.

The menagerie had a thousand moving parts. There was a vast assortment of horses, carriages, wagons, exotic animals and birds. Tents had to be erected in the blistering heat of summer or the pouring rain of the storm…and taken back down again, stored, and packed away so they would not tear on their way to the next town just twenty or thirty miles away over rocky, bumpy, narrow roads. Every man and beast needed to be fed every day, at least twice a day. Food had to be bought along the way, procured by an advance agent. The elephant alone could put away 400 or more pounds of hay every day and this menagerie had two elephants, six one-hump camels, one hundred dappled grey horses to pull the wagons, and several show ponies. It goes without saying that all the lions, tigers, bears and birds required food too, and lots of it. Every living creature in the caravan required good clean fresh water and it was a constant struggle to find enough to satisfy the thirst of so many every day.

It is an odd hodgepodge of men and boys that work a roadshow. A few veteran men come back year after year. They know how to run a show and they command a small army of young boys that "ran away to join the circus." The boys usually don't stay very long because the shine wears off the adventure quickly with twenty-hour-days that are often muddy, dusty, and sometimes hungry.

Charley learned to be more efficient in all aspects of the traveling show. He learned to prioritize and organize his responsibilities. Under Langworthy's guidance, he coaxed animals into doing as he wanted rather than forcing them. Over the summer he strengthened habits of rewarding good behavior and ignoring bad. He took the principles he learned about horses and applied them to the boys who worked under him. He learned how to lead them, so they worked better and stayed on longer than others before them. He did not just send the boys to muck out cages and hope they got it right, he showed them.

One afternoon in early June outside of a small town in Connecticut, Bolivar the Asian 'war elephant' became agitated, broke from his chain and took off running. Langworthy and Charley went after the errant behemoth on horseback with Turk running closely behind. An elephant can run fifteen miles in less than an hour, so by the time the men mounted their horses, the elephant was out of sight.

"It's amazing that he can move that fast!" hollered Charley to his search companion. "It's a good thing we have Turk to track him," he said.

It wasn't long before Charley felt foolish as all get out. A dog's nose was not needed to follow the escapee. A four-ton bull elephant leaves his mark on the landscape. Giant footprints left the road entering the forest. Broken branches and elephant-sized footprints marked his path through the trees. Where the trees stopped, the cornfield began. Row upon row of perfectly spaced foot-tall corn was marred by a newly plowed elephant pathway to the other side of the field. They could see him standing in the middle of the farmer's garden. The neat picket fence meant to keep the deer out of the vegetables was knocked over, leaving a hole the size of an elephant.

Turk was the first to reach him. He approached the elephant, stood in front of him, barked sharply several times in succession, turned on his heels and walked out of the garden. Bolivar followed him meek as a kitten. It was as simple as that.

Charley had come to know Bolivar and appreciate the intelligence of the giant. He could be aggressive and then you had to get out of the way. But he could also be gentle and even funny. He'd seen Bolivar throwing the ball for Turk to fetch and watched as the dog brought the ball back and dropped it in front of the elephant. Sometimes they played like that for hours. Langworthy claimed that elephants were complex creatures and Charley had come to understand that, firsthand. He still didn't know if he wanted to be an elephant trainer, but he surely did respect them.

The menagerie accountant reimbursed the farmer for his losses and threw in free admission tickets for good will. The elephant had to be fed anyway, so it was not such an extraordinary expense.

Other things happened in those couple of months, but nothing as exciting and harmless as Bolivar's escape and recapture. One of the dapple-grey horses stepped in a prairie-dog hole and broke his leg. There was no saving him. He had to be shot. John-John lost a couple of fancy chickens to a coyote; at least they thought it had been a coyote. Nobody was sure and there was no time to investigate. The show had to get down the road. The chickens were dead anyway. The camels went through a bout of dysentery, probably because the hay they'd purchased along the way had weeds in it. It was messy, but not fatal and they were over it in a day. The lion cage wagon lost a wheel just as they were starting off for the next town. It wasn't a dramatic failure. The wheel just slowly collapsed sideways, and the wagon halted. The wheel wasn't the problem though. It was the axel clip that failed. Luckily the place they were just leaving had a blacksmith that could fashion a new clip. The caravan was a couple of hours late leaving town, so they had to travel most of the night to make the next town in time for the show.

The crew and animals were all ready for a two-day stand when they got one in Buffalo, New York.

The first day, July 9th, was a very good day. The crowds were festive, loud and abundant. The second day was entirely different. That's when news of the death of President Zachary Taylor got out. The morning papers reassured, in a paternal tone, that Millard Fillmore would be a good president. He was already sworn in. The men of the menagerie knew of the death before the newspapers printed it.

There were always show people coming and going with news before newspapers had time to make it official.

The menagerie opened on schedule at 2:00 p.m. and again at 7:00 p.m. However, the ambiance that should have been gay and exciting was quiet and subdued, more of a wake than a holiday.

Charley thought the adults looked shocked and out of kilter. He watched them get glassy-eyed and stare blankly before seemingly shaking it off and moving on to the next attraction. He thought of how his own two horses had halted when the lightning flashed right in front of them and how they stopped in their tracks and listened and waited for him to say that everything was all right. Perhaps these people were waiting for someone to say it would be all right.

The caravan moved on to a new town the next day and the troubles of America were left behind. There were limited newspapers to read and even less time to read them.

As they entered the next town, G. C. Quick's Automatodeon whistled out beautiful tunes, much nicer than the previous year's atrocity of Spaulding and Roger's. Bolivar and the six camels, wearing colorfully embroidered blankets, pulled the beautifully decorated organ wagon slowly and deliberately through the small city.

The town's children followed the procession of gaily painted wagons filled with exotic creatures. Tents went up without a hitch and the shows opened at two and seven. Mr. Langworthy showed off his prancing ponies with monkey riders to an appreciative audience. Bolivar became the star of the show when he carefully lifted Langworthy on his four-foot-long ivory tusks and then set him down gently.

The audience went from adoring the gentle pachyderm to fearing the ferocious felines. They were certain Mr. Brooks would be killed as he stood alone in the cage with the nine lions, tigers, and leopards. He was not. He came out just fine, both times.

G.C. Quick's menagerie moved to Vermont for the month of August. Bolivar was happy to stay with the caravan, his dog and Mr. Langworthy. The caravan's biggest accident wasn't catastrophic. A fifty-gallon water barrel broke loose and fell off a wagon and knocked into the cook's wagon. They had to stop to re-band the wheel and replace a couple of spokes, but those things were easy enough to fix. They had spare parts for just such things.

News and gossip from other shows arrived with circus and menagerie travelers, men that found the need to go somewhere for one reason or another. Sometimes they had to pick up a spare horse, a new tent canvas or some other show necessity. The unspoken rule was that if you were a traveling menagerie or circus man, you'd be welcomed in to eat and bunk with others of your kind along your way.

August news was delivered by an animal man attached to the "Raymond & Company and Van Amburgh's Long Established Menagerie" which was currently in Canada. The event was with regard to Mr. Beesley, a lion tamer that had been with the "June, Titus & Company Menagerie" last season. This season he was alternating shows with Van Amburgh and going by the stage name of "Signor Hydralgo."

"We were in Toronto for a couple of days and everything was going okay. Hydralgo got in the cat cage to do his seven o'clock show," said the traveling man to the men around the dinner table. "Hydralgo was managing those kitties just fine. All of them hopped right up onto their platforms, except the tiger. The Bengal wouldn't budge. He just sat and stared."

The man leaned back in his chair. "Signor tried several times to get that tiger to jump and when he refused, Hydralgo flicked the tip of his whip to convince him. The cat jumped all right, right on top of Hydralgo! There was the tamer, pinned flat on his back with a tiger standing on his chest about to tear his throat out when Van

Amburgh showed up. He rushed into the cage and saved the day."
He paused for effect.

"Van Amburgh got that tiger to get off and go to the other side
of the cage. If he hadn't, we'd have seen a man killed that day."

Mr. Langworthy was quick to point out to all who would listen
that losing one's temper and whipping an animal was ineffective
and dangerous.

It occurred to Charley that tigers were probably the most unpredictable and dangerous of the cats. This was the second near-fatal
accident he'd heard of this season. If he ever became a big cat man,
he was going to stick with lions.

There is a certain strength in the camaraderie that develops between
the group of men aspiring to keep a show on the road and to keep it
healthy and profitable. Loyalty for one another grows as each crisis is
shared, conquered, and the caravan moved forward. Charley had made
many friends this season, but his friendship with John-John was the
strongest. Between Charley dealing with horses, wagons, maintenance,
and boys pumping air into organs and John-John tending his flock,
there was little time for their friendship to grow, and yet it did. They
were oddly different. Charley was slim, dark-haired and just over five
foot five inches tall. John-John was well over six feet in his socks and
the scales back at the zoo measured his bulk at two-hundred-fifty.
Both were quiet-natured. Both were soft on animals.

On the welcomed occasions when the menagerie stayed in one
place for two days, there was a little more time to relax and catch up
with friends. In mid-September, there was such a night in a beautiful
wooded area of Vermont. The sky was clear and although the air had a
little nip in it, it was still pleasant. The animals were bedded down for
the night and all the visitors had gone home. The younger boys who
were unable to stay awake late had already crawled into their blankets.

The last scrap of daylight vanished just as Charley and John-John finished cleaning out the fancy-chicken pen and laying down fresh straw. The birds were sleepy and protested grumpily even as the young men took themselves out and locked the cage.

"Are your birds all doing okay this trip?" Asked Charley as they walked along.

"Pretty much, except Minnie. I'm a little worried about her."

"I'm sorry, John-John, which one is Minnie?" asked Charley.

"The pea-hen, the little one. There're two girls and the one peacock. I'm worried because she hasn't laid any eggs yet. She is young, but she should be laying eggs by now," he continued, mostly talking to himself, "I hope she hasn't got one stuck or something." He sighed, "It's God's will, either way, but I sure hope she's okay."

Charley stopped walking and turned to his friend, "John, I'm sure that little bird is going to be just fine. You take good care of them," and then he added, "Why don't we go check and make sure right now?"

John-John nodded, and they set out for the peacock cage. The little peahen was perched beside the other female with her eyes closed. When John-John reached a hand up to see if she was okay, she let out an odd chortle and adjusted her feet on the perch. John-John lifted the bird gently, weighing it in both his big hands, and then returned her to the perch.

"She seems just fine," grinned the bird man. "If she had an egg, she'd be a little heavier. Maybe she's still too young for egg-laying. Every bird is a little bit different." He smiled at Charley and added, "Let's go see if they have anything left from supper, eh?"

They could see the circle of men ahead of them to the left of the row of wagons. The campfire illuminated their faces with its flickering golden glow. The pair walked on over to the back of the cook's wagon and fumbled around in the dark, looking for leftovers. Finding a pan of bread pudding, they each carved out a big piece. They filled their tin cups from the water barrel and walked over behind the trees, close enough to hear what the older guys were saying, but far enough away to be unnoticed.

There was a traveler amongst the men tonight. Neither John-John nor Charley recognized him. He had buckskin pants and shirt and a scraggly beard that came down to a point. His mustache was wet from drinking beer and he wiped it with his sleeve. Everyone else in the circle was bent forward, listening to what the man had to say.

Because the boys were tired and hungry, they sat quietly for a few moments and just ate the bread pudding. They could hear the voices of the group around the fire, but it took a few minutes before they actually paid attention. Once they started listening, they were spellbound.

The man had just returned from Africa where he'd been hunting down and capturing animals for menageries. He was an agent who knew the old guys in the circle and Charley heard Mr. June's name mentioned. He spoke of giraffes and rhinos and lions and cheetahs. He told stories of the hunt, the captures and finally, the delivery by boat to America. John-John listened closely as the man told of great flocks of grey parrots they had seen and how beautiful they were when they flew up, crimson tails like red beacons against the sky. He'd captured some four or five years back and brought them back to the American Museum. "Merlin," thought John-John.

"I've captured damn near every creature there is in that country and I'm telling you," he paused for effect, "That was one determined elephant.

"What do you mean by "determined" Cyrus, was it one of those big African bulls? How did you capture it?"

Cyrus grew taller and puffed out his chest. He appeared to enjoy the attention he was getting from the men gathered around him. "Well, the first thing you have to do if you're going to go after an elephant is get some help from the locals. They know the land and they know the animals way better than we do." He took a swig from his jar and wiped his face with his sleeve again, "We visit the local chief and pay him to buy the services of some of his men."

"We go out looking for a young one to capture. A young elephant is easier to manage and transport than a big one and besides, they train easier." He looked around to make sure everyone was listening and continued, "The blacks usually know where to find the herd, so we follow them. When we find a baby elephant, we have to steal it from its mother."

"How do you get the elephant to let go of her young'un? Inquired one of the fellows. "No mama gives up their young without a fight".

"Well, we distract her. The hunters harass the baby, so the mother is watching us. The blacks sneak up behind her when she is looking at us and they use their machete knives to cut the tendons in her back legs. She falls on the ground then, can't walk, can't stop us from capturing her baby."

"This particular elephant came after us, crawling on her front legs. She was determined to save her baby. The blacks had a terrible time killing her. She killed a couple of them in the fight."

"What happened with the chief when he found out his men were killed?" asked the same man, "Did you have to run for your lives?"

"No," he laughed, "He did not care one bit about the dead men because he was already paid for them." Answered the man.

Tears rolled down John-John's face. He saw nothing but the horrific bloody scene painted in his mind by the terrible man. The nightmarish spell he was under was abruptly broken by wretched sounds behind him. He turned to see Charley spilling his guts all over the forest floor.

John-John went and grabbed a hold of the back of his friend's belt to keep him from falling into his own spew. Moments later, without speaking, they parted ways to go get some sleep before the new day was upon them. Neither slept.

Just before dawn, Charley sought out Mr. Langworthy.

"I heard the hunter at the campfire last night. Do you know him?" Charley asked.

"Yes, I know him." He studied Charley's face for a moment before he continued, "I wish I could change the way they do things, but there is money involved. Men can be terrible evil when money's involved."

The young man's eyes were swollen, and his face was ashen. "I don't think I can do this anymore," he said gesturing toward the menagerie. "How can anyone allow awful things like that to happen?"

Without waiting for an answer, Charley reached out to shake Langworthy's hand.

"Thank you." He took a deep breath and continued, "I will never forget what you've taught me. I appreciate it." He started to go when Langworthy put a hand on his shoulder to stop him.

"We can't change what happened to those animals. What's done is done and no one can change that," said Mr. Langworthy. "The only thing we can do is to treat these animals well, here and now," he said pointing to the ground to emphasize his point.

"And furthermore," he said pointing at Charley, "You could be a great animal man. Those animals need kind people like you and those boys…" he pointed to the boys just rousting out for breakfast, "those boys need men like you to teach them how to respect these creatures."

Charley was dumbstruck. It felt like there was a hurricane swirling around him and his head was the eerily still eye-of-the-storm. Everything was too quiet. It was as if he were simply waiting for the high winds of emotion to blow him to pieces.

"We'll meet again, I know it. Good Luck, Charley White," Langworthy said quietly as he walked off to check on Bolivar, Turk at his heels.

CHAPTER EIGHT

15 MARCH 1851
FABIUS, NEW YORK

THE COLLAR OF CHARLEY'S COAT was turned up and the earflaps of his wool hat were pulled down. His hands were stuffed deeply into his pockets. Only his eyes and nose were exposed to the sting of the cruel spring storm, yet the wind still got in and did its dirty work. He was freezing, from head to toe, so much so that he had to hold his stomach muscles tight against the disabling shivers that would slow his journey back to his father's home and the welcoming fire.

Wet slush was piled three inches deep on the field and even heavy leather boots were no match for the penetrating, bone-chilling mess he was walking through. God in heaven, he hated winter.

"Beware the Ides of March," he thought and laughed, as he broke into a gallop toward the house, slush splashing up around him wherever his feet landed.

He stomped his feet on the porch and shook off what he could of the wet snow. He opened the door, went into the mudroom, unlaced and took off his wet boots, unbuttoned his soggy coat and made his way inside to the inviting warmth of the little kitchen.

"Mind your wet boots, Alasco!" reminded Johanna, his stepmother. He didn't mind her. She was kind and a hard worker. Everyone else had taken up calling him "Charley" instead of "Alasco." She had refused to compromise on the matter. The boots were delivered to the rocks in front of the fire and the coat hung from one of the hooks to the side of it.

"Hello, mother. It is nice to come home to you and the fire," he remarked as he toasted his palms in front of the crackling blaze, "And what is that smell? Is it roasted chicken?"

"Fish," she answered, "fish and taters," she answered smiling sweetly back at him. No sooner had she gotten the words out of her mouth when another's steps were heard on the porch.

"Ben! Ben!" she hollered, "Get yourself in here out of the cold!" She turned and looked at Charley, "Go help your brother get his wet things in, please." He did as she requested because that is how he was raised; Be polite. Do as you are asked. Be grateful. Don't argue.

"Hey, Ben!" called Charley, "How's it going, old man?"

Charley laughed at his little brother when he saw him. The wet snow covering his dark blonde hair was melting quickly and running down the boy's face in small rivulets that disappeared into his shirt collar.

"Darn it!" Exclaimed Ben. "I forgot my hat. I'm soaked, front to back."

The boys wrangled the dripping coat off, gave it a shake and then Charley took it to the fireplace hook. It could drip on the rocks without causing any harm. Ben pulled his shirt off and hung it on a separate coat hook, crossed his arms in front of his chest and ran his hands rapidly up and down his arms to increase circulation and make his skinny, fourteen-year-old body warm.

As Ben disappeared through the curtain to the other room to get a dry shirt, Emily and William (twelve and eleven) were noisily stomping off their boots on the porch. William walked right through the mudroom and made half a dozen steps into the little kitchen before his mother hollered at him.

"Get those wet boots off and by the fire! Don't you dare track up my floor!" William did an about-face and headed out again. Emily, grateful her mother had not noticed that she had not removed her shoes either, stepped back into the darkness of the mudroom.

Coats neatly hung by the fire and all four pairs of boots drying on the rocks, the children talked of their day. The older boys worked at their father's sawmill six days a week, so although this was a Saturday, it was a workday. They worked from eight in the morning until six in the evening unless the weather was too bad. Their father, Benajah, worked seven days a week to keep the mill running. Johanna, his wife, made him take time out for church on Sunday, though. She insisted that it was important to balance work and prayer. The younger children went to school during the winter. There was no school on Saturdays, but there were other chores to do. This Saturday they'd been sent to chop wood, after which they ran to the store to buy flour for her.

It was William James White's eleventh birthday. His mother, born Johanna Hubbard, was forty-three and a baker of cakes. She'd taken the flour the children brought back and sifted it into the batter she had waiting in the bowl on the sideboard. She expertly scraped the finished mixture into a greased cast-iron skillet and slid it all into the belly of the hot kitchen stove. Glancing at the clock as she wiped her hands on her apron, she announced to the children that dinner would be ready as soon as their dad got home.

The cake had come out and was cooling on the cupboard. Dinner was now keeping warm in the "warming oven." The table was set, and milk was fetched from the well house and poured, all around. The children, hungry and ready for William's cake, sat in the kitchen awaiting their father. The clock struck seven and the seconds ticked noisily by until, finally, stomping could be heard on the porch. Moments later the door swung open and a smiling Benajah White stood there, boots and coat in one hand, and a wrapped package in the other. He set the package on the corner of the table (which Johanna immediately removed to the extra chair in the corner) and delivered his dripping outerwear to hook and rock as per custom.

Benajah nodded at his family, "Shall we eat?"

Johanna and Emily fetched the meal from the warming oven. She had promised fish, but she had just been teasing. Instead, she had sacrificed one of her laying hens to William's special day. She had artfully baked the rubbery old hen to scrumptious tenderness and its savory aroma filled the tiny house with a warmth and joy that only a mother's cooking can impart. William's favorite mashed potatoes came out in a pottery bowl and in the middle was a melted lake of salty sweet cream butter. Johanna had opened one of her precious jars of applesauce and another of salty pickles and at the last moment, she produced fresh rolls from the bread box. It truly felt like it was everyone's birthday!

As William opened his package, the one his father brought home, Johanna brought the cake over to the table. Emily got small plates for dessert and passed them around. Dessert was a very special occasion. Johanna did her magic with the hand beater and a bowl of whipping cream.

"A knife!" exclaimed the birthday boy! "It's a beauty, dad!" William hugged him around the neck, breathing in the sawdusty smell of his kind father. "Thank you, dad! I shall take very good care of it."

Johanna stuck a candle in the middle of the chocolate cake still encased in the skillet. Benajah lit the candle, bowed his head, and in his beautiful deep fatherly voice began to pray. "Thank you, dear God, for our wonderful William who turns eleven years old this day. May he live a long and happy life, Amen."

When the prayer was over, William stood and blew out his candle.

"Did you make a wish?" asked Emily. "What is it?"

"Yes, of course I did… but it won't come true if I tell you!"

The house was warm and toasty. Bellies were full. Chocolate cake and whipped cream melted in the stomachs of a happy family. William went to sleep with his knife, sheathed of course, under his pillow.

One never knows what tomorrow brings, thought Benajah White. We must be grateful for today. Charley had been gone five summers in a row, only coming back when the menagerie road season was over. Benajah knew that the boy's need to travel would overpower him any day now and he would leave again for parts unknown.

+ + +

As soon as young Ben finished school the previous year, he had started working at the sawmill. He had been anxious to grow up and be independent and had felt pretty darn happy to get that first payday and hold the money in his own hands. The shine wore off quickly. He had grown restless. He was going to be fifteen in November. Time was running out for him to become a traveling man like his big brother.

When Charley arrived home the previous fall, he found his father's rented house already overcrowded. Although Benajah insisted there was plenty of room for him to stay, there really was not. The problem was easily solved. The neighbors, Mr. and Mrs. Johnson had raised their own brood of five and every one of them had moved out of the big house. They were happy to rent Charley a room and even happier to have a young one in the nest again. The extra income didn't hurt their feelings, either.

But as June rolled around, Charley made his decision; He was not going back to New York City. He let his parents and the Johnsons know he was heading north to work on the canal. He wasn't sure how long it would take to get the perfect job, but he knew he would find work right away. Even with the massive influx of Irish immigrants the past few years, there were still more rough ship and dock jobs than men willing to work them.

He had said his goodbyes to his own family the evening before. Mrs. Johnson, his landlady, had fixed him a big hot breakfast and presented him with a sack full of sandwiches to take with him on his trek to Syracuse. She was, after all, first and foremost a mama. After breakfast, Charley put on his coat and boots, hoisted the leather saddlebag that contained his belongings over his shoulder, and picked up the food sack. He shook Mr. Johnson's hand and gave Mrs. Johnson a gentle hug.

"Take care now, Charley!" Mr. Johnson said. "You're welcome back here anytime."

"Thank you for everything," he answered. "Maybe I'll see you next year."

As he opened the back door and stepped onto the porch, a figure arose from the steps and faced him.

"Hey, Charley!" It was his younger brother Ben, carrying a sack of his belongings tied to a stick.

"What are you doing here, Ben?" He inquired, pulling the door shut behind him.

"I want to come with you. I won't be any trouble, I promise." He looked at his brother hoping to find confirmation that he could tag along.

"Have you talked with father about this?" asked Charley.

Ben had talked with both of his parents about leaving. They had known the day would come when Ben would demand his independence. If he had to leave them, they were happy he chose to do it when Charley was there to give him a hand.

Two young men set out for Syracuse on the morning of 1 June 1851. It was a beautiful dawn, crisp and cool with not a cloud in the sky. It was a twenty-five-mile walk to Syracuse. It would take a couple of days for them to get there unless of course they were lucky enough to catch a ride with a passing farmer.

Ben got a job working on the Western Lake Boat Line right away. A boat was docked at Syracuse and when Ben inquired, they hired him on the spot. Built much bigger and stronger than his older brother, Ben looked more like eighteen than fourteen.

Charley waved his brother off as Ben's boat headed northwest toward Buffalo. He then walked back to his own new employer, the American Transportation Company, to see when the ship he'd signed up on was scheduled to leave. It would be heading east toward Albany. Whereas his brother had signed on as muscle, Charley had been hired to manage the men loading and unloading the freight. The man who hired him was impressed with Charley's experience in moving menageries and managing boys.

"All right," thought Charley aloud, "if he thinks I can do it, I probably can." He was nervous though; He'd never been in charge of grown men and he'd never worked on a boat.

— CHAPTER NINE —

JULY 1851
BUFFALO, NY

WORKING ON THE CANAL BOAT was downright enjoyable as long as the weather was fine. A man could sit on deck and watch as the mules towed the boat up to the next lock. Charley's main job was to oversee the loading and unloading of cargo. The captain was still in charge of the weight and balance of the load, but he was teaching Charley and that heavy responsibility would be his by the end of the summer.

At first there had been some reluctance among the older men to follow Charley's lead. He was years younger than all of them. That resistance melted away quickly. If someone worked extra hard, Charley would make a point of rewarding them in one way or another. Maybe, at the next port, he'd ask the guy to do the counting and Charley would take the man's place in the heavy lifting. Not only did he roll up his sleeves and pitch in, he made a point of praising the men who did the best work. If the method worked on horses and menagerie boys, it was bound to work on boat hands.

So, the journey up and down the canal was pleasant. The work wasn't too stressful. There were no wagons to break down and no elephants to keep track of. He was well-paid, meals were regular, and he had made some new friends. Unfortunately, after just a few weeks the routine had become a little boring. Charley had itchy feet. He could not imagine spending his life hauling freight across the great state of New York.

Fully loaded and ready to go, the transport pulled out of Buffalo on the sixteenth of July and headed north toward Tonawanda for the purpose of retracing its route back to Albany on the Erie Canal. Just ahead of them was a flotilla of three small canal boats each bearing a colorful "Dan Rice's Circus" banner. Charley had seen posters for the circus in Buffalo, but there had been no time to see the show. Maybe, if they were lucky, the crew could see the circus in Tonawanda on the seventeenth.

Charley checked with the captain, and they were indeed going to layover in the port town until the early hours of the eighteenth. If the crew unloaded and reloaded in time, they could all go to the show, except the ship's guard of course. There was a show at 2:30 p.m. and another at 7:30 p.m.

They were done by noon and the crew scattered, some to find a glass of beer and others to make their way to the show. Charley's pace quickened as he drew near the colorful tents set up in the field ahead. He'd heard of Dan Rice, of course! His friend Jimmy who was now in Europe performing spent a winter with Rice in New Orleans. There was also plenty of gossip about Rice at the Zoological Hall. No stories were juicier than the misadventures of Dan Rice and his run-ins with his former partners and the law. Charley knew Dan's story, as did most everyone in the business. Rice had been a part of "Doc Spaulding's North American Circus," acting as both a clown and minstrel. Subsequently, he partnered with Spaulding. Spaulding's brother-in-law, Mr. Van Orden managed that show. In 1850 Rice bought them out, but he'd run short on money and borrowed from old Doc Spaulding to keep the show on the road. That was all well and good except Van Orden had apparently tricked Rice into accepting unreasonable terms. When Rice was unable to repay the debt within the terms of the agreement, Spaulding and Van Orden immediately sought legal remedy. Spaulding's victory in court left Rice with but one horse and a few loyal performers. Rice took his "one-horse show" on the road in spite of the devastating loss. Rice could spin a yarn though, so folks were happy to pay good money to hear him rant and rave about how unfair his adversaries had been.

Charley had been without news of any show's adventures for close to a year. He hurried toward the tents now hoping to find someone he knew. His pace slowed as it dawned on him that maybe he wasn't a "show" man anymore. The circus crew might just shove him off as an outsider.

"Only one way to find out," he murmured to himself as he made his way to the group of horses gathered off to one side. He would just walk on over to the boy tending the horses first and see where that got him.

As always, Charley made a point of whistling whenever he approached animals. It was a good idea to let them know he was there and not startle them. "The Widow MaChree" had stuck in his head since his days with Joe Pentland, and that's the tune he whistled.

Three horses, corralled by a temporary fence, turned to watch him as he approached, beautiful things, muscular and strong with enormous clear brown eyes. Each was loosely tied to a center pole where water and hay were plentifully laid out for them. A small boy, not more than twelve stood brushing the rump of the smallest animal, each stroke accompanied by a small cloud of horse dust.

"Ummmm, excuse me…" said Charley in the softest voice possible. "Is your boss around?"

The boy stopped brushing and came around to the other side of the horse to face Charley, "He should be around here somewhere," he offered. "Who are you? You looking for a job?"

"No," replied Charley realizing at the same time that he actually *might* be looking for a job. "I just wanted to chew the fat with him a minute… was with Van Amburgh and Quick's last couple of years… thought I might know someone here."

Just then a sturdy man not more than five and a half feet in height, built like a tree-stump and closing in on fifty, came out from the tent. He walked over to where the boy and Charley were standing.

"What can I do for ya, son? You have business here?"

"No, sir," answered Charley as he removed his hat and extended his hand. "I just wondered if anybody I knew was working for this outfit."

He shook the man's hand and proceeded to tell him where and for whom he had worked in "the business."

"Name's Jonas," said the man as he reached over and unlatched the gate on the temporary corral meant to keep outsiders from approaching the animals. We just put coffee on. Come in and sit a spell."

The smells of sawdust, straw, hay, horses, leather, liniment and sweat blended into a sweet perfume that met Charley's nostrils like a long-lost friend. The moment he stepped inside that gate; he knew he wanted back in.

Jonas offered him lunch and Charley took it. He wasn't hungry, but he had sorely missed the companionship of show folks. There was no one he knew here, but he still wanted to stay. He didn't want to go back to the boat.

He didn't have to pay the twenty-five cents to get in and watch the afternoon show. He went along with Jonas and helped get the horses ready and then stood in the shadows watching. The grand entry promised the crowd a brilliant show. Dan Rice led the procession, skipping ahead of the line of horses that followed him. There were adult male equestrians in fine attire followed by Maggie Rice, an equestrian in her own right and her two little daughters, about seven and five years old. The brass band initiated the grand entrance music and the string orchestra intermittently took over and played gentler snippets of upbeat tunes.

The tent was full to bursting and the excitement, palpable. Even the horses seemed caught up in the thrill of the pomp and circumstance as they high-stepped around the sawdust ring showing off their beautiful adornments.

After the grand entry and retreat, Levi North and his trick horse Tammany opened the show with a brief, but clever equestrian act to warm up the crowd. He was as graceful as a ballet dancer as he stood and did his acrobatic maneuvers on the padded back of his magnificent steed. His horse's bow beside his master at the finish was met with thunderous applause.

"He will return for his full act in a bit," Jonas assured. "This was just him giving the crowd a taste of things to come."

As North turned toward them to retreat from the ring, Charley noticed a gash on the man's forehead with an accompanying bruise the size of a silver dollar.

"What happened to his head?" whispered Charley. "That looks like it hurt. Did he catch a hoof?"

Jonas shook his head 'no' and went back to his task. The music changed and Jim Reynolds the clown took North's place at center ring. Reynolds got the whole tent laughing as he cleverly tumbled over barrels, his dog, and a 'pretend' lost soul who wandered across the sawdust circle, who just happened to be the young boy that brushed the horses. The dog stole the show in the end. He was small, mostly white and only about knee high, but his antics were so well synchronized with his master's the crowd was captivated, as was Charley.

The band music changed again, this time the strings produced a classic melody. A big bay horse, led by the gentle instruction of a smiling young woman, danced in time with the hauntingly beautiful refrain. The crowd was enchanted by the grace and precision of the horse's movements. When the act was over, there was another standing ovation.

The brass band pumped out bright energizing music as the bay horse retreated and the tattooed man entered the ring. He wore only short britches and a pair of pointy brown leather shoes. All over his body were black inky marks in varying designs, arrows here, lines there, even a bowed line of what looked like "chicken-scratchins" under his left breast. The man's milky white skin stood in stark contrast to the dark patterns etched into his small statured body. His right hand was untouched and looked odd with its lack of adornment. The string band took up and began to play the old Irish tune, "Gary Owen." The tattooed man lifted his bright white unadorned right-hand into the air and with feet as light as a feather, danced an Irish gig. It was so unexpected! The crowd loved it.

Jonas finished cinching the trick saddle onto a small horse and turned to tell Charley about North's injury.

"Dan hit him with a bottle last week, cracked his head. Don't say anything, though. They've made up." In whispered tones, Jonas proceeded to fill Charley in on the latest escapades of Dan Rice. The previous week a pair of equestrians had decided to quit and make their way over to another outfit. Dan Rice and Levi North were partners, but seriously disagreed as to how to handle the defectors. Levi wanted to just let them go. Dan wanted to force them to stay and fulfill their contract. Dan lost his head, picked up a bottle, and hit Levi with it. A local judge fined Dan one thousand dollars for assault. Dan, in turn, filed a lawsuit for breach of contract against the two equestrians who left.

"Dan's a great guy," Jonas continued, "but he can get emotional. I guess that's why he is good; He wears his heart on his sleeve. Passionate. Just stay clear of things that upset him," he added.

The music changed yet again, and the brass band heralded the arrival of Dan Rice himself to the ring. He stopped in the center and greeted the crowd. He bowed and waved as he turned a complete circle, making certain he included all in his salutation. His voice resonated throughout the arena in a beautiful deep clear baritone. He thanked the folks for coming, told a few short and funny stories, and then promised the audience a magnificent show. The band played a happy melody as he retreated and the youthful equestrians Omar, Willie, and Master Jean burst onto the scene. They did their horseback riding stunts with amazing precision and skill.

Next Dan Rice reappeared, this time with his horse Excelsior. Charley had been fascinated with Mr. Langworthy's horse-training skills, but what Dan Rice had been able to get Excelsior to do was beyond belief! The horse could count by pawing the earth with his hoof. He bowed, turned circles, pranced, played dead, and was trained to throw his head back and "laugh" at Dan Rice's jokes. After a particularly bad joke that was aimed at insulting a horse's proclivity for passing stinky flatulence, Excelsior turned around and raised his tail at the jester as if to "pass gas" in his direction. The tent was filled to capacity and the laughter and applause was so loud, the canvas quivered.

Rice introduced his "beautiful wife" Maggie who rode gracefully around the sawdust ring on her big black horse. He had a white blaze and four perfectly matched white socks. The horse kept perfect rhythm as Maggie rode frontwards and backwards and did several hops from saddle to sawdust and back to saddle again. Each move was elegant and precise and matched the soft notes and upbeat tempo of "Messrs. Messemere and Gessing" of New Orleans' fame.

The band changed music. Riding into the ring to join their mother were La Petite Elizabeth and La Jeune Kate, Rice's own daughters. The girls exhibited advanced horsemanship for such fledgling equestrians and were richly rewarded with thunderous applause. The audience could "see" their own children in these little girls, and one could wager that riding lessons for children would be on the increase in Tonawanda, New York.

The music changed again, and Dan Rice reappeared and made his way to the middle of the sawdust circle. Charley wondered how a man dressed in tight red-white-and blue striped trousers and puffy shirt wearing pointy shoes and a top hat could command such a serious presence, but he did. His large angular face was accentuated by serious dark eyes and a long wavy chin beard that came down to a point. He wore no mustache and the sides of his face were clean-shaven. His head appeared too large for his body. Perhaps that was the reason folks were drawn to stare at him. The "magnetic light" shone directly upon him and its glare increased the dramatic effect of the actor and orator. His commanding baritone voice filled the tent once more. With precise and perfect articulation, he recited a poem of his own creation, one that told the story of how Van Orden and Spaulding had swindled him the previous season and left him with only a one-horse-show.

"You have to admit," Charley told Jonas, "he makes me believe that he is telling the truth about what happened."

Jonas smiled and patted Charley on the shoulder, "That's why he is good, Charley. He's easy to believe."

The acts continued until the two-hour show was complete. All the entertainers, including the juggler and the tattooed man, re-entered the ring for a final bow. Dan Rice announced that there would be another show that evening. "Come back at 7:30," he urged, and promised the audience new things to see, not presented in the matinee just witnessed. The audience roared with appreciation and clapped loudly as the showmen retreated to the shadows once again.

"Do you need a job," asked Jonas of Charley as they made their way out of the tent.

"What do you have in mind?"

"Well, first of all, we can't pay much. We need a guy to help move the show and do odd jobs. Likely as not, you'd get a chance to do most all the jobs involved in the show. Something you might consider?"

Charley stopped walking and thought for a second, "I've got a job on a boat that's leaving in the morning. I'd have to ask the captain if he could manage without me."

Jonas nodded, understandingly. He liked this kid.

"Alright if I check with my captain and come back and let you know before the second show?" asked Charley.

The two parted. Jonas went back to his work and Charley returned to the boat and waited for his captain to get back so they could talk. His mind raced as he gathered his few belongings and readied them for travel. He would have to get a letter off to his family and let them know where he was headed. He needed to get word to Ben so he didn't look for him on every American Transport Company boat on the canal.

The captain did not arrive back at the boat until half past five in the afternoon. By then, Charley had convinced himself that he wasn't needed for the journey back to Albany. The boat was fully loaded with freight destined for New York City. There would be no loading or unloading of any cargo for the next few days.

When he finally talked to the captain, the response was all he could have hoped for:

"Charley, I would prefer it if you stayed put. You're a good worker. On the other hand, it is never a good idea to have someone on your boat that don't want to be here," he paused. "So, you should go."

"Are you sure, sir? I don't want to leave you in the lurch." Charley answered, hoping for reassurance that he had the captain's blessing to take off.

"Go! Get your stuff and I'll fetch your pay," said the captain as he turned to step up into his cabin. "I'll meet you back here in five minutes."

He brought all Charley's pay and told him that if he wanted to come back and work for him, he was surely welcome.

The twenty-minute walk back to the "Dan Rice's Circus" took a little more than an hour. Charley stopped, bought some letter-writing supplies, wrote a quick note to his family, and sent off a letter all before he walked into the back entrance of the circus tent.

He wasn't sure what he was getting into. There was a lot of uncertainty with the Dan Rice outfit. He did not know how long the show would survive. Today they had filled the tent to capacity during the two o'clock show, but Rice had a sketchy reputation.

"Charley!" Welcomed Jonas. "So? Are you coming with us?"

"Yep," answered the nineteen-year-old man, "Just tell me where to leave my stuff and what to do next."

After the evening show, they broke down the tents and got everything loaded onto the canal boats. The men, women, children, horses, and the little white dog settled in for the overnight float on the Erie Canal.

✛ ✛ ✛

By the evening of twenty-first of July the little flotilla of three circus canal boats was safely docked in Rochester, New York. They had already entertained two other small towns along the way and Charley had a pretty good handle on what needed to be done in the little circus. It wasn't much different than moving a menagerie except you had more people and fewer animals.

The afternoon exhibition on the twenty-second in Rochester was packed, everything went as planned and a profit was assured. There was a bit of a worry about the evening show, though. There was competition; Jenny Lind, accompanied by the famous showman P.T. Barnum was in town. The "Swedish Nightingale" would be singing across town at the Corinthian Hall at the same time as the circus performance.

The bluster was that tickets to Jenny Lind's show were so limited and in such great demand, that old Barnum had held an auction to sell the tickets to the highest bidders.

"Clever bugger," Jonas muttered to Charley as they finished getting ready for the evening show. "Them tickets cost six dollars to begin with and that auction business just drove up the price." Strangely enough, Jonas was an opera fan and even a decent tenor himself. He had saved up the money to go to the show as soon as he found out Jenny Lind would be in Rochester at the same time as the circus. After setting up tents the night of the twenty-first, he walked into town to buy his ticket. Once he got there, he heard about the auction. The next day, Jonas was broody and unhappy.

"I ain't paying no ten dollars to hear anybody sing," he muttered to Charley and anyone who would listen. He finished tending to the harness he was adjusting and continued, "But, I sure do wish I could hear her sing just one song. They say she sings like an angel." Jonas had grumbled through most of the afternoon show.

Dan Rice was a generous friend. He thought of old Jonas as his own uncle. He knew full-well how deeply Jonas wanted to go see this Jenny Lind. All the tickets had been auctioned and theoretically there should be none to buy, but Dan knew there must be at least one 'speculator' willing to sell a ticket on the street

After dinner, Dan Rice motioned to Charley to come over to where he was in the cook tent. Charley did so, having no idea what the circus owner wanted of him.

"Jonas says you're okay and can be trusted, that so?" he asked.

"Yes sir, I mean, I do my best sir. Something you want from me?" asked Charley.

"I would, young man. Now listen," he said as he handed Charley a pouch with silver dollars in it, "I want you to go see if you can find a ticket to this Jenny Lind concert." He paused and watched warily as Jonas appeared and then disappeared again into the other end of the tent. "There are twelve dollars in this pouch to get a ticket. If you can't find one, just bring it back. Don't tell Jonas," he said conspiratorially.

Charley took off immediately and went into town. It wasn't long before he saw a man trying to sell a ticket to the concert. He walked over and listened as several people offered the man seven and eight dollars for the prize but were denied.

He observed the man for several minutes. He stood alone after the last ticket-seekers walked off, disgusted. Now was his chance.

"I'll give you eleven dollars for that ticket and not a penny more," Charley announced.

The man looked up and down the young man in front of him. "You don't have eleven dollars, but if you did, I'd give you this ticket."

Charley put his hand in his pocket where he had already liberated the dollars from their pouch. He took the coins out, one at a time, until he had eleven in his hand.

"Well, I'll be darned!" laughed the man. "You got yourself a deal!" He handed the ticket to Charley, took his fist full of dollars and headed off toward the tavern.

Charley rushed back to the circus. It wasn't long before both the Jenny Lind concert and the circus show would start. He found Mr. Rice, gave him his pouch with the silver dollar in it and produced the prized ticket. Rice pushed the hand with the ticket back at Charley.

"Go give that to Jonas and tell him to get his backside over to that concert before it's over with." Rice nodded at Charley, "Go! And don't tell him where you got that ticket," he laughed.

That evening was the first time that Charley took Jonas's place in the tent, ushering in the acts and double-checking harnesses, stirrups, and saddles. The tent was full to bursting and the crowd was lively and appreciative. Although one could argue that the circus was just a job done for money, it truly was a labor of love. And, the loud appreciation of a delighted audience only inspired the actors to rise to even greater levels of excellence. Rochester loved the "Dan Rice's Circus."

That night, after everything was reloaded onto the canal boats and ready to continue east, the crew gathered around on the deck of the lead boat. Jonas, rapt from his experience in the presence of the Swedish Nightingale, related his experience to his friends using every single adverb in his vocabulary to describe the talent of Jenny Lind and the large orchestra.

"I don't know which ones of you got together to get me that ticket, but I'm beholding to you all," Jonas said soberly. "I feel like my "cup runneth over" in both the experience tonight and in knowing that I have such faithful friends." He lifted his coffee mug to those around him and said, "Thank you."

After a few awkward moments of silence, one man uttered, "Charley did a great job with the show tonight, Jonas. You should've seen him!"

Jonas nodded at Charley and added, "Thanks!"

Tired and in need of some sleep before the next day's show, the crew slipped off into the night in search of their blankets and a soft place to rest their heads.

— CHAPTER TEN —

3 AUGUST 1851, SCHENECTADY, NY

SUNDAY WAS A DAY OF rest for most and if you were a member of Dan Rice's outfit, you got the day off. That's not saying that you sat around and did absolutely nothing. Horses still had to be taken care of and everybody had to eat. Occasionally it was necessary to travel on the Sabbath.

Today they were docked in Schenectady. They would set up the circus tents tomorrow morning, but for today, they were free. Dan Rice considered himself a man of the bible. It was his custom to invite the troupe to sit and listen to his sermon after breakfast on Sundays. This day was no different.

The morning air was fresh as August was still young and had not thus far succeeded in weighing down the world with oppressive heat and humidity. Weeds along the shore had yet to wilt and the sun was still a welcomed sight in the morning, although its popularity was waning. The little canal boats were almost motionless in the mirror-like water. There was no wind or current to disturb the peace.

The early risers were assembled. Some sat cross-legged on the end of the dock while others perched themselves upon baggage stacked on the nearest boat. Dan Rice emerged from the cabin, not attired in his showman's striped britches and top hat, but in his "everyman's clothing." Humble, quiet, almost drab, he found his way to the front of the assembly with bible in hand and began to speak in his loud, clear, voice.

"Let us give thanks to almighty God for this day and our lives in it."

The assembled answered, "Amen."

Dan followed the doctrine of the "New Jerusalem Church," and in the manner of a sincere and fine orator communicated his beliefs to his audience.

"And we may be assured if we put away our evils and look to Him in the way He has pointed out to us in His word, He will manifest Himself unto us as He does not unto the world…." He then implored, "Let us then approach the consideration of this subject with becoming reverence. Let us put away from us every thought, every affection, every tendency of the mind which would in the smallest degree obstruct the light of divine truth."

A violinist from the string orchestra began to play "Amazing Grace." They let him play the introductory notes and then joined in singing the well-worn hymn with reverent passion. A small white butterfly fluttered and dipped amid the congregation as if it wanted to catch the scent of each and every soul. A pair of mallards floated silently by, a procession of half-grown chicks behind them. Charley liked the sermons and the gatherings on Sundays, but the day of rest reminded him that he sorely missed his own family.

Later that night around the campfire, he shared his feelings.

"Jonas?" he'd asked, "I know you love working the show, but don't you get homesick sometimes?"

"Of course, Charley," everyone gets a longing for the home-place and the people they care about." Jonas stopped stirring the campfire and gave his full attention to his young friend.

"Once you've been on the road, there is no going back to the way it was. You change while you're away and the people you left behind also change. When you go back to visit, you just don't fit back in the same way." Jonas cleared his throat and started stirring the fire again, "It's like trying to get the egg back into the chicken, Charley… it don't fit."

Jimmy, the tattooed man, approached from behind Jonas, found himself a stump to sit on and immediately started stirring the coals with the long skinny stick he'd brought with him.

"Feeling homesick, Mr. Charley?" He asked.

"A little," he answered, "I don't know if it is homesick or me just wishing there was somewhere that I felt like I was home."

"Home is where you make it lad. The sooner you figure that out, the happier you'll be." He swept his arms all around himself. "This is home today. My friends are here, I have a little money, a full belly, and good health." He turned to Jonas, "Isn't that right, Jonas? Right here, right now… this is home!"

The older man nodded his agreement. He had once known a wife and was blessed with two little girls. Cholera had claimed them, one after the other. He'd sold his farm and joined a traveling show to take care of horses. Yes, sadly enough, this was his home.

"Where's your family Jimmy," asked Charley.

"I do not know if they live and breathe. I have not set eyes on them since I ran off nigh on thirty years ago." He stirred the fire slowly with the point of his stick and watched as sparks lifted off and disappeared into the night.

"I had a wife once. She had two children by me, but I've not seen them since I left the island."

Charley, not wanting to pry, stared silently at the fire.

"Go ahead Jimmy," urged Jonas, "We're in need of a good story. Tell us about your life. Start from the beginning."

It did not take much urging for James Francis O'Connell to talk about himself. He was, after all, Irish by birth and blood, by God!

"Where should I start?" he began. "I was born in Dublin in 1808 or 1809. I know it was November because that's when we celebrated my birthday. I don't remember much about when I was a "bairn" except for going to a boarding school with my two older sisters. When I was about seven or eight was the first time I remember meeting my parents. My uncle took us to Liverpool where they were performers in a traveling circus. I thought it was a wonderful and exciting thing to travel with my parents, but apparently they were not as happy as I was. After about a year I was taken away to London to live with another uncle."

Jimmy kept his eyes on the fire and Charley could have sworn he saw the ghost of a young boy in the face of his friend. He supposed a man was only as strong as his most vulnerable moment. Neither time nor tide can erase some moments of profound disappointment.

"Uncle didn't pay me much attention and didn't seem to notice the hours I spent at the docks instead of at school. I made friends with a ship's captain and one day when I was twelve or so, I left London on his ship. I never worked so hard in all my life, but I loved every day of it." Jimmy stirred the fire thoughtfully as he stared at the glowing red coals.

"The ship I was on took barrels of whale oil from one place to another. We sometimes transported people. Once we took a hundred or so women to Australia. They were taken from prisons in England and shipped off. It was a long voyage and I got to know some of them. A few were just poor and had been thrown in jail for their debts. Others were of more serious circumstances such as theft, prostitution and there was even one that committed murder. She had done away with her husband who beat her. She walked with a limp and one arm hung crooked because it had healed wrong."

He stirred the fire again.

"I believe the new land offered a chance for happiness for many poor women that had known a terrible life. For others it meant being forcefully dragged away from their home and families through no fault of their own. Who knows if it was right or wrong to ship them there?"

"Did you marry one of those women Jimmy? "Asked Charley.

The Irishman laughed, stopped stirring the fire and looked up at his two friends.

"I was a real man back then, working and living on that big boat. Proud I was… but as me uncle used to say, a cat is always dignified until the dog comes by. I was scared of 'em. Tough women they were. No, I didn't have the courage, Charley."

"Give me a minute," muttered Jonas as he stood to leave. He returned with three cups half filled with warm beer.

"This story calls for a little refreshment," he said raising his cup. The others raised theirs. A moment of silence followed as the three friends drank.

"Go on. Go on!" urged Jonas. What happened with the wife?

Jimmy cleared his throat, set his cup on the ground, retrieved his fire stick and began stirring as if to conjure up long ago memories.

"We shipwrecked on a coral reef off the Carolina Islands where as far as we knew all the natives were cannibals. Two of us made it to the shore of one called Pohnpei. To be honest, I don't know what happened to the others." Jimmy stirred the fire before continuing.

"We were dragged ashore by a group of women. We did not understand the words they spoke or the gestures they made. But, after showing us the tattoos on their legs, arms, chests and bellies we understood they were mighty proud of their markings.

"Those women led us to a little hut at the head of a tranquil bay. It was lush and green and cooled by a breeze off the water. If one could forget the pain inflicted there, you could not dream of a more perfect place."

"These same women did the dirty work. They put George in one corner of the hut and me in another. One woman drew designs on my arms and legs which was not unpleasant. Then came the stick with thorns and the bowl of black dye. Two women held me down while another dipped the thorns into the long bowl and repeatedly drove the ink-dripping-nails into the design."

"I feared that if I screamed, I would be killed. George on the other hand screamed his bloody brains out the entire time and ended up with only a few small tattoos while most of my body was covered." He showed his arms and legs in the light of the fire. "I suppose my courage was appreciated by the tribe for as soon as my wounds had healed, a young girl took me to her hut and proceeded to tattoo my chest." Jimmy raised his shirt and traced what looked like a chicken's footprints under his left breast. "I had no idea at the time, but this girl was the chief's daughter and by marking me, she married me."

"I lived a nice life, being the son-in-law of Ahoundel-a-Nutt, but leaving the island was always my most ardent desire. The tribe convinced us that all the other islands had cannibals and we would be eaten if we stepped foot on their shores. We learned a little of their language, became less afraid and earned more trust from the chief. After five long years a ship passed close by and we swam for it."

"Don't you wonder about your wife and children?" Asked Jonas. He would do anything to have his family back.

"Of course, I wonder, but I know they are as I left them. My son will probably be chief one day. My wife has likely taken another to her hut. It is just as well I am gone."

"But how did you get to Rice's outfit?" asked Charley.

"Well, now I got myself eventually to Canada and then down the coast to New York City. I've been in lots of different shows since '34. I even showed at Barnum's American Museum some winters. I wrote a little book about my adventures, which I sold after exhibitions called 'The Life and Adventures of James F. O'Connell, the Tattooed Man.' I can get you a copy when we're back to the city… having some printed up for next season."

Jimmy laughed softly, "You would be surprised how the ladies like to look at a man with tattoos and how the gents like to read about my adventure with the "voluptuous virgins" who tattooed my naked body."

"And, you will never go back to that island, Jimmy?" Asked Charley.

"No, son. It's like Jonas said, you just don't fit back in once you've left."

✛ ✛ ✛

Hearing about the escapades of Dan Rice was one thing, living with his adventures was an entirely different story. The tents were set up and everything ready for the matinee, a show that would not include Dan's partner, the one Dan had recently assaulted, Levi North. Levi had taken his trick horse and joined another outfit called, "The People's Circus," run by Johnson. The troupe, or what was left of it, was just now waiting for Dan Rice to get bailed out of jail. Once he was back, they could start selling tickets.

It had been a dramatic two weeks for "Dan Rice's Circus" because the leader of the enterprise had been jailed twice for slander. As part of his act, he would give his account of what happened between himself and old Doc Spaulding at every show, an oration that brought both laughter and respect for the large-headed man. Unfortunately for Dan, a lawyer for Spaulding went to the show in Albany. When he heard Dan's side of the story which included Spaulding and his brother-in-law living sordid lives that included prostitutes and mistresses, he reported the "slander" to the police in Albany. By the time the Albany authorities caught up with Dan, the troupe was in Fonda. They arrested him and hauled him all the way back to Albany. He was bailed out in time to catch up with his show in Whitestown.

And, did Dan Rice learn his lesson from the arrest and thousand-dollar-fine? Obviously, he did not for today he was again in jail, this time in Whitestown. He had given the same rendition of the same accounts of Spaulding that got him into trouble in Albany. The same lawyer that filed a complaint in Albany had followed the troupe to Whitestown. He filed another lawsuit for slander. By the time the authorities caught up with him, they were in Oriskany and Dan was hauled back to Whitestown to answer for his transgressions.

Dan Rice did not make it back to Oriskany in time for the afternoon show. Perhaps it was just as well because the weather was stifling. And, although the big tent offered shade, there was a fundamental lack of any breeze. The audience would have baked.

By evening, the man of the hour rejoined his circus as if nothing had happened. If he was shaken by his adventures, he did not show it.

In spite of everything, Dan Rice commanded loyalty with what was left of his troupe. They traveled westward again on the canal and Mr. C. H. Castle, agent extraordinaire, made certain that the show was well scheduled and advertised before they arrived in each new town. By the time they made it back west to Buffalo, they were all ready for a nice, relaxing two-day stand.

There had been an obvious need to reorganize the show to exclude North and his horse. Extra time, effort, and rehearsals had been required. Rice and company came up with a comedy drama where a young Mr. Jean Johnson, an equestrian of fourteen nimble years, would act out the love escapades of Don Juan. Dan Rice played his faithful servant, Scaramouch. As the advertisement told it, "The first scene introduces the youthful Don, who is about to set out on a visit to some lady love.… The pantomimic show features a shipwreck and an escape from death for the young hero."

Buffalo had gone well, both days. With fresh coinage in the coffers, the show set out for Cleveland at midnight on the thirteenth of September. All of the circus, animals, baggage, tents and most of the troupe were safely loaded upon the steamship, "The Empire State." The three canal boats were tied behind, one after the other.

Charley stood on the front deck of the massive boat enjoying the moment, the enormity of this voyage. He had dreamt of being spirited away on a big steamboat and exploring the world. The seven copper pennies he had saved as a child had been spent long ago, but the dream was still with him.

The night was sticky, humid, and very warm, but if he was going to be able to work tomorrow, he thought he'd better settle in for the night. The crew was not given a bunk to sleep in but found their bedroll comfortable enough when laid out upon the folded canvas of the circus tent. Charley made his way between the snoring figures of his workmates and found a place to stretch out. The bedroll was under, not over, his youthful strong body. It was too hot for covers. He was asleep before his head hit the rolled-up coat he used for a pillow.

He dreamt of being lifted by an elephant, lifted and lowered, rolled and turned. It didn't hurt, but his stomach was in his throat. He awakened just in time to lean out away from the canvas and vomit all over the wooden floor of the ship.

The vessel was heaving and lurching, forward, sideways, high up and then down again. Charley ran to the deck and hung onto the rail and vomited again.

"What the heck!" he muttered in between the heaving. He looked around and saw not one or two, but several of his comrades also hanging onto the rails and in the throes of being involuntarily separated from their supper.

The wind was howling, a strong steady gale of relentless power. The ship was rising and falling into the gigantic waves of Lake Erie. The hot air they'd fallen asleep to had become mean and cold and the rain drove into their faces like tiny little knives.

In spite of the wind and rain and the already emptied stomach, Charley's belly heaved and lurched. He felt sweaty and weak and unable to hold onto the rail much longer. A strong hand reached out and grabbed him. A muscled arm wrapped around his waist and he was steered back into the cabin. The stillness brought on another bout of heaves, dry heaves, nothing left to come up. Jonas held onto him, so he didn't fall face-first onto the wooden deck.

"Jesus! Boy! You almost went off into the water!" Charley swallowed a couple of times and looked up at his friend.

"Thanks. I don't know what happened to me."

"You got seasick, kid! Now try to stop puking and help us tie this stuff down," commanded Jonas.

As the gale blew, the circus trunks, supplies and paraphernalia slid across the wooden deck in concert with the obnoxious way the boat was riding the waves. The tent poles, normally fast in place because they were so heavy, rolled back and forth and threatened to break the leg of anyone who dared try to stop them.

Stomach still lurching, Charley dived into the situation and assisted the others in securing the deck. Work took his mind off his stomach, but as soon as the work was done, the retching began again. He made his way to the cabin door and went outside. He hung on to the inner rail and made his way to the back of the steamship. The rain stopped. A misty full moon peaked out from between lifting clouds and Charley tried to keep track of it. If he could just keep his eyes on something steady, his stomach might stop.

The gale had died down to a simple steady wind, but the Lake was still in turmoil. The water was choppy and every now and then, there was an enormous wave. The ship would dip what felt like twenty feet and then immediately climb the distance back up again.

A giant wave met the bow of the steamship, perhaps the last big remnant of the summer storm that caused the boat to rise and then dip precipitously. Charley, at the stern, held onto the inner rail with all his might. The three canal boats lined up behind the steamship followed their master down into the watery hole. In the blink of an eye, the steamship traveled up the other side of the dip, but not all of the canal boats made it back up. The last boat in the towline dipped under the water just as the steamship was rising. The drag on the submerging boat broke loose the second boat in-tow, which caused the first boat to break loose as well.

Charley watched in horror as all three boats disappeared from sight. He dragged himself around the inner rail and into the cabin to sound the alarm. It wasn't just three boats that had gone missing. There was one man on each boat in the towline.

It had been the last great wave that broke the boats loose. Lake Erie was still agitated, but no longer dangerous. The steamship set about with all hands-on-deck, looking for the boats set adrift and those that had manned them.

They found all three men and got them aboard the "Empire State." The third boat was gone. The second boat they found at "Sturgeons' Point" wrecked. The canal boat closest to the ship and the last to break loose, was undamaged.

The steamship made its way on to Cleveland, Ohio a day late for the scheduled exhibition.

Everyone was exhausted. Few words were exchanged as the steamship was unloaded at the dock at the Port of Cleveland. A separate dock was found for the surviving canal boat on the Cuyahoga River which was the northern terminus of the Ohio Canal. They had but one canal boat to hold the circus paraphernalia that required three.

They'd have to buy a boat or two before they left Cleveland and continued their journey down the Ohio Canal to the Ohio River. For now, they would have to get all of their things to the exhibition field and set up the tent for the afternoon show.

After everything was moved to the field and the tent set up, cook fixed breakfast for the pale-faced survivors. As soon as the scrambled eggs and pancakes were on the inside of the crew and performers, the dark mood of the tent changed to one of relief.

"Well boys," remarked Jonas. "That's one for the record books! Damn lucky we all made it out safe and sound." He raised his coffee cup to all around and said, "Here! Here!"

They were used to adversity; there was always some kind of trouble out on the road. Their survival together, bonded them together… made them family.

Charley White did not think this was the particular family he wanted to be part of, not as long as they traveled steamboats across rough water. He planned to jump off and find another show, one that traveled by land.

He caught Jonas as he was leaving the dining tent.

"Hey Jonas. Got a second?"

Jonas had suspected that Charley had had enough the second time Rice got arrested. Charley was a good kid, but he seemed to prefer things to be even and steady. The Rice show was anything but….

"If you think that you can move on without me, I am going to jump off here and head back." He'd rehearsed it in his head. "I don't think I was cut out for a river show." He went on to blame his distaste on the seasickness, but in truth, Dan Rice's outfit was just a little more exciting than he felt comfortable with.

"I can't get your hold-back pay, Charley. Hell, I'm not sure Dan has enough money after the fines and steamboat ride to pay any of us." Charley knew about hold-back pay. Road shows employed boys and those boys generally didn't stay the whole season because the work was hard. An incentive to keep them from beginning to end was to hold back a part of their pay until the last show, ten or twenty percent. Charley had forfeited his hold-back pay the previous season when he left the Quick show early.

"That's fine, Jonas. I don't expect the hold-back pay. I hope I can get this week's pay though." Then he added, "I don't know how I'll make it back to Buffalo, but I am not stepping on another lake boat, no sir!"

Jonas would continue with Dan Rice. It was his home, shabby as it might be. He knew there was no money to pay out this week, but Charley didn't have to worry about that. Jonas went off as if he was finding the show's banker, but he did not. Instead, he took off his boot and dug out some money, his own savings, counted out what Charley was owed and headed back to find the boy.

"Here you go son," he said as he handed Charley the money. "Sorry to see you go, but you gotta do what you gotta do."

Charley took the money and shook Jonas's hand. "Thank you, Jonas. Maybe I'll see you around sometime."

"That you will, my friend, that you will," he replied. Jonas turned and headed back to the outfit… plenty of stuff to do before the first show and then he'd have to go look for a boat to buy before they could continue their route.

CHAPTER ELEVEN

SEPTEMBER 1851

HE STOPPED WHISTLING ABOUT MIDWAY through day-three of his tramp to Buffalo. The relief and optimism he enjoyed the day he walked away from the Dan Rice show in Cleveland had melted away like snow on a sunny day. In its place was the stubborn tunnel-vision of self-preservation. He was hot, tired, and hungry. While he knew that Buffalo was a good two hundred miles northeast of Cleveland, he had envisioned an easier journey, one with less walking and more frequent wagon lifts from kindly passers-by.

The gale they survived on Lake Erie in the wee hours of the morning on the fourteenth of September had not confined its destructive energy to the water. The storm pounded the eastern shore of the Great Lake leaving in its wake twisted piers and half-sunken ships. There had been few wagons as the road to offer Charley a ride because roads had been damaged, washed out in some places and littered with fallen trees in others. Whenever someone did offer him a ride, he took it. A mile on a wagon was a mile off his feet. Besides he enjoyed the company and, more often than not, the driver would share his lunch.

He followed the shoreline north. It was not only the shortest way to Buffalo, but there were businesses, docks, roadhouses. The more populated the area, he reasoned, the more rides he could get.

Charley reached out with his boot and kicked a rock down the road. The only ride he'd been offered on this day was on a boat. He wasn't quite ready for that.

Dawn of the fifth day, he reached Erie, Pennsylvania. The harbor town beckoned him. He liked the water, so long as he himself was on dry land. He walked down the length of a gently sloped hill to the waterfront. Sea gulls called as they circled the fishing boats hoping for an easy meal. Early morning sunshine sparkled off the surface of the lake. Calm, he thought. He scanned the western horizon and marked that the harbor was protected by a long peninsula. He walked out on the dock and removed his boots. He carefully laid out his socks on the deck to dry. He sat down and rolled up his pantlegs. An involuntary sigh of relief escaped him as his swollen feet met the cold water. He removed his shirt, rolled it up and placed it under his head as he lay back onto the warm boards. He slept.

+ + +

Six days later when he finally ran into the Buffalo River just south of city of Buffalo, he had worn substantial holes in the soles of his boots. He was pretty sure he stunk to high-heaven, and he had to tighten his belt. The sun had just broken the horizon and, by his reckoning, the twenty-fourth of September in the year of Our Lord, 1851.

Charley stopped at the water's edge and removed the leather saddle bags he carried for his necessities from his shoulder and laid them on the ground. He peered into the water of the slow-moving river and caught sight of himself. His wavy dark hair stood on end and pointed in every direction. He needed a haircut and some soap, but for the moment wetting the unkempt mop with his hands would have to do.

He scooped the chilly water from the river over his head and finished the maneuver by scrubbing his face with his wet hands. He did this several times over until his hair was saturated. Then, he spread the fingers of both hands and swept the hair straight back, making sure that every strand was neatly tucked behind his ears.

His plan for the morning was to find a hot breakfast. After that, he would fix some insoles for his boots. The flaps on his saddle bags would have to be sacrificed. His little knife would work just fine. Good blade. Sharp.

A last glance at his reflection reassured him that he was presentable enough to go into town. He started off, refreshed and inspired. Once on Main Street, the smell of bacon and biscuits led him to his destination. The Commercial Hotel stood in front of him. As he lifted his foot onto the lowest step, he stopped dead in his tracks. A boy standing in front of the door selling newspapers was calling out, "Last day of Barnum's Museum, get your paper, get the details."

Charley looked at the buildings around him. Sure enough, there were posters for the show plastered high and low all over the street he'd just come down. He did not need to buy a newspaper to find out that Barnum's Museum would be at Swan Street and South Division that very day. The information was literally all around him.

He made his way past the paper monger, ordered breakfast, ate it quickly and made his way back out onto the street in a matter of minutes. All of a sudden he had spring in his step and the fatigue of the past ten days fell away like water off a duck's back. He got directions from a passerby and headed off to find the show.

He saw it from a long way off, an enormous canvas, round with vertical red and white stripes and at the top, giant blue stars! Charley drank in the details with hungry eyes. The show tent was a colorful American flag accentuated by individual flags belonging to other countries. As he got closer, he saw that two American Flags draped the front entrance while a third larger American flag flew high above on a towering flagpole.

There was little movement about the tent as the hour was early, barely nine. The advertisements said there were shows at two and seven. "Backyard," he murmured to himself as he made his way through a gathering crowd of curious kids. There they were, the crew, gathered in a side tent eating breakfast.

A guard came up to him before he got near enough to see if he recognized anyone. "You can't be here," he growled as he positioned himself between Charley and the tent. "Now get on out of here and wait for the show like everybody else. Got it?" he asked.

"I'm a traveler," stated Charley, unintimidated by the guard.

By rights, the guard should have immediately asked Charley questions about what show he worked for and where he was going. He then should have taken him to the manager where he would have been fed and sheltered so he could continue on his way. The guard was having none of it.

"You're just a fakir!" He took Charley by the left shoulder and spun him around into the opposite direction. "Now get yourself out of here and don't come back unless you have twenty-five cents in your hand for the show."

Just then a man called from the dining tent, "Charley White! Is that you?"

The guard and Charley both turned to face the big straw-haired man that came after them.

"Charley White, well I'll be darned! What in heaven's name are you doing here?" asked John-John the bird man. John-John nodded at the guard, assuring him that Charley was no intruder and dwarfed his friend in an exuberant bear hug. He scrubbed the smaller man's head with his knuckles and stepped back, grasping Charley's shoulders with both hands.

"Hi John," smiled Charley looking up at his friend. "It's good to see you, too!"

+ + +

A man dressed in all black stood by himself in the far corner of the dining tent, his gestalt unremarkable, thus his presence largely ignored. Built like a proverbial brick outhouse, but well under six feet, Lewis B. Lent observed. Most of the menagerie crew had polished off breakfast and sat slurping coffee and gabbing amongst themselves. Waiters busied themselves collecting tableware for washing and stacking for the next meal.

Since Lewis's fiasco of investing in the gold mining adventure in California in '49, he had become more prone to looking-before-leaping into any decision. Near-death experiences where you lose money and forfeit your pride force you to acknowledge your mortality.

He had returned to New York from San Francisco via horseback and carriage over endless dusty roads, some of them barely a trail, rather than take another packet boat around Cape Horn. Why tempt Fate? When folks asked him about his adventure, he pretended not to hear. He didn't want to relive a single moment.

Next summer he would be once again managing this show of Barnum's. The Asiatic Museum and Menagerie consisted of a dusty collection of wax figures, a tidy little menagerie, and a pride of lions "tamed" by Mr. Peirce. There were also a few oddities like Mr. Nellis the armless man, a fat man, and Tom Thumb with his little carriage. As the manager, he was responsible for everything that went into making the show profitable. Today he was observing. It was important to observe carefully and make any improvements as soon as possible.

Lewis noticed the big blonde kid, John-something, the fellow in charge of Barnum's birds. He was talking to a young man foreign to the camp, yet familiar to Lewis. If he stared long enough, he'd remember. He never forgot a face, a favor, or a slight. He'd been working with menageries since his father started one in the mid 1820's. He was thirteen when he helped with that first string of camels, and he had more experience in show business than most anyone. He had also made and lost more money than most men see in a lifetime.

The name came to him, Charley…Charley White, the kid that was good with horses. That's the kid that pulled the Sands & Lent wagon out of the mud near Syracuse, he thought. He straightened himself, reached over and stubbed out his cigar, brushed his coat off and walked over to the young men.

"Well, if it isn't Charley White from Syracuse," he smiled as he held out his hand.

Charley stood to greet his old friend, "Yes sir!" he exclaimed. He shook Lewis's hand and stepped back. Waited.

"Where in the world have you been, Charley lad?" he asked. "Have you been with any shows since I last saw you? Have you trained a horse to fetch your slippers yet?" Lewis laughed as he asked, and his eyes twinkled. He remembered how well he liked this boy.

"Well, sir, I've just left the Dan Rice show as they were headed south through Ohio.

"And, why did you leave Dan's show, Charley?" asked Lent. It was always important in judging a man's character to find out why he left his last employer.

"Well, if I was to be honest sir, I don't think I'm cut out to be on a river show. A storm on Lake Erie cured me of wanting to live on a boat, sir."

Lent stepped back, crossed his arms over his chest threw his head back and burst into laughter. He put a big hand on each of Charley's shoulders, looked him in the eye and said, "We seem to be of the same mind, Charley! I don't much like boats and storms either."

"Are you looking for a job," Lewis asked.

"If you're the boss, I sure am," Charley answered quickly.

Lewis pulled on his chin beard a moment, pondering the question. Where best could he use him, for certainly the boy was a good asset. He closed his eyes momentarily as the nexus of an idea formed in his head.

"How about I come back between shows? You stick around, give this guy, John is it? A hand with his birds, and we can have supper together, here, about six."

Lewis turned on his heal and left without waiting for an answer. He'd have to think this out a little bit before deciding how best to use Charley's skills. As soon as he got back to Philadelphia, he was getting married. Her name was Mary and she was an angel. At thirty-eight it was way past time to settle down, build a nest and start a family. California had reminded him that time was flying away. His zest for life was never greater, but he needed to be serious in his planning.

If he was going to properly manage every angle of the show next season, it might be good to have a man he could trust to deliver his messages between all entities in the show. He could not be in two places at once, but with a good, smart, trustworthy fellow like Charley, he could have greater control. And, if he was clever and Charley worked out well, Lewis might have adequate time to spend with his bride to produce offspring. Ah! He'd loved his own father so much that the mere thought of his own son made his heart swell.

Six thirty came and went and Charley began to believe that Mr. Lent had forgotten. He was disappointed, but he'd faced disappointment before, and it hadn't killed him. Just as he pushed his plate back and started to get up from the table, the man arrived.

"Are you finished eating, Charley?" He asked without waiting for an answer. "Come with me. I want to talk in private."

Lewis B. Lent walked slowly and deliberately out of the tent and toward a small black carriage that awaited him. He had made his assessments of Barnum's outfit and was about to depart for Welch's in Pennsylvania this very night.

"I have an offer for you, Charley." Lewis said very seriously. "I've given it some consideration and I want to try an experiment. If you are willing, I would like to personally employ you as my right-hand man to help me carry out my responsibilities. I don't just manage this show. I have many other irons in the fire both on the road and in Philadelphia. I can't be two places at once, but I could send you to deliver my orders and instructions. What say you?"

Lent's deep brown eyes peered intently at his young friend as he waited.

"Mr. Lent, I've worked for you before and I would gladly work for you again," answered Charley.

"Well!" smiled Lewis. "Then, I guess we have a deal," he said shaking Charley's hand.

Lost in his own deep thoughts, Lewis turned to step up into the carriage to take him off into the warm summer evening.

"Ah ha!" he exclaimed as he turned once again to face his young friend. "We'll have to discuss wages and such, but I haven't time now. Stay here and help with wherever they need you to do until we get this outfit safely back in New York City. We'll meet there and I'll pay you. You can find a place to stay with your friend John until I get there, am I right?" He asked, this time waiting for an answer

"Yes Sir! I'll see you in a few weeks, sir."

Charley watched as Lent's carriage pulled away, parallel puffs of white dust rising after the wheels marking his departure. His youthful heart swelled in his chest. He felt warmth, happiness, adventure, and best of all, he felt like he was home.

CHAPTER TWELVE

THREE YEARS LATER
NOVEMBER 1854
NEW YORK CITY

TWENTY-TWO-YEAR-OLD CHARLEY WHITE HAD SEEN a lot during nine seasons in the business, so it didn't bother him at all that this show was ended. Partnerships were always breaking up and reforming somewhere else in different combinations. For three years running he had traveled with Barnum's Museum and Menagerie during the summer and then spent winters at the American Museum in Manhattan.

Mr. Nellis the armless man, Mr. Lengel the lion king, Tom Thumb and the military band were all scattered to the wind now, looking for new employment. Mr. Lent had expressed an eagerness to flee back to Philadelphia where he not only had a wife and two small children (named Lewis and Mary after himself and his wife), but he also had a business to attend to. He and his partner, Rufus Welch, owned the "Welch's National Circus and L. B. Lent's New York Circus Combined."

Lent had offered Charley a job in Philadelphia helping to rebuild Mr. Welch's theatre which had burned down the past June. However, Charley wanted to spend winter in Manhattan where he could meet old friends and maybe get a chance to travel up to Smithville to visit his family.

He listened now, only mildly interested, as the auctioneer rattled off numbers and pointed at bidders, slamming down his hammer when the bidding petered-out and a sale was made. Today the entire menagerie was being sold off. The partnership of P.T. Barnum, S.B. Howes, S.E. Stratton (Tom Thumb's father) and Avery Smith was dissolving, bit by bit, as the animals were auctioned off by Hammond, the Tattersall's auctioneer. Charley's job was to get the creatures from their holding areas to their new owners. Once done, he was unemployed.

It had been a tough year. Bad weather all season had hamstrung traveling shows all over the northeast. Barnum's had suffered a terrible loss early on in April when lightning struck the tent during foul weather in Ohio. One man was killed, several were injured, and the tent was shredded when it blew down. They had to send back to Connecticut to get a new canvas.

According to Mr. Lent, it was Barnum who dissolved the partnership because it was not profitable enough. Everyone agreed that Barnum must know more about failures than most anyone. The showman had stuck his fingers in a great many pies the past year, none of which seemed successful. He and a partner started an illustrated newspaper, which failed after a few months. He had attempted to restore the Crystal Palace to a profit, and the venture fell flat. And, Barnum's fire annihilator was an abysmal failure (at least according to the newspapers). Of late, Mr. Barnum spent most of his time on the road lecturing people (for a fee) on the virtues of temperance (trying to get all states to adopt Maine's strict prohibition law) without any great success. The biographical book he had just published, *The Life of P.T. Barnum*, was already getting bad reviews and selling at a discount. Barnum was losing money everywhere except the museum, which was still doing a very good business.

The hammer slammed the auctioneer's table and the man in charge bellowed, "Seven Elephants, known as Pizarre, Mogul, Fanny, Canada, Jenny, Mary, and Tom Thumb are sold to Mr. S. B. Howes for twenty-three-hundred-dollars, cash money!" The Ceylon elephants had cost three thousand dollars apiece when they were brought to America but feeding stock over the winter was expensive, so it was better to let them go. The giants could each consume at least two bushels of oats and a hundred pounds of hay a day.

Barnum had purchased the giraffes, Colossus and Cleopatra for himself. Charley had already organized their removal to the American Museum. Windows had to be removed at the back in order to facilitate the ingress of the graceful couple. A display had been set up for them in the center, open area of the five-story exhibition hall at Anne and Broadway.

Charley watched as bidding opened for the lot which included the big cats, camels, monkeys, an alpaca, a bear, a zebra, a wolf, a spotted hyena, an assortment of parrots and various wagons and canvas.

"Who will give me fifteen hundred dollars?" asked the auctioneer, "Fifteen hundred dollars," he repeated and looked around the crowd.

The right hand belonging to Mr. Titus rose above the crowd, and the auctioneer continued, "Who will give me two-thousand dollars for this lot? It's worth at least ten times as much!"

Mr. Howes put in a bid and the auctioneer continued his chant, raising the price by five hundred dollars as the bidding heated up between Mr. Titus and Mr. Howes. Finally, the bidding stalled at thirty-five hundred dollars. The hammer hit the table and the auctioneer awarded the sale to Mr. Howes.

Today the remainder of the hardware, including the two miniature ornamented wagons that "General Tom Thumb" had ridden in the past four years, were auctioned off. The hand-painted portraits of the little man were still in perfect condition and the gilding (repaired every season) was still in good stead. Still, the two wagons sold cheaply, one for thirty-five dollars and one for ten.

Nobody wanted the Rhinoceros. He didn't travel well, took up too much space in the museum, and although it cost a small fortune to bring him to America, the public just wasn't interested. He would likely find a home at the zoo, at least for the winter.

Charley went around and shook hands with the parting showmen, some with animals in tow and others, empty handed. He knew most of them. It was a small world, this family of travelers.

After the crowd dispersed, Charley delivered the last two cart horses over to a livery in the Bowery, got his receipt and headed out for the museum.

From a distance, Barnum's American Museum looked like a gigantic birthday cake. There it stood with its five layers of gaudily decorated outer walls, splattered with posters advertising the wonders one could witness inside for just twenty-five cents. The roof was bedecked with well-spaced flags from all nations. The American flag being at least ten times the size of the others flew on the Broadway side directly over the entrance. "BARNUM'S MUSEUM" was painted in oversized letters along the sides of the first and third floors. Between the windows were cameos depicting monkeys, snakes, elephants, bears, birds, and a plethora of people and creatures that one could find if you just went inside.

Charley walked around and reached the back entrance just as icy pellets of sleet slapped against the back of his neck. He knocked. The guard recognized him and let him in.

The warmth of the wood-paneled hallway that led up the back stairs was welcoming and familiar. This place was the closest thing Charley had to a permanent "home." His friends either worked here or came by on a regular basis during winter months.

He reached the landing on the third floor and made his way over to where "The Happy Family," one of Barnum's special projects was kept. He had bought the entire exhibit, the hundred or so animals, from Scotland in toto. The creatures were exhibited in a very large elongated cage that was tall enough to allow the birds to fly and perch well off the floor. The enclosure housed both predator and prey animals in the same space peacefully, thus the moniker "Happy Family." Mishaps (one animal eating another) were kept to a minimum through ample feeding and careful tending.

The familiar gestalt of a large man in overalls bent over a workbench turned as he heard Charley approach. John's round face broke into a grin as he recognized his friend.

"God Bless you, Charley White! How are you? When did you get back?" he asked as he shook his friend's hand. Observing the baggy pants and gaunt face before him, he asked, "Are you hungry? I'll be done here in a few minutes and we can go get some dinner. Boy! Marika and the kids will be mighty glad to see you!"

While John finished, Charley went down to the first floor to find Mr. Greenwood. Although Barnum was owner and general manager, it was Greenwood who managed the day-to-day of the museum and it was he who would keep Charley employed this winter, he hoped.

Mr. Greenwood's door was open. He and another man were in a deep discussion over some papers scattered across the desk between them. Both men were pointing, noting, and nodding for several moments before Greenwood looked up.

"Charley! Welcome back!" Greenwood stood and shook Charley's hand. "Can you come by in the morning, say eight o'clock?"

"Yes, sir. I'll see you then," he replied smiling. The two friends met at the exit and walked a few blocks to John's place. Both men scraped the mud off their boots outside the front door before walking up the stairs. When John opened the door, the warm coziness of the room radiated out to greet them. Four pairs of bright blue eyes lit up as they realized that "papa" was home. The older twins were just over two. The younger twins were a year younger.

All four boys rushed their father, the little ones crabbing their way across the floor and pulling themselves up onto his pantleg. He knelt down and hugged his children, perfect little replicas of himself and his wife.

Marika née Johnson, the mother of this golden-haired tribe, came from the kitchen wiping her hands on the pinafore she wore to protect her dress from cooking and sticky little fingers.

"Boys! Boys! Let papa come in." They ignored her even as she lifted the smallest ones away from John's legs. "Anders… Anton… Jakob… John-John let papa get his boots off and sit down. He's tired, you know, yes?"

Marika laughed and turned to Charley, "Come in! Valkommen!" she said smiling. "Come in! Sit! The food is nearly ready!" She turned and walked back to the kitchen, her straight back, the perfect posture of a prima ballerina.

John had a wonderful life, even if it was a little chaotic. Three years earlier he had been put in charge of "The Happy Family" exhibit. One day he noticed a pretty girl who stayed for hours in front of the exhibit, watching the animals and scribbling in her little book. Some weeks later he saw her again and he came out from behind the exhibit and they talked. She spoke little English, but John was smitten. He would teach her. Marika was a recent immigrant from Sweden. Her family arrived in New York too late to get established in Minnesota before winter. She was seventeen, nearly six feet in her stockings, bony (but with ample feminine endowments) and blessed with a sort of kindness Charley had only seen in one other person, his friend John. They had married just before Christmas. Twin boys arrived after the correct number of months and before the two little ones could walk, another set of identical little boys arrived.

John had a long and trusted record with Mr. Greenwood and the American Museum. He had been working there since he left the G.C. Quick show in 1850. And, although he was a faithful employee, he did not earn the attention or confidence of P.T. Barnum until February the previous year when he helped facilitate a successful show near and dear to the heart of the master showman himself.

The Metropolitan Hall burned to the ground three weeks before it was supposed to host the very first National Poultry Show. Mr. Barnum was the president of the newly formed society. Upon his suggestion the show would not be cancelled but would instead be held at his very own American Museum at no charge to the society or the exhibitors.

The museum had five levels if you didn't count the basement. All five levels were chock full of animals, oddities, portraits, wax statues, and bits and pieces of everything one could imagine. In addition, there was the lecture room, a theatre where plays deemed wholesome enough for women and children were performed five times daily.

The decision to house the poultry exhibition at the museum was made January 20th and the start date was February 13th. Making room for hundreds of cages full of birds of all varieties on such short notice was nigh on impossible. Mr. Greenwood tasked John with the project and John got it done.

For a whole week, the museum was filled to bursting with turkeys, chickens, pigeons, pheasants and even (God knows why) a pig, a sheep, and a dog. Most importantly for Mr. Barnum, the museum was filled with customers who paid the twenty-five cents to come in the front door. Being pleased with the results of the highly successful poultry show, Barnum immediately scheduled the show for the following year. John was delegated to manage it.

Charley's function at the museum was much different. He was a skilled carpenter, thanks to his father. Mr. Greenwood depended upon him to build and repair everything in the oversized establishment. He constructed showcases for animals, oddity collections, partitions for portraits, and displays for natural history exhibits. Whenever a new play would come into the lecture hall, it was Charley who built the wooden structures that held the various elaborate scenes painted to illustrate the story.

The plays were mild as everything violent or course was removed from the script before it could run in Barnum's. Since the intent was to attract women and children into the museum, the plays had to be moral and righteous. They often portrayed social dilemmas. And although Charley could have watched all of the performances for free, he rarely did. He wouldn't have watched this one if it weren't for the fact that his carpentry had failed during the earlier show.

The mechanism was beautiful in its simplicity. There was a wooden frame the width of the stage and eight feet high. A wooden "spindle" was placed upright just inside the frame on either end of the stage. Each spindle had a "cup" at its top and bottom to allow the spindle to rotate freely.

The spindles supported a cotton canvas painted to look like a river. The canvas was seven feet tall, twice the length of the stage, and the ends were sewn together to create an endless loop. Charley had created a gear and crank on the bottom left spindle so that one man could turn the crank, move the fabric, and make it look as if the water was flowing. It was ingenious until the gear broke. Charley had hastily fashioned a new one, but there had been little time to test it, so he stayed to make sure it held.

His attention was inadvertently drawn from the mechanism to the actual production. The story was *Uncle Tom's Cabin* and its focus was slavery, a subject he avoided thinking about. Slavery was not right but didn't know what he could do about it. There'd been an incident in Virginia last summer where a farmer accused Mr. Lent of luring a young black boy away. There was a big brouhaha about how the traveling show was stealing slaves, but the boy had never come near the show. The incident died down, but it left a bad taste.

Winter 1855 brought the return of the poultry show. John organized everything, including getting Charley to build safe pens for the larger birds. John's father from New Jersey was still a chicken farmer. He brought several of his Cochins to show off in hopes of winning a portion of the offered five-hundred-dollar prize bounty. It happened that Barnum (still president of the National Poultry Association) was close by when John's wife showed up with their two sets of twin boys. It was right then and there that Barnum hatched the idea of a baby contest. He was always looking for a new way to draw in customers.

Advertising started right away for a contest to be held in June. They would find the handsomest children of different ages and reward them with cash and notoriety. Charley helped build a viewing area where mothers and their beautiful children could be on display for the museum visitors to see. He built a partition to create a place behind which the mothers could tend to their children's needs in private. A select group of women would choose the most handsome child in each age group, the best set of twins, triplets, or quadruplets, and the fattest child. Oh, there was scuttlebutt. Righteous citizens disapproved of displaying children like animals in a menagerie, but their concerns (so freely offered in newspaper opinions) only further advertised the venture, making it wildly successful.

By the end of August 1855 Mr. Greenwood's job as assistant manager evolved into one of part-owner (with Mr. Henry Butler) of Barnum's American Museum. Mr. Barnum bragged that he sold the collection for twice what he originally paid for it. He expressed publicly his eagerness to try new things. He got his wish. By the end of 1855, Barnum was bankrupt.

He had lent his guarantee for the Jerome Clock Company to borrow no more than one-hundred-ten-thousand dollars. The deal was struck in exchange for a promise that the company would relocate to Bridgeport, Connecticut and provide jobs for his beloved city. It turned out that the clock company was heavily in debt (a fact they hid from Barnum), and they ran up loans to the tune of over half a million dollars. Barnum was on the hook.

While Barnum was scurrying around to find his financial feet, Mr. Greenwood ran the museum as he always had, with care and efficiency.

Charley was lifted from simple cart man and carpenter to caretaker of the lions and other large animals. The first time he put on a show for the public, he was in absolutely no danger. He simply entered the cage of a very old lion, carried in a bucket of blood, and stood by as the toothless beast lapped it up.

By the summer of 1856 John and Marika were expecting another child and given her history of having twins, John was a little concerned. It wasn't easy to feed four growing boys while living in the city and although another child was welcome, money was a worry. He was planning on moving his family back to his father's chicken farm in New Jersey. Even if there wasn't much cash on a farm, there was usually enough to eat.

One day while tending "The Happy Family," John noticed a little girl sitting on the floor outside the exhibit. She had a sock on her hand. As he got closer, he noted the sock was a puppet with black button eyes and red chain-stitching for a mouth.

"Now Eliza, you need to eat your breakfast!" said the sock puppet to the little girl. "There'll be nothing more till supper, so if you don't eat, you'll go hungry."

"Well," answered the little girl seriously, "Then I'd better eat, or my tummy will hurt."

The sock puppet nodded up and down and gave the little girl a kiss on the cheek before noticing the big man standing over them.

"Hey little miss. Who are you?" asked John as he squatted down in front of her. "Are you and your friend having a picnic?"

"My name is Eliza, but my sister said no one's supposed to see me." She made herself as small as possible and held the sock puppet over her mouth.

"Why shouldn't anyone see you, Miss Eliza? Where is your sister? Are you lost here?" asked John.

"Nancy is selling programs for Mr. Barnum downstairs. She said I am not supposed to be here, but I have to be somewhere, don't I?" she asked, looking up at the big man.

"Why yes, you do!" He answered giving her a big grin. "We all have to be somewhere! Are you hungry?" he asked. For John, food was always a priority.

"A little bit, but Nancy said if I'm good we can get a bun on the way home." The sock puppet came to life, looked at Eliza and said, "Yes! That's right Eliza! We're going to get a sweet bun. I hope it is a sweet bun, don't you?" asked the sock.

Not waiting for an answer, John motioned for the little girl to come sit at the table behind "The Happy Family" exhibit. His lunch was already spread out, an apple, a sandwich, a piece of cake, and a bottle of milk. He poured milk into a cup and put it in front of her. He took half the sandwich and laid it beside the cup.

"Go ahead now, you eat," he urged." John sat back in his chair and pointed his half-sandwich at her. "You need to eat if you want to grow up big and strong like me!" He laughed.

Although food was not in abundance at home, Marika packed extra lunch for John's daily guest from then on. Eliza helped her new friend with cleaning up after "The Happy Family" and kept him company while her sister Nancy sold programs in the lobby of the American Museum. When her sister was done for the day, she came to fetch Eliza and take her home. Everyone was happy.

Charley knew of Eliza for he often took his own lunch sitting at John's table behind "The Happy Family" exhibit. He missed his own little sister, Emily. Although Emily had turned eighteen this year, he thought of her as that little girl of eight he left behind when he joined the traveling shows. He enjoyed listening to little Eliza as her animated freckled face lit up when talking about some adventure of hers. She was like a little hurricane lamp of sunshine in a scrawny, red-headed little-girl-body.

One day Charley was working in "The Happy Family" exhibit repairing some perches just before closing time. He was balancing precariously on a flimsy ladder trying to fasten the end of one pole to the wall brace when he turned and saw her…a pretty young woman he would later know to be Nancy, the older sister of little Eliza.

Charley did not find women easy. He had avoided them since that girl in Fabius married the widowed farmer. Mostly he kept himself busy, but sometimes things would go quiet and the loneliness crept in. No one waited for him with a hot supper at the end of the day.

It started innocently enough. Charley began walking Eliza and her sister home to their boarding house where they lived with their mother. It was always dark by the time they headed out and the city was dangerous. The girl's father was off in the Army. Even with the money he sent back to them, they didn't have enough to live on. That's why Mrs. Spaulding worked as a home nurse and Nancy worked at the museum.

Charley grew more fond of Eliza and Nancy as the days, weeks, and months went by. He continued to walk them home every night, even when summer provided ample light.

By Thanksgiving 1856, Mrs. Spaulding was facing an impossible situation. Her husband had quit sending money. The elderly couple she cared for insisted she move into their house, or they would get another nurse. There was not enough money to keep the rented rooms, and Charlotte's employer had no room for her little girls.

Charley came up with the solution; he married Nancy so she and Eliza could live with him. It was meant to be a platonic relationship, but their friendship and close proximity soon brought about intimacy.

On the 29th of August 1857 Nancy gave birth to Charles Henry White. He was welcomed into the world by his grandmother Charlotte who delivered him, his six-year-old Aunt Eliza, and his dad, Charley.

The father is often made to feel unnecessary in the care and handling of newborn infants. This was especially true in Charley's case. The Spaulding women were tightly bonded by past suffering. Charlotte Spaulding had given birth to three baby boys who all died in infancy and then her husband, Liberty Spaulding, left them. Charlotte, Nancy, and Eliza were survivors and when Charles Henry was born, they circled their wagons to protect him. He bore his father's middle name and the middle name of two of Charlottes' lost sons.

Charley did what he knew best, he worked. Mr. Greenwood kept him employed seven days a week helping run the great conglomeration that made up the entertainment venue. He did carpentry, deliveries, a lion show, and he helped train dogs and show them. He was always looking for more odd jobs.

After Mr. Welch died thus ending the Welch-Lent partnership, Lewis B. Lent moved his family to New York City where he ran Lent's Great National Circus. This circumstance was most helpful for Charley because he picked up extra work with Mr. Lent.

Abraham Lincoln was elected in November of 1860 and the political discourse was loud enough to even reach the inner sanctum of the museum. The papers predicted war. Several southern states had left the Union and when Douglas lost the election to Lincoln, the crack between north and south widened. War was inevitable.

CHAPTER THIRTEEN

1861 NEW JERSEY

JOHN MOVED HIS WIFE, FOUR sons and newborn daughter Sylvia to New Jersey. He reasoned they would be better off living in the countryside. Marika could grow a vegetable garden and John could help his father on the family's poultry farm. John wanted his children to experience running barefooted, tending chickens and growing their own food.

Charley decided New Jersey would be a good place for his growing family, too. In late March he drove a wagon filled with household items, his wife, child, and sister-in law and left Manhattan for Jersey City. Nancy was heavily pregnant, so her mother followed a week later.

The three women, Charley and three-year-old Charles Henry lived in a small apartment a ten-minute ride from John's place. If war broke out, the two men had a strategy. John would stay on the farm and aid the war effort through producing food. Charley would sign up and go to war. Everyone believed any such conflict would be resolved after a few weeks, a few months at most. John would watch over Charley's family until he got home again. Charley was ready to fight for his country just as his friend Michael had done. If he joined the militia, Nancy would get five dollars a month of his militia pay and have access to the nest egg he had saved by working multiple jobs.

Charlotte would be living with them and her income as a midwife would help keep them until he returned home again.

After moving his family, Charley made a hasty trip to Smithville to see his father. He wanted to say goodbye, just in case… Benajah had taken on an apprentice carpenter, Madison Fitch, whom Charley disliked intensely. To his great disappointment, his sister Emily married him. The newlyweds and Charley's youngest brother, William lived with Benajah and Johanna. Charley's brother Ben was married and living in Sterling.

April 12, 1861, war erupted. Members of the South Carolina Militia fired the first shots against the union soldiers at Fort Sumpter and took the island fort for the south. President Abraham Lincoln called for seventy-five-thousand volunteers.

On 19 April 1861 Charley took the ferry from Jersey City to Manhattan where he signed up with the New York State Militia, Volunteers. He was assigned to Company G of the New York Volunteers, a part of the 9th Regiment.

Chapter Fourteen

26 May 1861
New Jersey

William Albert White was born at home in Jersey City. His grandmother was there to deliver him. The newborn's father was already in New York with his uniform, bedroll, and kit ready to muster out the following day.

Washington Square
Manhattan
New York

In spite of glorious sunshine, the seriousness of this day weighed heavily upon him. Charley was part of the Ninth Regiment assigned to the 83rd Infantry, Company G, New York Volunteers. Because he believed there was a chance he could die, he had signed up as volunteer "Alasco C. White, age 29." Whether being married or buried, one should use one's Christian name.

The entire Ninth was gathered at Washington Square under Colonel John W. Stiles for the purpose of being inspected by the Union Defense Committee. After the inspection, the troops were ordered to assemble the following day at two o'clock whereupon the regiment would remove to Washington D.C.

The regiment assembled as ordered and formed a line on Fourteenth Street. Since this was a state militia and the governor of New York (Edwin D. Morgan) had not sanctioned the regiment's choice to fight for the federal government outside of New York, all state-owned firearms were left behind.

The regiment was very orderly assembled until a throng of well-wishers descended upon them delivering prayers, hugs, kisses and the like. Sisters, mothers, and sweethearts showered their loved ones with small gifts of scarves, hankies, socks, and knives. Charley felt a pang of sadness. He had not seen his youngest child, nor did he know if mother and child had lived or died through the labor. He had been compelled to leave to join his company before the child was delivered. He stood alone among hundreds of men. His wife had not been angry that he left. She had seemed indifferent to his departure.

The call to "Fall In" was given. The band and drum corps started up and the troops marched up Broadway to Cortlandt Street and climbed en masse aboard the Jersey Ferry to cross the Hudson into New Jersey. The distance was covered in minutes. As the loading ramp bridged the gap between ferry and wharf, the band struck up "The girl I left Behind Me" and the men began to disembark, cheered on by the shouts of well-wishers lining the shore.

Over the din, Charley heard a loud and familiar voice shout his name.

"Charley, Charley White! Hey Charley!"

Turning toward the voice, he saw his dear friend John, his straw-colored mop a head above the throng as he waded through the crowd toward his friend.

"You have a son, Charley" shouted the man when he was still a few yards away. "He's fine! Nancy's fine!" He bellowed out joyously as he arrived.

Charley was unable to stop and talk. His company was moving to board the train to Washington. John walked with him and gave him the blessed details.

"She named him William Albert, like you wanted. He is a prince," John continued, "with a full head of hair and a pair of good lungs on him. Screamed like the dickens when he came, he did!" John slapped his friend on the back one last time and broke off as they reached the train. Charley turned to John.

"Thanks John! Take care of them, won't you?"

As the train was moving out, John kept pace with it and the window behind which his friend was sitting.

"God speed, brother! Be well. Stay Safe!"

Charley watched as John faded into the distance. I have another son, he thought. He was a little sorry to leave his family behind, but he knew they were safe in John's care.

By five in the morning the train had made its way to Camden, New Jersey. The men disembarked and marched across the Delaware River to Philadelphia where they boarded another train to Havre de Grace. They crossed the Susquehanna River on the Ferry Boat "Maryland" and continued their journey to Baltimore and Washington D.C. On the 30th, the regiment marched to the arsenal and lined up to receive their Harper's Ferry smooth-bore buck and ball muskets, caliber .69. Once outfitted, the regiment was paraded before President Lincoln, his cabinet and General Scott. The Ninth Regiment would defend the capital, replacing the Seventh, at Camp Cameron on Harper's Ferry Road.

Most of the recruits had never served in any capacity. Many had never held a gun, much less shot one. A regime was dictated as to when and how the men would rise, retire, eat, train, and pray according to the orders of J. W. Stiles, Colonel Commanding. The green soldiers did as they were told, however the night watch was fraught with fear and paranoia. It was impossible to tell friend from foe in the daylight, and even more uncertain after dark. More than one hapless bush was shot to pieces when leaves rustling in the wind failed to respond to the command, "Who goes there?"

Company G was led by Captain Atterbury, First and Second Lieutenants Hendrickson and Wickham. They were, with Alasco Charles White, one hundred and three in number. Mid-July they marched to Darnestown and after a few days there, made their way to Point of Rocks. The bridge across the Potomac River was destroyed by rebels. On the 3rd, Company A and Company C were dispatched to Sandy Hook a village across the Potomac from Harper's Ferry. On the fourth of July when the soldiers returned, it was found that the dispatched soldiers had been fired upon by rebels across the river. Three were wounded and one killed. The "baptism by fire" of the Ninth was done.

Shock reverberated through the regiment. War was real. Death came by the enemy's hand, a fellow countryman. Charley had experienced fear, but this was different.

They laid the dead man, John E. Banks, in a coffin. His head rested upon a pillow of daises plucked from a nearby field. He had been shot through the heart. His remains were shipped by train to his relatives in New York. They all felt the loss keenly because although they had only been together a short while, bonds in war form quickly and the steel threads of kinship bind them. All for one. One for all.

A second man, Ernest Geidecke of company A, died of his wounds. He was shot in the stomach and took hours to die. It was awful and there was nothing that could be done.

The men were marched to Sharpsburg, Williamsport and finally camped near Falling Waters. Charley was dismayed at the ineptness of his own company of men. There was chaos at every turn. The boy volunteers from the city had few skills to help them survive a life on the move. Charley, on the other hand, had several years of experience living with tent shows. He also had experience leading boys. It was only natural that a man of twenty-nine would reach back into the ranks of seventeen-to-nineteen-year-olds and help guide them.

When Charley traveled with Lent, his job had been to act as a go-between for Mr. Lent and every entity that made up the show. He had checked in on everyone from the cook crew to the wax museum curator. He observed the conditions of the menagerie from poultry to elephants. He relayed orders from Mr. Lent to forward men that bought supplies and to those who traveled ahead slapping posters on the side of every available barn. If there was a problem in the town they had just left, it was Charley who was sent back to relay a message of apology and a check for damages. He was nobody's boss and yet, from a management point of view, he was able to see just how a successful show needed to run.

So, from the position of a lowly private, Charley became a mentor to the younger men. He showed them how to make and break camp efficiently. He led them in well-organized camp and travel routine, setting up, breaking down, fires, cooking, and routines of personal hygiene. He taught the horse-handlers how it was better to entice the horse to do their will rather than force them. He showed the boys how to scavenge for small things that would make their lives bearable. A scrap of leather in the rucksack could aid in keeping the contents dry and, if needed, the scrap could be used to repair the soles of worn-out shoes. The young men were eager for guidance.

Charley's leadership did not go unnoticed. By mid-August he accepted his first promotion to Corporal. As a private, he was paid eleven dollars a month. His pay was raised to thirteen dollars. The army sent five dollars a month to Nancy directly. Now they could send two dollars more. He was quick to arrange it.

General McClellan had been named by President Lincoln to head most of the Union Army. He immediately noted the condition of the unseasoned troops of the regiment and ordered them to learn soldier discipline. While learning to be soldiers, they were marched up and down the Maryland side of the Potomac River, keeping the enemy at bay. Although they did once venture south of the river into Charlestown and near Bunker Hill, they took no enemy fire. The rebels had moved south for the winter.

Winter camp was made near Frederick City and was named Camp Claassen. Most of the local residents had fled, believing the war on their doorstep would envelope them. The ones who stayed treated the soldiers to a buffet dinner on Christmas Day. Boxes arrived from loved ones filled with food and necessities like mittens and sox. Charley received a letter from his wife, filled with descriptions of his sons, Charles and William. They were waiting for him. A letter from his friend John confirmed that all was well.

Many men went on "French Leave" and were promised severe discipline upon their return to ranks. Corporal Alasco Charles White lost no men to this folly.

A man was executed for the assassination of another, Major Lewis. All three thousand men encamped in the area were required to witness the hanging just after Christmas.

Camp Claassen was healthy. According to Surgeon Charles S. Tripler, medical director of the *Army of the Potomac*, the "Potomac Forces" had a remarkably low sick rate. Jaundice broke out, but other illnesses associated with military camps were somehow avoided. A baker in Frederick picked up the camp's flour each morning and returned it as freshly baked bread every evening. Some believed this was the source of their good health.

Company G commanded by Captain Hendrickson was sent out on picket in early March. They marched to Charlestown where the inhabitants were hostile and then on through Bunker Hill. Near Winchester there were several skirmishes. No men were lost. They continued marching on, the men almost shoeless. Those who listened to old Charley White, had leather in their sacks to help fill the holes in their soles. At abandoned camps, they scavenged for more. They marched toward Manassas junction where they witnessed first-hand the total devastation of war. Every tree and fencepost had been scavenged for firewood. Bridges were destroyed. A graveyard was discovered with over one hundred new graves dug and filled with the Eleventh Alabama Volunteers. Measles had killed far more than bullets that winter.

In May, the company spent most of the time on boats steaming up and down the Potomac. Charley maintained his composure by not eating if the water was rough. Nothing to vomit meant shorter bouts with seasickness. On the 27th the sun shone brightly and there was little wind. They journeyed past Mount Vernon without seeing it. There was too much brush between the home of George Washington and the river. The band gathered and played the Star-Spangled Banner as they made their way past Fort Washington. By noon they reached Alexandria where they boarded a train and disembarked at Manassas just after midnight.

He was the old man within Company G. Leadership was hard to come by. Most men were too young to know anything or command respect. June first, Charley was promoted to Sergeant. His pay was raised to seventeen dollars. He immediately made arrangements for Nancy to receive the extra pay.

July 1862 Henry Halleck was appointed the new Commander in Chief of the Union Army by President Abraham Lincoln. No clear-cut changes were noticed with the exception of a general sense of increased aggression in pursuing the enemy. General Major John Pope was put in charge of the Ninth (as well as the combined forces of several other scattered forces) and tasked with mounting an offensive against Richmond.

Robert E. Lee's army led by General Stonewall Jackson and James Longstreet outmaneuvered Pope's army. The rebels moved in behind the Union forces, stripped them of their supplies and then outgunned them at the Second Battle of Bull Run on August Twenty-Ninth.

A very badly defeated Ninth regiment was forced to retreat back across the Potomac toward Washington D.C. All supplies had been stripped, backpacks filled with personal items gone. Coats, extra socks, blankets razors… everything was gone. The men, conquered, limped back to Union territory. The Union force that fought at the Second Battle of Bull Run had been cut in half by the rebels.

On the fifteenth of September, with some supplies replenished, a new offensive was mounted. They were ordered to march to Boonsboro and then to Keedysville near Antietam Creek. An allowance of two crackers per man for the day's ration was doled out. On the sixteenth, a full ration was issued, and the men were positioned near Sharpsburg.

All eyes were watchful. Every avenue of escape was evaluated. If they needed to fall back, they must not fall into a trap of the enemy. Three stone bridges crossed the Antietam. The two they had already passed were in ruins as was the one that lay crumbled before them.

September seventeenth, Company G was ordered to occupy the East Woods east of the Dunkar Church. There they would clear the forest, pushing the rebels back to an open corn field where they would be vulnerable and more easily overcome. The air was cool and made soft by the morning fog. The sky was clear and becoming lighter by the moment as the sun crept up above the horizon.

Charley put his hand into his jacket, feeling for the photo of his wife and two sons, a treasure only recently received by long delayed post. Reassured that it remained safe, he inspected his gun and leather cartridge pouch, buttoned his shirt up tightly around his neck and double checked the laces on his shoes. He fumbled in his pocket for Michael's knife. It too, was safe.

"Ready?" He asked in hushed tones to his men.

"Yes sir," They answered in unison.

"Let's go!" He replied.

They crept into the woods before them, outnumbering and out-gunning the enemy. The rebels would get off a shot and run like the dickens, falling back into the forest and finding sanctuary behind another tree. Charley's men advanced. Adrenaline pumped and the men pursued the enemy with righteous vigor. Seasoned now after a year of army life, their effect was dangerous and efficient. Charley kept an eye on his men, watching for trouble, finding none, he kept pushing forward. The haunting sound of bullets, their pop, pop, pop as they were discharged toward the enemy was mesmeric. The air, so recently morning-sweet, was filled with the sulfur stench of smoking gun powder.

He stopped suddenly. His left arm no longer gripped the fore end of his rifle and the weapon dangled stupidly in his right hand. His stomach tightened as he looked to see the trouble with his left arm. It took a moment to realize that a musket ball had ripped through his arm below the elbow. Everything went quiet as if he were under water, sitting on the bottom of a lake. Noiseless. He got himself behind the safety of a large tree, laid his rifle on the ground and inspected the wound. Serious. Bleeding. Could die. He removed his belt, his good luck belt from Jimmy, and pulled it tightly around his upper arm. Jimmy was dead, he'd heard...died in Singapore in an accident. He supposed he was dying, too. His eyes slid shut.

The sounds of battle returned and with it, awareness. Charley checked the tourniquet... holding. He pushed his back hard against the tree and pushed himself to standing. The others had run past him in their pursuit of the enemy, one came back to find him.

Tom Johnson startled him.

"Are you shot, sir?" the boy asked rhetorically. Tom stood directly in front of Charley and observed the condition of his leader, tugged on the belt tourniquet and waited for instruction.

Clear headed now, Charley instructed the boy to take the remainder of his buck and ball ammunition and continue pursuing the enemy. Charley could make it back to camp on his own. His legs were fine.

There is something that happens to the human spirit when in spite of horrific pain, the mind compels the body to escape danger and survive. The arrival at camp was a blur. The pain, held at bay, came screaming into focus as Charley fell into the arms of his comrades. A bottle of whiskey was produced, of which he drank deeply and choked upon and spat out.

Charley and the other wounded were removed to a barn north of the battlefield where doctors and volunteers administered to the fallen. As he lay in a state of helplessness, he watched as a field surgeon removed a man's leg. He saw the blood squirt as the artery was cut and watched as the doctor scrambled to stem the bleeding. He heard the saw scraping through living bone and watched as a man lifted the leg away as if it were simply a log to be laid on the fire. When it came his turn, a field surgeon removed splintered bone from his arm, a process which Charley watched with interest under the numbing effects of chloroform. The ball had shattered the outside bone of his left arm, just below the elbow. He hoped he would not lose his arm.

He was taken by ambulance to Frederick, Maryland. The journey was arduous, the pain excruciating. He hoped for another dose of Dover's powder. It came too late and he passed out before reaching the make-shift hospital. Hundreds had been wounded at Antietam, but they were the lucky ones. Hundreds died.

Charley's wound was awful, but comparatively minor compared to those of the wasting bodies around him struggling with gut wounds, amputations, blindness, and diarrhea. The diarrhea was the straw that broke the camel's back for some. They could live through the pain and disfigurement, but the diarrhea drained their strength unrelentingly. This malady Charley did not escape. After a month in hospital, he was thinner than he was at twelve and his arm was not healing. They saved the Dover's powder for those in greater need. Charley suffered. Whiskey was offered as an alternative. He took it whenever he could get it.

At the end of October, he was deemed unfit to return to duty. Furlough was granted for sixty days.

"Alasco C. White a sergeant of Captain Hendrickson of Company (G) Ninth Regiment of five feet five inches high, light complexion, blue eyes, brown hair…born in the town of Brookfield and enlisted in New York…unfit for duty…ulna badly punctured, the wound not improving…to prevent loss of limb…patient is apparently failing… unfit for duty.

December 17, 1862 he was discharged from duty.

"Sergeant Alasco C. White…florid complexion…cabinet maker… disability three fourths."

He returned to New Jersey by train. The war went on without him.

CHAPTER FIFTEEN

1863

CHARLEY OBSERVED THE PEOPLE GATHERED in the little farmhouse. They patted him on the shoulder now and then, said kind words and brought him warm soup. He knew who they were of course. That was his wife Nancy, his boy Charley and the little one was William. John, he had known the longest and yet… they were strangers. He felt nothing.

He'd arrived back in New Jersey broken, weak, and thin as a stick. They took care of him, fed him, covered him, tended to his ruined arm. He was grateful. Only the disability pension he received kept him from feeling completely worthless. They were all living at John's farm. John chopped the wood and provided food and shelter. Nancy and her sister helped John and his wife tend the chickens and more recently, turkeys.

Although the wound in his arm had finally started to heal over, the whole thing was stiff…not the skillful wielder of carpentry tools it was before. John had tasked Charley with milking cows the day after he got back. The effortless skill of his youth was now arduous labor. He resented doing it.

Before the war, he worked at as many jobs as he could to save money to buy a small farm. There he could live with his family and do carpentry work for cash money, just as his father had. When Charley enlisted, John's name had been added to the bank account so that he could give Nancy money as it was needed. It was New Year's Day 1863. He had been back in New Jersey only a week and his bank account was down to five dollars. He himself had spent most of the balance the day before.

Charley had never touched a drop of alcohol in his life until the day he was shot. Alcohol was the nectar of the devil; his father had preached. No good ever came from a drunken man, he had heard from Barnum and the temperance preachers that abounded in New York City. Charley had learned that alcohol was indeed his friend. Over the past three months it had numbed the hurt of his mutilated arm and made him drowsy, so he slept instead of vividly obsessing over the men of his company who died at Antietam and those who were brutally wounded. Over half of the twenty-three hundred union soldiers he fought with at Antietam were killed, wounded or missing. It helped him forget momentarily that some were still out there fighting while he was here, being coddled.

He'd rented a place on Newark Avenue near the waterfront in Jersey City and opened a liquor store. He'd used most of his bank account to order a supply of liquor, pay the first month's rent and give New Jersey their twenty-dollar-license fee. There were a lot of wounded soldiers like him. He would have lots of good customers, including himself. Nancy, her sister and the two boys stayed on the farm with John. Charley slept in a back room at the liquor store, going to visit his family only to deliver money and supplies.

He'd written to his father to let him know that although he was wounded, he was okay. He got a letter back right away. He and Johanna would pray for Alasco's arm and they hoped it would return to normal. Ben was still in Hannibal; his wife and two boys were doing fine. So far, the government thought his farming was more important than having him go to war, so he'd been left alone. Charley's little brother,

William had mustered into company E of the 114th New York Infantry in August. "Your prayers for him would be appreciated." Emily, his baby sister, was struggling. Charley's no-good brother-in-law, James Madison Finch, had signed up for the New York Infantry a year ago, but had deserted in early April. Emily and her little Florence, who was now two years old and cute as a button, were staying on a farm with Fitch's relatives. In September she had given birth to a boy she named Floyd. If anyone knew where Fitch was hiding out, no one was talking. If you have a spare dollar, his father had asked, you might send it to your sister. She is destitute.

A stray dog had stopped on the doorstep of the liquor store one cold day in February. Charley fed him half of his own supper and the dog stayed. His name was thereafter, "Lucky." Business was good throughout the summer and autumn. Lucky guarded the store when Charley wasn't looking. Charley was certain the dog was a terrier mutt of some sort because although he was a smart animal, he was stubborn as all get out. If Charley had too much whiskey (to numb the pain in his arm), Lucky would lick his face until he woke up sufficiently to close the store and fix supper. There was only one day a week where Charley didn't seek pain relief and that was Sunday. He didn't go to church, but he did clean himself up, lock the store and take a ride out to John's poultry farm. Lucky liked to chase the chickens, which wasn't very helpful. He was only welcome there if he learned to leave the birds alone. Charley taught him to leave them be. You could see the dog wanted to chase the chickens, but if he did, he didn't get that bit of meat Charley held back in his leather treat pouch. Lucky's eyebrows worried about the birds the whole time, but he restrained himself. He liked playing with the children and that was encouraged. By summer of '64, Charles Henry was almost seven and little William Albert was a wild three-year-old. Dogs like nothing more than energetic kids to play with. Lucky liked Sundays and usually beat Charley to the door when it was time to head out.

John worried about his longtime friend. He still didn't weigh much more than a hundred pounds and the circles under his eyes were darker and deeper than they should have been on a thirty-three-year-old man. He had let his beard grow scraggly and his hair was untrimmed. The more he tried to reach his friend, the more alienated he became.

15 August 1864

Someone knocked on front door of the liquor store. Lucky reacted immediately, barking incessantly and running circles around Charley while trying to herd his master to the source of the banging.

"All right! Easy, boy!" soothed Charley. "Take it easy. Let's go see who has come knocking." A trill of terror traveled up his spine. No one came to knock on his door before sunrise on a Sunday. Did something happen to his family? To John? What?

"Who goes there?" shouted Charley through the solid oak door. "The store is closed, what do you want?"

"Open the door, son" came the soft-spoken answer.

"Get back and sit," he said to Lucky as he pointed a finger at a spot on the floor beside his right boot. The dog sat, looked at his master and waited.

Charley unbolted the door slowly. He had not seen his father for three years, but there was no doubt that it was him. Benajah stepped over the threshold and closed the door behind him. He sat his bag down on the floor and wrapped his arms around his first-born son. Charley sobbed.

John had sent for him. Nothing he had tried himself had helped a thing. Charley had remained in limbo, making a living but not really living his life. Although the arm was better, Charley continued to use whiskey. He isolated himself from his family, his friends, and even the people he had known in the circus. Writing to Benajah had been John's desperate attempt to bring Charley back to life.

Charley fixed a fire and put on coffee to boil. He sliced bread and broke eggs into a bowl to scramble them. He avoided eye contact with the man sitting in the chair, preferring to "do something" rather than exchange random conversation. Lucky sat and watched the men, first one and then the other. Only the sound of forks clinking against plates broke the silence as they ate. Charley did not know what to say to his father and Benajah was evaluating his son.

"Clean up. We will go to John's house, yes?" said the older man. "I want to see my grandchildren." He reached down and opened the ties on the bag he'd brought and withdrew a shaving kit and a pair of scissors. "Wash yourself and I will cut your hair."

Charley did as he was told. He washed his face and hair in the kitchen sink as his father watched. Benajah cut his hair and admonished the dog not to run through the cuttings. A towel had been soaking in a pot of water on the stove. Benajah removed it, wrung out the excess water and wrapped it around his son's face. As Charley soaked, Benajah whipped up foam in the shaving kit and readied the straight razor. He shaved his son. His hands were gentle and confident.

Benajah, Charley, and Lucky rode the short distance to John's farm in the liquor store cart pulled by a horse called "May." It worked. Benajah had reached down into the darkness and retrieved his son. Now it was up to Charley to regain his feet.

Charley closed his liquor store, boxed up what inventory he was unable to sell back to the distributor, and moved out to the farm with John. He slept in the barn in the hay loft. Although the farmhouse was enormous, it was filled with John's family of six, Nancy, her two sons, and her little sister, Eliza. Nancy and Charley had been apart for too long. There was never a question about him sleeping in the barn. It didn't matter. When he wasn't working alongside John on the farm, Charley was gone.

He spent a good deal of time between Jersey City and New York, looking for work. He could no longer work as a carpenter because of his arm and he'd promised his father (and it was a good decision) to stop selling and drinking alcohol.

There were no suitable openings for him. Although he'd been with Barnum before the war, times had changed. There were so many people in the business camped out in the northeastern United States waiting out the war, every job had two applicants. Lent had been in town in July with his Equescurriculum, but was now off in Illinois with his combination of four circuses. He could have found work with Lent, no matter what, but there was no catching up to the show in time to prevent Charley's bank account from reaching zero. He had responsibilities.

On his way back to the farm from Manhattan, Charley passed the recruiting office of the New Jersey Volunteers. His arm was not great, but perhaps he could carry a pistol instead of a rifle and rejoin the war.

Charley signed the very day that he walked into the recruiting office. He took the oath as a Second Lieutenant and was assigned as a recruiting officer for the 41st Regiment, New Jersey Volunteers. The assignment lasted only days before he was reassigned to the 39th Regiment, Company D. Although his arm was crippled-up, his leadership skills were much in demand. Most recruits were still under twenty years of age and Charley was an experienced officer of thirty-two years. Nancy and the boys would be financially taken care of, Lucky stayed with John, now a welcomed guardian of poultry, and Charley had purpose.

The 39th spent most of the autumn and winter near Petersburgh, Virginia until they were ordered to take Fort Mahone. The 39th won the battle and took the fort, but the cost was high. Ten were killed and about seventy-five were wounded. Charley was not among those who fought having been told to remain at the rear and support the casualties. He obeyed the order as he understood that a crippled man could get in the way of healthy men and cause more trouble than good.

Robert E. Lee surrendered his army at Appomattox on the ninth of April 1865. A cowardly group of Confederate sympathizers in New York conspired to kill their nemesis, President Abraham Lincoln. John Wilkes Booth, an actor, sneaked into Ford theatre and shot Lincoln in the head on the fourteenth of April. He died the following day. Booth escaped but was soon trapped in a barn not far away from the treasonous act. Sadly, he died from a bullet wound and was not made to suffer the fear, humiliation, and agony of hanging. Four of his co-conspirators did hang, one of them a woman.

The 39th returned to New Jersey and disbanded in June.

Nancy was not at the farm with John. She had taken the boys to stay with relatives in Massachusetts while she made a life for herself in Jersey City. She had left word with John that she no longer wanted Charley in her life. So, there it was. No wife. No children. And, although Lucky the dog was glad to see him, his allegiance was to John now. He was an excellent poultry guard.

Charley braced himself against a new round of self-pity. He gathered his old carpentry tools from John's barn along with the few cases of whiskey he had left over from the old store and loaded them into his little wagon. He hitched May to the front and drove away. He had heard that Richmond was in complete ruins. Surely, he could find a job helping in the reconstruction.

Charley hit his stride in Richmond, Virginia. He opened a modest liquor store and hired a young black man to help him lift and carry. At the store he met people and spread the word that he knew how to build. While his arm limited him physically, muscle was easy to hire in post-war Virginia. Charley gathered a crew of young hungry men and showed them how to rebuild houses, barns, and furnishings. His apprentices flourished under his tutelage and although none got rich, they earned money and learned a trade. Dollars flowed steadily into Charley's pocket.

Equestrian shows, menageries, and circuses struggled throughout the war years. Unable to risk traveling routes in the south, they saturated the northeast and Canada with entertainment. If shows had not consolidated, there would have been several hundred of them competing for the same audiences. L.B. Lent's Equescurriculum ended up being a conglomeration of seven different shows that included gymnastics shows, menageries, Grizzly Adams' Acting Bears and an act of FOUR GREAT CLOWNS, not the least of which was Joe Pentland himself, Charley's old friend. Barnum's American Museum, still anchored in New York City, fought to survive the war years. The world class entertainment that had huddled down in New York City meant stiff competition for the interest of the paying public.

Just months after the war ended, audience-craving road shows began venturing south and when one came to Richmond, Virginia. Charley was first in line to buy a ticket. It wasn't a show that he knew or had heard about, but it reminded him of the little show he began with back in Syracuse. Right then and there he knew he wanted back in.

Charley made his way to the backyard of the little circus before the finale. Almost the entire show was already folded and loaded, ready to travel immediately to the next town. The crew was so busy packing up, it took a minute for someone to notice Charley and stop him.

"Hey!" Shouted the guard as he shook his fist at Charley. "Yes, YOU!" He pointed at Charley's chest. "You don't belong back here, get out!"

Charley never took a step after the guard shouted. He watched, unafraid, as the burly man approached him, puffed up and menacing in his demeanor.

The guard loomed over Charley as he came to a halt directly in front of the intruder. The intention was intimidation and it usually worked.

"I'm a traveler," remarked Charley, and in a sense, he was. He was an animal man, a show man, and the war had just interrupted his journey with the business.

"What show?" asked the guard, "and where are you headed?"

"May I talk with the manager?" Asked Charley without backing down. I have business.

The manager did not have a job for Charley. They didn't have a menagerie and they already had a horse guy.

The boss man and Charley talked a short spell as the band blared out the happy refrain that indicated to the crew that there was just one more encore before wrapping it up. Charley asked the man if he knew the status of some of his old employers hoping he could gain some insight as to which of them might be in need of an animal man.

Barnum's American Museum had burned to the ground, seven months prior. Everything, including the lions, was gone. Barnum had already opened a new American Museum on Broadway, but the circus man did not know what he had in the way of menagerie as yet.

"Your friend Lent sold off the Equescurriculum combined circus. He bought the New York Circus and announced his desire to come off the road and stay in New York. They have four clowns and a bunch of equestrians, but I don't think they have much of a menagerie."

"If you're looking for lions, you probably ought to get up to Girard Rice is wintering up there. With all of the wartime consolidations it's hard to keep track, but I believe Van Amburgh and Dan Rice were in cahoots for a while and then Thayer & Noyes' Circus came into the picture." The man paused, scratching his head and thinking.

"You know Van Amburgh kicked the bucket in November, right?" asked the man in charge.

"No sir, I did not know that," replied Charley. He hadn't liked Van Amburgh much, but this man didn't need to know that.

"I think his lions are being shown by that Langworthy fella up in Pennsylvania. If I was you, I'd head up to Girard. Might want to wait until spring though," he added laughing, "Damn cold up there now." The manager wished Charley best of luck and walked over to his crew to get them moving a little faster.

Charley's spirits sank. For a moment he had thought he could just ditch the liquor store and head out with the circus that night. Dumb idea, he thought dejectedly. He didn't belong in Richmond, Virginia. None of his people were here. He was restless. In spite of the fact that the past seven months had been busy and his construction business lucrative, he wanted out. Richmond had raised liquor taxes to where folks could barely afford to buy from him anyway. Time to get rid of the liquor store. Yep. It was time to dissolve his life here and go back up north.

CHAPTER SIXTEEN

NOVEMBER 1866
RICHMOND, VA

TAXES ON LIQUOR HAD GONE up so much since Charley stocked his little store in Metropolitan Hall that his inventory was now worth about thirty percent more than when he'd bought it. It was easy to sell off and that chore was done and tied up in a day and a half. It took longer to wind down the carpentry business.

He had led his crew of apprentice carpenters for sixteen months. Most of them were pretty good at the basics of building and there was plenty of work for them in Richmond. They didn't need him. Nine months after the circus came to town, he paid them and bade them farewell. He just said he was "going home," and they all agreed that it was a worthy endeavor. He sold his horse May and her wagon to one of the young men. He bought a train ticket and headed north.

He went first to Jersey City and found John, his wife and now seven children. They were all glad to see him, even Lucky the dog. Nancy was living with her mother and sister in New York. She had divorced him citing "abandonment." The boys were living in Massachusetts, still with their mother's relatives. She was polite when he asked after Charles Henry and William Albert and even gave him a photo of them. There was no hate. It was uncomfortable, but nothing more.

He took the train to Massachusetts. Charles Henry was already nine and remembered him. Five-year-old William cried. He didn't like strangers. Charley gave "Uncle Monty" and "Aunt Susan" money for the boy's keep and slipped young Charles Henry a silver liberty to hide away in case he ever needed it. Charles Henry solemnly accepted the dollar and followed him out to the road when he left.

"Come back soon, dad," he said as Charley turned to leave. "I know how to read and write. If you write, I will write you back." A lump swelled up in the boy's throat and tears streamed unchecked down his cheeks. Charley wrapped his hand around the back of his son's neck and drew him into his chest and held him there for a moment.

"You'll do just fine, son. Go to school. Learn things. I'll be back. I promise."

Charles Henry reluctantly pulled himself away from his father's embrace and made his dad promise once again that he would come back as soon as he could.

The liquor store owner, animal man, circus traveler, clerk, soldier-carpenter-father, made his way to upstate New York to visit family. His father and mother were well, but age was showing on Benajah. He was sixty years old now, living on a small farm just outside of Smithville. William had suffered from his time in the war and although never wounded by bullets, he grieved from a sadness so deep he could not speak of it. He lived with his parents, helping on the farm.

Sister Emily was the family's greatest concern. The son-of-a-bitch she married had come back to fetch her after he deserted and dragged her and the children out to some godforsaken place in Michigan. There was no way to protect Emily from her drunken husband when she was a thousand miles away.

Benajah was glad to see his eldest son and derived great pleasure from the photograph of Charley's boys. William smiled a little when he learned the youngest was named William but said nothing.

After a week, Charley headed out. On his way to Girard, he made time to stop on a farm near Granby where brother Ben lived with his wife and two little ones. The war had been easy on Ben according to his father. He had mustered in five weeks before the war ended and saw no battles.

Charley had been to Girard, Pennsylvania once before. After leaving Dan Rice in Cleveland in 1851, he had walked most of the way to Buffalo. Girard was about halfway between the two cities, just south of Erie where he'd rested on the dock soaking his sore feet.

Jonas was the first to spot the boy-turned-man when Charley walked up to the winter quarters of the Dan Rice show the first of January 1867. The elderly man, now totally white whiskered, stood and held out his hand.

"Well, I'll be! If it isn't Charley White! How are you, boy?" Asked Jonas.

"You are a sight for sore eyes, Jonas! Sit. Tell me what is going on around here. Where's James? He still around?" Asked Charley scanning the tent.

Jonas closed his eyes for a second and took a deep breath, "We lost James in New Orleans winter of fifty-four. God rest his soul." He took a deep breath, straightened his back and stared at Charley. "Now where in heaven's name have you been, boy?"

Charley relayed the highlights of the past fifteen years… the Barnum years, the war years, the relatively short marriage to Nancy and, of course, he showed him a picture of his sons.

"Fine boys, Charley. You're a lucky man. Now, what can an old fool like me do for someone as worldly traveled as yourself?" Asked Jonas.

Charley smiled at his old friend, "I want back in, Jonas. I want back into the business and I want to work with lions, if I can find some to look after." He added quickly, "Of course I would prefer to travel by land." Both men laughed, remembering that stormy night on Lake Erie.

"Rice doesn't have cats or any other menagerie animals now. We had 'em during the war. Van Amburgh's menagerie was here in '65, but the animal man…Langworthy…left with his critters soon as the war was over. Thayer and Noyes' circus also went out on the road with part of the Van Amburgh collection. As far as I know, Thayer and Noyes' still have some animals they're wintering across town. They might have some lions."

Charley's heart skipped a beat. He said his goodbyes to Jonas and made a beeline over to Thayer and Noyes' winter quarters.

It turned out the show did have lions, five of them. The biggest male was uneasy and paced back and forth eyeing the stranger. Two of the males were youngsters, born in captivity. They rubbed up against the bars of the cage looking for affection. The fourth male was very old, his glorious mane thin and no longer impressive. He opened his eyes, observed Charley, closed his eyes and resumed snoring. The female was in a separate cage. She was sleek, her amber eyes clear and watchful. The sides of her belly bulged out. She was obviously very pregnant. When the Thayer and Noyes' circus was consolidated with the Van Amburgh outfit, Langworthy tended to the needs of the lions. When he left, all of his expertise left with him. James Thayer was glad to meet Charley because although he possessed only limited experience with lions, he was yards ahead of the rest of them.

March 1867 brought five lion kittens and newsprint notoriety. The Erie Dispatch wrote, "It has been a difficult task to rear young lions in this country, but the keeper, Charles White, is confident…." Charley relished his new life. The only concern was that Thayer and

Noyes' had little money to pay his wages. And, they were considering selling off the lions. They didn't have a man to show them and they were expensive to feed. Cash from the sale would enhance their advertising budget for the coming road season. On the other hand, a lion show was a good draw and boosted ticket sales. It was a dilemma.

Charley had half the value of the adult male lions in cash money. A bargain was struck whereby Charley would care for the lions and show them all summer. In return, if the season was good and they made most of their stands, he would own the lions outright.

Charley got a costume made, a roman gladiator outfit with paneled skirt and a tight-fitting shirt with short sleeves. He grew a mustache and goatee but kept his hair short-clipped so as not to obstruct his vision when he was in with the lions.

In April, the eighteen-month-old-elephant Hiram, died. He had just been delivered by train from New York three weeks earlier. The female lion and her cubs were summarily sold for cash to pay for a replacement elephant. Dr. Thayer left immediately for New York City to deliver the lioness and retrieve his new elephant.

They got on the road in early May and toured through New York and Pennsylvania. Charley was "Professor Charles White the Lion King" and grandiose advertisements illustrated him lording over the big cats. The old lion, bereft of teeth, was no more ferocious than an old house cat. He rode without restraint in the wagon during the spectacle and sometimes walked on a leash. The two young lions learned quickly and were compliant. Charley rewarded good behaviors with food, just like he had done with his horse. Nero, the virulent male at the height of his glory, shocked audiences with his ferocious roars. He resisted training. Ticket sales remained good-to-exceptional. Newspaper accounts glowed with appreciation. What a thrill it was to see the lion king in the cage, feeding the felines raw red meat with his bare hands. Everything went stunningly well until the fourth of July during the second show in Rochester, New York.

Charley got in the cage with his four lions and commanded the beasts to go to their respective places within the cage. Nero refused to budge. Charley snapped the leather tip of his whip on the lion's hip to encourage him to move to his place. Instead of being encouraged, the four-hundred-pound lion sprang upon his master. He knocked Charley to the ground and held him there with the full weight of his enormous forepaws. He locked his jaws upon Charley's shoulder and sunk his teeth deeply into flesh and bone.

The audience watched in horror as the lion shook Charley like a rag doll. He lay limp on the floor of the cage, as Nero continued to grip his shoulder. Mr. Noyes grabbed a metal bar, ran into the cage and hit the lion on the head with great force. The surprised animal released his hold and Charley was able to regain his feet. His performance with the lions continued as if nothing had happened. When finished, Charley walked out of the cage without saying a word.

His memory of being hustled out of the tent and taken to the National Hotel by carriage was vague. Dr. Whitbeck reduced the fractured bones in Charley's shoulder and upper arm while he was semi-conscious. His condition was critical and Dr. Whitbeck did not expect him to survive.

Three weeks later, Charley walked out of the hotel and caught up to the circus and his lions. On the twenty-fourth of August, he made his first public appearance by entering the lion's cage and simply feeding them with his bare hands. His ordeal had made him famous and newspapers immortalized him for having survived an attack by such a great beast, a beast that this man dared be unarmed within a cage even now.

Nero wasn't born vicious. Most probably he had been whipped into submission by an earlier handler. When Charley grazed the animal with his whip, the lion's reaction was reflexively defensive and violent. He trusted no man. Charley was going to change that, but it would take time and patience.

They continued to travel through Pennsylvania. The lions were a good draw, so an illustration of the lion king and his lions adorned the center panel of Thayer and Noyes brand new twenty-two-foot-wide-poster in Harrisburg, Pennsylvania. The same glorious illustration decorated the sides of the bandwagon. They were famous.

In November they put up the tent in Washington D.C. and then wintered in Baltimore, Maryland. Charley got word in February that his father had passed away. His dying wish was that his sons would try to help Emily. The brothers dissolved their father's estate and moved their mother to relatives in Homer. Charley went back to his lions. Ben returned to his family. William headed to Michigan to look for his sister.

In March they got word that Barnum's Museum on Broadway in Manhattan, the new one, had burned to the ground. The weather had been so abnormally cold, the fire hydrants froze which allowed a small fire to become an inferno. All the animals were lost, even the two whales and the two African lion kittens Barnum bought off Thayer and Noyes the previous year. They all knew the risk of having a show and what a knife's edge of survival they lived on. The 1868 spring route started in Pennsylvania in April. Thayer and Noyes' Circus continued to methodically wind its way through Ohio, New York, Indiana and Ontario.

In early August Charles W. Noyes, circus proprietor, got word that his infant son had died from Scarlet Fever. He rushed home from Bowmanville, Ontario to his wife and remaining children in Syracuse. Sam Stickney filled in as equestrian director until Noyes could return.

Business in Canada had been good all summer. Seeing an opportunity to foster good will, Mr. Thayer generously donated ten percent of their gross receipts for the evening show in Toronto to aid the starving people of Red River Settlement. The settlement's crops had been stripped by grasshoppers; even vegetable gardens had been eaten bare. Doc Thayer planned to return to in the future and the donation insured his welcome.

Back in New York State, the outfit continued to have good receipts. On Friday the sixteenth of October they were in Titusville, New York. They sold over twenty-six-hundred tickets for the evening show. The tent was filled to capacity and the show had just begun when a bank of seats filled with women and children collapsed injuring many, one critically.

Mr. Noyes did not return to the partnership in spring of 1869. Doc Thayer, by himself, called his company to assemble in Girard, Pennsylvania before May first. The new venture was billed as "Dr. James L. Thayer's Zoolohipposzonamadon!" and boasted a circus, pantheon, and menagerie of trained animals. The big draw this season was a den of four baby lions. Another menagerie had owned the mother lion. She died when the kittens were just a few weeks old. They got them for next to nothing because they were so young, so it was unlikely any would survive. Charley White, the animal man, was Doc Thayer's secret weapon. The kittens thrived under his care.

The 1869 season was a slow-moving financial disaster. Every place they put up the tent another, bigger show, had just left. G.F. Baileys & Company's Big Show was a hard act to follow. They didn't just have African lions, but also tigers and black-maned lions. While Doc Thayer could only afford small print advertisements, Baileys bought two full columns and filled them with sketches of exotic animals and equestrian feats. Audiences were meager at best and every day the losses mounted. Doc Thayer had not been able to pay his suppliers, crew or performers. Creditors caught up with them in Ohio in November and the Hamilton County Sheriff seized the show. Everything was auctioned off, sold to the highest bidder. Even Charley's lions had been sold to satisfy the debts of the show. However, once Mr. Thayer produced a document stating that all of the adult lions were the sole property of Professor Charles White, the sale was reversed. The four six-month-old kittens were appraised at forty-one-hundred dollars. However, they belonged to Mr. Thayer and wouldn't help Charley's finances one darn bit.

Charley let it be known via The New York Clipper that he "could be engaged to train and perform animals." He needed cash. Lions eat expensive meat and needed to be housed during cold New York winters. On the 27th of November, the same day that his paid advertisement went to press, Charley ran into Jimmy Reynolds.

Jimmy and Charley had little in common. He was a clown and Charley an animal man, but they had known one another a long time. Both had worked for Dan Rice and Doc Thayer. Currently what they had in common was unemployment.

"Hey Charley!" Hollered Jimmy as he approached. "Did you find work yet?"

"Not yet," Charley admitted, "Have you found something?"

"Yes. It won't last but a couple of months, but could tide us over until next season, interested?" He asked.

"I'm all ears," He replied.

"My uncle James, whom I am named after, has a southern show. I wired him about those of us available to work. He said I should bring you and come on down to South Carolina." James looked at Charley questioningly. "It's just for the winter, though."

Jimmy waited for Charley to digest the news and then added, "And he is willing to pay the freight on your lions if you can get them down there right away."

Without further ado, the two showmen and Charley's four male lions made their way to South Carolina and joined the "Reynold's

Immense Menagerie and Gymnasium, Enlarged and Improved." Receipts were good, but by the end of March, the show was headed back to Mexico with its menagerie, Juvenile Mexican gymnasts and Juvenile Silver Cornet band.

Jimmy and Charley got invited to join the "James Robinson, Great Circus and Animal Show" and were performing in Richmond, Indiana by the fifth of May. Lipman and Walters owned the show and Jimmy Reynolds was a good friend of Mike Lipman. They added two female lions to Charley's show. The full length two-column advertisement in the Richmond Weekly Palladium was topped with a sketch of "Mr. Charles White, the emperor of LION CONQUERORS!" and his "SIX TRAINED NUMIDIAN LIONS."

They spent June wandering through Kansas, playing to enthusiastic crowds. James Robinson and his international awards for his bareback horsemanship dominated illustrated advertisements now. Charley and his lions were mentioned only in small print.

The James Robinson's agent perpetuated a hoax which garnered a lot of attention. The hope was that it would generate business. The story released to the newspapers relayed a terrible accident in which the band members (riding atop the lion's cage) met with an accident which caused the wagon to collapse. Many band members were reportedly killed, and Professor Charles White came to the rescue of the remaining trapped men. The New York Clipper magazine admonished the James Robinson's show for putting out such a hoax and called for all the newspapers who repeated the story to make an apology and retract the story. Nevertheless, the story was reprinted in innumerable newspapers. The story did not increase ticket sales.

In mid-September a telegram caught up with Charley in the city of Chicago.

To: Charles White c/o James Robinson's Show

From: P.T. Barnum

New York, NY

Re: Offer of employment

I am starting a new Project.

Need man to manage dangerous beasts.

If you still own lions, we will pay top dollar.

Please reply soonest.

Charley said his goodbyes to the James Robinson's show, loaded his lions onto a railroad car and headed for New York City. He'd pick up his oldest son for the winter months and who knows, he thought, thirteen-year-old Charley might want to learn the business and stick with him.

PART 2

CHAPTER SEVENTEEN

1861 APRIL
CINCINNATI, OHIO
ANNA MARGARET MATCHETT

SHE SAT IN A MAROON and gold upholstered wing backed chair facing the fireplace. If it weren't for the tiny seven-button black leather shoes that stuck out in front of her on the footstool, she might have gone unnoticed altogether.

The boarding house fit her budget and was a reputable refuge for an unmarried woman such as herself, but it was drafty. Her room was good for sleeping with the fat feather tick she'd brought down with her from Ontario but sewing fine stitches up there was out of the question. Jagged embroidery made with stiff hands and shivering shoulders had just meant an hour of carefully pulling out stitches to begin over again. The silk would not hold up to mistakes. This job would pay for her rent, but she would not get paid if she ruined the fabric.

She had quickly found her spot in the parlor in front of the fire. Warm as toast wrapped in the oversized chair, she settled in, her brown eyes sparkling in the cheery firelight. With lips pursed in concentration, she deftly pushed the threaded needle down through the fabric held tightly in the embroidery hoop and brought it back up through in a single movement. She imagined she was playing a fiddle and the needle was her bow. The motion needed to be smooth and confident, not jerky and off-key. She hummed softly, an Irish ditty her mother taught her. The humming stopped as she leaned in toward the firelight and examined the completed rosette. "Good," she confirmed aloud, and leaned back in her chair.

"Looks very fine to me," said a man's voice.

Startled, Anna pulled her feet from the footstool and sat forward in the chair all in one fluid movement. Her smallish pale face framed by neatly pinned blonde braids peered around the side of the chair.

Her eyes met those of a slender young man standing in the doorway. She could feel the heat rising in her cheeks as he stared back at her with beautiful blue eyes framed in luscious long black eyelashes. When she realized she was staring she dropped her gaze to her work.

"I'm sorry if I disturbed, sir." She stood up, gathered the shimmering cloud of pale blue silk and headed toward the door. "I'll leave you to the fire, sir," she said as she swept past him, down the hall and up the stairs. Once in her room, she closed the door and leaned back on it. A deep breath in and a slow breath out. She shouldn't be unnerved. He was just a man and he wasn't dangerous. She didn't know why she pardoned herself. She wasn't a servant here; she was a boarder. She didn't know how long they had actually stared at one another, but she remembered him in startling detail. The nose was slender and long. The smile was crooked, not like he was sneering, but more like he was laughing at some private joke. Long, beautiful fingers. Had she really stared at his hands, too? Anna stomped her foot lightly as she headed across the room to lay the nearly completed frock in the cloth-lined basket.

The little clock by the bed told her it was almost six o'clock and soon time for supper. Although not fancy, the food was decent. Breakfast and supper were included and since Anna never ate lunch, she was always hungry for the evening meal. But, she wondered, what if that man was there? She dreaded the thought of meeting him again.

"I shan't eat dinner," she muttered as she finished washing her hands in the basin. She dried them carefully on the little white towel with pink embroidered roses. "I'll just light the lamp and write a letter to mother instead," she mumbled to herself as she opened the door to the hallway and, in contradiction, made her way down to the dining room. He won't be here, she reassured herself. He was just passing by.

The dining room glowed with the light of three lamps, one at each end of the long table and one on the sideboard. Plates and cups were stacked on the near end of the sideboard and silver-plated utensils lay in a wooden box, divided to separate spoons, forks and knives. Anna was first to the dining room. She breathed a sigh of relief. The handsome stranger was nowhere in sight. A dark-haired young couple came in, wrapped in each other's arms and made their way to the table. Anna knew them, newlyweds from up north, like her, but they hailed from Quebec, not Ontario. "Frenchies," she thought. They were moving to Minnesota in the spring. A few others trickled in, a recent widow waiting for summer to travel to relatives in New York, a single girl who worked in the hotel down the street, dear old Mrs. Simms and a traveling salesman who was in Cincinnati to sell pelts and leather goods. The double doors to the kitchen knocked open and cook brought in the day's meal, a large iron pot of chicken and dumplings with carrots.

The residents lined up to fill their plates from the sideboard. Anna waited until the rest had taken a portion before she stood and filled her own plate. She believed she was youngest, and her mother had brought her up to respect her elders. Once she was seated at her place at the table, Mr. Pendergast spoke. "Shall we bow our heads and give thanks?" Anna liked the family of strangers that filled the dining room and she felt happy with the tradition of saying grace every morning and evening. She had no family close by, save this oddly matched group. She silently added to her prayer, "Please God, keep my mother safe."

They ate quietly with only the clinking of tableware and rustling of napkins to fill the silence and mutterings of "please" and "thank you" as the bread, butter, and jam made its way around the table. Anna passed on the bread and jam but helped herself to a generous helping of beautiful sweet cream butter. With all her feminine finesse and good manners, she deposited the golden prize atop the soft warm dumpling in the center of her plate. Her eyes sparkled with pleasure.

The double doors from the hallway opened and a tall, middle-aged woman with upswept brown hair entered the dining hall with a letter in hand. She was the house mistress and never ate with the guests. And, although she entered from the hallway as if she were a leisurely proprietress, everyone knew that she had just left the kitchen from another passage. Mrs. McCarthy worked all day, every day, cooking and cleaning and making breakfasts and dinners for her guests. She was a warm and rosy-cheeked Irish immigrant, a widow and mother of two young sons. Mrs. McCarthy usually left letters in the cubby out front for the guests to retrieve, but she knew that Anna was anxious to hear from her mother. She dropped the letter into Anna's waiting hands and nodded in the affirmative. "You'll be wanting this right away, lass!"

Everyone stared at Anna, waiting. It wasn't proper to stop in the middle of dinner and open mail and Anna was a stickler for etiquette. Her mother had drilled manners into her. Never compromise. She slid the letter into the front of her pinafore and smiled at the others. "This must mean that she is doing well."

The letter nearly burned a hole through the fabric, but she continued to eat and be gracious at the table. When the others stood to go sit in front of the fire, Anna slipped up to her room. She closed the door, turned the key and made her way to the bedside table. She lit the kerosene lamp, adjusted the wick, and sat in the wooden chair to read her letter. Carefully, she opened the seal and lifted out the folded sheet.

New Orleans, Louisiana
March 15, 1861

Dearest Anna,
I am safe and well and I pray you are the same. It has been nine months since I laid eyes on you and I miss you so.
No longer am I the nanny for the O'Rourke family. They lost two of their children this winter and believe the hot sticky weather here caused the sickness. In response, they traveled back to Canada.
Now I live with the family Burke. They have a dairy farm and there is plenty of work to do. There are no children to teach, so I help on the farm. The Burkes are from Ireland as are most of our neighbors. It is wonderful to be with kinsmen, but I do so long to be near you.
The men here talk of war. Louisiana has already seceded from the Union. They believe it is unsafe for you to travel. I know you planned to come to New Orleans soon, but I implore you to stay there where you are safe. I know Mrs. McCarthy will take good care of you.
I will write soon.
God be with you,
Mamaí

Anna carefully folded the letter and placed it in her diary. Resting her hand on the leather cover, she closed her eyes and whispered a small prayer. The change of plans was disappointing, but she knew in her heart her mother was right. The talk of war between the states was everywhere, every day.

She had been on her own since her mother left Ontario in August of 1860. An Irish family and a few of their closest friends had decided to uproot and move to New Orleans. Warmer weather and the promise of cheap farmland had enticed them. They needed a nanny, preferably Irish, and Anna's mother, Margaret Slingsby, age 40, was available.

Margaret had been ready for a change for a long time but raising a child on one's own without a husband required having steady employment as well as courage. It had been difficult, hurtful even.

In 1842, when the Peterborough community found out that their new Irish schoolteacher had given birth to a child out of wedlock, the council was severe, quick, and unbending. Anna was born on the fourteenth of August. Margaret was unemployed on the fifteenth. She was allowed to remain in the teacher's quarters until the end of August. Anna was two weeks old when she and her mother moved into the big household of a wealthy local family where Margaret could tutor the children and do household chores for room, board, and a small wage.

Anna's father had lived on a nice farm with his legitimate family and had also been a teacher. That's how he met Margaret in the first place. When Anna was born, he publicly acknowledged her as his daughter, gave her his surname, and worked diligently to regain the trust and respect of his family and friends. While everyone was aware that he had fathered a child out of wedlock, no one spoke of it. He was a good man, and an Irish immigrant, which made him popular in the predominantly Irish community filled with non-Catholic immigrants. Sandy Matchett, although never a rich man, had never failed to send a small monthly stipend to his former mistress to help cover the expense of raising his daughter. Tragically, he died in winter of 1852 at the age of forty-two. Anna was nine. The stipend stopped, but Anna was already working in the Lytle household in the Monaghan North division of Peterborough County. She did chores while her mother taught and took care of the children. In her father's will was a provision whereby Anna would receive fifty dollars from his estate when she reached the age of eighteen. All other monies and property were left to his wife and seven legitimate children.

On the fourteenth of August 1860 Anna turned eighteen years of age. She retrieved her inheritance from the bank and tucked it safely away. She did not need to spend it immediately. She had worked as a servant and seamstress for as long as she could remember and had no trouble supporting herself.

The situation in Peterborough had been isolating and hard. Even though Sandy Matchett's legitimate family never voiced open resentment toward Anna or her mother, they and their acquaintances shunned them unbendingly. When Sandy Matchett died unexpectedly and included Anna in his will, not one word was uttered by the family about it. They just sold a small bit of land to get the cash for the bank to hold in trust for her until her eighteenth birthday. Mrs. Margaret Matchett, the legitimate widow, was elevated by the local society to near-saint status the moment her husband died. To worship the one meant a need to reject the other, which left Anna and her mother coldly shunned.

When Margaret Slingsby left for New Orleans, she had no idea of how lonely life would become for her daughter. In spite of the societal isolation, Anna had been engaged and expected to be married by Christmas. The new couple would have lived in Montreal, far away from the old rumors. Anna had been studying to become Catholic and join the church so that she and Jean Baptist could be legitimately married in his church. Just as Anna was nearing the point of conversion, she was unable to commit. She just did not want to become Catholic. Her fiancé, unable to go against his family and church, withdrew from the marriage agreement.

So, Anna suffered alone in the autumn of 1860. The isolation in Peterborough was complete. She made her decision to leave the evening after Jean Baptist turned his back on her. She had stared into the abyss, and decided that somehow, she would make her way to New Orleans. She was well-educated and had always worked to make her own money. All five feet one inch of her grew resolute in her decision and she talked herself into being confident. She was eighteen now. What could go wrong?

She booked passage in late November from Peterborough across Lake Ontario, through Buffalo and across Lake Erie. From there she traveled from Cleveland through Columbus and finally, to Cincinnati. She found the boarding house her mother had written to her about and inquired about a room. None were available when she arrived, eleven days before Christmas. The owner of the household, Mrs. McCarthy, took Anna in anyway. There was always a spare bed for "family," and Anna could sleep there until she traveled on.

The next morning, when Anna went to book her passage to New Orleans on the riverboat, the price was higher than she had bargained for. To add insult to injury, the ticket-seller refused to accept her money. She was compelled to find a bank to exchange her fifty in Province of Canada money for thirty-seven dollars and fifty cents in American money. The balding, black-vested clerk told her there was a twenty-five percent charge to exchange the money. Anna had no choice but to accept it. She tucked her diminished "nest egg" into her glove and returned to the boarding house. She found Mrs. McCarthy in the kitchen, doing up the breakfast dishes. When the older woman saw the look on Anna's face, she dried her hands on her big apron and walked over to her.

"Sit down, Anna. Tell me what has happened," she encouraged.

Anna closed her eyes for a moment and took a deep breath, letting it out slowly to allow the calm to come back to her. She sat, pulled her money from her glove and laid it on the table.

"I don't have enough money," she said. "I can't travel until I have enough American money! What shall I do?" Her lip quivered a little bit before she sniffled, blew her nose resolutely, and regained control of her emotions. "Do you know of any post available?

Mrs. McCarthy was eager to help. She had always wished for a daughter and welcomed Anna without hesitation. A room would open within a fortnight, so Anna would have a more permanent place to stay. She would have to charge her for the room and board, of course. She needed the money to run the house and feed her two half-grown sons. However, Mrs. McCarthy knew a lot of people and since Anna could sew and mend, she would find employment easily. Meanwhile, she could stay on the cot in Mrs. McCarthy's room.

Mrs. McCarthy did find work for Anna through her network of shopkeepers and friends. It started with small jobs mending and darning, but when people recognized the fineness of her needlework other opportunities started to emerge, like those of sewing fine lady's dresses with delicate embroidery and customized details. Wealthy Cincinnatians could pay well for such luxuries and the work suited Anna. It was so much more fun to make a beautiful gown than to mend a working man's pants or socks.

Anna had a lot of orders, but she could only do so much in the hours given in a day. Mrs. McCarthy suggested Anna use her inheritance to purchase a sewing machine. That machine would make the long seams go much more quickly and Anna would have more time to concentrate on the fine needlework she was so well-paid for.

Anna wanted to hang on to every single penny but could see the logic of investing money to make more money. After six weeks she had only added three dollars to her "nest egg," after room and board and that was only because the first two weeks Mrs. McCarthy had not charged her anything. At this rate, she might never make enough money to get to New Orleans. If she could make more garments, she would make more money. On the other hand, if she bought a machine, it would take all of her money. How long would it take to recover the cost of the machine?

It wouldn't hurt to look at sewing machines, she concluded. She could use the machine for a few months and double her income. She could then sell her machine and travel to Louisiana.

She looked all over Cincinnati at the different shops. There were many types to buy. Some were more expensive than others. Some looked as if they would fall apart at the drop of a hat. She liked the "Grover & Baker" machine at forty dollars and the "Singer" that was priced at fifty. She preferred the "Singer."

After a week of her going back and forth, the shopkeepers knew her by name. They were competitive and had tried to offer her special deals, even payment options. Anna held out, looking, comparing, making note of weight, size, and threading apparatus. She was thorough. She was absolutely going to get the most efficient machine at the cheapest price. The "Grover & Baker" machine on West Fourth Street was a good machine and in her price range, barely, but she simply *wanted* the Singer.

Sales after Christmas were slow. When the snow fell like icy daggers in mid-January, few customers came around looking to buy sewing machines. As Anna walked round and round the shiny new Singer machine, the salesman approached her.

"Miss Matchett, I wonder if you would be interested in a used Singer?"It is less expensive, and I guarantee that it will work. I have gone over it myself."

Anna's ears perked up when she heard that.

"Follow me," he instructed, and she did. In the back of the room, behind the counter on a wooden work bench stood a small black Singer sewing machine.

"It is last year's model, but in good condition. I've gone through it, oiled it and made sure everything is just like new. Interested?"

"Yes, please," answered the girl, "but does it come with a written guarantee?"

"Well, it is in perfect condition and only turned in because the woman who owned it died after her husband bought it." He knew he shouldn't have said that. People never want things that belonged to people who died. It was bad luck.

"But, for forty dollars you can have it, a written guarantee and I'll throw in a box of thread, two extra needles, a can of machine oil, and a nice pair of scissors!"

Delivery was made the next day. And, although she only had fifty cents left to her name, it was the happiest day of her life. Perhaps it was because she had a beautiful new machine and lovely new scissors. Perhaps it was because it represented her father's gift. In her heart she knew that this machine was the key to changing her life forever.

She shivered involuntarily and said aloud in her empty room, "Thank you God, for this. I don't know what plans you have for me, but I feel that my life will be good, and this is the start. Let Your will be done." She laid herself upon her bed, pulled the duvet up to her chin and slept.

+ + +

The mending jobs were endless but were accomplished efficiently with the Singer. Patches went on quickly and securely. Seams were repaired with straight, even, tight stitches. The stack of items in her basket, each with its own note describing the owner and the job, was replenished every day. And then there were the dresses ordered by prominent women in Cincinnati to take up her time. She did the fine work in the morning when the light was good and her mind fresh. She mended and darned before daylight and after dark when candle and lamp provided barely adequate light.

Mrs. McCarthy answered the door and took in the orders, carefully writing down the names, tasks, and description of the articles. Anna fetched the piles from the front corridor, completed the tasks and returned them to the basket. Mrs. McCarthy would hand off the completed garments and collect the money. Anna almost never met the people for whom she completed patches and repairs. If there was a new garment to be made and they left an old shirt, skirt or pair of trousers for Anna to use as a pattern, she had no need to meet them. Occasionally she would have to meet a lady and take measurements for a new garment, but it rarely happened.

One customer left a very odd set of clothes that needed repairing one day. The top item was a shirt that resembled a man's undergarment, long-sleeved, white, but with a deep "V" in the front and the bottom hem was decorated with a bright red zig-zagged ribbon. There were great gaping holes under both arms. "Hmmm," thought Anna aloud, "I believe an inset from underarm to hem would work." She sat the garment aside and reached into the basket for the trousers: "What in heaven's name!" she squeaked as she lifted the pants which seemed to be missing the legs. Upon closer inspection, she found the pantlegs were no more than sixteen inches from waist to hem. The short dark blue muslin pants had no button to close the top. Instead a thin brown cord was threaded through the waistband that could be tightened and tied on the side to secure the garment in place.

Anna read the note she found under the garments: "Donovan, William A.; Please mend shirt and pants and make new set with the fabric provided." She lifted out the blue and white muslin from the bottom of the basket and tested its weight and thickness with expert hand.

"That'll do," she said to herself as she carried the lot with her to the kitchen to seek out Mrs. McCarthy.

Seeing her friend bending over the bucket peeling potatoes for dinner, Anna approached her, holding out the note. "Who is Donovan and what kind of clothes are these, Mrs. McCarthy?"

A smile formed as she lifted her eyes from the potatoes and met Anna's gaze. "Oh Anna, he is a circus man, a friend of the family, born in New York City, but of Irish parents. I hope you don't mind doing the costume. He needs it rather quickly, at least the repair. Can you do it?"

Anna softened and shook her head "yes." She would do anything for Mrs. McCarthy, anything. "Of course, I will do it," she said, "as quickly as possible."

The days flew by and the money Mrs. McCarthy kept for her in the safe piled up. By mid-March, she had forty dollars and a new letter from her mother telling her to "stay put" at Mrs. McCarthy's.

April 15, 1861

News travels fast, especially in a boarding house where people are coming and going all of the time. It had been a tumultuous year in America with the election of Abraham Lincoln and his views that slavery should not expand to new territories in the states. Anna only got bits and pieces of information about American politics when she happened to overhear Mr. Pendergast discussing things in the drawing room with other gentlemen. He quickly stopped talking whenever she entered the room. He believed that women should not be subject to such coarse affairs as slavery and assassination threats on the president. Anna was very happy to live in her world of thread, needle, and sewing machine and only became alarmed when she heard that war had been officially declared and young men from Cincinnati were asked to fight against the southerners. What made it exceedingly real to her was the public request for seamstresses to step forward and help dress the army of men needed to go to war and fight for the Union. Would she be making shirts or trousers for a boy who would be shot through on a battlefield and left to die in his new clothes?

She didn't want to hear about war, but could not help herself. She listened at the doorway to catch Mr. Pendergast's opinions. She read the newspaper for old Mrs. Simms whose eyes had grown opaque with cataracts. Mrs. Simms wanted to hear about the war. Her grandson had volunteered to join the Union Army for three months. He was mustering out in a week and Anna had been frantically sewing to get his wool trousers with suspender button loops and cotton flannel shirts ready. She did this for old Mrs. Simms and it was done for honor, not money. War had become personal for her.

Busy is as busy does and Anna was always busy sewing and stitching order after order that dear Mrs. McCarthy took in for her. She had dressed and made herself ready for the day before daylight and finished the circus man's new costume before breakfast. A quick look in her hand mirror confirmed that every strand of straight blonde hair was still tidily tucked under her morning cap. She snuffed the lamp, picked up the costume and headed down the stairs. She would pop into the kitchen and tell Mrs. McCarthy the garment was ready, deposit it into the "finished basket" in the hall and proceed to the dining room to enjoy a cup of tea before the others came down for breakfast.

As she made her way down the stairs, the warm air from the fire grew more cozy with each stair descended. "Lovely," she whispered. A finished job was always a good feeling. Doing this favor for Mrs. McCarthy made the prize even sweeter.

"Mrs. McCarthy," she called as she opened the door to the kitchen, "I've got the costume ready!"

Anna stopped dead in her tracks. The handsome young man had been talking to Mrs. McCarthy. Both stopped talking and gave Anna their undivided attention. "Oh dear! I'm so sorry to have intruded," she said as she turned to go, "I'll come back later."

"Anna!" called Mrs. McCarthy, "Come back!"

Anna stopped and turned around.

"You're welcome to come in Anna! This is William, my friend, and the owner of the costume you're carrying."

William's eyes sparkled as an easy smile spread across his face, "Lovely to meet you, Miss Anna. It is a pleasure to make your acquaintance," He proclaimed while bowing deeply in front of her. Once again they stood for what seemed like an eternity, staring at one another. The fact that they had already met in the parlor was their unintended little secret.

Mrs. McCarthy, keen to get on with it, cleared her throat, and said something about having to make breakfast. She turned to the workbench and began breaking eggs into a deep earthenware bowl.

The room was toasty, smelled of freshly baked muffins, and glowed with the light of the small fireplace and a large hurricane lamp on the kitchen sideboard. Seconds seemed like an eternity and finally William broke the silence between them, "So, you've finished the costume! Wonderful. I have to admit that the repair you did on the old one was excellent! Thank you!" He had babbled. He knew he had babbled, but he loved her from the moment he had laid eyes on her more than a month ago.

"Oh!" Anna giggled, something she really wished she hadn't done. "Here," she said as she handed the bundle to him.

Fingers accidentally touched. Hearts leapt. Cheeks flushed. Time stopped.

Anna had not felt her heart race since the day her finance proposed to her on her seventeenth birthday. The magic disappeared sometime between then and when he withdrew his proposal. She had been relieved when the fading relationship was finally declared dead. She had forgotten the enchantment of romance, but her fires were easily lit. William was handsome and his smile, delicious.

Blushing, she pulled back away from William, eyes lowered, afraid he would see the smile on her face and the warmth of her cheeks. "Um, it was a pleasure to sew for you, Mr…."

"Donovan!" he replied, "William Albert Donovan, at your service." He bowed again and asked, "And your surname, Miss Anna?"

"Ah!" she laughed self-consciously, "It is Matchett. I am Anna Margaret Matchett of Peterborough, Canada West…" at your service, she added without knowing why. It sounded ridiculous. She felt faint and turned to leave the kitchen.

"Wait, please Miss Anna Matchett of Canada West," he called after her.

She stopped with hand on door and turned to face him.

"Would you like to go for a walk this afternoon? The weather is nice, and there is a park close by. We could stop for tea somewhere." He waited, eyes to ground, believing she would say no.

"I can meet you in the hall at two this afternoon," she replied quietly.

"Wonderful!" he replied as the door closed softly behind her. She had gone without another word.

He had arrived quarter to the hour to fetch her. She had been ready for an hour, waiting in her room. At precisely one minute before two she exited her room to meet him. Their gazes met when she was halfway down the stairs. He walked forward to greet her. He held out his hand to assist in the last step and she took it. It was if they had done the same for a lifetime. His hand felt warm and safe encompassing hers. Her hand, soft as a rose petal, felt perfect in his palm.

They had gone for a stroll under the blossoming trees and talked about childhoods. He had lots of brothers and one sister. His parents still lived in New York City, where Mrs. McCarthy had made their acquaintance before marrying Mr. McCarthy and moving to Ohio. Anna had, of course only half-siblings she had never met. She did not reveal any of that to him, but only remarked that her mother was in Louisiana and her father had passed away long ago. There was no need to elaborate. Now was time for positive, gentle, friendship and only good things, less personal things, should be revealed. He took her for a soda at Hannaford's Druggist. They each had a "Dew-Drop Cream" and giggled as the unfamiliar bubbles tickled their noses. Neither had experienced the strange sweet drink before. As they laughed together their eyes met and Anna knew that she wanted this sweet funny man in her life forever.

A month went by and William showed up at the boarding house nearly every Sunday. Sometimes he could stay hours. He and Anna would go out for long walks together and he would eat supper with them. Other times he barely had time to have something to eat before he was forced to leave so that he could get back with his troupe in time for the next day's show. He usually brought other circus member's mending for Anna to do during the week and picked up the sewing from the previous week.

That last Sunday in May, Donovan did not show up at Mrs. McCarthy's boarding house. His circus, the Antonio Brothers, was too far away for him to make a round trip in one day. Anna had grown used to her new beau showing up every week, and for six weeks in a row he was out on the road. He sent letters from every place he visited.

She had never heard of most of the towns like, Eaton, Hamilton, Circleville and Lancaster. The last letter was from Columbus. She did know where that was because she had traveled through there on her way to Cincinnati. She kept the letters tied with a blue satin ribbon, tucked away in her trunk.

She expected that she would not see him until October when the season for circus travel was over. But, in spite of the distance between them, she felt closer to him with every letter. His optimism shone in his letters, and he always made her laugh.

The traveling show life was not without problems. Because the circus did not want to venture into Kentucky or any other seceded state for fear of being swept into the throes of war, business was poor to terrible for The Antonio Brothers. They had returned to quarters the sixth of July to regroup. A debt of over three thousand dollars had been rung up and the talented troupe of performers needed time to reorganize before they could go out on route again. William had two weeks of unemployment to wade through, so he returned to Cincinnati to find part-time work and to visit Anna.

A crisp knock on her bedroom door wakened Anna from her daydream, "Yes?" She called forward as she put down her sewing and moved toward the door. Standing in the doorframe was William, all five and a half feet of him, lithe and well-dressed, and smiling from ear to ear.

"Anna!" His beautiful face softened when he saw her, and he acted out an exaggerated deep and flamboyant bow. As he came up again, his left hand reached forward with a handful of daisies! When she took the flowers into her hands, he put his hands around hers and held them there for a moment.

"May I come in?" he asked.

"No! You may certainly not!" she scolded. "I will meet you on the front porch after I've put these in water." Her eyes sparkled. Her heart skipped a beat. She was really very glad to see him.

William nodded his acquiescence, turned on his heels and made his way down the stairs, whistling.

His proposal came without warning. She wasn't prepared for it. They had been sipping lemonade while swaying back and forth on the suspended porch swing. Although they were careful not to touch one another as they sat there, Anna could feel his nearness. It made her stomach feel odd and she wanted to move closer to him. Of course, she did not.

William sat his glass down on the little table and took her hand in his. Smooth as silk he slid to his knees in front of her and gathered her hands into his own. She realized her mouth was open from the shock of it and acted quickly to close it again. What in the world, she thought to herself? What was he doing?

"Anna Margaret Matchett, dear Annie, I am a simple man. I do not make much money and I travel with a circus. But, if you would honor me by becoming my wife, I promise to look after you and love you all of my life."

She was silent, a million thoughts rushed through her head and no words came out.

"Annie?" William asked, searching her face for some clue as to her thoughts. "Would you be my wife?"

Two days later, they were married by Justice of the Peace William Lusby on Tuesday, the ninth of July 1861. Mrs. McCarthy and kindly old Mr. Pendergast accompanied them for the ceremony and a celebration at the boarding house was enjoyed after.

Annie, her new husband, and all of her belongings including her Singer sewing machine joined the troupe two weeks after their nuptials and they all headed for St. Louis, Missouri in hope of a profitable stand. For the first time, she watched her husband perform his gymnastics act. She observed most of it with her hands in front of her eyes, afraid to watch him balancing between two ten-foot ladders using only his feet to hold them together. He did handstands, one hand on the top rung of each ladder. He treated the ladders as if they were stilts and walked around the show circle, waving at the audience. He pulled a fabric rose out of his vest as he saw Annie and tossed it to her, expertly. His sense of balance was amazing. And, as a finale, he did a full circle flip, releasing and regaining the ladder so quickly the two did not separate and fall leaving him nothing to grasp hold of. She loved him but was now truly impressed with his talent. She loved his lithe body and how it could wrap around her easily and comfortably. She no longer felt alone in the world with him in her life. And the most surprising thing to her about joining the troupe was how they welcomed her. They just immediately pulled her in and made her a part of the big working family that traveled, ate, slept, and worked together. No longer did she feel the empty pit in her stomach caused by being apart from her mother.

No one in a traveling circus was idle. Everyone lent a hand wherever and whenever needed. There was food to be prepared, tents to erect and deconstruct, horses to tend, costumes to wash and mend, and a myriad of carefully orchestrated details that kept the wagons on the road and the troupe clean, well-dressed, and healthy. In August and September, they traveled hundreds of miles and gave shows every day except Sundays. Some days there were as few as twenty in the audience. At others, like in Chicago where audiences were large, the troupe put on two shows a day, three days in a row. There was much less work on days when they didn't have to travel.

Anna helped with everything she could, but her greatest gift to her new family was her ability to sew, mend, and create new costumes for people and horses alike. She learned the little dances performed between equestrian acts and experienced the absolute joy of performing successfully in front of an appreciative audience. At first, she had been afraid she would make a mistake, but Antonio Migasi, one of the owners, assured her she would do just fine. "After all," he said, "these people don't know what the dance is supposed to look like. Even if you do make a mistake, how would they know?" He added, "Remember, these people will probably never set eyes on you again. Don't be embarrassed. Have fun."

Mid October the Antonio Brothers show featuring Melville's Australian Circus stopped touring and made their way to winter quarters. Anna and William spent a week at Mrs. McCarthy's boarding house in a conveniently empty room before heading out to New York City where Anna would meet her in laws. William had previously worked at small jobs during the winter and joined shows in New York theaters when he could. It had been his habit to stay at his parents' home until he went back out on the road in the spring. This year he hoped his family would welcome both him and his bride to the small apartment in Manhattan.

They did. They welcomed their new daughter with open arms. Although it was cramped quarters, Anna relished the warmth of her new family. She embraced life in New York and felt very much at home. She felt beautiful, alive, and loved. In fact, for the first time in her life, she had put on a little extra weight.

Chapter Eighteen

Nine Years Later
Manhattan, New York
December 26, 1870

Annie Donovan rose from the table and pushed in her chair. She picked up her bone china teacup decorated in delicate pink roses and put it on the sideboard. There was no putting it off; it was time. The evening hour marked precisely one year since her dear William took his last breath. For the past twelve months she had not allowed herself to sink down into the depths of sorrow. She had held her heart at bay. There had been a need to survive and for that, she needed to work. Between working and sleeping, she had cared for her little boy, William Albert Junior. At seven, he was resilient. His grandmother Maggie lived with them now and for him, twelve months was long enough to mend. For Annie, it would have to suffice.

She went to the bureau, opened the top drawer and selected a starched white handkerchief from a stack that lay neatly ironed and folded. A single pink rose was embroidered on one corner. William always brought her wildflowers during the summer when they traveled with the circus. His favorites were the pink, five-petaled, wild roses with bright yellow star centers. He was a romantic and Annie blushed remembering how she loved him for it. She started to close the drawer, changed her mind, and reached in for a second identical handkerchief.

This evening was the beginning of a planned wake of sorts where Annie would go through her husband's things and mourn him. Her mother had taken young William for a few days. They would be back before the new year. Then she would start anew, sorrows put to rest.

She sat in front of the vanity mirror and observed her own reflection. She was dressed in widow's weeds, black hat with netting, black gloves, shoes, and shawl. She tidied the errant strand of blond hair that routinely escaped the bun fashioned at the nape of her neck. With all the grace of the queen of England, she rose from her dressing table, collected her handkerchiefs and made her way to the excursion trunk where William's things were stored.

It was small, wooden, with leather straps, and had been with them throughout their marriage. The Initials "W.A.D." were burned into the top, William Albert Donovan. It had once contained all their worldly needs as they traveled with exhibitions. When their son was an infant, it occasionally functioned as a cradle. Every single dent and stain was a memory they had shared.

She placed one gloved hand upon the lid and the other reached to open the latch. She paused, retracted her hands, removed her gloves and once again reached to open the trunk. She wanted to feel everything. The lid, left closed for an entire year, nonetheless opened without resistance. She stared. On top was the soft gray shirt she had made for him of wool flannel. She touched it, fingers closing around the soft cloth, and buried her face in the fabric that still held his scent. The sobs, great and horrible started from deep in her bowels and exploded from her throat with such force she fell to her knees.

"Oh William!" she howled.

It could have been minutes. It might have been hours. It was still dark when she awoke, arms wrapped around the shirt. She bunched it up and shoved her nose into it and once again breathed in all that was left of her husband. Disoriented, she reached for the little watch still tucked safely inside the pocket of her dress. She could not see it of course; the room was in total darkness. Somehow, she had made it to her own bed and slept.

She shivered, sat up and pulled the flannel up over her shoulders. She'd freeze if she didn't build a fire soon. "Practical matters," she muttered as she made her way to the hearth. In moments she had the fire kindled and the wall-clock told her the hour was five in the morning. She had slept quite nearly around the clock wrapped in the memory of her dearly departed.

The trunk was still there, standing open, waiting. First things first. She would fix a nice strong cup of tea. After breakfast (she found that she was starving), she would tackle the contents of the trunk. In the weeks before the death anniversary, Annie had created a book in which to paste memories of her life with William. She padded and upholstered two thin-cut pine boards with two holes drilled in the top. She had embroidered wild roses on the front cover and in perfectly neat stitches wrote "William Albert Donovan 1832-1869. To fill the book, she had fashioned large squares of bleached linen that she starched hard and ironed flat. Drawing the whole thing together would be two leather strings threaded through the linen and the boards. She procured glue from the hardware store. The idea was to lay out all of the clippings from William's gymnastics career, organize them and then paste them onto the linen sheets. She could relive and celebrate her life with her husband as well as mourn him finally and completely. One day when she was dead and gone perhaps her grandchildren would look through the book and remember him.

Annie dragged the table closer to the parlor stove and made several trips to move the contents of the trunk to the table. She lit an oil lamp and placed it at the far corner in a deep pie tin. She worried about lamps falling over and catching the apartment on fire. William had teased her that she should join the Manhattan fire brigade because they could learn a thing or two from her about fire safety.

She sipped her milky tea (sweetened with two sugars) and nibbled at the thick-crusted bread just warmed on the iron plate over the stove. The butter was sweet and smelled of summer. Annie smiled, savoring every bite.

She had slept in her clothing and a thorough freshening-up was in order. She poured hot water from the tea kettle into a basin, undressed and commenced her morning toilet. Once finished, the weeds were once again taken on and little black shoes were buttoned anew. She looked into the mirror and a newer, younger Annie stared back at her. She felt a sliver of guilt as she marveled over the good effect of having a peaceful night's sleep, the first in a year.

There came a knock at the door, a knock she knew well. It would be young James delivering coal as he did every day. She opened the door and let the boy empty his bucket into the box by the little stove. He held out his hand for payment and looked up at her.

"Miss Annie!" he exclaimed! "You look so happy today. Is it your birthday?"

"It's not," replied Annie, "And it is Mrs. Donovan, young man. Now take this," she handed him a penny, "and get on with you." She smiled at him, a sort of watery (but genuine) smile, and escorted him out the door.

The stack of things she had assembled amounted to a collection of newspaper clippings, employment records, and small mementos. She had meticulously kept every possible scrap. It had not been a perfect life, but they had loved each other.

They had married shortly after the war started and traveled together with the Antonio Brothers through Indiana, Illinois and Wisconsin. William performed and she sewed and mended. Sometimes she danced. It was fun, exciting, and seemed a lifetime ago. The first thing she pasted onto the linen page was their marriage certificate, the second, a small clipping from *The Woodstock Sentinel*. The advertisement illustrated "The Antonio Brother's Great Show & James Melville's Australian Circus Combined" as they would appear in Illinois.

Her finger traced the print, "W.A. Donovan, in his new and terrific act, entitled L'Echelle Perilleuses." William did dangerous balancing exercises between two ten-foot ladders. Her heart caught in her throat as she relived the first time she witnessed him do his somersault between the free-standing ladders. By the end of October, they were in Brooklyn, living with his parents. William found a job with "Stickney's National Circus" at the Bowery for the winter. Annie sewed and mended costumes sporadically as word of her skills got around the entertainment community. For her, the most memorable costume that first year was one she created for Joe Pentland, the clown. It had broad stripes of heavy red and white cotton. The costume included a cap which made his head look abnormally small and his ears, abnormally large. It was meant to be silly and it was.

Mr. Pentland had been the first to notice that Annie was "with child." As she measured the circumference of his head to make his new hat, a high-pitched voice with a thick Irish accent had risen out from nowhere asking, "Might you be expecting, Mrs. Donovan?"

At the time she had not known the clown could throw his voice. Annie smiled remembering. It certainly wasn't a proper thing to say to another man's wife, but if it really wasn't him, then how could he have been guilty of a faux pas? Joe was always polite, and no one ever heard a course word escape his lips.

Her smile faded. Mr. Pentland was not doing well these days. He had gone from a jolly, clean-shaven man dressed in wildly bright colors to a somber man with heavy mustache clad in the blackest of clothing. "Oh Joe," she muttered aloud, "What could have gone so wrong?"

The clock on the wall ticked off the moments loudly and a slipping grinding gear growled as the hour was about to be struck. Gong, Gong, Gong, Gong, Gong, Gong, Gong it declared. It was already seven.

Annie became lost in her thoughts as she sorted through the memories laid out on the table. The summer of sixty-two had been both sad and joyous. William went on the road without her. She was expecting and travel would have been too dangerous for her. He left with the Antonio Brothers in late May. He had learned the trapeze over winter and did a combination act with a man by the name of Ashton. She was frightened of the trapeze and as she waved him off that spring, she wept believing he would surely die from a fall. The trunk had but one newspaper clipping from that year from Madison, Wisconsin. Although William had written every week, he had only sent home one advertisement. By the time the show returned to New York, their son was already four months old.

Winter in New York City had been difficult. As the war raged on and circuses were unable to take southern routes, New England suffered from a glut of equestrians, dancing bears, and unemployed gymnasts. The veteran circus man, Lewis B. Lent, organized an extravaganza consisting of seven exhibitions and three circuses. The New York Clipper article Annie pasted into the book next took both sides of the linen sheet and the front of a second one. The "Equescurriculum" advertised itself as an immense and unparalleled combination.

Annie prepared a fresh cup of tea, this time pouring the steaming liquid into a large ceramic mug. She was out of milk, so she dropped in three teaspoons full of sugar and stirred lazily. Being careful as to not spill on the Clipper article. She read through it slowly, saying aloud the names of outfits she'd shared the road with, off and on, for several years. The "Leaping Buffalos" had not been her favorite. They had stunk. However, Mr. Langworthy's dogs had been a delight. He had asked her to make costumes for his pony-riding monkeys. She had done so, but had acquired a distinct dislike for the spidery little things. They were too clever for their own good. Derr's educated Bull she had little to do with, but she had fashioned jackets for Wallace's troupe of acting bears. And, of course there was good old Joe Pentland. His tagline was "The Jester Shakespeare Drew," and the advertisement to build up his act was a full two paragraphs long.

They'd left their infant son with William's parents when the grand caravan left for New Jersey in April of 1863. With the enormity of the Equescurriculum, Annie was employed full-time to take care of wardrobe needs. It was a magnificent undertaking to move the great lumbering enterprise on the road and Annie was thrilled to be a part of it. They had started off traveling around New York state, Auburn, Seneca Falls, Geneva, Lancaster, Buffalo, and Lockport. Mid-June the parade of wagons entered into Canada West and entertained the population of thirty-eight different cities and towns. On August ninth, just five days before her twenty-first birthday, the show stopped to honor the Sabbath by the Otonabee River just shy of Peterborough. Although Annie had been gone from her hometown for over two years, it seemed a lifetime ago. When she left for Cincinnati, she was a child feigning courage. Now she was a wife, a mother, and a paid employee of a grand traveling circus. As the show paraded, act after act, in and out of the giant tent in Peterborough the following day, Annie waited in the wings to be at the beck and call of gymnasts and equestrians alike that might need a stitch or button. She observed the audience and looked for familiar faces. She saw a few, but they were not looking for her, so she remained invisible to them.

"Are these my people?" she had whispered to herself. And the answer was immediate and clear: No. Her eyes glazed over as she took herself back to that evening in Peterborough.

She looked around her, watching as Joe Pentland pulled on his hat and tied it under his chin. He was the definition of good clean fun.

Mr. Wallace was in the middle of the finale with his troupe of acting bears. They were dressed in the little red waist coats she had made for them. It was not she who had measured these great hairy beasts, but Mr. Wallace himself. She watched as William approached the ring entrance to wait with the other equestrian artists. They exploded into the ring in a grand entrance upon the backs of fine horses, all eight of them, waving and smiling and demonstrating perfect routines of equestrienne gymnastics. Besides her own husband, there were the Madigans, Virginie, Mr. Morgan, Charlie Shay, Mr. Derr, Gonzales, Forrest, King, and Rochelle.

Each man charged, in turn, to the center of the sawdust circle and dazzled the audience with amazing calisthenics. At intervals some tumbled in the center of the ring while others circled the ring on horseback, jumping, tumbling, and seemingly flying through the air. James Madigan, with the assistance of a loud drum roll from the orchestra, successfully completed three backward somersaults in a row on the back of his horse. The audience stood and a deafening roar erupted from the crowd at every accomplishment.

This segment of the show was fast paced and dizzying. As the horses were led away to awaiting liverymen, the ringmaster presented himself to center ring and while exaggeratedly clapping his hands, incited the spectators to give the retreating athletes a greater round of applause.

The prop crew delivered balancing ladders and platforms to the ring. Others climbed the ropes to the rooftop, to release the trapeze apparatuses. The ringmaster presented the athletes once again and encouraged more applause. The band played lively music as the two climbed the ladders to the trapeze platforms.

Some of these gymnasts were experts on the trapeze, others balanced on ladders, and some were perfection at vaulting and somersaulting. William had evolved to performing somersaults on the back of a running horse as well as on trapeze and ladders.

As always, she sat with eyes glued to the ring, literally taking in every exciting moment of the show and, as always, was relieved when William returned from the ring unharmed.

After the gymnasts did their first turn, the jugglers and balancers took the ring. The pace slowed and the audience was able to catch their breath after the thrills of extreme gymnastics. Following this came Mr. Langworthy and his trained dogs. Annie had fashioned small coats for the stars of the troupe, a little dress for the small black and white terrier that was both very smart and very eager to please. She was always on last before the grand finale because she was best. Mr. Langworthy had taught her to stand on her hind legs and do ballerina-like circles for the audience before hopping on hind legs onto and off of small boxes.

As each act entered and exited the arena, they nodded at Annie, a signal that they did not need her needle to fix anything at the moment. There were several individuals employed to make certain that costumes were kept in good order, but Annie was the one who always sat ready at the entrance.

"These are my family," she muttered to herself as she shook herself form her daydream. She brushed a tear from her cheek and pasted the final bit of the big 1863 article into the book. This sorting through memories was a tiring task. Her head spun as she recalled the antics of one friend and the hearty laugh of another. Time slipped away unnoticed as she daydreamed about the days of old. She put more coal on the fire and decided to simply lie down on the settee, close her eyes, and remember. Again, she slept the slumber of an innocent. When she awoke the feeble December daylight had turned darkness. Winter nights were so long.

"Goodness," she said to her own reflection in the vanity mirror. "I'll need more energy than this if I'm to get it done." Annie carried the oil lamp to her bedside, stood it carefully upon the pie-tin and lowered the wick until the light was extinguished. The Manhattan Gas Light Company had run lines throughout her Thirteenth Street apartment house, but she didn't trust the flammable gas. Tomorrow she would have to walk the half block to Fourth Avenue and buy more lamp oil. Just now she was exhausted and fell asleep almost before she closed her eyes.

She imagined a bird was singing sweetly outside her window. As sleep left and reality took its place, Annie smiled at the illusion. Spring would come again, for now it was a pleasure just to dream of it.

The pile of clippings covered the table from corner to corner. They would have to wait. Annie received her coal then left for the store. The morning was brilliantly sunny and surprisingly warm for the 27th of December. It took less than five minutes to get to the grocer, but she took her time checking the apples for wormholes and deciding which loaf of bread she should buy. Since William wasn't home, she bought only a pint of milk, but added a quarter pound of sweet butter to her basket and a small jar of strawberry preserves. She had a sweet-tooth and this week she did not have to be a motherly example. On the way back, Annie caught herself humming an Irish melody from her childhood. She wasn't sure if she should feel guilty about being lighthearted. It had been such a long, sad year.

Annie climbed the three flights of stairs to her apartment, added coal to the stove and put the kettle on. It was soon whistling up a storm. She pushed the mementos away from one corner of the table and sat her breakfast down. Unusually hungry, she had boiled two eggs and toasted a thick slice of bread that she covered in butter and preserves. The feast was completed with the porcelain mug filled with sweetened milky tea.

Annie cleaned up, refilled her tea mug, and sat back down at the table to begin again.

The season of 1864 was a difficult one. She thought about skipping it and moving on to the next year but decided it needed to be done. In February that year her second child was stillborn. It was hours before the doctor could get Annie to stop bleeding and it took months for her to recover any color in her cheeks. It would take a lifetime for Annie to get over the death of her baby girl. They christened her Margaret Anne and she was buried in Green Wood Cemetery in Brooklyn. Annie had been unable to attend the funeral. She was still fighting for her own life at the time.

The war dragged on. By March Mr. Lent had successfully reassembled the great "Equescurriculum" show. The advertisement published the first of June in *The Chicago Daily Tribune* was another oversized clipping that would require several pages. The consolidated show still had seven exhibitions and three circuses, but some of the names had changed. Grizzly Adams from California now had a troupe of trained bears and the band was Charles Boswold's Opera Band. Having injured a shoulder, William could no longer execute the most daring of his gymnastics. He was reassigned as one of the "Four Great Clowns" and they called him the "English Gymnastic Clown." Joe Pentland led them. They spent most of the tenting season in Illinois. It was wet, cold, and miserable almost all summer. Young William stayed in Brooklyn with his grandparents. Annie worked again in wardrobe and tried to support William as he transitioned from headliner gymnast to clown. It was a depressing year, in the world, in the war, and in the Donovan family. When the Equescurriculum once again returned to New York City, Annie went to live in Brooklyn with the Donovans. William took off for Tennessee with "The Howe & Norton's Circus." Tennessee was very close to the war and Annie worried that her husband would fall victim to a bayonet or bullet. William was determined to overcome his injured shoulder and prove himself capable. Perhaps he was also glad to leave his sad and depressed wife behind for a few months.

By January of 1865, William was home again in Brooklyn and immediately went to work at the American Theatre at 444 Broadway in lower Manhattan. Sometimes Annie noticed the smell of alcohol on his breath. He said it was just a little medicine to limber his shoulder so he could perform. She believed him. She didn't notice it often.

William's mother passed away on Ash Wednesday, the first of March. Young William would spend the tenting season with family friends, George and Tryphena Hill in Brighton. The couple was childless and would take no money for boarding little William for the summer.

Mr. Lent headed out to Ohio with the 1865 version of the Equescurriculum in early April. James Robinson, the famous equestrian rider was one of the stars. Grizzly Adams was still along and William was once again assigned to be one of "Four Great Clowns." The war ended on the 9th of April and they heard about it in Cincinnati on the 10th. They were still in Cincinnati celebrating when it was reported that President Abraham Lincoln was shot dead in the Ford Theatre on the 14th. So much relief and joy, then such disbelief and sadness left circus performers and audience alike stunned.

They continued on through Ohio, Michigan, Wisconsin, and Iowa before heading back to New York. When they did return home at the end of October, the city had changed dramatically. The population that had moved in and hunkered down to wait out the war had left for home.

Lent auctioned off the Equescurriculum in Ohio and bought "The New York Circus." He rehired Donovan and Pentland as well as most of his pre-war troupe. He brought Annie along for wardrobe.

They were winter-employed, and all was settled except for the lack of a place to live.

William's father had died over the summer. His household in Brooklyn had been liquidated and the apartment, vacated. They were forced, for the first time in their married lives, to find an apartment of their own for the winter. They chose Manhattan and a cramped three-room apartment on the third floor near the entertainment district on 13th Street. It was less than a block from "Lent's New York Circus."

The winter was spectacular! Boosted by post-war optimism, the circus did great business in the Hippotheatron just across from the Music Academy on 14th Street. William's shoulder was still giving him trouble, but Mr. Lent kept him employed as an extra clown to Joe Pentland. His name was not in the advertisements though, something that cut deeply.

The newspaper article Annie had decided to save did have her husband's name in print. He was listed as one of a dozen artists of "acknowledged ability" to the New York Circus. He remained one of the four great clowns led by Joe Pentland. "From the Hippotheatron Buildings, 14th Street, opposite Academy of Music, N.Y.," the clipping read. Annie smiled. It seemed like yesterday that they had been introduced to the Hippotheatron. What she had liked most about it was the size of it. The ring was almost as big as a canvas tent and had three separate places for seating, dress, pit, and orchestra seats. The roof was high and the walls made of metal. They believed it to be fireproof, something that calmed Annie's fears. It was also decently warm. It had modern, highly effective steam heat.

Their tent season started in Brooklyn and was slated to run May 28th through June 2nd. From Brooklyn, they had dared do something quite new. They loaded the entire circus onto a train and made stops in Connecticut, Massachusetts, Maine, and New York State. Because there was no menagerie associated, there was no spectacle or parade in new towns. That cut down on the number of spectacular costumes needed. It was less work for Annie and amounted to a considerable savings for Mr. Lent.

Annie held the advertisement clipping closer to the lamp. "Brook. Daily Eagle, 24 May 1866" was written in faded ink on the top of the paper in her own neat hand. She savored the printed names and descriptions, each one an acquaintance and someone who shared her life with William. Mr. James Robinson was there and his son Clarence, who was only five. Clarence had played "beeswing" in the "Sprite of the Silver Shower" and was everybody's darling. He had ridden in the legendary equestrian spectacle in the Hippotheatron alongside the great Levi J. North. Mr. North's performance was stunning in spite of his advancing age.

"Hmmm." Thought Annie aloud while inspecting the tips of her fingers. The fabric she had used to make the fairy costumes was woven with threads of silver. It had tested the strength of her character. She'd ended up with thimbles on three of her fingers to escape injury from the harsh material. The costumes were beautiful though, catching the light perfectly to convey the legend of fairies.

Carlotta De Berg, an equestrienne, had earned Annie's admiration. Her gymnastics on horseback were every bit as good as what the men did, and she did it with pure grace. The amount of ridicule she had been forced to endure on her struggle to stardom was in her own words, "Worth every bit of the trouble." She'd earned the respect of the other athletes even though she was a woman.

The Madigans, and Levantines were there then and one of the Stickney's. Cooke, Forrest, Messenger, and someone by the name of Francois Lee and of course William. Below the list were Joe Pentland and Professor Chas. Boswold's Full Opera Band.

Annie smiled as she carefully glued the back of the clipping. She and William used to waltz behind the curtain between acts as the band played. That was before he hurt his shoulder. "Good times," she uttered aloud as she neatly glued the clipping in place.

As pages were made, glued, and ready, Annie placed a heavy book on top of them to guarantee that they didn't pucker. The first pages were dry and ready, so she carefully removed their weights to use them on the new ones. She had only two thick books, her mother's family bible and a Noah Webster dictionary inherited from William's folks.

When they returned from the 1866 tenting season, William's shoulder was worse. Annie, reassured that William was not taking too much alcohol, nevertheless kept an eye on him. Before performances she was witness to his dosing for the pain. He kept a bottle in the kitchen and a small glass for measuring. He gave himself two-fingers of liquor in the glass and swilled it down while making a terrible face. He acted like he hated the stuff, but it was "to make him safer when he did his act" by relaxing the shoulder and letting it work. She never found out about the second bottle William kept with his things at the ring until much later.

Winter of 1866-1867 was spent much as the winter before, with Mr. Lent in the big metal building. Annie sewed beautiful costumes for the Christmas ballet and pantomime and enjoyed the company of other seamstresses whose work she orchestrated and checked.

The tent season started again in mid-May when they took off by railway for Connecticut. The clipping she had for the tenting season was from Columbus, Ohio. She had written 10 July 1867 in the corner. William was not listed. Mr. Lent had explained that it was expensive to list all of the fine talent in the show, so he only listed a very few. William hadn't liked it, but he never mentioned it again. Carlotta De Berg's name and illustration were prominent, showing the star doing ballet on the back of a galloping horse. The new child wonder was on the tightrope that year. "El Niño Eddie, the child wonder." Annie sighed. She had missed little Clarence and his bareback-riding father James Robinson. They'd moved on. Also new that year was the Runnells family. They were gymnasts and equestrians. They had spent time in Paris performing. Annie had studied Bonnie's French costume carefully as the fashion and fabric was very interesting. James Madigan was the only brother listed and only two clowns made print, Pentland and Croueste. And, although they traveled by train and had no menagerie, a street parade was added. Mr. Lent admitted that parades drew visitors. Annie sewed for the spectacle and for the first time, her income surpassed her husband's.

In New York City, William dosed himself for his painful shoulder at regular intervals with alcohol. He worked for Mr. Lent all winter before making plans to go to California with Sam Stickney for the tenting season. Sam was well known in the business. He was a for-midable hurdle rider before injuring an ankle that ended his career. Since then he had worked as a jester and had even been ringmaster for Lent one season.

Sam seized an opportunity to take over a small circus and take it to San Francisco, California. They were calling it the "Great Paris Exposition" and hoped the association with the real "Exposition Universelle" in France would be a good draw. People out west were hungry for entertainment and would pay top dollar to see the show. There was the potential to make good money.

William had come home one frozen day in February babbling excitedly that Sam had asked him to join the troupe. "He understands, Annie…" pleaded William, "He is giving me a chance!"

Anne recalled his face, full of excitement, more joy than she had seen in ages. He had held her hands in his and begged her permission to go try his luck. The past few seasons he had played second fiddle to almost every other gymnast at Lent's circus and this… this was a chance to be on top again.

She relented rather quickly as she recalled. She had loved this man with her whole heart, and he could twist her around his little finger with little effort. He was gone for the whole tenting season. She had not traveled alone with Mr. Lent that summer, but instead remained behind in New York. Her costuming skills were known in the business and she did not lack for work.

William sent a letter home in May with newspaper clipping from the *San Francisco Examiner*.

He was listed second among the athletes, right after Montague who was listed as the principal rider. At least his name was there, she thought. She read through the text and it dawned on her that many members of the troupe were women. "MLLE. MARIE, HANNAH, ELLEN, CAROLINE, JENNIE, LA PETITE ROSA" were announced after which came John Saunders, "Premium Leaper, Double Sommersaultist." It had never occurred to her to be jealous of the beautiful athletic women that passed through William's life. Perhaps she should have considered the possibility....

"No!" she said to herself with clenched teeth, "He would never!" Annie recalled waving them off in New York in late March as they boarded the steamer "Fulton" for Panama and San Francisco. She had believed they had a lifetime in front of them when she gave him up for that one summer. Had she predicted his untimely death, certainly she would have kept him back.

There were no more advertisements to fit into the book of starched linen sheets. The next time William Donovan's name came into print was to announce his death.

She thought about the past year, 1869. Young William was seven and started school. Annie's mother came to stay with them. William still worked for Mr. Lent as a backup gymnast, but his shoulder got worse and somersaulting from horses was a thing of the past. He drank more, to quiet the pain, and was often unable to perform at all. More than once Annie held her husband in her arms as he wept, sorry to have failed her.

December came and with it, a new production at "Lent's New York Circus." Annie had worked for months measuring athletes and making fancy costumes. She had made a new costume for William, a fine one that glittered as he moved through his calisthenics. Her husband had exhibited well during the week leading up to Christmas and Annie sincerely believed he was on the mend. He performed on the 22nd. It was a Wednesday evening. She watched as he went through his routine and for once, never saw him wince in pain as he mounted the horse.

They rushed him to hospital on Christmas Day. Her mother had stayed with William. "Was it only a year ago?" she asked aloud.

She had fetched a guard from the Hippotheatron just down the street and it was he who brought a cart to transport him. William was delirious and oblivious to what happened around him. The doctor, she remembered with humility, smelled alcohol on William's breath and declared him drunk.

The agony of that day came crashing in on her and the tears flowed silently down her cheeks as she remembered every painful moment. She knew that William drank for medicinal purposes, but even when he drank too much, he recognized her. She had not believed the doctor. William never regained consciousness and, on the twenty-sixth, breathed his last.

She clutched the paper she had gotten from the authorities. They had written his cause of death as "alcoholic delirium tremens." He was thirty-five. Annie put the paper aside and reached for the clipping from the *New York Clipper* dated 8 January 1870. "Much better," she proclaimed as she read it aloud:

"William A. Donovan, gymnast, and a most excellent general performer, died very suddenly in this city on Dec. 26th of congestion of the lungs, and was buried on the 28th at Green Wood. He leaves a widow nearly destitute and a child. He was connected with the New York Circus where he has been for a long time. He performed for the last time on Wednesday night, December 22nd."

Annie Donovan carefully pasted the New York Clipper article onto a linen sheet and placed a book on top of it. She stared at the official paperwork for a moment before crumpling it up, walking over to the fire and tossing it in.

She had learned a lot this past year, sometimes she learned things she would rather not know. She heard whispers that someone gave William morphine for his pain the last night he performed and thus his performance was nearly pain-free. Had he taken too much? Is that what really killed him? She would never know, and her son would never be privy to the question.

The last thing to do was to visit the cemetery, which she did. She paid for a horse drawn cab to the ferry and then another to the Green Wood Cemetery in Brooklyn. The main entrance was gothic in appearance with two tall twin structures. She walked through and made her way to the Donovan plot where her husband, his parents, and baby Margaret rested. When she had paid her respects to the loved ones lying there, she returned home.

On the 31st of January her mother returned with William. There would be a celebratory glass of sherry and a formal toast to good health in the new year. She looked forward to it.

Her plans for 1870 were laid out. She had a new position as assistant costumer with P.T. Barnum. He was starting a new show and nothing he ever did was small. She would have plenty of work. Besides, she knew almost all of the performers, so it would be like rejoining family.

Chapter Nineteen

1 January 1871
Lower Manhattan, New York City

The route from her apartment to Fulton Street was usually bustling with cabs and carts and swarming with Manhattan's workforce. Today was eerily different. During her solitary journey down Broadway, she had seen only a handful of shopkeepers opening doors for deliveries and a solitary milk wagon.

She was not expected until the following day but would walk to the workshop a day early and get the lay of the land. There was nothing like foreknowledge to strip away jitters and the uncertainties of a new job. It was an enormous task before her; to work under Mr. Hamilton to deliver costumes for the new show led by Barnum, Coup and Castello. Mr. Lent had recommended her and while that boosted her confidence, this was her largest undertaking by far.

Annie shivered involuntarily as she counted off the seventeenth block; just three to go. She always counted streets, just as she counted the stairs and stitches. Twelve perfect locked stitches to every inch she sewed into any garment, eight loose ones if the fabric happened to be fragile or delicate, like silk. Counting things kept life in order, she thought, smiling to herself.

As she counted off the last city block, she turned left and walked down Fulton. Halfway down the street she spotted it:

Wardrobe Costumers

Help Wanted, Inquire Within

Mr. Fred Hamilton, Master of Properties and Wardrobe

(Barnum, Castello, Coup)

She tried the doorknob, rattled it, but it was locked. It was a Sunday, New Year's Day. Of course, no one was there. She looked around to make sure she was alone, cupped her hands to the glass and peeked inside. Nothing interesting was visible save a broad dark wooden staircase. So, she thought, the production room must be located above on the second or third floor. She would bring her most practical shoes. Just as she started to pull back from the window, a round moon-faced middle-aged man of her own height with a thick brown mustache appeared in the widow opposite. Annie let out a squeak and rocked back on her heels, dropping her black umbrella onto the pavement. She felt the blood fill her cheeks at her surprise and embarrassment. She hurried to gather herself and her umbrella but was unable to escape before the man opened the door.

"And who might you be, Ma'am?" He asked, eyebrows raised. "Are you seeking work here today?"

Annie lifted the black netting from her face and clutched the umbrella to her chest with both hands. She straightened herself to achieve her utmost height and did her best to appear dignified.

"Indeed sir! I am Mrs. Anna Donovan, hired to be first seamstress-in-charge under Mr. Hamilton's management. If you please, sir, I've come to inspect the establishment and conditions under which I will be working."

The mustache twitched as the man stared wide-eyed at the woman before him. Under all that black was a strong woman with a lively spirit. The round man laughed softly and opened the door wider.

"My name is Mr. Kowalski; please call me Karl. I too am an employee of Mr. Hamilton." He quickly added, "Do come in from of the cold, Mrs. Donovan."

Once inside, he continued, "I was told that it was highly likely that you would stop by a day ahead of schedule to view the sewing room. I've been watching for you since seven.

This, thought Annie, was quite acceptable. She followed Karl up the steps (thirteen), rounded the small landing (three steps) and proceeded up an additional bank of stairs (thirteen). Karl opened the door to the expansive room on the third floor which would, from tomorrow, be bustling with women employed by the costuming company cutting, sewing, and fitting costumes for the much-anticipated new traveling show.

It was all wrong! The entire south side of the room was windowed, which meant excellent light for cutting and sewing costumes, but some ignoramus had almost completely obscured the windows with cutting tables stacked with sewing machines still in crates and on top of them were heaped bolts of fabric that at first glance appeared to be a hodgepodge of shimmering gold, scarlet red and royal blue. The ceilings were high and the lighting further back from the windows was unacceptable.

Annie took inventory quickly. She noted the cutting tables were excellent and the sewing machines, new and modern. She could have ten women cutting and sewing simultaneously, but to be efficient, the room needed rearranging before the staff of professional costumers arrived in the morning sharply at seven, she hoped.

Karl watched as the young women circled the room, muttering to herself, lifting fabric bolts counting, scurrying around to inspect various corners of the large open room. He was fascinated. She was lovely. "It was like hen-chicken searching barnyard for bugs, it was" He related later to a friend.

Annie stopped right in front of Karl and waited for him to acknowledge her.

"Yes, ma'am?" he asked.

"You are at liberty to help me arrange the room for tomorrow?" She inquired in such a way as to make sure Karl knew it was more of a statement than a question. "Can you help me move a few things before you go?"

Karl surrendered immediately to the request believing that the job would take at most an hour and then he could curl up in the sun in his own room and nap the rest of the day away. He had already spent half the Sabbath awaiting Mrs. Donovan's arrival, another hour wouldn't hurt.

When they finished "rearranging a few things," the room had been transformed completely. Bolts of fabric were now stacked against the inside wall neatly arranged by color and fabric type. The cutting tables stood directly in front of the lovely windows and the sewing machines (unpacked) were lined up just inside from the tables, one after the other, neat and tidy. One sewing machine was placed right next to the window in the same row as the cutting tables. This would become Annie's station. From there she could observe and direct the pattern cutting and assembly of costumes.

She would bring vinegar and newspapers tomorrow and wash the windows. No time was left today. Satisfied, she checked the watch pinned to the front of her dress and found it to be nearly four o'clock. It would be dark before she got back if she didn't leave soon.

Annie donned her coat and little black hat and slid the umbrella crook over her arm. Glancing back at Karl, she asked, "Would you be so kind as to see me out?"

Karl smiled and nodded. Of course he would see her to the door. They'd spent the entire day cleaning, sorting and assembling and he didn't mind one bit… best New Year's Day he'd spent in a long time.

"Will you be here tomorrow, Karl?" Annie asked as they parted ways at the front door.

"Yes, Ma'am," he answered smiling at her. "I am to see that you get everything you need for the next three months." Annie smiled, muttered a "thank you" and turned to walk back up Fulton toward Broadway. It had started to snow, but the two-mile walk melted away under her feet as her mind buzzed with the task ahead of her.

The next day when Annie stepped out of her apartment at precisely 6:15 to make her way to the costuming shop she found that Mother Nature had laid down a thick carpet of snow during the night. She would have to hurry if she was going to make it in time for her own seven o'clock starting time.

The omnibus on Fourth Avenue and Broadway was late. She waited a good ten minutes before it emerged from a cloud of densely falling snow. It progressed down Broadway slowly as the horses labored to draw the bus through three inches of wet snow.

When they finally made it to Fulton Street, the driver failed to stop. Although she had tugged on the "stopping strap" (which was attached to the driver's ankle) well in advance, he hadn't noticed it. She gave the strap a much harder, more deliberate yank. The driver noticed and let her off just past Cortlandt Street. She had two city blocks to backtrack and she was already wet and cold. No matter. This inconvenience was not the cause of her stress; being late to work was the reason. It was unacceptable.

Karl met her at the bottom of the stairs as she came in through the door.

"Mine Gott!" he exclaimed! "You are wet as drowned kitten and late. I was worried!"

Annie nodded to the kind middle-aged man, lifted her skirts and made her way up the stairs, grateful to note there were still only twenty-six stairs to climb.

She was the first woman to make it to the salon even though she was fifteen minutes late. She turned to find Karl staring at her.

"Well," she asked questioningly, "Were not the ladies supposed to come to work by seven o'clock, Monday through Saturday?"

Karl nodded in agreement; the ladies were indeed late to work on their very first day.

"Come," he gestured toward the coal stove on the far wall. "Get shoes off and dry feet by the fire. You need to warm yourself before you work."

He brought her a cup of tea in a big porcelain mug. He hadn't asked but had added a generous pour of milk and several spoons of sugar.

"Here. Drink and then we work."

Annie did as she was told. She had worked with show people often enough that the embarrassment most women would have felt at baring her feet in front of the fire was only a passing thought. Practicality trumped conventional modesty when they were all working, and this was one of those times. She must get warm. Mustn't fall ill.

By the time she finished the tea, her stockings were nearly dry. The shoes would take a good deal longer. The hem of her dress was soaking wet, but it could dry on its own

Seven of the ten women arrived to work within the hour. They were veteran costumers and heavy weather might delay, but not deter them. Before the day was done, the rhythm of cutting and measuring, sewing and pressing was already well established. As the day finished and Annie was putting on her coat to leave, Karl approached her.

"I will give you ride home, Mrs. Donovan. It is not trouble."

Annie didn't question the offer, but quietly rode home in Karl's horse cart. Although there was no canopy, he did offer a robe to cover her legs. The fact that he was falling in love with her never crossed her mind.

January disappeared into February and March arrived with ice and more snow, but nothing could hinder the steady progression of getting the big show ready. The thriving metropolis buzzed with the gossip of Barnum's great new adventure. The New York Clipper chronicled the building crescendo that would eventually become "P.T. Barnum's Great Traveling Museum, Menagerie, Caravan, and Hippodrome."

An army of men (and women) and animals were training and organizing all over the greater New York area for the coming season. As the ladies from the costuming company cut and sewed on Fulton Street, Annie orchestrated the entire production. It was also her job to travel to all those in need of costumes and fit, measure, and adjust those costumes to perfection.

Karl drove her around so she could fit and adjust everything from headdresses for elephants (eight feet tall and six thousand pounds) to formal attire for Admiral Dot (twenty-five inches tall and fifteen pounds) and his entourage. Several times they caught the Fulton Ferry to Brooklyn to Carll & Cortelyou's stables on Hicks Street near Atlantic where most of the show horses were stabled and near where most of the equestrians could be found and fitted.

Today they had crossed the New Jersey Ferry to Jersey City where trained monkeys were measured for gold trimmed red jackets and Mediterranean style red fez hats with gold tassels. Annie didn't care for monkeys, but the trainer had controlled the animals well while she took measurements and it had gone off without a hitch.

When they finished Karl asked, "Mrs. Donovan? Would you mind if we stop at barn near here so I can look in on old friend? It is on way to ferry and won't take long time."

The day was sunny and still. The wind from the Atlantic Ocean had stayed offshore and although there were mountains of work to do back at the sewing room, Annie acquiesced. "Extra time in the sunshine is welcome, Mr. Kowalski, so long as it won't take too long."

Near the docks not far from the ferry, Karl reigned in the horses and parked the cart beside a weathered square, one-story building. He hopped out and made his way around to the other side to offer a hand to Mrs. Donovan.

"But," Annie remarked, "I can wait out here, Mr. Kowalski as you said it would only be for a few minutes."

"No, no Mrs. Donovan. Come in and see lions, tigers and leopards. Meet Charley," he said, gesturing toward the building.

Annie followed him into the barn. It took several moments for her eyes to adjust from the brilliant sunshine to the darkness inside and she hesitated to move until she could see her way forward. In front of them were several enormous cages made of iron bars. The ground within them was covered in a thick layer of sawdust. The shadowy figures of the occupants were barely perceptible, darker shadows within the shadows. The silhouette of a man filled the door on the opposite side of the expanse. He hollered at them, "Who goes there? State your business!"

"Karl… Karl Kowolski… here to see my friend, Charley White."

The shadowy figured walked toward them purposefully with the quiet grace of a trained athlete. He threaded his way through the cages, acknowledging each occupant as he passed.

"Karl!" He extended his hand to shake Karl's. "How are you, my friend? I haven't seen you since before the war!" he declared, "And who is this?" he nodded toward Annie and smiled, "Is this the Missus?"

"Uh, no Charley! This here is Mrs. Donovan, head costumer for company." Turning to Annie, he continued, "Mrs. Donovan, my very good friend, Mr. Charley White."

Charley stepped forward and bowed slightly from the waist.

Even in the half-light Annie caught a glimpse of the wounded spirit that stirred within. His expression was soft, his posture, unassuming. Her instinct told her to hold him, to comfort him.

She willed herself to look away, did a slight curtsy and said, "Pleased to make your acquaintance, Mr. White."

Charley smiled. "The pleasure is all mine, Mrs. Donovan."

He showed Karl and Annie around the den of cats explaining that most were hand raised by humans and although tame, the wild still lived within them and they could be very dangerous. The tiger, he said, was never to be trusted.

Annie was surprised when one large male lion walked over to the side of the cage where Charley stood and offered the top of his head for a scratch… which Charley provided seemingly without a second thought. When Annie asked why it was such a dark room for the poor animals, he explained that it was "naptime." The barn doors were thrown open morning and evening but were kept closed otherwise so the cats would relax and not become agitated. "They sleep about twenty hours a day," he added.

"Well," Interjected Karl, "We have to go. Mrs. Donovan measured the monkeys for jackets and needs to get back and deliver numbers to costumers." He nodded at Annie to be certain of her agreement and then shook Charley's hand again.

"We'll be seeing you more often next month, I guess, once the show's started," Charley said in parting.

He walked them out, squinting as the sun broke through the opened door. Annie turned to wave goodbye, but Charley had stepped up beside her to help her into the cart. His hand was dry and slightly rough, but warm, firm and steady. Had she imagined it, or had he held her hand just an instant longer than necessary?

As Karl guided the horse-cart toward the ferry landing, Annie rode silently beside him lost in her own thoughts. She relived the moments she had spent in the barn, playing over and over again in her mind every moment. There was something mesmerizing about the way Mr. White, Charley, moved…and his eyes were kind, but watchful and intelligent.

Karl was shaken. He had seen the spark between Annie and Charley. You'd have to be a moron to miss that, he thought. And he was right. Long after Karl and Annie had left the barn, Charley White stood in the sunlit doorway and watched the road they had departed upon, hoping, he guessed, that she would come back.

The whole of greater New York City buzzed with activity as shows that had wintered in the city made ready for the tenting season. Gymnasts and equestrians practiced, horses were re-shod and trained, exotic animals were procured, and wagons were ordered and outfitted.

The Barnum enterprise consisted of not less than one hundred wagons, two hundred and fifty horses and two hundred and seventy-five teamsters. There were some one hundred and fifty employed to wrangle tents, cook, and manage the show.

The Clipper announced that P.T. Barnum was proprietor, W.C. Coup was manager, and Dan Castello was director of the hippodrome. Harrison was put in charge of the "Exposition of Living Curiosities" and Jakes was to maintain the Automatron mechanics. While General McDonald was made master of the menagerie, Alasco Charles White was made "The Dominant Hero of Wild Beasts."

The great show was advertised using both newspapers and a free, throw-away paper of sixteen pages called *The Courier* which described and embellished the new circus. An adult would pay just one entrance fee of fifty cents to gain access to the circus, menagerie, museum and sideshows.

They opened in Brooklyn on Fulton near Hoyt Street on the evening of April tenth. While many believed it would have been advantageous for them to open in Manhattan, it was impossible. Barnum had, for a payment of twelve thousand dollars, vowed to Mr. George Wood of the Wood Museum not to exhibit any shows with his name attached in New York City. In other words, he agreed to not compete. In the end, the starting exhibition place was of no consequence. That first Monday evening the show was a sellout and remained so for the six days they showed there.

The show moved en masse to Greenpoint and then to Williamsburg just blocks away from their starting place on Fulton Avenue in Brooklyn. The next moves were to Jersey City and Hoboken.

The short hops provided an opportunity to smooth out hiccups in the moving process before setting out on the open road in earnest. By the time they headed to Paterson, New Jersey, nearly thirty miles away, the processes of collapsing tents, packing up, moving creatures and humans and setting it all back up again in the new place was practiced and somewhat efficient.

Sunday 23 April 1871
13th Street, Manhattan

Annie stood in front of the little mirror in her apartment and inspected her well-groomed image with a critical eye. A small face with nicely arched eyebrows compensated for slightly too-thin lips. Although her twenty-eight-year-old expression was set and firm, her small brown eyes sparkled ever so slightly exposing her inherent good humor. Annie was an optimist, a hard worker, and disciplined. She stood on her tippy toes and looking in the mirror again, adjusted the brooch and chain that fastened the front of her fancy black travel dress tightly at her neck.

"Mama! Mama!" came little William's voice ahead of the young boy's feet which propelled him into the room. "It's working, Mama! The arm is healing! I can feel it!"

Grandma Margaret, Annie's mother and William's nanny while the Barnum show was on the road, had taken the eight-year-old for his smallpox vaccine ten days previous. The scab had formed beautifully before young William scraped it off in a fit of itching. The pit formed by the vaccine and subsequent injury was taking its sweet time to heal and William was not leaving it alone. Last evening Annie had come home from the show in Hoboken to spend one night before the show headed to Paterson, New Jersey some twenty miles away. This was her last time to see her son until the tenting season was over. She brought a present for William. She had fashioned a single shoulder board like President Ulysses S. Grant wore on his uniform during the war. It had four beautiful white Army General Stars sewn onto a dark blue background and was framed with a broad border of gold. It had a loop to hold it up on the shoulder cap as well as two thin straps (one with a button and one with a loop) to fasten it around his arm. After washing the wound and smearing it with honey, she attached the general's insignia to William's arm, covering the wound.

She told him that generals were brave men and disciplined. They listened to the field surgeons and did as they were told, "Leave the sore alone to heal."

The costume had the intended effect. William imagined he was a general in President Grant's army. His chin lifted a little higher and his shoulders stiffened to attention. Although he disciplined himself to not uncover the sore and look, he was certain it was better because he was a brave army general.

Annie gave last minute instructions to her mother for the summer including how to reach her on the road should it be of dire necessity. She spoke gently to her little boy, reiterating the need for him to be a brave soldier and be nice to his grandmother. Annie took one last look at her image in the hall mirror, made sure all her buttons were fastened and tidy, put on her coat and picked up her small bag. She opened the door to leave, turned and smiled at her family.

"I will be back soon. *Slán*. Stay safe," she whispered as she closed the door behind her.

— CHAPTER TWENTY —

CHARLEY WHITE HAD HIS HANDS full being the "Dominant Hero of Wild Beasts" at Barnum, Coup and Castello. He had three assistants Abdul Zid, Karl Shishak, and Mial Zaldad to help him care for, move, and show the most dangerous animals in the menagerie.

While the hyena, panther, jaguar, polar bear, sun bear, and leopards were new to his stewardship, the lions were old friends. Barnum had bought the whole pride from him and then hired him to tend them. A weight lifted from his shoulders; He still had the cats, but no longer had to worry about finding work to feed them. He had his cake and was eating it, too.

The 25th of April two new tigers arrived by boat from Liverpool. Abdul and Mial had gone to New York harbor to fetch them and bring them back to the menagerie currently set up in Morrison. That next morning when Charley heard that a circus wagon had been struck by a train and several died, he thought the two full-grown Bengal tigers must have perished along with his two assistants. He awaited word in grim silence as he tended the animals. It wasn't until late afternoon that the two assistants arrived with their precious cargo, all in good health. They had been delayed, but it was not they who had perished.

A cook wagon loaded with supplies, a driver and five employees had been headed for Elizabeth to set up for the 27th of April. The five men riding in the back of the wagon were sleeping, as was customary for a moving circus wagon. What was not expected was for the driver to also fall asleep and fail to stop at the railroad tracks. The two mules were obliterated by the passenger train as they crossed in front of it near Cranford. Four men were killed outright and a fifth died later.

Barnum, up in Bridgeport at the time, gave orders to have the deceased returned to their families with all possible haste. The wardrobe department immediately set out to deliver black "mourning" armbands to the staff. When Charley saw Karl Kowalski at the tent entrance, his heart skipped a beat; maybe Annie was with him? She was not. He took the bands and after thanking Karl, headed back to work. The show would go on. Expenses don't stop. Animals still needed to eat.

The Barnum, Coup, and Castello show had become a rumbling giant of perpetual activity. With the exception of Sundays (the day of rest) and bigger cities where they sometimes stayed for longer than one day, they travelled daily to a new town. In Providence, Rhode Island they had a two-day stand; they showed both Friday and Saturday, the second and third of June.

Before the end of the last show on Saturday night, some of the wagons were already on the road traveling the eighteen miles to Fall River. Drivers, keepers and crew slept in crowded tents in close proximity to their wards. They would only sleep once they had safely arrived at their new destination.

Management, wardrobe, athletes, equestrians and entertainers spent the night in hotels in Providence. Some would attend a local church on Sunday before making their way to the next stand.

By 9 a.m. Monday morning June 5th the whole kit and caboodle was assembled just outside of Fall River, Massachusetts.

While menagerie and museum wagons made ready for the grand exhibition, wagons loaded down with tents, poles and supplies (along with their assigned crews) headed out for Mr. Hood's lot on Highland Road where the show would set up.

One division of the circus that did not display itself openly was the "Marvelous Human Phenomena." Part of the draw to get people to buy tickets for the show was their insatiable need to stare at human oddities. Giving away the sight of them in a parade would be self-defeating. The whole show had been well-described in the "Advance Courier" and wherever they went people were waiting in line to see thirteen-year-old Admiral Dot (twenty-five-inch-high dwarf dressed in military uniform and riding in a miniature chariot with small ponies), the French Giant who was over eight feet tall, Annie Leak the armless girl, the Infant Esau (Annie Jones, aged seven) the little girl with long dark hair all over her body and of course, the fat couple, John and Mary Powers. They arrived in unmarked wagons incognito, blending in with the wardrobe, dining, and tent wagons.

The parade wagons lined up neatly in a preordained order. Ten camels were harnessed to the front of the "Chariot of Orpheus" bandwagon to lead the procession. There were thirty shiny new lacquered wagons in the procession and an abundance of beautiful horses, and costumed riders. Some of the wagons had automated mechanical features made to move by gearing them to the wagon's axel. One such wagon had a rosebud that opened revealing a statue of cupid. Another, the "Temple of Juno" supported a bejeweled throne (adorned with a dazzling queen) and sporting a telescoping canopy that rose to thirty feet in the air. Two men with long poles positioned themselves just in front of it to "lift" any telegraph lines that might be drooping down in the path of the wagon. Halfway back was the "Car of the Muses" which was a smaller wagon (about twelve feet by eight) which had two mirrors (one on each side), four knights in shining armor (facing outward from the four corners of the platform), and a small brass band (with their backs to one another) all facing out toward the crowd.

Everyone focused on pulling off the best, well-organized extravaganza possible. The public, intrigued by what they saw and heard, would follow the procession to the ticket wagons. The quiet low-key buzz of activity was disrupted only by the random snorts and growls from ready horses and restless lions and the metallic warming-up toots and peeps of the band preparing to belt out lively, happy music through the primary streets of the lucky town.

The wardrobe cart started at the back and made its way systematically up the line of parade wagons handing out sequined costumes for both man and beast. The elephant and camel blankets were beautiful, sewn with silk and metal thread to shimmer as the animals paraded. The procession was a show of extravagance and attention was given to every detail. Charley caught a glimpse of Mrs. Donovan as the wardrobe process began just in front of him. He hoped she would look up, but she did not. Instead, she concentrated, lips pursed, eyes focused, hands ever busy, discerning, touching, observing every beautiful garment entrusted to her care. Once the trunks were empty, the wardrobe department would proceed to the grounds to set up their tent where garments were repaired, stored, and washed. As the procession concluded at the lot, Annie and her ladies would be waiting out front to take back the costumes. The delicate regalia would once again be neatly folded between layers of tissue paper and returned to the trunks, ready for tomorrow's exhibition.

They had been on the road for fifty-five days and shown in thirty-eight different towns. With the exception of the train accident, all had gone well. Receipts were far better than expected and management was euphoric whenever they had time to be. Charley had kept an eye out for Annie since Brooklyn. He hadn't meant to, but he did. He looked for her in the dining tent, but only caught a glimpse of her on rare occasions as she came in or went out. All departments were segregated. Management had their table. The menagerie (including

Charley and his assistants) had a different table. The equestrians, clowns, and other entertainers were given their own assigned areas to sit. As soon as the grand procession was over, costumes returned and wagons secured, everyone went to the newly erected dining tent and ate the noontide meal. Waiters brought food and drink to every table in a preordained sequence and then systematically collected the dishes for washing. There was no opportunity for Charley to bump into the little mistress whose snappy brown eyes had caught his fancy.

The show tents opened at 1:00 p.m. and 7:00 p.m. every day although business had been so good there was talk of increasing to three shows a day. Shows commenced at 2:00 p.m. and 8:00 p.m. They had started out with two exhibition tents in Brooklyn in April but had quickly added a third before they left New Jersey. There was the hippodrome tent for racing and competitions, the menagerie tent full of animals, and the museum tent with all its curiosities, human, dried, preserved, and mechanical. The "nut" or breakeven point for the show was $2,500 a day. They could accommodate 5,000 people at a time at 50 cents per adult (25 cents per child under nine). They had made expenses every day and often nearly doubled what they needed.

The outfit did have extraordinary expenses now and then, so it was good to have a little extra. On the morning of the eighth of June in Plymouth, Massachusetts one of the elephants got loose. He lumbered off through fields knocking down fences and crops and ended up raiding the pantry of a clergyman. Compensation was doled out immediately to pay for trample-damages, for the contents of an entire bag of cornmeal and for the three tubs of milk the pachyderm slurped up.

1871 June 12-17
Boston, Massachusetts

By the time they made it to Boston for a five-day stand at the fairgrounds, everyone was grateful for the reprieve. It was not a vacation of course as there were still two shows to put on every day. However, the time normally spent traveling and parading was happily spent sleeping, socializing, and repairing equipment. Not only did they have five days in Boston (and six nights), but their very next move was less than three miles away and the next five stops after that were five miles or thereabouts. This densely populated area provided plenty of customers and a bounty of time saved. Charley was a little bored. When not tending his "dangerous animals" or inspecting their wagons, he had little to do. He did have a gladiator costume he wore when he fed the lions publicly in the menagerie to the great appreciation of the awestruck audience, but he only wore it twice a day for an hour, so it wasn't often in need of cleaning or repair. The animal cages and wagons were maintained regularly, so there was nothing to do there. For years he had struggled to keep up with the rigors of big cat ownership and he wasn't used to being idle. He walked the lot quite often and found himself outside the wardrobe tent watching the entertainers come and go as they prepared for the next show or turned in their costumes after the last show. He watched young women hauling buckets of water to do laundry and then a bit later, he watched as they hung clothes on lines just outside the tent. In five days, he had caught but one glimpse of his new fascination. She had come to the tent door her arm wrapped protectively around the waist of a willowy woman gymnast. As the lithe young woman prepared to walk away, Annie caught her arm at the elbow stopping her retreat. Charley watched as Annie spoke earnestly to the young woman, her hands flying about her in an attempt to convince the delicate creature of some profound truth. The young woman nodded over and over again while wiping away plentiful tears. Annie reached up and patted the child on her shoulder reassuringly. As the young woman walked away, Annie's eyes followed her. She must have felt Charley's gaze upon her for she relinquished her attention on the young woman and turned to stare directly into the bright blue eyes of her admirer.

Charley's stomach flipped a somersault. Unable to break from her gaze he walked forward. Having no idea what he would say to her, he quickly made something up.

"Hello, Mrs. Donovan," he bowed slightly in front of her. "How are you getting along? I was wondering if there was anything I can do for you." He had no idea why he had said that. One department did not ever offer to help another without being asked by management or…at least being asked by someone.

"Mr. White?" Annie asked as if she was unsure who he was when, in fact, her own heart was fluttering alarmingly. For the moment she utterly forgot the girl who just left with an enormous bruise given to her by her new and impatient husband.

"Yes," he answered, "Charley White, a friend of Karl's… with the lions," he stammered.

"Oh yes, of course…. We are doing very well, thank you, but it is very kind of you to offer," she continued, her eyes sparkling with restrained laughter. "I believe we suited a costume for you to show your lions! Does it hold up well, or do you need repairs?"

Charley did not recall the rest of the exchange, except that Annie assured him that if she should need his assistance, she would ask. When he got back to his tent, Karl was waiting for him. There was bad news. Their mutual friend of old, Mr. Langworthy the elephant trainer Charley worked with when they went on the road with the Van Amburgh and GC Quick show, had died of dropsy a few weeks back while (still) working for the Van Amburgh Menagerie in Tecumseh, Michigan.

Such joy at meeting Annie and such sorrow at the loss of an old friend, all in the span of a few minutes, was overwhelming. He thanked Karl for the news and went off to pet his lions. Mr. Langworthy had taught him kindness for all animals. And, he reckoned, animals were often kinder than humans.

Although the next towns were very close to each other, there was a new one every day and they all required a procession with pomp and circumstance. There was little time for tending to the affairs of the heart. But, he still looked for her at every parade, at every meal, and he took every opportunity to pass by the wardrobe tent. At night, she slept in town in a hotel while he slept in a menagerie supply wagon next to his animals.

If there was little opportunity for show people to socialize on the road, there was even less opportunity as they traveled through Maine. Starting in late July, they began putting on three shows a day to accommodate the hordes of visitors that showed up to buy tickets.

1871 July 29
Waterville, Maine

Visitors had taken special excursion trains and traveled up to eighty miles to catch the show. Some trains arrived on Friday night for the Saturday shows. They came from as far away as Bangor and Gardiner. One such train was twenty-seven cars in length and packed with people coming to see the circus in Waterville on Saturday, the 29th of July.

By 9 a.m. it was apparent that even if they filled the tents with five thousand souls three times during that day, not everyone would be accommodated.

Waterville had a populace of less than five thousand people. The day of the show, the number more than quadrupled. The railroad had only just been completed through the little town and locals were anxious to encourage commerce. Town authorities erected huge tents in the field adjacent to the circus to provide shade and a resting place for the throng of visitors. They arranged for barrels of fresh water (and ice) to be delivered and replenished at regular intervals. Liquor sales were suspended so as to avoid controversial behavior.

Barnum, Coup and Castello, in an attempt to accommodate the extraordinary number of visitors, decided to run continuous shows from nine o'clock in the morning onward. It had never been done before. It was only the arrival of a summer storm that brought a heavy downpour that closed the show at nine o'clock in the evening. For athletes, clowns, costumers, and animals it was a true blessing that the following day, July 30th, was a Sunday

The season took them through Maine, New Hampshire, Vermont, and many towns in New York. In Syracuse they had seating capacity for nine thousand and the tent was filled at both exhibitions. By the time they arrived in Rochester, they were again giving three shows a day to satisfy the crowds. In Buffalo, not only were the tents filled to capacity, but Barnum was giving temperance lectures in town. Coup and Castello were important certainly, but it was Barnum's name that sold tickets.

On October 28th when they closed out the tenting season in Harlem, the outfit had visited one-hundred-fifty-five cities and towns. There would be little time for resting before they opened again at the Empire Arena near the center of the Rink at Third Avenue and Sixty-Third Street. (Barnum had paid Mr. Wood twelve thousand dollars to cancel their agreement so he would once again be able to have his show in New York City.) They expected great crowds and many amusements were planned, complete with new costumes made by New York costumers. The workforce scattered like minnows in a pond. They had the weekend to visit family, eat, rest, do laundry and get ready for the winter run on Monday. Charley headed to New Jersey to visit his two sons living with his ex-wife. Barnum was already up in Connecticut babbling on and on about what a great summer it had been. Coup and Castello were scheming and had been for weeks about how to reach more large towns next summer. Annie Donovan got into Karl's wagon to be driven home to her Thirteenth Street apartment. She hadn't seen William for months. He had turned nine on July 26th while she was away. As she rode in the cart, she closed her eyes and could see his face. It dawned on her that she missed him terribly now that she had time.

CHAPTER TWENTY-ONE

EMPIRE RINK
MANHATTAN, NY
DECEMBER 1871

THE ANIMAL AREA WAS A bloody slaughterhouse, no other word for it. Diablo the hyena had wreaked havoc during the night when he'd gotten out of his cage. The prey animals unfortunate enough to be in its wake, were either dead or dying when Charley got in that morning. Thanks to assistance from a pair of the Digger Indians, Diablo was sleeping off his escapade in a cage with iron bars securely located within the confines of another larger iron cage. The Fiji Island cannibals couldn't face their fear of the African dog and ran off to the arena to hide when all hell broke loose. The Digger Indians from Yosemite gave Barnum's customers an idea what real Indian life was like because they truly were full-blooded native American Indians. They knew how to survive in the wild and had grown up around mountain lions and grizzly bears. It wasn't the first time they'd come to Charley's aid. They yearned for the wilderness and the life they led with their tribe. Working in the menagerie when they weren't acting in the show made them feel more at home. Besides, they were darn good with the creatures. They had a knack for it.

Charley turned to his son, "Not a word to your mother," he declared. As soon as he had gotten back in town at season's close, he'd gone to New Jersey to see his sons, Charles Henry and William Albert. Fifteen-year-old Charles Henry was being a typical teenager, not something his mother was happy about. Not only did he continuously annoy and tease his thirteen-year-old little brother, but he was constantly in trouble.

First and foremost, the boy didn't get on with his stepfather, Alexander Beaks. Beaks was just fifteen years older than Charles Henry and they butted heads at every turn. The apartment in New Jersey was overcrowded and there wasn't a lot of money to throw around. Nancy's little sister, Eliza still lived with them. Eliza was twenty, not married yet and a wild-eyed redhead. Nancy was afraid for her virtue having been given the responsibility of rearing her own sister to adulthood.

When Charley showed up to see if his boys wanted to come stay with him in the city and work, he got an earful. He was told the money he sent was not enough, they needed more. William needed a special teacher. He wasn't quite right, had never spoken much, and had taken to sleeping most of the time to avoid his brother's torments. Charles Henry had been caught stealing that summer and while the grocer let him off with a warning and paying for the fruit, it was still stealing. To add insult to injury, he came home drunk after spending the Fourth of July with a neighbor boy and showed no remorse.

Charles Henry went with his dad that same day and William was left to recover from whatever ailed him. He had refused to leave his bed to even greet his father. Nancy, in spite of wanting someone else to handle her eldest son, was an almighty protector. "Keep him away from those lions and make sure he gets a bath once a week, promise?" She'd demanded.

Well, work remedies most ailments of childhood. Busy hands keep a kid from being a nuisance. He'd put the boy to use helping to feed animals and muck out cages. There was always too much work to do and not enough hours to do it. In the beginning it was more work having the kid help than not having him there at all. He had to teach him and make sure everything was done right. Charles Henry thrived in the menagerie even if he was a little overly proud that his dad was now not only the "Lion King," but also "Master of the Zoological Department."

Charley stood, hands on hips observing the carnage. "We have to clean this mess up quickly, son," he said. "The animals are on edge and the smell of fresh slaughter makes them unpredictable. We gotta calm 'em down."

He threw a canvas tarp over the outer cage holding the hyena, so the other animals didn't have to live with the deadly stare of the predator. Several men began the gruesome chore of gathering up the dead. The hyena had tried its luck with a tiger and lion, but the big cats reciprocated, and the hyena had big bloody wounds on its rump, both sides. He'd recover. The zebra and camel fared less well. While not killed outright, they were mortally wounded and had to be put down. Two monkeys had stood no chance against Diablo's deadly jaws. One of them was Monty, Charley's favorite.

The famous Mr. Bergh of the Society for the Prevention of Cruelty to Animals had paid a visit to the Rink to inspect the conditions under which the animals were kept. Since Mr. Barnum and Charley agreed wholeheartedly that kindly treated animals not only lived longer but were more pleasant to be around, the menagerie was well-kept. Mr. Bergh, after his detailed inspection, gave a hand-written report to Mr. Barnum which indicated that he too was pleased with the conditions under which the creatures were kept… with one exception, the hyena. Now the hyena is a vicious predator and for years had not only been kept in a cage, but also anchored by a chain to the floor. It wasn't cruel. There was plenty of chain so the animal could move around all it wanted within the cage, but it was necessary because the animal was so dangerous. He could kill people. Mr. Bergh insisted the chain be removed. Mr. Barnum conceded that possibly it was a good idea. Charley had only shaken his head and followed orders.

Christmas came and Christmas went and nothing much changed in the menagerie. Hordes of bored New Yorkers trekked through day in and day out, some of the nasty ones throwing whatever they had in hand at the animals to get their attention. If Charley had his way, there would be thick glass between his animals and the taunters, but the visitors paid the bills, so they had to live with it.

The shows in the arena would continue from eleven in the morning until ten at night right on through the sixth of January. The new season and show would open at The Empire Rink the first of April. Although it would appear that the whole outfit had twelve weeks off to rest and recuperate, that was the last thing they had time for. Before the tenting season commenced, a whole world of things needed to get done. Wagons needed fixing, horses needed re-shodding, a grand entrée needed to be organized, costumes needed to be designed and fitted, and the different entertainments needed to be choreographed and practiced. And, in particular this year, a whole gigantic show had to be put on rails. In total there would be sixty railroad cars plus passenger cars with sleeping quarters attached, divided into two trains of thirty-three, each being pulled by two engines. Everything from animal cages to parade wagons needed to fit on the rail cars.

As the menagerie animals relaxed free from the prying eyes of the public during the winter hiatus, Charley and his son worked to ready their wards for the daunting summer of travel ahead. Animals that had been loaned out to the zoo for the winter were reunited with the rest of the menagerie on 3rd Avenue and 63rd street. All of the creatures needed to get used to being moved by the crew again. Horses, both the performing and wagon-pulling variety, had to be conditioned to living on the rails so they didn't spook and kill themselves. They practiced loading and unloading the led-stock, good practice for both man and beast. They loaded and unloaded the oversized lion and tiger cages to determine the best way to facilitate a smooth transfer.

An army of 130 working men (not counting management) worked day in and day out to execute the plan. Not only would every single animal travel and sleep on the trains, management, performers and crew would as well.

Annie Donovan, still under the management of Fred Hamilton, Master of Properties and Wardrobe, rarely saw her manager. She was given a list of costumes to be made and he expected her to get it done. It was a good arrangement for all concerned. She was good at organizing and it made her happy to coordinate not only the maintenance of the current wardrobe, but to arrange for the assembly of the new one. She had learned from the previous season which New York costumers were good and which were not. Her knowledge about fabric had grown deep through the past nine years in wardrobe. Even if her name was not on the list of management or assistants, she was happy, nearly autonomous, and confident.

She was a widow with a young child, but she was not destitute or helpless. She was self-supporting and proud. Today was Valentine's Day, the 14th of February 1872, exactly six months to the day short of her 30th birthday. She stood on tiptoe and turned the wall calendar to find August 14th. It fell on a Wednesday. Good. She could ignore it much easier than she could have if it had fallen on a Sunday

She was dressed as usual in her widow's weeds. She had discarded the veil and gloves, kept the fancy black parasol and had added a few black chiffon ruffles to wrist, waist, and hem. "Not quite mourning clothes," she thought aloud while inspecting her appearance in the half-length mirror in the dressing room. Pinching her cheeks hard enough to bring on a little color, Annie laughed at her own image in the glass. While she wasn't tall or elegant and was entirely incapable of riding a trick horse in the circus, she was passably attractive. Her small Irish face was adorned with lovely brown eyes and framed by soft blonde hair skillfully contained in a knot at the back of her neck. The lips although small were perpetually held in a position which indicated to the outside world that she held a very juicy secret. Should the half smile ever leave her face, there would be no one to see it. While she would gladly share her happiness, any sadness she might feel would remain hers alone.

"Mama!" Came a boy's voice to break the reverie. "I couldn't find the blue velvet you wanted; can you help me?" He asked.

Annie turned at the sound of her son's approach. He was the love of her life and at nine years of age, still an innocent child. He was the spit of his father, slim built, delicate, black straight hair and startlingly beautiful blue eyes framed in long black eyelashes. "His father's son," she whispered aloud to no one. She had missed him last season. She did not intend to leave him behind again, but she would not have to. He was old enough this year to stay with her and be her official helper, someone to fetch things, deliver things, and keep her company. Besides, they were going to travel by train, an easier and safer method of transport than wagons.

"I'll be with you in a moment, William" she said turning back to her mirror. In front of her on the vanity tray lay a stickpin three inches long with a small globe on top. Inside the clear bauble was a tiny rose made of dark pink glass. Because it reminded her of the wild roses her husband used to bring, she had splurged and bought the pin from one of the glass blowers that routinely set up outside the show tents. The pin was beautiful and was appropriate given that it had been more than two years since poor William passed. She gathered the top front of her dress at the collar and deftly fastened it with her pin.

"There!" She exclaimed to her waiting child, "Let's go find that velvet, shall we?"

25 April 1872
Philadelphia, PA

They had enjoyed four whole days in Philadelphia. The weather had held up making life easier for man and beast alike. Costumes stayed nicer when their owners weren't traipsing through the mud, but that wasn't the sole reason that Annie Donovan was happy. She had slept the sleep of the innocent for three nights, three nights where the blessed train wasn't moving. Naturally life was easier when all of your things stayed in one place while you lived day-to-day, but she was not used to trying to sleep while the train chugged forward, its iron wheels bumping over the spaces between the rails… clickety-clack clickety-clack clickety-clack all night long. She and William had slept, head to toe in the wide bunk in their spot in the women and children's sleeping car. Young William slept soundly only awakening when his mother shook his shoulder in the morning to get dressed for breakfast. Annie on the other hand, had only slept fitfully since they left New York. She had hoped that once they got out of New Jersey, she would be used to the sounds and feel of a moving train at night. Tonight was just a one-mile journey to West Philadelphia. There they had a two-day stand, so she reckoned she could rest easy for a couple more nights. She would never complain to a living sole. She had seven ladies working with her to keep the wardrobe top notch. They looked to her for leadership and if she wanted them to be positive and pleasant then she needed to remain positive and pleasant. After all, their show, "The Greatest Show on Earth" as it was now advertised, should also have the best wardrobe on earth.

By the time "P.T. Barnum's Great Traveling Museum, Menagerie and World's Fair consisting of Museum, Menagerie, Aquarium, Aviary, Polytechnic Institute, International Zoological Garden, and Dan Castello's Chaste and Refined Circus" had traversed Pennsylvania and was headed off toward Baltimore for the May Day show, the train sounds were familiar and comforting. The moving train meant the day's work was done and it was time to rest. Sleep overcame most just after the single short whistle that signaled departure and the initial bursts of steam signaled the laboring engines were hauling the iron horses and her thirty-three cars down the track. By the time the two steam engines had produced enough momentum to achieve optimum traveling speed and the chug-chug-chug rhythm was achieved, most were fast asleep. The trains followed one another, thirty-three cars and two engines took the lead and another train in the same configuration followed just after. The railroad crew depended heavily upon steam-whistles and toots to maintain order and safety.

What woke the sleepers on the train was the danger-proclamation of four very-long steam whistles and the brakes squealing on the wheels beneath them grinding the train to a sudden halt.

Her first thought was "accident" and the second was "there was no crashing sound." Annie's train was able to stop its progress before running into the back of the twin circus train in front of it.

Whispers and words came bumping out from behind the sleeping berth curtains, robes were hastily wrapped around night-clad shoulders and pairs of bare white legs dangled out, their attached feet swinging like dual pendulums.

"What happened?" Asked one of the wardrobe girls to no one in particular, "What should we do?"

"Wait," said Annie, "Someone will be by to tell us what is happening." And just as she said that a heavy fist pounded on the entry door.

"Cover up, ladies, I'm coming in," hollered the familiar voice of Karl Kowalski, Mr. Hamilton's right-hand man.

Karl opened the end door leading into the sleeping area. Annie thought he looked as wide as he was tall standing there in the half light. He held his lantern up high so the women could see him.

"Train-One missed a switch or something. We don't know yet what the situation is. Train-Two is just fine. We stopped in time. I will come back in a few minutes and tell you what needs to be done. For now, please remain inside. We think some animals got loose, no telling yet." Karl nodded at Annie as if seeking her concurrence.

"Yes, Mr. Kowalski," we shall stay inside our car and await further instructions," she stated clearly and with authority. "Ladies, be so kind as to light one or two lanterns so we don't stumble over one another.

Sleep had been replaced by apprehensive fear of the unknown. What happened? Was anyone hurt? Train-One held most of the animals and the animal act performers as well as the men from the railway crew and equestrian performers. Train-Two was management, the cooks, and the women and children. They had just left Erie Pennsylvania on their way to Corrie. The hour was just past one in the morning.

The windows on the left side of the train in the seating area were crowded with the former occupants of the sleeping births. They could see movement of lanterns dancing down the hill in front of them. A great bright railroad lantern lit up a wider area and they were able to see men crawling over the tops of rail cars. The outline of one must have been Karl Kowalski for his size was unmistakable. Using imagination to see between the pricks of light from the lanterns, the ladies conceded it must have been animal cages on the cars that had crashed down the hillside.

The date was the seventh of June and daylight arrived about five o'clock. As the dark cloudy night turned to gray morning, the ladies in Train-Two began stirring again and peering curiously out the side windows. Immediately apparent were three rail cars lying in disarray in the ditch below the tracks. Men and mules were attempting to lift the lion cages back up to the track for reloading. Nothing that Annie could see was covered with a blanket, so no dead were immediately apparent.

"Cover up ladies" Came a shout and a banging from outside the sleeping car door, "I'm coming in," bellowed Karl. He waited the long count of fifteen as was customary and then opened the door, took off his hat and began speaking.

"We are lucky. No man died last night. Some lions got out when cages crashed, but Mr. White moved animals to different cage. We will go soon." Karl cleared his throat. "I am sorry. Two baby kittens were killed, but one is all right and is with mother." He cleared his throat yet again, "Do not worry. Mr. Coup said we will be in Corry for second show. Breakfast will be when we get there." He looked at Mrs. Donovan and nodded, "All right?" He asked quietly, put on his hat and departed the way that he had come.

By the time they reached Corry the whole crew had heard some version of the story. A railroad engineer had missed the switch and the leading train jumped the tracks. Both locomotives and several cars derailed. Two of Mr. White's Asiatic male lions were set free when their cage door sprang open. Although most shrank from the ferocious growls of the frightened kings of the jungle, Mr. White simply fastened a narrow leather strap around each lion's neck, one in turn, and led them calmly to a secure enclosure. The lioness was more of an issue. Two of her three cubs lay dead at her feet on the floor of the cage. One kitten, alive and mewing piteously, was being lifted in its mother's mouth repeatedly and put down again as if she did not know if she should take him and run or just protect him right there.

Finally, Mr. White, being well known to the mother, gently took up the kitten in his arms and carried him to an awaiting cage. The lioness followed, seemingly relieved to be led to safety.

The whole outfit sang the praises of Mr. White, his calm demeanor and control over the animals. His very presence, they insisted, calmed the animals and made them docile and compliant. Mr. White's son, a good half-foot taller than his father, strutted around for days as if it were he himself that saved the lions from disaster. Annie caught sight of the hero as he took breakfast with his menagerie crew. He could have dined at the management table but chose to stay with his people. Charley looked up from his meal in time to meet Annie's gaze. Their eyes locked. Each, overcome with embarrassment, looked away in an instant.

+ + +

Annie Donovan's son, William Albert Donovan, Jr. was not a brave country boy. He was curious, but not brave enough to give in to his curiosity. He wanted to see the lions that Mr. White took care of, but the closest he could talk himself into getting was the door of the menagerie tent in between shows when the public wasn't around. Charles Henry saw him and walked over.

"Hey" he said, "I'm Charles, who are you?"

"My name is William Donovan Junior, sir" was the polite reply he had been taught to give.

"Who do you belong to," asked the older boy, "are you that wardrobe lady's kid?"

"My mother is Mrs. Donovan, sir" answered William "and I am not a kid, sir, I am a boy and I will be ten years old next month so I am nearly a man." Annie Donovan did not allow her son to use slang words and she insisted that everyone older than he was would be called "sir" or "ma'am."

"Well, hear hear!" Exclaimed Charles Henry laughing at the boy, "You really are something, aren't you!" He laughed a little extra. "Do you want to see the lions, or are you scared?"

"Will they bite?" Asked the younger boy looking up at his elder.

"You bet they can bite" answered Charles seriously. "But you should not get close enough for them to get at ya. Dad won't even let me pet them yet." He sighed with sadness. "So, want to come closer or not? Are you chicken?"

No matter how scared he was, he could not let a dare like that go by.

"Sure," he said, chin jutting out in defiance as he moved a few steps closer to the cages.

Whether it was because Charles Henry liked William or because he was just homesick for his own little brother, he was both kind and instructive. For fifteen minutes he led William around the cages introducing him to the big cats.

"That big one is Jim," said Charles Henry. "He's more than twenty years old and dad says he's the oldest lion he's come across." He watched as the big male lion sauntered over to the side of the cage and backed his rump up against the bars. "He's looking to have his butt scratched," laughed Charles Henry, "but dad said not to pet him. Dad's the only one that pets the big cats. They aren't safe."

William was glad he was not allowed to touch the animal, but he was enjoying having Charles Henry for company. He spent most of his time with the women in the dressing room tent and in his life had not had many opportunities to meet other boys except at school.

A big man approached the two boys, a man both boys knew on sight.

"Hi there Mr. Donovan!" Said Karl Kowalski as he approached William. "Your mother is looking for you! You'd better skedaddle on over to wardrobe and check in with her!"

William started heading out of the tent but stopped to wave good-bye to his new friend. "Can I come back again?" He asked. Charles Henry nodded and waved the boy out. He knew about mothers that worry too much. He felt a little sorry for the kid… being in the constant company of a bunch of women.

On the thirteenth of June in Canton, Ohio there was a death among the crew. A railroad man by the name of Henry Forney drowned while bathing in a creek. They put his body in a wooden box hastily nailed together and transported him to Canton to be shipped home to New York. Charles Henry, now a somewhat frequent companion of young William Donovan, managed to sneak into the freight car where the body was held. He might not have had the courage to open the box and look at the dead man by himself, but once he'd roped William into tagging along, he had to do it. Willian did not want to look but did not want Charles Henry to think him a coward.

Now both boys had seen a dead body. Without a word (not needed) about keeping their secret, the two parted ways and made a beeline back to their own places on the train. Annie did not know why her son was so quiet and preferred to stay in the tent after that, not venturing out to visit his new friend or look at the animals. She did understand he was lonely. Options were limited, but she knew of another child, a little girl, who was frightfully alone most of the time, Annie Jones, the seven-year-old bearded child sometimes called the Infant Esau.

Wardrobe had been asked to make repairs to little Annie Jones's dress, the one she wore when she was on display with the other human oddities. Although the garment had been well constructed with every feminine ruffle and bow, it had begun to strain at the seams as the slender child grew.

While fitting the mended costume, Mrs. Donovan began to feel a sort of motherly empathy towards the shy little girl with hair every-where it shouldn't be. Even though the girl's mother traveled with the show and kept her daughter company, there was an unmistakable air of loneliness about the Infant Esau. It was a sadness no good mother could ignore. Mrs. Donovan would do something to make it better. She invited little Annie Jones to have "tea" with her and William in the wardrobe tent.

One Sunday afternoon the tea was arranged with milky tea and small cakes that Mrs. Donovan had wrangled out of the cook's supply. The magic of friendship was kindled and the seven-year-old adored William. Annie Jones was quiet, sweet, and soft spoken and William loved her like a child would love a kitten. Although the curiosity department and wardrobe department did not normally socialize in any way on the show grounds or in the dining tent, an exception was made for the children. They played games together, sang songs, and even took their meals at the same table. Everyone was happy, the mothers and the children. It would be a long summer which was better spent with a friend.

They made their way through Ohio stopping only in the larger cities, most of the time for just one day with three shows in each city at 11:00 a.m., 2:00 p.m., and 8:00 p.m. before moving on. Saturday the thirteenth of July brought another death to mourn, that of one of the drivers, Mr. Charles Carter. It was a freak accident, one which Charles Henry would never forget. Mr. Carter had taken his team to the aqueduct in Hamilton to give them a good drink and a much-needed bath. He rode the lead horse into the water and the others followed. Charles Henry had run along beside them to help herd the horses should they need guidance and watched in horror as Mr. Carter drowned. The horse he was riding walked into a sunk spot and Mr. Carter fell off. The horse, spooked by sinking into the mud, kicked Mr. Carter in the head and the poor man never had a chance. Other drivers were waiting their turn in the aqueduct with their teams and hastened to pull Mr. Carter from the water, but it was to no avail.

His head was clearly bashed in and even though it appeared that he tried to swim to the surface a few times, they realized he was dead the minute the hoof struck him.

The evening show went on as normal. It was Saturday, and the only night scheduled in Hamilton. The Silver Cornet Band played the same happy music as if nothing had happened and the Burnell Brothers presented their side show in their separate tent for only fifteen cents extra. Mr. James Melville, Frank, and George all smiled and flew through their equestrian feats as if they hadn't a care in the world. The tumblers tumbled and little Miss Minnie Marks wowed the crowd with her child equestrienne act. The lion tamer thrilled the audience early on with his fearless handling of the full-grown male lions and then later that same talented man delighted the show goers with the acrobatic antics of his five-dog crew of little white terriers. People clapped and laughed as Admiral Dot, the dwarf, drove his miniature carriage around the ring pulled by miniature horses.

The museum opened to all and showed off its stuffed birds and automatron wonders, the Fiji Cannibals and Digger Indians, Annie Leake the girl with no arms and the Albino family… all without ever whispering a word about the loss of life in the town's reservoir.

Sunday the big tent was turned into a funeral venue where Reverend Starr gave a touching sermon. Mr. Barnum paid for a plot in Greenwood Cemetery. The hat was passed and $200 was gathered to buy a headstone for poor Mr. Carter. The funeral procession was dark and glamorous, Mr. Carter's team and wagon were draped in black, and his cap and coat lay upon the back of his favorite steed. Six attendants wearing badges of mourning walked beside the wagon that bore the coffin.

It was the first funeral Charles Henry had ever witnessed and he hoped his last. William, just two weeks shy of his tenth birthday had seen two funerals before…his father's and his baby sister's. He was profoundly saddened and his friend, little Annie Jones, was there to comfort him. She sat beside him throughout the funeral and held his hand in her hers.

The show moved through Ohio, Indiana, and Missouri without any big problems. They blanketed the big cities in Illinois, Iowa, and Minnesota before steaming through Wisconsin, and in October, Michigan.

Charley White got the okay from Mr. Coup to take a temporary leave from the show after the last stand in Detroit. (Charles Henry would look after the dogs and the menagerie crew could see to the lions.) As the two show trains chugged off toward New York City, Charley boarded a local train north to Hadley to meet his sister who had turned thirty-four in his absence. He had not set eyes on her since before the war when her drunken husband went AWOL and dragged her off to Michigan. It had taken five years for the family to find her. When William reported back to his family that she was in Michigan with her husband Madison Fitch and her three children, they were all relieved to know she was still alive.

Charley came to Hadley and found his sister on October 31st. The rented house they were living in was too small to hold two adults and three small children. Madison, now going by the name of James to avoid being arrested for deserting the army, came home from his day's work drunk and combative. He threw open the door to the shack and asked who the hell his wife was entertaining. He'd seen them through the window by the light of the lantern. It took a good five minutes to convince the enraged husband that Charley was indeed his wife's big brother. For three days Charley stayed and kept company with his little sister. She was thin and haggard, and he worried she was unwell. "James" went to his carpentry job for several hours each day leaving the siblings time to get to know one another again.

James Madison Fitch was not only a drunk, but he was also a mean drunk. He whipped the horses and came after the children with willow sticks. Emily showed Charley scars on her ankles where her husband had beaten her (where it didn't show) under her long dresses.

"Leave him, little sister," Charley had begged. "Pack up the children and we will catch a train back to New York. I can take care of you. Ben and I and William can help you get back on your feet."

But, she would have none of it.

"He has been trying harder and promised just last night to stop drinking." She sighed. "I am his wife and I am supposed to stay with him until the day we die," she added dropping her gaze to hide her shame.

It was with a heavy heart that Charley took his leave on the third of November, 1872. Each of the children clutched the circus-candy tightly that their Uncle Charley had given them as a parting gift. He stopped on the porch to say his goodbyes and slipped a packet to his sister.

"If it gets bad, you need to leave. There is enough money to get you out of here and to send a telegraph to me. I can send tickets. You just have to ask."

Charley held Emily at arm's length by her shoulders and saw the little sister who adored him when they were younger. The light was gone from her eyes and the joy from her face. There was nothing more he could do except pray she would stay safe.

CHAPTER TWENTY-TWO

JANUARY 1873
MANHATTAN, NY

ANNIE BADE EVERYONE GOOD NIGHT, pulled on her overcoat and wrapped the thick wool scarf around her head and shoulders. It wasn't far to walk home, but it was Manhattan and although only five o'clock, it was dark, windy, and cold. She didn't notice the street sounds or shopkeepers closing up for the night. She was five layers deep in thought, planning an impossible task.

Barnum, Coup, and Castello held their meeting in the auditorium at the Academy of Music. Everyone showed up believing they were henceforth unemployed and would need to find work elsewhere. Oh boy! Were they ever wrong! Barnum had a plan; He would rebuild. Bigger. Better. The Greatest Show on Earth would not only rise again, it would outshine every other show on the planet!

The nightmare had come without warning about four in the morning on December 24th, 1872. The Hippotheatron on Fourteenth Street burned to the ground. The inferno consumed the circus building, neighboring Grace Church, and the old Lawrence mansion. It was only through the valiant efforts of firefighters that more of the city was not destroyed.

The Hippotheatron, long occupied by L.B. Lent's New York Circus had been purchased by Barnum in August. When "P. T. Barnum's Great Traveling Museum, Menagerie, Caravan, Hippodrome, Polytechnic Institute, International Zoological Garden, and Dan Castello's Mammoth Circus" returned from a profitable season on the rails (while other shows floundered losing money to bad weather and presidential-election-malaise) it settled into the vast iron building across the street from the Academy of Music. For Annie it had been a delightful autumn. Not only was the new winter venue just three blocks from her apartment, she had been promoted to "Wardrobe Mistress."

Her proud confidence was short-lived for when the building went up in smoke, her livelihood went with it. The details of destruction were painfully articulated in full-page articles in every newspaper. Rumors spread that the fire marshal (who inspected the building in November) had deemed it unsafe and ordered improvements. Although untrue, it added another layer of darkness.

Two elephants, Betsy and Gypsy, and one double-humped-camel escaped the inferno. The rest of the animals perished. Among the dead were the giraffes, monkeys, a sea lion, leopards, lions, polar bears, innumerable small animals, all of "The Happy Family" collection and Charley White's little band of trained dogs.

Also consumed by the fire was the new wardrobe for the play *Bluebeard* (which had opened to great success at Thanksgiving), the band instruments and the costumes of all the performers. Admiral Dot's fine miniature wagon, the ponies that drew it and all his regalia… all of it was gone.

There were blessings to count: The show's horses were kept in stables far away on Eleventh Street and a portion of Barnum's menagerie was rented out to a circus touring the south. The absolute saving grace was that no human life was lost.

Barnum was in New Orleans when his building burned. His response to (son-in-law) Mr. Hurd's telegram was that they could get more animals from Europe in short order, and they would be ready to go by the end of March, April latest.

They had just under eleven weeks to create a whole new show. All departments were full-steam-ahead gathering, organizing, procuring, planning, and working long hours. Barnum had already hired a costume company, but it was up to Annie to orchestrate the resurrection of the wardrobe department.

Four weeks into the undertaking something terrible happened. A friend died, a contemporary, a colleague, someone they all knew. Where there had been a frenzy of activity, there was stunned silence as the news spread. Dazed in the vacuum of their own mortality they were cruelly reminded how fragile life is and how abruptly it can end.

February 10, 1873
Brooklyn, New York

The drawing room at 317 East Seventeenth Street was small and overcrowded. Ladder-back chairs arranged around the walls faced the humble wooden coffin snugged up against the inside wall. As visitors came in through the front door, they were ushered to one side where they waited to walk by the coffin and look upon the deceased.

"Old Joe Pentland" never made sixty. His brain rotted out from under him and in less than a year, he was dead. Annie stood silently waiting to pay her last respects. When her own husband fell and injured himself in 1862, he could no longer perform the extreme gymnastics that made him famous. It was Joe who took him under his wing and got him a spot as one of the "four clowns" in L. B. Lent's Equescur-riculum. She owed Joe a lot and yet when he became ill, there was little she could do. She had visited him once at the lunatic asylum on Blackwell's Island, but his mind was gone, and he did not know her.

Pressing forward onto the toes of her boots, Annie peered over the edge. Expecting to see a withered old man void of humanity, she was surprised to see the translucent smooth face of a youngish man. Having been artfully groomed for his final journey, he appeared to be resting peacefully.

She moved along and graciously accepted the chair just vacated by a gentleman who saw her coming. Those that followed gathered silently against the wall. As she looked around, it was obvious that she knew almost everyone here. Many were old friends from the war years, people who had traveled with Joe Pentland and L.B. Lent in his conglomeration show.

Those were lean years because shows could not travel south for fear of being overtaken and their horses conscripted for the war effort. As a result, the northeast was over-saturated with entertainment. To beat the competition and stand above the crowd, L. B. Lent consolidated several shows, as many as ten, into one monstrous production called "The Equescurriculum." It went on the road for three seasons in various combinations. The extraordinary size was enough to draw customers into the tent.

Joe Pentland had led the troupe of clowns. He was masterful at entertaining the audience between equestrian and gymnastics acts, a true professional worthy of working in concert with the likes of James Robinson and Madam Louis Tourniajre.

Lent's endeavor made no one rich, but it did provide a way to make a living during deplorable times. Many of the once-in-a-lifetime conglomeration were here this gloomy day. Greetings were kept to glances and nods. They'd lost one of their own to an unspeakable disease. All wore the expression of "but for the grace of God, go I…"and held their hands folded in front of them in respectful silence.

The sermon was short and to the point, God's will had been done and even though Joseph Pentland had lived a moral and temperate life, God had taken him home. God rest his soul. His wife Jane would need their support.

As the final prayer ended, six men rose and carried the closed pine coffin out to the waiting hearse. There were no fresh flowers. It was February. Annie had fashioned a small bouquet of roses from scraps of red velvet which the minister placed upon Joe's coffin before the door closed and he was carted off to Brooklyn's Cypress Hill Cemetery on Jamaica Street. It was a miserable day; freezing rain, blowing wind, slushy streets; and yet a dozen carriages filled with mourners followed Joe home to his rest.

Charley White made his way quickly across the graveyard in a desperate attempt to get to Joe's funeral before it was all over. Tasked with rebuilding the menagerie meant that he had little time for anything else. Today he had met a ship in the harbor that delivered a pair of zebras. He was responsible to ascertain if the offloaded animals were all there and viable. All went as planned this time, but he had been present when shippers tried to say an animal was delivered that wasn't. Occasionally creatures died at sea or were simply butchered to feed the crew. Charley would not miss old Joe's funeral for anything… and yet he had, at least the first part. There hadn't been time to get to the house, but he damn-sure was going to make it graveside.

Annie stood with the mourners and watched as the preacher spoke his final words. Dirt unearthed when the grave was dug had refrozen, but he managed to knock some loose to throw on top of the coffin. "Dust to dust, ashes to ashes," he proclaimed solemnly. "Rest in Peace." The preacher took off his hat and walked around asking for donations for Joe's wife and talking with the assembled. Even though Joe had made over two-hundred-thousand-dollars in his lifetime (according to the papers), he died a pauper. His wife Jane was destitute.

Charley approached the preacher and dropped a twenty-dollar bill into the hat before turning to face the group of huddled mourners. Most knew him and nodded, some shook his hand and others asked how it was going with the rebuild. He caught sight of Annie standing alone near the gravesite and made his way over to her.

"Mrs. Donovan?" he asked quietly as he approached, "How are you? Are you on your own here? May I escort you back?" he inquired.

"Mr. White," replied Annie, "Yes, yes of course, thank you" she replied.

She slipped her fingers through the crook in Charley's arm and without a word they made their way back to the carriages. Even through gloves she felt the warmth and sinewy strength of the man who guided her between the monuments.

When they made it back to the carriage path, they found Lewis B. Lent himself standing beside his big black covered carriage. The owner and manager of "The New York Circus" (scheduled to open the last day of March on Madison Avenue) was a commanding presence in spite of his sixty years. His face lit up as he recognized the pair approaching, arm and arm.

"Charley!" he exclaimed with enthusiasm while simultaneously turning his attention to the little woman. "Mrs. Donovan, my dear lady, how are you?" he asked sincerely.

Annie looked up into the face of the man who stood up for her when her husband died three years ago. Lent had arranged for the funeral, purchased the plot in the cemetery, and kept her employed in wardrobe. He had been there to watch over her until she was able to manage on her own.

"Mr. Lent," she said, "It is good to see you even under such sad circumstance."

Lent turned to Charley and held out a hand, but when Charley offered a hand in return, Lent only laughed dwarfing his younger friend with a generous bear hug.

"And you!" he remarked staring into Charley's face, "You have made something of yourself with Barnum, haven't you! "Professor

White! Or is it Colonel White today?" Lent laughed all the while patting the smaller man on the shoulder with enthusiasm. "And how is that arm, son?"

Charley answered solemnly, "It still works, sir in spite of lions, tigers, and bears!" There was no need to mention the bullet that ruined his left arm below the elbow, rendering it as stiff as an iron rod or the terrible bite he got from the old lion in '67 that froze up his right shoulder. They knew each other's past. There is something precious about old friends that mere words cannot adequately describe.

"You come back to work for me when you get tired of Barnum's hoopla, anytime Charley, any time at all." He said in all seriousness.

Turning to Annie, his voice gentled, "You are welcome to our show and to my home, dear Mrs. Donovan. But I am not going to worry about you now that I know you are in Charley's good hands."

Charley froze. Annie fumbled for her handkerchief. Before either could clarify that the two of them were not a couple, Lent turned his attention elsewhere. This was one of those times of meeting and greeting old friendships too long left in the wilderness.

"Mrs. Donovan, will you be returning to the Rink today? May I offer you a ride?" Barnum, Coup and Castello had brought their two elephants, single surviving double-humped camel and all relevant employees to the Rink to begin the process of rebuilding the show. For the past three weeks, there had been a flurry of activity. New cages, seating, props, hippodrome…everything needed to be rebuilt and ready for reopening the end of March. Mrs. Donovan had her own area in a back room filled to the rafters with sewing machines, bolts of material, wardrobe women and distraught performers waiting to be fitted for new costumes. Karl Kowalski and Mrs. Donovan could be seen fleeting from one place to another measuring everything from horses to monkeys.

"Yes!" smiled Annie sweetly. "No time to waste. …Most kind of you, Mr. White."

Charley offered his hand and helped her into the carriage. Her movement was fluid and feminine and yet agile and deliberate. She literally exuded robust health and quiet strength. A whisper of roses met him as he ascended to the driver's seat and closed the side door. Wordlessly they drove the distance to the Rink. Karl met the carriage at the side door as if he had been waiting for her and helped her descend. Charley felt an unfamiliar pang of envy.

"Thank you, Mr. White. Good day!" She said while turning to Karl obviously discussing something urgent that must be done as soon as possible. She disappeared inside as Charley drove around the corner, parked his carriage under the shelter and walked into the Rink, leaving the team for his men to take care of.

Most everyone was off eating lunch when Charley came through. The exception was Jimmy who was in the process of leading Betsy and Gypsy to the arena.

"Hey," called Charley. "Where are you taking them?"

Jimmy halted as did the two docile female elephants in his charge.

"We're just heading over so wardrobe can measure the girls for their new dresses," laughed Jimmy. Gypsy reached down with her nimble trunk and removed Jimmy's hat and showed it to Betsy.

"Hey!" Said Jimmy. "Give that back!" He admonished trying comically to snag the stolen hat from the elephant.

"Gypsy," said Charley White softly. "Give, please."

The elephant lifted the hat one last time, placed it on her own head for a moment and then gently lowered it back down.

"Thank you, Gypsy. Good girl," he soothed, patting her on the cheek. He handed the hat to Jimmy.

"Why don't I lead them out," said Charley. "You've got a cage to fix before you pick up that load of feed from Barley's."

"C'mon girls," he encouraged and without hesitation the behemoth ladies followed after their trusted friend.

For the past two seasons it had been Karl and not Annie who stood on a ladder and measured the elephants for decorative blankets and headdresses. For two years Annie had been irritated that the costumes never fit correctly and needed adjustments. This year she insisted upon measuring the giants herself. A seven-foot wooden ladder stood ready. Two of the girls from wardrobe waited, one with pencil and paper and the other to assist Mrs. Donovan in stretching the tape. Karl stood nearby, a nervous look on his face. The elephants arrived, their huge feet making no sound whatsoever on the sawdust covered floor as they gracefully crossed the arena.

She smiled as he approached, "Mr. White, you've brought the elephants! It is nice to see you again so soon," she remarked, blushing.

"Good afternoon, Mrs. Donovan," he nodded in return. He led Gypsy to one side where she could nibble on hay and watch as Betsy got measured. He loved the female elephants, so gentle. They had become even more precious, if that was possible, since surviving the fire. They were best friends and always kept together.

Charley stood in front of Betsy, a very large Asian elephant, and watched as Karl stood a ladder next to her. He had done this before and was savvy in the ways of elephants so as not to spook her. Sitting in a chair a few feet away was Annie's son, William. He was thin and frail, dark, and quiet. He looked nothing like his fair-haired mother and was so pale Charley wondered if the boy was healthy.

With all the dignity Annie could muster, she ascended the ladder beside the elephant. She had taken on an acrobat's britches under her dress and had drawn up the folds of her skirt out of the way of her legs (so she wouldn't trip) and fastened the fabric with a series of knots. She had planned for this fitting and was determined to get it right the first time. Building an entirely new wardrobe from scratch meant she would have to be efficient.

Karl handed up a small tin bucket which Annie hung from a nail on the side of the ladder. In the bucket were bits of chalk and a long cloth measuring tape.

After carefully feeling for and finding the center point between the elephant's shoulder blades, she put an "x" on the spot with the chalk. Using the same eyeball-and-feel method, she made white crosses on the elephant's forehead, rump, and strategic points along her sides. She did the same dots on both sides of the patient animal as Charley fed her quarter apples and talked to her. When Annie climbed down from the ladder Charley spoke to get her attention.

"You can pet her," he urged. "She likes to have her cheek stroked." He could tell a lot about people by the way they connected with the animals. Did she understand the intelligent creature she was outfitting, he wondered?

She was not an "animal person," per se. She had not been raised with them and apart from sewing costumes she had little interest in elephants. On the other hand, she felt a growing respect for this docile creature that just stood quietly eating apples while people climbed around her and fiddled with chalk and tapes.

Annie walked over to stand in front of the elephant. She looked to Charley one last time for reassurance before reaching up to touch the elephant on her cheek. It was one thing to measure a beast's backside and quite another to put yourself in front of the end that could bite. Betsy, familiar now with the movements of the wardrobe mistress, did not move away when Annie touched her. Instead, she reached out her long trunk and drew in the scent of this curious human.

"Warm. Dry. Your skin feels a bit like giant corduroy," Annie murmured. She looked up at the sleepy, half-closed eyes of the enormously pampered elephant. "You'll do," she reassured the creature stroking her one last time before returning to her measuring.

Charley's son came carrying a fresh bucket of apples. He was nearly sixteen and fancied himself a grown man. "Hi dad," he said handing the bucket over, "Need anything else?" Before Charley could answer, his son's attention was drawn elsewhere. He had caught sight of young William Donovan.

"Hey Willie! Wanna come help me muck out? I'll pay ya!" Charles Henry felt sorry for William. He reminded him of his own younger brother, also William… also a lad inclined to hide silently in a corner.

William's eyes lit up and he stood from his chair, looking first at Charles Henry and then at his mother.

"May I go with Charles?" He asked hopefully.

Annie answered, "Yes. Of course. Be careful," and then she added, "Please send him back before six for supper."

"Yes ma'am," answered the older boy. William sprang across the room and followed his friend out of the arena like a faithful puppy.

28th of March 1873
3rd Avenue near 63rd Street
Manhattan, New York

The dining tent buzzed with excitement. Four-hundred-eighty employees (more than double from the previous year) plus entertainers would be served three meals a day in this cookhouse for the next eight months, but this meal, this moment, was extraordinary; This was the breakfast before the first parade, the first show, the first demonstration of the comeback-power of Barnum since the fire nearly wiped "The Greatest Show on Earth" off the planet for good. This year's show, "P.T. Barnum's Great Museum, Menagerie, Hippodrome and Traveling World's Fair" had managed the impossible. Newspapers referred to Barnum as "Phoenix" T. Barnum as the show, like the phoenix, had quite literally risen from the ashes.

There was always much to do. Work was laid out in exact allotments to be accomplished at precise times by specific people. Without keeping the schedule, the entire scheme would collapse. Breakfast was at 07:30 and tables cleared by 08:30. This morning was no different. Seats were assigned and folks ate with their own departments. The tent crew, menagerie, ticket takers, door keepers, performers, human curiosities, wardrobe… they all knew exactly where they should be. One waiter per table brought their plates, filled their cups, and cleared up after. Delicious hearty meals were provided free to all employees. (It was part of the pay.) No matter how demanding the job, three times a day one could look forward to a respite in the dining tent. Today they found sliced cold beef and fried bacon, boiled and fried potatoes, pancakes, toast, butter, jam, eggs, and oatmeal served with milk or cream. Managers had their table, too, as far away from the kitchen chaos as possible.

Annie sat at her assigned place at the manager's table. At thirty-one she was not only the youngest present, but she was also the only woman. Frank Whittaker (equestrian director), Horace Nichols (ringmaster) and Doc Thayer (head ticket taker) sat across from her. Doc was telling some tale of a bygone era while Horace and Frank nodded and muttered in agreement. She was out of her depth here. She had never owned a show, led one, or even ridden many horses for that matter. They had nothing in common with her except the need to make the show a success.

She lifted her teacup with both hands, closed her eyes and drew in the steamy scent of freshly brewed English tea infused with milk and two sugars. She focused on quieting her racing thoughts and reassuring herself that today would go well. The herculean effort of the past three months had born fruit. The costumes were ready. She smiled, opened her eyes and lifted her cup to the gentlemen around her as if to offer up a "toast" and whispered "ready?" but no one noticed. Although satisfied with her life, she was a bit lonely. Even William, soon eleven, spent little time with her. When he wasn't in school, he was running errands for wardrobe or off with Charley White's lad in the menagerie. Her mother who had been a welcomed companion after her husband's death had moved to Cincinnati to live and work with her friend Mrs. McCarthy in the boarding house.

Charley White was under a lot of pressure, but would never admit it. Advertised as "Colonel Charles White, Lion King and Elephant Performer, Superintendent of the Zoological Department," it was he who was tasked with rebuilding the menagerie. All winter Barnum had animals coming in from all over the world to every port in New York City using a multitude of carriers. Keeping up with the boss's proclivity for abundance in animal procurement was no easy task. But it had gotten done and here they were starting the season, bigger and better than before.

He made his way over to the manager's table. Before him were not only friends he could trust with his life, but the pretty little wardrobe mistress, Annie Donovan. His assigned place was, most fortunately, between Fred Hamilton (Master of Properties) and his best friend Frank Whittaker, opposite Mrs. Donovan.

The waiter gestured with the coffee pot and Charley nodded. The waiters knew the habits of those they served and were motivated to please them in hopes of generous tips.

The meal was served up in exactly the same manner as it would be for the next 700-plus meals of the tenting season. Management was served first. The dining-room chatter quieted so precipitously as the diners dug in that the clattering of pots and pans in the kitchen could be heard with great clarity in all corners of the enormous tent.

Annie found herself watching Charley eat. When he looked up, he smiled and held her gaze. Her heart did a little somersault in her chest. Embarrassed, she smiled back.

"I am quite excited to see the parade," she said to him and anyone who happened to be listening. "Everyone has worked so hard to get ready and now… here we are!" She thought to raise her cup again in a toast as would seem appropriate but hesitated. Her enthusiasm was, after all, earlier ignored.

As if he'd read her thoughts, Charley stood and pushed back his chair. He raised his cup in the air and addressed the entire table, "To success!" Surprisingly everyone stood and raised their cups. The sentiment carried throughout the tent and hundreds chimed in, "Hear! Hear!"

Charley turned to Annie, "Might I see you again at dinner then, Mrs. Donovan?"

"Indeed, Mr. White!" she said as her heart did that flip-flop thing again.

Charley had not felt the warm flush of female enchantment for so long, he had forgotten the euphoria. He had observed her for two years and although he had tried to be near her as often as possible, opportunities had been few and far between. Since she was promoted to management, they could be together at least three times a day.

He headed back to work. More than thirty of the fifty cages of animals had to be ready and lined up outside before eleven. Thank God it wasn't raining. The end of March could be good or evil and *not raining* was a blessing.

"Damn!" he exclaimed as he walked through the door to the menagerie. There was a quarter inch of water all over the floor. "What the heck…" he muttered as he made his way through to find and fix the problem. "Always something…."

At precisely 10:45 a.m. William Cameron Coup (age 37, ambitious and prematurely balding) was positioned atop an eight-foot platform outside. With a whistle around his neck and a clipboard in his hand, he was ready to direct the day's big parade. On the clipboard were typewritten sheets listing every element of the parade in order of appearance. In some places were inked-in-additions and crossed-out-deletions. Every participant knew which wagon or group they followed. It was up to Coup to whistle and wave everyone in with precision timing.

The procession would extend three miles and take (if timed correctly) fifteen minutes to pass by any one point. Today they would have two street parades. This one would traverse a little more than fifteen miles. An abbreviated parade was planned for the school children between two and four o'clock.

This first procession's primary objective was to travel from Central Park to City Hall Park and back again with well-planned side street excursions.

Their designated route took them down 3rd Avenue to 48th Street and then a crossover to Lexington where they would continue south to 21st Street. There they would cross over to 3rd Avenue and follow it south on Bowery all the way to Chambers. Before the procession arrived at Chambers and Chatham, Barnum would appear and address the crowds. As Barnum disappeared up Broadway the procession would follow to 14th, cut over to 5th Avenue as far as 59th Street, then march to 8th Avenue where they would turn south again. At 14th Street they would turn east to go up 5th Avenue as far as 42nd Street where they would cut over to 2nd avenue and finally back to the Rink at 63rd Street and 3rd Avenue where they had begun. Almost every unit was mounted and thus a pace of five-miles-per hour could be maintained. Even so, it would take three hours at the very least

When they got back to the Rink, workers who had already eaten their noontide meal would take care of the animals and make sure the procession was ready for the afternoon's short run. Those that had been in the parade would eat, get ready once again, and then go out to indulge the school children. This afternoon route would be limited to one third of the original, but it would still be a long day. The first show wasn't until tomorrow, Saturday the 29th of March. Today was a grand demonstration meant to entice paying customers to their door.

At eleven sharp, Coop blew his whistle and the immense golden Apollo bandwagon filled with twenty-four musicians drawn by eight camels and four piebald horses rolled onto 3rd Avenue pointed south. The band played a sprightful tune as a troupe of cavaliers on horseback dressed in silver mail and sporting plumed helmets of dazzling solid silver followed directly behind. From the side came the rainforest wagon carrying a small tribe of "Amazon" women scantily clad in jungle costumes. The shuffling hooves of a dozen sure-footed trick ponies followed with child-sized riders dressed as jockeys. The ponies would perform small maneuvers throughout the procession.

Then came one of the most beloved wagons, the enormous twenty-four-foot-long mirrored steam calliope. The moment its wheels touched Third Avenue, the steam-filled pipes whistled and tooted joyfully.

The elephants were signaled in next and being well-practiced they took their place without fuss or bother. Each of the pachyderms sported a gigantic red brocade blanket trimmed with six inches of golden metallic lace which sparkled and danced in the sun as they walked. On each head was a corresponding forehead adornment made of the same materials, but with much more detail. The gray giants were each led by a turbaned dark-skinned handler dressed in Far East Indian attire. Betsy took the lead, being the largest of the three. Gypsy followed because she and Betsy were best friends, and Cindy the new elephant came last.

Coop whistled three sharp notes and the Garden of Eden wagon rolled onto the street. The Robin Hood riders decked out in snappy red and green costumes came right behind. Next in was the Chariot of Orpheus bandwagon with its complement of minstrels drawn by six white horses with dark lavender plumes on their proud heads. The minstrels were first-class musicians, black men given an opportunity to perform at Barnum's behest. Behind the minstrels came Jim. He was an old lion and content to ride in the silver cage for the duration, no matter how long it dragged on. On top of his cage was an Automatodeon, a figure of a ferocious lion that would turn its head, lift one paw, and appear to roar at the crowd. After the king of the jungle came twenty-nine cages of rare and exotic animals including a polar bear. Coop had arranged to have two polar bears brought from the arctic, but one had gotten loose in the city and the police shot it. That memory brought a fleeting moment of sadness for the veteran circus man. On top of the cage of rare birds was another Automatodeon depicting two roosters that would spar the entire route. Museum wagons followed bedecked with portraits of dignitaries and presidents from all over the world.

There were many menagerie animals too delicate, rare or dangerous to take part in the procession, but the last in line to draw a lot of attention was indeed very dangerous. The snake-den with glass sides rolled forward. In clear view for all to see was a Hindu snake charmer handling a live cobra and kissing and fondling it as if it were a beloved pet.

The Chariot of the Sun shone bright and golden in the late March sun as it was drawn onto 3rd Avenue by three elegant white horses commanded by a helmeted Roman warrior. A lineup of gilded and painted wagons followed, eight with statuary and eight with tableaux.

Barnum, temperance lecturer and moralist had insisted the painted wagons be decorated with altruisms and depictions of the Bible, not the least of which was a life-sized portrait of "The Last Supper." Coup signaled the last wagon of the group onto the road, one that proclaimed Barnum's personal message to the masses. On one side was painted "My ambition survives the fire" and on the other, "Three times but not dismayed."

The Temple of Juno (thirty feet high) joined the parade with several more museum wagons some of which sported Automatodeon, life-sized figures whose movements were driven by hidden wires and gears (designed by J.L. Lukes).

Gilmore's famous Jubilee Band would bring up the rear. Music was the heartbeat of the parade and the band's brilliant performance was the most perfect ending to the procession.

The abbreviated afternoon parade for the school children went off without a hitch. New York was properly primed and excited to come see the show.

29 March 1873
The Rink

As the cast and crew polished off supper in the dining tent, a crowd gathered out front. By 6:30 p.m. the entertainment-hungry public had filled the forecourt of the American Institute Building (Rink) and overflowed into the street and around the block.

The doors opened at seven. By 7:30 p.m. Doc Thayer closed the ticket window. They were sold-out. About two thousand patrons were turned away.

Annie, Karl, two assistants, Annie Wood and Mrs. Stewart and the seven others who made up the wardrobe department were doling out costumes for elephants, camels, horses and the like. Once the animal men got what they needed, entertainers collected theirs.

The year's theme was *The Grand Bashaw's Court,* also known as *The Halt in the Desert.* The overall effect was mesmerizingly beautiful. Costumes reflected the rich colors, satins, silks, and gilded opulence of the exotic east.

At five to eight everyone was lined up in back ready to go. Inside was a large oval hippodrome track with two show rings inside. First came the knights in glittering medieval armor who would fill the two circus rings, one with white-knights on white horses and black-knights on black horses in the other. The trained elephants, Betsy and Gypsy would lumber around the track clad in their red brocade blankets and headdresses meticulously embroidered with glittering metallic thread. Five camels would follow and then costumed men on foot and on horseback representing different regions of the mysterious far east. There were turbans, headdresses, banners, and balloon-britches galore. Just as Fritz Hartman's orchestra began the pre-entrée overture, Karl tapped Annie on the shoulder.

"Boss wants you out front," he said pointing out the door to the arena.

Her eyes darted around in panic as she assessed if everything was ready, and they could do without her. Karl reassured her.

"We'll be fine without you, miss. Everyone's ready. Go!" He urged.

With a final look, Annie tidied her hair and with both hands lifted the front of her skirt to give her feet freedom to move quickly and hastened to answer the summons.

She found management, including Mr. Barnum, muddling about in reserved seating. Coop and Castello were there along with Mr. Hurd and a few others. Dan Castello waved when he saw her, and she made her way over to him.

"Mrs. Donovan, hurry! Hurry!" He gestured at a seat for her as trumpets and trombones heralded the entry. All management was requested to be present for the premier evening. They had done their jobs. Now they should be seen watching their victorious grand entrée marking the triumphant season start many believed would never happen.

It's hard to let go and just enjoy the fruit of one's labors. A cook is always tasting to see if there's enough salt and spooning the gravy to make sure it is just right. Such as it was with the little wardrobe mistress. At first, she didn't see the pageantry, she saw ingredients and questioned their perfection. As Betsy walked by…was her head-dress straight… did her blanket shift a little to one side? Were the ballooning britches of the dark-skinned elephant handlers too short? The scrutiny continued until the tempo of the music and the excitement of the parade overwhelmed her concerns and she was able to enjoy the spectacle. It *was* grand! Coming in last were the "human curiosities." In front was Admiral Dot, the California dwarf, clad in his snappy military uniform riding in his miniature carriage drawn by four white ponies. Following him were young Charles Tripp the boy without arms, The Aztec children, Zip the man advertised as "What is it," Zaluma Agra, The Circassian lady with her voluptuous hair, and four Fiji Cannibals scantily clad with turkey leg bones in their bushy black hair. Last, but not least, was the albino boy riding alongside little Annie Jones. She was the seven-year-old bearded-girl and younger friend of Annie's son.

They circled the hippodrome track two full turns before exiting. Annie, glowing with pride, rose from her seat. Costumes needed collecting and repacking to be ready for Monday's matinee spectacle.

"Mrs. Donovan," Came a familiar voice. "Your costumes were perfect!"

She turned to him. "Why, thank you, Mr. White! …very kind of you." She smiled and curtsied playfully, "Your animals paraded very handsomely," she added.

She had not seen him arrive. He must have slipped in at the last moment. She felt a little shiver. Had he been watching her while she was unaware? She shook her head to clear it. She had to get back to work. She took the tête-à-tête with her, like a sweet caramel melting on her tongue, back to wardrobe.

Out in the arena, the show was ready to begin. Dan Castello was in position to direct using a simple bell. With it he would signal in and out the acts which would be performed in the two rings (simultaneously) as well as every other aspect of the show including clowns and music. Even the ringmaster, Horace Nichols took direction from Master Dan.

Everyone kept an eye on the show's progress including wardrobe. It wasn't as if they had never seen it all before, they needed to get their part in the timing correct. A successful show is a finely tuned mechanism. All of the pieces must be designed, engineered, assembled and executed with precision to create the magic the public had come to expect from P.T. Barnum.

While the triple bar act was performed in Ring One, the Bushnells did their balancing wire act in Ring Two. While Romeo Sebastian executed athletic pad riding skills, Dave Castello did gymnastics on bareback. The Mathews Family acrobats jumped and twisted in one ring while Lazell & Milson entertained in the other. Signor Sebastian demonstrated his trick horse in one ring while Dan Castello showed-off his own trick horse in the other.

As the clever steeds were taking their synchronized final bow, the chant, "Barnum! Barnum! Barnum!" erupted at one end of the arena and spread throughout the building. The clapping and foot-stomping shook the building. Mr. Barnum took to his feet and entered the ring, waved, and smiled. In a short speech he thanked everyone for coming.

After the interlude came the juggling of cannon balls, D'Atalie with his iron jaw, Lucille Watson and Helena Cook (equitationist and equestrienne), the horse-riding goat act and finally the elephants, Gypsy and Betsy. Gypsy worked with Charley White in one ring while Betsy went through her paces with Frank Dooley in the other. Both pachyderms performed *au natural* as their costumes were safely tucked away in wardrobe.

Each performance was ten to fifteen minutes in duration, so by the time Jerry Hopper (stilts) Dave Castello and George North (Indian horseback riding), Sebastian and Frank Barry (bareback riding), and the comic scene "Jockey and Traine" was carried out with Nathan, Castello, and Aymar, the time had come to call it a day. The audience was invited to pass through the museum and look at paintings and stuffed birds, watch a live demonstration of Faber's talking machine or visit the human curiosities or the menagerie before the lights were turned off and doors were locked precisely at ten o'clock.

20 April 1873
In Transit from New York City
To Norwalk, Connecticut

THE CALL TO BOARD THAT evening had been orderly and efficient. All local accommodations were either sublet or locked tight until the occupants returned from the summer run. Annie was content and ready to get on the road. The three weeks since the show opened had gone fine, almost entirely without problems. Any issues with personnel and equipment had been worked out while the show was still in the greater metropolitan area where supplies were abundant.

The new rail cars bought and customized for sleeping were grand. Well, she only had the experience of this one car, but she was pleased. The sleeping berth was comfortably situated with thick dark curtains and a cubby specifically made to keep personal items. Although it was dark outside, it was still too early to sleep. They would make it to Norwalk before bedtime. She was happy to just sit here looking out the window reflecting on the weeks gone by. The other unmarried ladies were busy getting to their places and stowing away their gear. They weren't allowed to take much with them. Only upper management got a trunk.

The comforting sounds of the steam engine up ahead could lull even a colicky baby to sleep, she thought as she relaxed in her seat. William was no longer with her on the train. He was almost eleven and no longer allowed in the women's car. He would bunk with the men. She was proud of him. He had grown up these past few months. He worked most days after school mucking out animal pens or running errands for wardrobe. He also spent a lot of time with little Annie Jones playing pick-up-sticks and cards. The odd little girl was lonely. Who could blame her? It was kind of William to spend time with her.

The train was to set to leave the station at eight. At seven fifty-nine, a courier burst into the railway car carrying a parcel wrapped in brown paper and tied with a string.

"Mrs. Anna Donovan?" hollered the young man, "I have a package for Mrs. Anna Donovan!"

Surprised, Annie stood up and waved. Two long raspy train whistles sounded, the steam engines belched, and the train jerked to a start. The courier handed her the parcel, turned, and fled out the door. He'd been promised a dollar if he could deliver the package in time.

Naturally, all eyes in car four were trained on that package. Girls often got surprises from beaus, and everyone knew it was disrespectful to watch someone open a private package…but dear Mrs. Donovan had never received a present and neither did they know of a mysterious suitor.

She removed the heavy outside paper to reveal pink tissue paper. Nestled inside was a silver whistle attached to a sturdy silver chain with a clip. The miniature instrument was delicately etched all over except for one tiny smooth square which had been engraved with "Anna." The ornament was meant to be attached to a chatelaine. She read the note aloud for others to hear.

"When my need arose for assistance, you were there to help. If you ever need anything, just whistle. Your humble servant, Lewis B. Lent."

Also included in a packet were 10 seated liberty silver dollars, one for each of her assistants.

The gifts were a thank you for the emergency assistance rendered willingly by the close-knit members of the New York entertainment fraternity. When the storm came to Manhattan on Saturday morning the 12th of April, it dumped heavy wet snow that knocked down every single tent belonging to "The New York Circus." Barnum's was still at the Rink, so the only tent they had up (which succumbed to the storm) was the dining tent. Every able-bodied soul rushed to rescue Lent's show.

Charley White and his men helped round up menagerie animals and got them to warmth and safety in temporary shelters. Once the property crews at Barnum's resurrected their own dining tent, they rushed over to the New York Circus at Madison and Fourth (between 26th and 27th streets). There they worked together with Lent's outfit to get the tents back up. Annie opened her wardrobe department to L.B. Lent's and between the two crews every garment was saved, cleaned, and made ready. The esprit de corps got Lent's show up and running in time for Monday's morning show.

The first stop of the circus train was Norwalk, Connecticut. There was a parade and three shows, one at ten, one, and seven. Everything went smoothly in spite of the rain and snow. The wet weather continued, but caused little hindrance until Woonsocket, Rhode Island. The afternoon show was cold and miserable but sold out. Just after the evening show the center pole of the museum pavilion broke and knocked over nine quarter-poles. The next day was Sunday, so there was plenty of time to get things repaired and travel the sixteen miles to Providence for a two-day stand in fair weather. Friday the ninth they were met with strong winds and heavy rain and one of the performers got sick. The Frenchman Edward D'Atalie also known as the man with the iron jaw did his act, went back to the railcar, and passed out cold. He couldn't catch his breath and died of pleurisy while enroute to Boston. A high mass was said for him at St. James Catholic Church and several from management and the equestrienne department attended. The next fatality was a conductor who was killed while coupling railcars together in Salem.

The hauls in the northeast were short and most stands were single until they had traversed Maine and Massachusetts and landed back in Albany, New York. There they enjoyed a two-day visit with sold out audiences, fourteen thousand seats sold for all six performances. The only dark spot was when one of the waiters (John Haggerty) was arrested by one of Mr. Barnum's detectives, James McLaughlin, for stealing a chicken from a local farmer. Mr. Barnum did not tolerate drunkenness, thievery, or brutality. The first (drinking) was grounds for immediate dismissal, the second (thievery) required an immediate arrest and the third (hitting an animal or a woman) meant a twenty-five dollar fine for first occurrence and dismissal if it happened again.

The fourteenth of June, they found themselves in Vermont and spent a leisurely warm Sunday just outside of Burlington on Lake Champlain. After breakfast, Charley suggested they take a lunch and walk along the lake. Annie's son, accompanied by little Annie Jones, tagged along. This day was a sunny afternoon skipping rocks and catching tadpoles and everything a normal child would love about summer. The next day was another train ride and another workday.

They were outside of Albans, Vermont and all were tucked away in the sleeping cots at midnight when a knock came on car number four. The porter opened the door to find the menagerie man's son, Charles Henry White standing there.

"I've come for Mrs. Donovan," He whispered. "My dad sent me."

The porter verified that the boy was who he said he was and told him to wait while he went after the wardrobe mistress. She awoke immediately when the porter spoke to her from the other side of her sleeping curtain.

Annie, dressed in her nightgown, deftly took on a dressing gown and came to the door of the train. She conferred with young Charles Henry, nodded at the porter, and stepped out into the night air.

The boy led her to the animal tent, lantern in hand. Inside was dark save the glowing light in the far corner where Charley squatted down on his haunches beside a deer. The animal was resting on a bed of straw cleaning off her newborn fawn. Annie stood and watched a moment before approaching.

"Mr. White," she whispered. "Shall I come closer?"

Charley turned and even in the shadows she could see the smile on his face.

"Yes," he whispered softly, "come see the new baby."

Annie walked up behind him, being careful not to startle the animal. The tiny fawn laid there helplessly being gently licked by his mother.

"He is an albino, Mrs. Donovan, truly a miracle." Indeed, the fawn appeared almost transparent.

"May I touch him?" She asked surprising them both. Was she becoming a person who felt kinship with animals?

"In a minute. First, he needs to stand and suckle," answered Charley. "The bond with his mother and first milk is vital for him to survive."

They watched for several minutes. Charles Henry returned to his cot leaving them alone in their vigil. The tiny fawn was becoming more alert and struggled to find his legs. The mother stood and nudged him, encouraging him to rise. When at last he stood on four wobbly legs, his first instinct was to seek out his mother's udder. Annie looked up at Charley and saw the innocent face of a young boy. What a sweet, kind, wonderful man, she thought.

"Oh Mr. White," she said. "It is a little miracle, isn't it?"

Charley smoothed the long strand of hair from the side of her forehead (for it was let loose for the night), leaned over, and kissed her. It was so simple and so right. They were both shocked and pulled back before leaning in and kissing once again.

"Mrs. Donovan?" He asked. "May I call you Annie?"

"When we are alone…Charley." His name sounded strange to her own ears. "I would be pleased."

He escorted her back to car number four, knocked on the door softly and bade the porter to take her in to the safety of her own cot. As he returned to his own accommodations, Annie involuntarily let tears slide from her eyes. It was happiness.

They met at breakfast, lunch and dinner and always addressed each other formally as if they had no relationship, but everyone knew. The wardrobe mistress had a twinkle in her eye whenever the menagerie man walked in. And he, the quiet lion tamer, softened his gaze when Mrs. Donovan was nearby.

June and July took them through New York and Pennsylvania and finally into Ohio. In every instance the show was a near sellout with an average of about ten thousand in attendance at every show.

In Cleveland there was a private show at the behest of Mr. Barnum. His friend's son had been stricken with a crippling disease and could not attend the circus. Barnum thought they should take the circus to the boy for no boy should miss out. Charley took some of the animals to the boy's house. All three elephants, five camels and a few horses made the pilgrimage, and all performed some of their tricks as the child watched from his second story bedroom window. Annie had ascertained the general measurements of the boy and had quickly made a Ringmaster's jacket for him to wear for the occasion.

In Cleveland the weather was fair, and they sold out all four days before moving on to Hamilton, Ohio on the 25th. After the matinee in Hamilton, a group of more than four hundred followed a band playing solemn music to the sacred grounds of Greenwood Cemetery. They paid homage to Charles Carter, their friend who last year had led his horses to the reservoir for a bath and was killed in a freak accident. An abundant arrangement of beautiful flowers was laid in front of the Scottish granite headstone newly placed there bearing his name. Doc Thayer spoke of his good character. The sun was setting as the group made its way back to the circus grounds for the evening show.

They missed a morning show in Lafayette, Indiana due to a train delay in Zionsville and it rained in Danville, Illinois the following day. It was of little consequence. They were averaging ten thousand souls per show and profit was, at least for the time being, realized.

August took them to St. Louis for a week. It would have been a glorious reprieve from travel had it not been for the death of one of the canvas men who was run over by a stake wagon on Sunday. George Lynch was a young man with a wife and two children three hundred miles away in Kansas City.

There wasn't much time for anything but work six days a week. On the seventh, there were personal things like laundry and bathing to take care of. Nevertheless, relationships had time to grow.

In St. Louis one of Annie's wardrobe girls showed up with a black eye. Upon questioning, she tearfully admitted that her husband (horse tender) had gotten drunk and hit her. Annie, as head of her department was bound to report the incident, but the girl begged her not to.

"If James loses his job, Mrs. Donovan, we'll be destitute! Please," she begged," Please don't tell on him. If he is fired, I have to leave with him!" Annie was between a proverbial rock and a hard place.

"Don't breathe a word to anyone," Annie told her sternly. You sleep in car four with us tonight. Give your husband time to stew. I must think," She added, and went about her work.

Later than evening after the last show, Annie met Charley in the menagerie tent. It was still early enough to be a righteous meeting, but private enough she could manage a secret conversation. As the two leaned over the rail and admired the albino fawn now doubled in size, Annie told him of the incident and asked his advice. It was quickly decided.

"I will speak to James's boss," he said quietly. "I'll suggest that we report this man for hitting his wife one time. That is a fine. But, if it happens again, he will be fired." Charley continued, "I don't think that boy is a drinker or short-tempered. Frank would have mentioned it." They both knew that if James messed up again, Frank Whittaker would fire him.

"Annie," he said changing the subject, "we'll be in Chicago for a week soon. Could you reserve the Sunday we have there to spend some time with me to look around the city?"

"Yes Charley, that would be nice!" She smiled and added, "Shall we invite our sons to join us?" She asked with a twinkle in her eye.

"Um, let me think," he said seriously as if he were pondering the meaning of life. "No," he laughed. "Let's just spend a few hours together in Chicago and find a nice place to eat."

Annie giggled…she hated it when she did that, but he loved it….

August 14, 1873
Thursday
Illinois

It was her birthday. Thirty-one years ago, she was born an illegitimate child in Peterborough, Canada West. She was not ashamed of her birth, but she never told anyone. She dressed in a black skirt with matching bodice made of cotton with the underskirt made of crinoline. Her under-bodice, made of cream silk taffeta was trimmed at the top with lace that she herself had tatted. At her waist was her silver chatelaine where her scissors, thimble, pins, pen, and paper were readily available. The little silver whistle from Mr. Lent was clipped to the center. She fastened her glass rose pin at her throat just under the ruffle of the under-bodice and then inspected her image in the large tin mirror of the wardrobe tent. She turned and observed her backside and patted her derriere. "I don't need a bustle," she giggled, "I have ample padding without one."

The morning passed seemingly with no one remembering that it was her birthday. How should anyone know, she thought. But still, it was a bit disappointing that even her son had forgotten. The afternoon show was a grand success. Everything went as planned and no one got hurt.

The dining tent was pleasantly cooler than normal after a rain shower had dampened the mid-August afternoon. Today they would get fried chicken for dinner. Annie knew by the aroma coming from the kitchen that today was going to be her favorite meal. Charley came to the table and sat opposite her, as usual, and smiled warmly at her.

"And how are you this fine day, Mrs. Donovan?" He asked.

"Very good, Mr. White," she smiled a little shyly, "And how are you?"

Just then the bell rang signaling the beginning of service. The waiters came bearing trays to tables and Annie's suspicions were confirmed. Fried chicken, mashed potatoes, a lovely cool lettuce salad and condiments were delivered. What luck, she thought! Now, if they come with apple pie and ice cream, I shall be very happy with my birthday indeed!

There was only modest conversation as everyone ate. It had been a busy day. Everyone was hungry and the food, delicious. The waiters gathered the dishes, coffee and tea were brought, and the waiters came out with desert. It was not apple pie, it was peach, but there was ice cream.

Mr. Castello arose from his chair and with his knife banged on the side of his glass to get everyone's attention. He had a speech

"Ladies and Gentlemen: I have been appointed on behalf of the performers and others, to perform a duty in which I take a great pleasure. It is that of rewarding true merit, which never seeks reward, but sooner or later is sure to gain it...."

"Mrs. Donovan—good lady. Your friends and admirers have been observing your actions with extreme vigilance of late and concluded that you are deserving of being made a member of the chain-gang, which sentence we trust you will willingly bear. I have therefore been requested by them to present you with this beautiful gold watch and chain, as a mark of their esteem for you as an honest upright and true woman. You will observe that in many respects it resembles yourself; it has a pretty face, and its hands, like yours, are in continual motion. You will also observe that each tick of this beautiful piece of mechanism marks our time nearer and nearer to the grave; and when our Heavenly Father takes you to himself, leave this token to your noble boy, of which you are the widow mother; leave it with these admonitions; tell him it was a hard-earned treasure; tell him it was earned by honesty, perseverance, and industry; tell him it was a gift from his mother's friends to her and is a legacy from her to him..." and he added, "We know that you are grateful and that you will ever cherish the gift as the voluntary offering of your associates and friends."

He raised his coffee cup and said, "To your health, dear lady. Happiest of birthdays and may you enjoy a hundred more!" The dining room cheered and raised their cups, standing to applaud the wardrobe mistress.

They had not forgotten. Charley beamed and she smiled back shyly. She arose from the table and attempted to regain her composure, gold watch and chain in hand. She looked about her at those who smiled and waited to see her reaction.

"Very kind of you. Thank you," she said in a clear voice. "Thank you," she curtsied slightly and sat down.

The show made it to Bloomington and Juliet for one day each before landing in Chicago for a week, the 18th through the 23rd. Sunday, the 24th was the day set aside for the rendezvous. Charley took a horse and cart and met Annie at the east side of the Washington and Elizabeth junction. She, being the wardrobe mistress, had access to nice apparel despite the fact they weren't given much allowance for personal belongings. She had polished her leather button pumps to a mirror-like finish and taken extra care with her miserable hair. What did one do with thin straight blonde hair? You could have three feet of it, and it would still fit into a thimble. She was nervous. "Courting" she thought and giggled. It was silly, but she felt happy. When Charley drew the cart near, she was astounded to see him decked out in gentlemanly attire. The jacket hung loose about his shoulders and the pants were overlong. While he looked fine indeed, it was obvious he had either never had the suit fitted or it belonged to another. Never-mind. She was happy.

He hopped down from the cart and came to assist her. She gave him her lace-gloved hand and felt a rush as he took it and steadied her ascent.

"And how are you this fine day, Mrs. Donovan?" He asked before starting off.

"Annie," she corrected. "I'm very well, thank you," she nodded to accentuate her approval. "And you, Charley White, are you well? Are your creatures all well-tended?"

Charley laughed, transferred the reigns to his left hand so he could pat her gloved hands as they lay folded genteelly upon her knees.

"All is well, dear Annie!" He signaled the horse to proceed east on Washington Avenue.

"I have directions to Jackson Park. We can walk the shoreline and enjoy the breeze off the lake." It sounded rehearsed and it was. "For lunch, I've reserved a table at John Wright's Restaurant at the Palmer House on Wabash Avenue."

"Wonderful!" rejoined Annie. "It's so nice to be out today…" her voice trailed off, not knowing what else to say.

They arrived at the park and found a place to leave the horse and cart where, for a small price, a man would watch over them. Charley helped Annie down. She slipped on a cobblestone and nearly toppled over. He caught her about the waist to steady her and there they were, face to face… and profoundly embarrassed.

"Well!" Annie giggled nervously. "Thank you, Mr. White, for saving my honor!" She withdrew her hand, stepped back, smoothed her hair, and made as if to begin walking toward the great lake.

"Charley," he corrected, more to himself than to her, "My pleasure." He whispered.

"Charley," she conceded.

She took his offered elbow and they walked across the park, arm in arm, enjoying the quiet nature and the sunlight peeking through the trees. As they approached a bench, Charley asked if she'd like to sit a while and she did.

"You look lovely today," he said. "It's nice to meet when we aren't working or eating!"

They sat staring at the lake. He reached out and took her hand in his. Neither spoke. Neither could. After a bit, Annie withdrew her hand gently to reach up and remove her hat. Charley did the same. When he had his hat securely resting upon his knees, he turned to her.

"Annie, I like your company. I wonder, do you feel the same?" He asked and he watched for her response.

"I do, Charley," she replied shyly. She paused and stared at her hat.

They relaxed in comfortable silence watching the birds play in the wind over the shoreline of Lake Michigan.

"We should go," he said quietly. "Yes," she answered.

The Palmer House loomed in front of them, at least seven stories high and crowned with a decorative bell tower with windows facing every direction. The grand structure sprawled out over the greater part of a city block of downtown Chicago. The restaurant, newly opened, shone in the noontime sun. The immaculate windows sparkled under colorful green and white striped awnings. The brass door handles shone as doormen dressed in black greeted patrons and opened doors for them with their white gloved hands.

Charley and Annie were seated at a table for two persons by the window facing Wabash Avenue. The spotless table linens starched and white met with the approval of the wardrobe mistress. Would others have appreciated the quality of the fabric? Likely not, but this just added another measure of joy to her day.

The ambiance of the dining hall was festive and grand. The room was filled with gentle folk dressed in their Sunday best. Perhaps some were celebrating a birthday and others just enjoying a day away from their own home and stove. Charley and Annie were always working to put on a show complete with parades and spectacles. Neither ever had time to enjoy the pomp and circumstance themselves. Today they did. A cellist and violinists created delightful parlor music on a small stage at the far end of the hall. They breathed in the wonderful aromas of fresh bread and roasted chicken as they watched other tables receive their fare and made toasts to one another with glasses of sparkling wine and cider. When their own crusty bread arrived, Charley offered Annie the first bit. She daintily served herself a generous portion of butter. He smiled. He knew her love of butter and sweets. They ate across the table from one another every day. Awkwardness faded as they partook of their meal. It was good, although they both agreed, not measurably better than was served up in the Barnum Hotel every day.

They requested iced cream and coffee for dessert. He wanted strawberry. She preferred chocolate. The waiter smiled and said he would return with a surprise. He first brought a carafe with steaming hot coffee and small pitcher of warmed frothy cream. He left again and came back with a covered silver serving dish. He placed a small bowl in front of each of his guests along with fresh white napkins and silver-plated spoons. He poured their coffee, Annie's first, and then gracefully added the cream and sugar as they indicated. Then he smiled and with dramatic flair raised the compote-cover to reveal the glass dish inside filled with ice cream. "Neapolitan!" he announced. "It is three flavors, strawberry, chocolate, and vanilla all in one!" He gestured as if he were the ringmaster at Barnum's. "*Buon appetito!*" He declared. "*Bon appetit!*"

When they had finished their desert and the waiter refreshed their coffee, Charley turned to the woman beside him.

"Do you think you could marry someone like me," he asked simply.

"I could," she answered.

"Will you do me the honor of becoming my wife?" He reached across and took her hand in his and looked at her hopefully.

"I will," she answered, smiling at him shyly.

He pulled a little white box from his jacket pocket and sat it down in front of her on the table.

"I had this made for you, Annie Donovan."

She looked at him a moment before reaching for the box. She pulled the end of the little red ribbon that held it closed and gently removed the top. Nestled inside on a pink satin cushion was a silver heart-shaped locket chased and engraved with delicate leaves and flowers. When she lifted it out and turned it over, she found that it was engraved in a beautiful script, "Annie."

"It's beautiful," she whispered as she ran her thumb over the exterior

"Open it," He urged.

Annie sat the locket carefully upon the table so she could open it. He watched intently as she inspected the clasp and finally loosened the lock. She gasped when she saw what was inside.

"Oh, my goodness, Charley White!" She whispered, "Oh my!"

Several around their table had paused their revelry to watch. It was obvious that this couple was sharing a very joyous time, and joy is something grand to see. Even the very formal waiter had paused with white-gloved-hands folded to see the opening of the locket.

The inside of the silver heart locket was a work of art. The whole of the interior was lined in rich yellow gold. On one side was mounted a brilliant diamond on four little golden prongs.

Charley put his arm around her shoulders and said, "You have a heart of gold, Annie Donovan and the strength of a diamond."

Those who had been watching in stealth now openly showed their pleasure. They clapped and muttered "bravo" and "hear-hear." The violinist brilliantly caught the mood and started a melody of love which the cellist quickly joined in on. Realizing that perhaps enough was enough, the waiter went about his business and quickly asked nearby diners if he could help them, leaving the newly betrothed some semblance of privacy.

The day had been an oasis, an island in a sea of activity that made up the tenting season. They decided to keep their commitment to themselves and not make any formal announcement until they were safely back in New York. The cat was soon out of the bag though for the following day the little locket was securely fastened to Annie's chatelaine alongside the whistle Mr. Lent had given her. To the outside world, it was just a little locket of silver. Only she and Charley knew that it was not only a token of their affection, but a financial resource should she ever need it. When asked from whence it came, Annie confided in her closest friends and her son, of course. Word travels fast in a travelling community.

Charley was no better at keeping their secret. Upon returning to the menagerie, he had confided in Frank Whittaker and asked if he would be his best man when the time came. He also needed to tell Charles Henry before he heard it from Annie's son.

On the second of September they got word that Lent's circus had suffered another accident. A Pullman car had come loose in St. Louis with forty persons on board. Mr. Ketch, the show's manager and ringmaster John McLean were cut and bruised, but no one was badly injured.

They were in Detroit on Saturday the sixth of September when Charley confided that he would be leaving the show for a couple of days to travel north. He explained to Annie about his little sister Emily living near Lampeer and how he wanted to make sure she was all right. "Alcohol," he told her, "has made Emily's husband difficult to live with."

Annie understood. They were a team now. His worries were hers and vice versa. He would rejoin the show in London, Ontario on September eighth.

From there they worked their way back home through Maryland, Pennsylvania and New Jersey. They set up in Brooklyn at the Capitoline building on October 13th for the week before moving on to Manhattan. Barnum had leased the grounds where Lent's had been in the spring at Madison Avenue between 26th and 27th Streets. There was some scuttlebutt circulating that Barnum wanted to build his own permanent venue there. Nobody knew what might happen after the season was over this year, but then they never did. The circus business was fluid and ever-changing.

CHAPTER TWENTY-FOUR

SUNDAY MORNING
NOVEMBER 9, 1873
MANHATTAN, NY

ANNIE PLACED THE MANTEL CLOCK on top of the linens in the wooden crate. It was the last thing she had left in her apartment, and the most fragile. She would hold it in her lap as they made their way over to 8th Avenue, Charley's place, after the wedding. His apartment was larger and a better location, but she had never set foot in it.

It was already nine and she would have to hurry. Kirk was due to drive her to the lot where she could get ready. Her dress and toiletries were already in the dressing room in the wardrobe tent. She had butterflies.

Once she got past the guards and into wardrobe, Annie found she was not alone. Two of her wardrobe girls were waiting for her.

"A woman shouldn't be left to tend herself on her wedding day," announced Lily the same girl whose husband had hit her and barely escaped being fired. Lily's abdomen was obviously bulging with the promise of her first child. James, her husband, had returned to the good side of sober and she had heard nary a negative word since. "Susan pressed your dress and…." She gestured to the trunk beside the dressing table "we managed to find a little something special for our mistress." The two girls giggled behind their hands as Annie caught sight of the delicate ivory laced undergarments laid out for her approval.

Annie giggled. The heat from her blush rose from her throat to her cheeks. While it had occurred to her that she and Charley would be man and wife, she had never allowed herself to imagine the moments ahead.

"Oh no!" she whispered breathlessly, "I simply couldn't!"

"Oh yes, you must" replied the ladies in unison. And, as ladies in waiting might attend a queen the two girls tended to their mistress as she washed and dressed, buttoned her shoes and applied the rare touch of powder and rouge. Susan, best at dressing hair, deftly brushed out Annie's fine blonde tresses before backcombing it a little for height and expertly pinning it atop her head in a feminine twist.

"Ahem…" Came a discreet cough from the other side of the curtain.

Lily rushed to see who it was and there stood Karl.

"May I speak to Mrs. Donovan, please?" he asked formally in spite of the fact that he knew them all very well after an entire season out of the road together in the same department.

"Miss Annie," informed Lily, "It's Karl and he'd like to speak to you."

Annie brushed the front of her skirt smooth, stood and removed the towel from her shoulders (which kept hair and powder from her dress) and turned to face the doorway.

"Of course! Come in Karl!"

Karl very formally approached the wardrobe mistress and stood before her, a small red velvet box in his hand.

"My friend, I want to wish you and Charley happiness. I have small present for you. I hope you will wear for wedding. It is tradition… something old, yes?" His rehearsed words still bore the endearing accent of a Polish immigrant. He opened the box and drew out a small hair comb.

"This was my mother's, God rest her soul." He said as he handed it to Annie.

It was a golden three-pronged hair comb made from Baltic Sea amber with three red garnets embedded in the shaft.

"It would be my honor," said Annie as she handed the treasure to Susan who deftly placed the comb in her mistress's hair.

"I will be out front with carriage when you are ready, Mrs. Donovan," he said as he turned to go.

Meanwhile on the other side of the lot…

His fancy white shirt fit perfectly, which was what was to be expected of a man betrothed to a wardrobe mistress. The little box containing his collar buttons stood open on the dressing table. The twin gold lion heads with ruby eyes stared at him, daring him. He did not have nimble fingers and he dreaded trying to put them on his shirt. His men had given him the unique buttons when they'd gotten back to Manhattan. Annie had arranged for a shirt so he could wear them.

"Charley!" Hollered Frank Whittaker as he pushed himself through the door. "What is the hold-up, friend? We're going to be late." Frank walked over to the table, picked up the box and deftly pinned Charley's collar down with the little lion buttons. In moments, the tie, vest, hat and boots were all assembled upon the groom and Frank was rushing him out the door.

They had about a five-minute walk to the Methodist Episcopal Church on 34th Street. There Frank and Charley were to wait on the front steps for Annie and Frank's wife Margaret to arrive by carriage.

Karl had taken the open carriage because the air was still, the sky was blue and Indian summer in New York was the finest anyone had ever witnessed. The men saw the carriage coming but Karl, appearing even more massive than ever in his vested suit and bowler hat, obscured the view of his passengers. When they pulled up in front of the church, Annie and Charley finally caught sight of one another. He was beautifully turned out, handsome, dapper, and snappily dressed. His eyes sparkled, as Annie would remember later and always. She was a vision of loveliness, perfectly dressed with shiny shoes and white lace peeking out from around her collar and sleeves. The golden hair comb shone brightly in the sunlight and wisps of blonde curls fringed her forehead. At thirty-one she was a woman in full bloom, a warm-hearted woman with an endearing giggle and twinkling eyes.

Karl climbed down and went around the carriage to escort Annie to the church. He took her gloved hand and walked her up the steps where he presented her to the man she was about to marry. He then returned to the carriage. Mrs. Whittaker joined her husband and the four of them entered the church together.

Karl waited outside while Alasco Charles White, age 41, son of Benajah White and Ivanna Hubbard of New York was joined in marriage by John E. Cookman (Clergyman) to Anna Donovan nee Matchet, age 31, daughter of Margaret Slingsby and Sandy Matchet of Canada. Francis and Margaret witnessed the marriage, the documents were signed, and the pastor led them to the front door of the church. He opened the double doors wide, went out on the steps and proclaimed, "Hear ye! Hear ye! For all the world and God to witness, I present to you Mr. and Mrs. Charles White!"

To the newlywed's surprise a small crowd had gathered. Friends, colleagues, one of Charley's sons and Annie's boy William were there to congratulate them. They clapped and cheered and crowded around to greet them.

Frank Whittaker had made reservations for a small reception and late lunch at the Fifth Avenue Hotel between 25th and 26th Streets. The revelers enjoyed a lovely lunch with a few speeches. Mr. Coup and Mr. Castello were both present, but Mr. Barnum was still overseas trying to procure a hot air balloon and pilot for next season. During the wedding party a few members of the animal department gathered Annie's things from her apartment and moved them to Charley's. Meanwhile, several of the ladies from wardrobe decorated Charley's apartment with ribbons and bows. They left a ribbon-wrapped-wicker-basket of delicacies on the table and filled the icebox with fruit, cheese, and champagne.

The plan was for Annie and Charley to spend the rest of the day alone getting to know one another before returning to work in the morning. Their plans were changed when Mr. Coup read a telegram from Barnum sent from Germany.

"Congratulations. Much Happiness. Two nights at Fifth Avenue Hotel as a gift for you. Blessings! P.T. Barnum."

When at last the celebrating was over in the dining hall, the newlyweds were further served by friends that expeditiously fetched the personal items they would need for the impromptu honeymoon. And, much to Annie's embarrassment several stayed to watch the couple sign the register as Mr. and Mrs. Charles White for the first time. The hour was seven and the day had been long. There was nothing to do but go to their room.

Room 207 had been made ready for them. An oil lamp burned, and the bed was turned down. Flowers had been delivered and placed on the table along with several hand-written notes, greetings from well-wishers.

Annie started to ask where they had put the wash basin and towels because she simply did not know what else to say. Charley put his arms around her and drew her near while gazing into her eyes.

Shush," he said while putting a finger to his lips. Then he kissed her, not a demandingly intense kiss of lust and need but rather a slow and easy delicious private moment of being home at last.

They kissed again and this time Annie could feel the heat rise in her. She felt the arousal of the man, a feeling she had almost forgotten, and it surprised her how quickly her body responded to the bidding.

They undressed one another slowly, both uncertain and yet hungry to proceed. Tenderly he reached out and removed the comb from her hair allowing her angel-soft golden tresses to settle softly about her shoulders. He gently lifted the hair from the side of her neck and kissed her there, breathing in hungrily the very scent of her.

He kissed her fully on the mouth for long and tempestuous moments. Instinctively she responded to his embrace as he drew her body tightly into his.

"Mr. White!" Someone knocked incessantly upon the door of 207. "Mr. White! I have a message for you!" A fellow from the menagerie had been sent to inform the boss that the dog Susie was in trouble. Susie was a great large Newfoundland, a gift to Charley after the fire destroyed all his performing dogs last year. She was just a year old, but already the favorite companion of the elephants. If they thought someone was going to hurt their puppy, they started to get upset. Usually, the offenders were just pretending to hurt Susie to get a rise out of the elephants, but they were, so far, smart enough to stop before anybody got hurt.

"What's going on," asked Charley through a crack in the door. He knew it must be important or they wouldn't have sent someone for him.

"Susie got out front and got hit by a wagon. The elephants won't let anyone near to see what's wrong with her."

"I'll be right there," he said firmly and shut the door.

Annie had heard everything and nodded at Charley when he looked at her apologetically.

"Let's go," she said pulling her skirt closed and fastening it. "No time to waste."

When they arrived, they saw three elephants standing around a prone black dog. The workers were keeping a healthy distance while they waited for Charley to get there.

"Sorry boss," said one of the guys, "We didn't know what else to do but come get ya."

Charley approached the elephants slowly talking softly as he went. Betsy stepped back and made an opening where Charley could get in to Susie. The dog lay on her side whimpering piteously and one of her hind legs was bent at an abnormal angle.

"It's broke," announced Charley. "Poor girl," he reassured as he got closer. "Get me a couple of boards and rope and I'll splint this and carry her inside," he directed. He had to come out of the elephant barricade to fetch the supplies. No one else dared come near.

Charley carefully applied a temporary splint to the broken limb and carried Susie inside, no easy feat because even though she was still technically a puppy, she weighed over 80 pounds. The elephants stood guard at the door while Charley worked inside. Annie joined him through a side door and helped fashion a better splint. Susie had broken the lower bone of her back leg when the cart ran over her. However, the bone had not gone through the skin, so Charley hoped that it would heal without infection.

Annie left and came back with blankets and some scraps of meat to soothe the wounded canine. Food, for a big dog, is quite often enough distraction to take their mind off an injury. The elephants seemed placated by the fact that Charley was there to take care of the dog and were led peacefully off to their quarters for the balance of the night. The members of the animal department who had been held off by the elephants bled off one by one and found their cots. Tomorrow was Monday, a busy day lay ahead. Charley and Annie sat by Susie well into the night, leaning against the wall, dozing off and awakening disoriented off and on only to rediscover that they were in fact married to each other.

At five in the morning a familiar voice reached them. Karl was an early-bird and generally showed up before anyone else in his department. This morning he had met the night watchman and been told of last night's events.

"This girl okay now?" he asked as he approached them.

"I'll just check," said Charley rising and going over to inspect his dog. Annie remained by the wall where she had spent the night. Karl walked over to her.

"Mrs. Dona…" he began, "Er… Mrs. White! Can I bring something? Cook can fix sandwich," He offered.

"Thank you, Karl," She answered, "I'm fine, just a little tired."

"It is not what bride expect, to spend night in barn with sick animal." Commiserated Karl

She thought for a moment as she observed her new husband. .

"That," she said pointing to the man bent over the wounded animal, "is why I married him. He is good and kind and honest with every person and every creature. He cares. I love everything about him, his dogs, his pet lions, well-dressed elephants and all.

"Karl…" she said looking up at her dear friend. "We must embrace the day for what it is and be grateful. Who knows what lies ahead?

Charles Henry White, Charley's oldest son, left the circus and became a railroad engineer. He married Hannah O'Connel in 1877 and they had several children.

William Albert White, Charley's youngest son has not been verifiably traced.

18 October 1879, Charley's little sister Emily Fitch and her three-year-old daughter Edith were shot and killed by James Madison Fitch in Michigan. Fitch died in prison.

Charley and Annie took in two little girls who were counted in the 1880 U.S. Census at St. Barnabas House (a shelter) in New York City. Elizabeth White and Emily White were listed as eight and nine years old and native to Baltimore. The girls were possibly the orphaned children of William White, Charley's youngest brother. The two grew up in the circus. Elizabeth married Edward Caron an acrobat and Emma (Emily) married Robert Bigsby, who would follow Annie (Mrs. Charles White) into leadership of the wardrobe department.

Charley retrieved the white elephant for P.T. Barnum in 1884. He was Jumbo's keeper as well.

William Albert Donovan, Annie's only son, married Annie Jones the infamous bearded lady in 1895. He died while the show was in

England on 2 August 1899 of tuberculosis. Annie Jones died on 2 October 1902, in New York, also of tuberculosis.

Charley White trained smaller animals (like dogs and goats) even after he retired from managing the circus menagerie. An newspaper interview from 1879 provided rare details of his early life. It was said that James Bailey had a special fondness for him. Charley passed 19 March 1909. Annie received his Civil War pension of $17.33 per month.

Annie spent the rest of her retirement years with her adopted daughter Emma. She departed this earth on August 15, 1935, one day after her ninety-third birthday.

From the time she joined Barnum until her retirement in 1907, Annie's birthday was celebrated with lavish parties while the show was on the road . "Mother White" as she was referred to was much loved. Several lengthy newspaper articles in 1905, 1906, and 1907 highlighted her long and successful career with the show. It was Annie who looked out for the well being of the women in the show for all those years.

Donna Lee Dicksson lives in Garland, Texas with her naturalized Swedish husband Peter and two African Grey parrots.

While researching her own circus great grandmother and writing the book, "Mattie Lee Price, the Forgotten Georgia Wonder," she stumbled across two circus characters who intrigued her. Pulling on the little red thread of lost history, she found a magnificent world of resilient and fascinating people and a story that needed to be told.

When not researching and writing, Donna is an avid photographer, gardener and homemaker. She is mother to two wonderful children and has three granddaughters and one great granddaughter.

At eight I wanted to be a clown. My teachers and parents were concerned and asked why.

My answer: "People take themselves too seriously. They need to laugh more."